Why had a woman like her—educated, poised, socially at ease—singled out a man like him from among the wealthy, erudite snobs milling about to grace with her attention tonight? His body language had stated clearly enough that he wasn't looking for company.

"Just trying to make conversation," she said.

"I'm not much of a conversationalist."

"No kidding."

The flirtatious sheen melted from her green eyes, leaving challenge blazing in its place and confirming his suspicions. She had an agenda. He just didn't know what it was.

Or what to do about it. Especially since he found the fiery reality of the warrior unmasked even more attractive than the façade of civility she'd worn before.

Temptation raked him with her razored claws. His kind were born with two undeniable compulsions: to protect humans from evil, and to procreate.

At that moment he didn't see anyone in need of protecting.

CARVED in STONE

Vickie Taylor

BERKLEY SENSATION, NEW YORK

THE BERKLEY PUBLISHING GROUP
Published by the Penguin Group
Penguin Group (USA) Inc.
375 Hudson Street, New York, New York 10014, USA
Penguin Group (Canada), 10 Alcorn Avenue, Toronto, Ontario M4V 3B2, Canada
(a division of Pearson Penguin Canada Inc.)
Penguin Books Ltd., 80 Strand, London WC2R 0RL, England
Penguin Group Ireland, 25 St. Stephen's Green, Dublin 2, Ireland (a division of Penguin Books Ltd.)
Penguin Group (Australia), 250 Camberwell Road, Camberwell, Victoria 3124, Australia
(a division of Pearson Australia Group Pty. Ltd.)
Penguin Books India Pvt. Ltd., 11 Community Centre, Panchsheel Park, New Delhi—110 017, India
Penguin Group (NZ), Cnr. Airborne and Rosedale Roads, Albany, Auckland 1310, New Zealand
(a division of Pearson New Zealand Ltd.)
Penguin Books (South Africa) (Pty.) Ltd., 24 Sturdee Avenue, Rosebank, Johannesburg 2196, South
Africa

Penguin Books Ltd., Registered Offices: 80 Strand, London WC2R 0RL, England

CARVED IN STONE

A Berkley Sensation Book / published by arrangement with the author

PRINTING HISTORY
Berkley Sensation edition / June 2005

Copyright © 2005 by Vickie Spears.
Excerpt from *Close-Up* copyright © 2005 by Virginia Kantra.
Cover art by Franco Accornero.
Cover design by George Long.
Interior text design by Kristin del Rosario.

ISBN: 0-425-20291-7

BERKLEY® SENSATION
Berkley Sensation Books are published by The Berkley Publishing Group,
a division of Penguin Group (USA) Inc.,
375 Hudson Street, New York, New York 10014.
BERKLEY SENSATION and the "B" design are trademarks belonging to Penguin Group (USA) Inc.

PRINTED IN THE UNITED STATES OF AMERICA

10 9 8 7 6 5 4 3 2 1

PROLOGUE

"Under the bed, Daddy! Check under the bed!"

Rachel clutched Mr. Mott, the pink rabbit who'd been missing one ear ever since the boo-boo with Mommy's sewing scissors last year, to her chest. Her toes curled off the smooth wood floor as she danced on the balls of her feet. The ruffle of her sleeveless nightgown bounced around her knees, and she hiked it up in one fist. It was a hot night. The smell of the rain Daddy said was coming and the rosemary bush Mommy had planted outside fluttered through her window on a breeze as sticky and sweet as cotton candy.

Daddy closed the door to her closet, having verified it as messy, but monster free, and knelt by her bed to inspect the dark space beneath.

Rachel giggled. She didn't really believe in monsters, but since her little brother Levi was born, bedtime was the only time she got Daddy all to herself, and she wasn't ready to give him back yet.

She might give Levi back, though, if they would let her.

Daddy lifted the pink bed skirt and bent his head. "No monsters here, either." He stood, pulled back the pink bedspread, and patted the pink pillowcase. At six years old, Rachel was definitely into pink. She had a pink bicycle and pink roller skates. But she didn't want to go to bed yet, even if it was in a pink bed.

Instead of climbing under the covers, she jumped up in the air and landed in a fighting crouch. Feet spread, knees bent, and both arms outstretched, Mr. Mott dangling from her grip on his one remaining ear, she pointed an accusing finger at the foot of her bed. "The toy box!"

Daddy gave her a look, but opened the lid and squinted inside anyway. Rachel chewed her lip and glanced around, wondering where else monsters might hide. If there was such a thing as monsters, which there wasn't. Unless . . .

"Daddy, can monsters be invisible?"

"Invisible? No honey-bug, there's no such thing as invisible—"

His eyes went suddenly wide. He swatted at the air, ducked and swatted again. "Hey! Stop that!" He swung at nothing, fell against the bed, and staggered toward her, yelling. "No! Ahhhhhhhhhhh, no!"

Rachel's eyes stretched open until she thought they would pop out of her head. She tried to scream, but her throat stuck closed. She tried to run, but her feet froze to the floor. Daddy twirled, tripped toward her. He picked her up by her stiff arms, his face still all twisty, and—

He tickled her.

Laughing, he dumped her on the bed and pulled the covers up to her chin.

Her throat opened. She gasped in a humongous breath and socked him in the arm. *"Daddy!"*

Daddy threw his head back and howled. "Listen up all you monsters, invisible and otherwise. I am the biggest, baddest, and only monster allowed in this house. All lesser creatures are hereby banished forthwith!"

Rachel wasn't sure what that last part meant, but she hoped the monsters listened.

Not that there was any such thing as monsters.

Yawning, she snuggled down in the puddle of cool

sheets. Daddy tucked Mr. Mott next to her and planted a sputtery kiss on her forehead before he left. At the door he paused and flicked off the light. "Sweet dreams."

"Don't forget to leave it open a crack." Rachel wasn't afraid of monsters, but she was afraid of the dark. She didn't have to worry, though. Daddy always left her door open a couple of inches so the hall light could get in.

Which is why, when she woke up hours later, yawned, dug a fist in one eye, and peeled back the other eyelid to find there was no reassuring glow shining in from the hall, her chest turned cold and tingly and a whimper pushed up her throat.

Thunder rumbled overhead—just clouds bumping together, Daddy had told her once, but the wind was moaning tonight, too. Trees scraped against the house like bony fingers. The storm and the darkness pressed down on her. She wanted to cry out for Mommy and Daddy, but she wasn't a baby anymore. She wasn't *the* baby anymore. They had Levi now, and he did enough crying for both of them. Besides, her throat had closed up again. Dark air was harder to breathe. She could hardly make a squeak, much less yell.

A beam of light slashed through her window from outside, and she heard people out there, their voices as angry-sounding as the storm.

In the hall Mommy and Daddy shouted in loud whispers. "We have to get out."

"It's too late."

"The children—"

Footsteps pounded toward her bedroom. Rachel pulled the covers up and squeezed Mr. Mott so tight she'd have strangled him if he'd been a real bunny. Her door flung open and a dark shape loomed over her, snatched her from warm covers into damp air. She shivered, gasped, then smelled a familiar spicy smell and relaxed in the strong arms.

"Daddy—" She reached for Mister Mott as Daddy

pulled her against him, but the rabbit fell. The toe of Daddy's boot kicked him under the bed.

"Hush, baby," he said.

She bounced sleepily in his arms as he jogged through the house. In the living room, candlelight flickered on the walls.

She thought he was taking her to bed with him and Mommy 'cuz the 'lectricity was out, and she smiled, 'cuz she didn't get to sleep with them much since Levi was born, but then Daddy stopped next to the little door under the stairs, almost invisible in the paneling. It was their secret place, the spot where they hid Mommy's birthday presents.

Rachel's smile crumbled as Daddy opened the creaky hatch and lowered her inside. She reached up to him, her lips trembling. "Daddy, no!"

"Please, baby. Do what I say."

Mommy leaned over with Levi in her arms. She looked at Daddy once, her eyes all shiny, and handed the baby to Rachel. "Take care of your little brother. And please, *please* don't make a sound. No matter what."

Then Daddy closed the door and left her in the musty-smelling cupboard.

In the dark.

Rachel gulped down her fear, trying not to cry and trying to remember how to cradle the baby. Mommy had never let her hold him without help before. She didn't want to break him.

Outside, thunderclaps mixed with the pounding of fists on the front door. There were shouts, men's voices, and then splintering wood. Daddy yelled for Mommy to run. Glass shattered.

Rachel wanted to scream, needed to scream, but Mommy had said to be quiet. Very quiet. Tears rolling over her eyelashes onto her cheeks, she jammed a fist into her mouth and bit down hard. The darkness in here made her ribs all sticky. She couldn't breathe. She needed light, just a little sliver.

Squatting with the baby balanced in one arm, she leaned forward, reached for the cabinet door. Her palm slid over rough, unpainted wood. She chewed her lip, her heart doing jumping jacks in her chest. The voices she'd heard outside were inside now. Saying bad things. Scary things.

But the dark in here was scary, too. Hand shaking, she pushed on the wood. The door opened an inch and candlelight slithered in. Shadows oozed like puddles of oil across the slice of dining room wall she could see. There were three figures, her mommy's shorter shape and two bigger ones, one of them she thought was her daddy.

"Get out of my house!" he yelled.

There were lots of voices in the background, murmuring and hissing like snakes, but she could only make out the words from one. ". . . don't belong here."

The shadow she didn't know raised an arm, pointed something at her daddy's shadow. Daddy's shadow jumped toward him. They mushed together into one bigger blob and crashed to the floor.

Mommy screamed. "No! Please—"

A big bang, like a firecracker, made Rachel's shoulders jerk. Mommy's shadow fell down.

For a moment all was quiet. Levi snuffled in Rachel's arms, and she rocked him and waited for Mommy to get up and tell her it was okay, the bad shadow was gone, that it had all been a dream. But it wasn't a dream, because she didn't wake up.

Something screeched like a cat that got its tail caught in the door, only louder. From the spot where Daddy and the bad man had fallen, a new shadow rose up. The dark figure was shaped like a man but huger than anyone she knew. The watery candlelight made it look like horns sprouted from each side of his head, and his fingers grew longer and longer until they looked like big claws. When he lifted his shadow arms, they weren't arms at all, but wings.

Rachel's heart tripped. She wanted to shut her eyes, but she couldn't. All she could do was squat in her hidey-hole and shake as the monster shadow rose until its feet—

claws—no longer touched the floor, and then flew through the air with the slow *whump, whump, whump* of heavy wings.

Someone Rachel couldn't see screamed. Others cursed, grunted. Footsteps scuffled across the wooden floor. Something heavy, like a piece of furniture, fell over. For a moment the light in the cupboard dimmed, then she heard a whoosh, and the room got brighter again. Rachel smelled smoke—not the waxy smell of a candle, but the bitter burn of a real fire.

Lightning flashed through the room, and that's when Rachel saw it—not the monster's shadow, but the real thing.

She stopped breathing. Her heart stopped beating. She didn't want to look at it, look into its shiny black eyes, but she couldn't look away. A forked tongue flicked from its pointy beak. Blood matted the gray tips of its wings, dripped from its claws as it swooped past her hiding place, knocking the cupboard door shut with its scaly three-toed claw.

She crashed against the far wall of the cabinet, crammed herself into the darkest, tiniest corner. Eyes squeezed shut, ears ringing with the echoes of people wailing and more firecrackers popping, she clutched Levi against her chest and recited the only prayer she knew, her lips moving but unable to make any sound come out.

Now I lay me down to sleep, I pray the Lord my soul to keep. If I should die before I wake . . .

ONE

Nothing reminded Nathan Cross he wasn't human so much as an attractive woman watching his every move from across a crowded room. She wasn't a regular at the Chicago Museum of Fine Art's patron's gala; if she'd attended before, he would've remembered. A woman like her made an impression on a man.

Even a man who wasn't really a man.

She had hair the color of sunshine, as light as his was dark, and she wore it rolled up in an old-fashioned chignon that lent her an air of classic elegance, yet appeared perfectly contemporary, thanks to the tendrils she'd left free to spiral around her face in spindly whorls. Her gown added to the impression of modern sophistication, flowing over her slender body like liquid emeralds, offering just enough shimmer to catch the eye without being gaudy, cut low enough to tantalize without being risqué.

But it was the slit rising above one knee, exposing a stiletto heel secured to her ankle by a single delicate strap, and her long, shapely calf that had Nathan's blood simmering as he waited for her next step . . . and his next glimpse.

Clenching his fist around the fragile stem of his wine-glass so tightly he was lucky it didn't shatter, he turned his back on her.

Curse his unholy nature, making him burn for something he couldn't have. He wasn't looking for a woman tonight—any night.

Nathan had only come for the art.

In art, in the muted pastels and dark dashes of oil, the raw emotion, he celebrated mankind's greatest joys, suffered the depths of its despair.

In art, he experienced humanity.

And if art were a cold mistress, she was at least a faithful one. Nathan had been born, lived, and died fourteen times, and through it all she'd remained his constant. Brought him peace in a way no woman could.

In art, he found his solace. Found his soul.

Refusing to spare the temptress in green another thought, he focused on the twelfth-century tapestry displayed in front of him. He was reading the placard detailing the history of the hanging—as if he weren't intimately familiar with its origins—when the scent of rosemary wafted past on a puff of conditioned air. His unnaturally sharp senses identified the fragrance as uniquely hers among the other women's heavier florals and musks, the zesty men's colognes perfuming the gallery.

Helpless to stop himself, he continued to stare at the placard, concentrating more on the shiny surface of the Plexiglas mounting than the writing beneath, until his vision blurred. The glass caught the reflection of the crystal chandelier overhead. Hundreds of individual bulbs coalesced into a single brilliant source, a midnight sun.

The sun bored a channel through time and space. Nathan swayed as his senses left his body, following the light, spilling into the tunnel of Second Sight, a kind of self-hypnosis that allowed him to see things his human eyes could not.

Within seconds the woman's image appeared in his mind's eye. He watched as she glided across the room behind him, wending her way through the gallery with frequent smiles and interludes of small talk among clusters of patrons, stopping a uniformed server for a fresh flute of champagne. She appeared to wander in no particular direction, and yet every click of her heels on the marble floor drew her inexorably closer.

To him.

Tall and slender, she moved with cultured grace. The emerald pendant bobbing in the hollow of her throat competed with eyes the same color for brilliance—and lost. She would have been the picture of female perfection except for one detail: Above her unflawed eyes, her left eyebrow arched at a slightly higher angle than the right, giving her face a gentle, crooked look he found endearing.

In women, as in art, it was the tiny imperfection that made a good work a masterpiece.

"Magnificent, isn't it?"

Her voice at his shoulder was curiously rough, in opposition to the smooth sophistication of the rest of her. The husky timbre swept the spurious Second-Sight image of her from his mind. With some difficulty he resisted the temptation to turn his head and take a look at the real thing. Instead he studied *Le Combat de Rouen*, the medieval tapestry on loan from Museé de Cluny that he'd come to see tonight. It had been a long time since he'd laid eyes on the pictorial record of the birth of his people.

"It's amazing how clearly the artist portrays the triumph of Christianity over paganism," the woman in green continued.

Nathan rolled the stem of his wineglass between his fingers. "Is that what it portrays?"

"The symbolism is obvious. The dragon is the embodiment of the pagan belief in magic and mythical creatures. The priest kneeling in the middle is using prayer to slay the dragon. Christianity slays paganism."

"Those don't look like prayers tearing that dragon apart with their beaks and fangs and claws to me." He didn't need to look at the tapestry to imagine the beasts doing battle with the dragon. He could hear the roars, taste the blood. He hadn't been there himself, but his forefathers had passed down the memory.

They'd made sure none of his kind ever forgot.

He didn't point out to the woman that the priest knelt in a faint, but visible, pagan circle, that some of the beasts had human faces, or that around the edges of the battle scene, only figures of women and children looked on from the streets of Rouen. The men were notably absent.

The woman rolled her shoulders subtly. "One might assume that the priest used prayer to call upon the beasts to do his bidding."

"One might assume that," he allowed. *If one didn't know better.*

Romanus had deceived the villagers of Rouen. Used their own magic to trick them. Their own religion to curse them.

Thanks to the bastard priest's treachery, Nathan and those like him were damned to forever carry a monster inside them, slumbering, but always ready to Awaken.

Always hungry.

Oblivious to the rage rising within him, the woman stared at him with cool green eyes. "The detail is incredible. There's not another work from this period with a range of color like this."

He calmed himself with a deep breath. Romanus was long dead and Nathan was too intrigued by a woman who recognized range of color in a medieval tapestry to ruin this night over something that had happened a thousand years ago.

"There is one," he said, aware of the danger of getting drawn into a conversation with her, but not able to stop himself.

"I can't imagine where."

He realized he was staring—and not at the tapestry— but he couldn't bring himself to look away from her. "Tibet."

"Doesn't count." Her eyes were as bright as her smile. "The Easterners had an unfair advantage. Silk thread."

"Unfair or not, they set a standard for color and pattern that the West wouldn't match for another two centuries."

"Three, at least."

"Perhaps."

She raised her glass in salute. "You know your hangings."

"As do you." A fact that honed a fine edge on his already-sharp awareness of her. Too many women cared only for their own beauty these days. Realizing she wasn't one of them had desire cracking and snapping like a whip low in his belly.

His breath deepened and the gossamer bouquet of rosemary surrounding her enveloped him, invaded him. Beneath it, his predator's senses caught another, headier scent: feminine awareness. She was as interested in him as he was in her.

He wheeled and strode toward the next exhibit, a gleaming broadsword with a gilded handle, before he completely gave in to this idiocy and asked her name.

Unfortunately, she followed.

She stopped too close behind his shoulder. Invaded his space. His peace of mind.

"Are you a collector or a dealer?" she asked.

"Neither." Although he sold the odd piece from time to time to make ends meet.

"You must be quite a patron of the arts to go all the way to Tibet to hang out at museums and look at tapestry. Do you travel a lot?"

"When it suits." He didn't bother to correct her assumption that he'd been to the museum in Tibet. The weaving he'd had in mind had hung in a great maharaja's hall; Nathan had been present when the prince unveiled the masterpiece he'd consigned specially for his maharani. But that had been many lifetimes ago. Literally.

"And does it suit often?"

"Often enough."

She frowned, a shallow furrow forming above the bridge of her impertinent nose. "Are you always so forthcoming with information?"

"Do you always ask so many questions?" Her curiosity put a chill on the heat her interest had stoked in him.

Why had a woman like her—educated, poised, socially at ease—singled out a man like him from among the wealthy, erudite snobs milling about to grace with her attention tonight? His body language had stated clearly enough that he wasn't looking for company.

"Just trying to make conversation," she said.

"I'm not much of a conversationalist."

"No kidding."

The flirtatious sheen melted from her green eyes, leaving challenge blazing in its place and confirming his suspicions. She had an agenda. He just didn't know what it was.

Or what to do about it. Especially since he found the fiery reality of the warrior unmasked even more attractive than the i. :ade of civility she'd worn before.

Temptation raked him with her razored claws. His kind were born with two undeniable compulsions: to protect humans from evil, and to procreate.

At that moment he didn't see anyone in need of protecting.

He clasped his hands around the stem of his glass to give them something to do other than twist in the curls that fell around her face in sunny ringlets. While he stood staring at her, the woman huffed out a breath. The furrow between her brows disappeared and her smile returned, somewhat chagrined. She wrinkled her nose ingenuously, and his body tightened like hardening clay.

She shifted her drink to her left hand and extended her right. "Well, now that we've had our first fight, I suppose I should introduce myself. I'm Rachel Vandermere."

Nathan left the delicate fingers untouched, not trusting himself to lay a hand on her. He'd always had a passion for beautiful things, and she was certainly a work of art with her golden hair and bejeweled eyes. But more than beauty drew him to her. There was something familiar about her. Something he recognized on an instinctual level, the way he'd recognized that she—unlike he—wasn't here just for the art, or interested in him simply for his knowledge of ancient hangings.

He felt a connection with her deep inside, weak but palpable. A synchronous vibration, like two tuning forks singing the same key. He almost felt as if he could reach out with his mind and touch her thoughts as easily as he could with another of his kind, but that was impossible.

There were none of his kind like her. No women, beautiful or otherwise.

The magic that made Nathan what he was passed only to male children. His people depended on human women to bear them sons, but female offspring possessed none of his race's unique characteristics, and were considered inconsequential, while male children were highly prized, for producing a son in this life guaranteed rebirth into the next. As soon as a boy child was born and suckled first milk, males of his race left their human mates, taking their sons with them to be raised among the congregation and learn the ways of their people.

Ways no human would understand.

Nathan had lived, died, and lived again many times in this way, but no more. He would not mate in this lifetime. There would be no male child born to him, and the price for this refusal to contribute to the survival of his species would be that his essence would not reincarnate.

This life would be his last, and he would live it alone.

He dragged his shoulders back, feeling the full weight of the course he'd set for himself. Suicide of the soul.

The woman in green still held her hand out toward him. *I'm Rachel Vandermere.*

It wasn't a name he'd soon forget. No matter how hard he tried.

Cutting his gaze away from her, he downed the last of

his champagne in one gulp. "And I'm late for another engagement," he said, and stomped toward the exit.

"Well, that son of a—" Rachel planted her fists at her waist and cocked one hip in a very unladylike pose. She tilted her head as if that would help her hear past the snickers filtering through the miniature transceiver in her ear and turned so that the art lovers ambling by couldn't see her talking to herself. "Did you guys get that?"

From the way the snickers exploded into laughter, she guessed they did.

"He's gotta be gay!" one of the guys in the surveillance van said. She couldn't be sure which guy. She didn't know the Chicago team well enough to recognize their voices.

"Or dead."

"An alien, maybe."

"No human would walk away from a babe with a body like—"

Rachel suspected the *thump* and *wuff* she heard next was Carter Laisson, the task force team leader, embedding his elbow into the speaker's lungs. Carter was State Department, a former marine, FBI agent, and CIA operative. Rachel didn't think he knew how to laugh.

"Enough with the Keystone Kops," Laisson's deep tenor warned. "Let's get a make on that guy."

"Coming up." The squeak of a chair on wheels and the sound of tapping keys gave the speaker away as the tech specialist. She thought his name was Otto. He'd put together a database of info on the ticket holders to the gala. Looked like it was going to come in handy. "You think Pretty Boy's our man, Rach?"

"Could be."

"What?" Carter Laisson sounded skeptical. Figuring that was his job, as the boss of the multiagency task force, she tried not to hold it against him. "You Interpol types can pick out an assassin just by looking at him?"

"Take a gander." She turned in a slow arc, giving the

tiny camera mounted in her emerald necklace a clear pan of the room. "We got bent old men, blue-haired ladies, community leaders. You see any other likely candidates for an international hit man? Besides, I just got this vibe from him—"

"What kind of vibe?"

"I don't know." She couldn't explain it; didn't understand it herself. "Like this buzz going off in my gut."

"Sounds like a case of the hots to me."

"Shut up, Otto," Laisson warned.

Someone else chimed in with a real helpful observation. "You wouldn't know the hots if your feet were on fire, Otto."

"He came in alone," Rachel said, as much to stop the quibbling as anything. This was her first assignment with team members from so many different groups, and every rumor she'd heard about interagency task forces was true. Seemed like they spent more time trying to prove who had the bigger, er, acronym on the back of their raid jackets than working.

She scanned the museum for other likely candidates. Found none. Then again, maybe she didn't want to. She couldn't explain it, even to herself, much less her temporary teammates, but there'd been something about Mr. I'm-late-for-another-engagement. . . .

She ran down the list mentally and out loud. "He kept to himself all night. As much as admitted he traveled a lot. And he got real nervous when I asked questions. Wouldn't even tell me his name."

"Nathan Cross," Otto spoke up, apparently finding the background check. "Born Chicago, 1970. Residence currently in same. Art history prof at Chicago University."

"You're kidding," Rachel said. "That guy is a *professor?*"

He didn't look like any teacher she'd studied under, with his black eyes and raven hair sweeping a good three inches over his collar, not to mention the way his anything-but-bookish shoulders filled out the tux attached to that collar.

A stray thought ended her accounting of his physical assets. His many physical assets. "How does an art professor afford his own tux and a gig like this?" Tickets had run five grand a pop.

"Family money?" Otto guessed. More key tapping. "Nope. Here we go. Ah, seems Professor Cross supports his lifestyle by selling a piece of fine art every three or four years."

"A thief," Rachel spat. "I knew he was dirty."

"Hold on. Exactly where he gets the art is a mystery," Otto said, "but none of it was ever reported as stolen. Seems he's just real good at finding lost treasures."

"Yeah, I'll bet he's real good—"

Carter interrupted, squelching her enthusiasm. "This isn't a Cultural Properties investigation, people. We're here to catch a killer, remember?"

"Hey, a bad guy's a bad guy," she grumbled. But the boss was right. Her days tracking the movements of antiquities smugglers and international art thieves for Interpol, the International Criminal Police Organization, were over. She'd been promoted to the big time—antiterrorism. All because she'd recognized a man making a seemingly innocent inquiry to the French consulate about the exhibit—and made a sudden trip to Chicago—as the reputed go-between for an infamous hit man, presumably scoping out the killing field for his boss.

France had shipped more than a bunch of musty old wall hangings to America with the medieval exhibition. They'd sent Secretary General Frederique DuBois to give the opening speech—a secretary who'd had a terrorist target on his back since he'd passed information on Al Qaeda to the United States.

Her job of connecting the dots from Al Qaeda, to the go-between, to the hit man, to DuBois had earned her a coveted field assignment for Interpol, an agency where even veterans were usually limited to chasing paper trails from the Central Bureau.

It didn't hurt that she was a knockout in a low-cut

evening gown, either, she supposed. Or that she knew her way around a museum. The task force assembled to protect DuBois needed someone who could blend into the art world. Walk the walk. Talk the talk. That was her.

Rachel was all for saving the life of a diplomat and preserving world peace, but she had personal reasons, as well, for wanting this assignment. Though the assassin she believed had picked up the contract on Secretary DuBois was suspected in seven political murders, no one knew what he looked like. Not a single photograph existed in the various law enforcement files on him. No witness had ever gotten close enough to describe him for a sketch artist. Rumor had it that evading law enforcement wasn't the only reason no one had seen William "The Freak" Bishop's face. He was supposed to be hideously deformed. Some called him a monster.

And Rachel had a long-standing interest in monsters.

A sleek fall of black hair, dark eyes as shiny and opaque as wet slate, and chiseled features—anything but hideous—popped into her mind with startling clarity and no warning. The image was so clear, it was almost as if he were there, inside her. Touching her mind. She had the oddest feeling he was thinking about her.

Her blood warmed instantly and coiled into an ache low in her abdomen. *What are you, Nathan Cross?*

He sure didn't look like a monster.

But then, looks could be deceiving.

Two

❧

Coat in hand, Nathan loped down the museum's front steps like a man possessed. The darkness called to him, summoned him home to the alleys and gutters where his kind belonged. Overhead, the giant gold-and-white banners hung along the front of the museum to advertise tonight's gala popped in the wind like the sails of the great ship that had carried a previous incarnation of himself to America many years ago. A new world, he'd thought when he'd looked upon the green shores. A new way.

Yeah, right.

He paused to look up at the monolithic museum, shining like Cinderella's Castle at Disney World under the spotlights set up for the gala. His gaze roamed over the towers and buttresses to the shadowed creatures suspended on them, shrouded in midnight mists.

Uneasily he studied the unholy amalgamations of man and animal. Nightmarish monsters with horrific visages, the agony of their existence timeless, ageless, the gargoyles were condemned to look down on human society, human life, for all eternity, but never to be a part of it.

They were his history, his heritage carved in stone, not the pretty human paintings and fine sculptures inside.

His gut twisted. Why shouldn't he succumb to the whispered urgings of the beast within him? Take Rachel Vandermere home with him and peel that green gown off of her inch by measured inch? Make love to her until dawn chased off the darkness of his soul?

What could be more human?

But then, that was the crux of the matter, wasn't it?

He wasn't human.

The fire in him squelched by the thought, he shouldered his way into his coat and drew the thick cashmere tight across his chest. He would forego a cab and walk the two miles back to his Lake Shore Drive condominium.

As if a brisk walk could wipe away the images of her burned into his consciousness. Just because he couldn't have her didn't mean he could make himself stop wanting her, any more than he could walk past a master's canvas without admiring the painting.

Nathan Cross was a man of fine tastes.

And Rachel Vandermere appealed to every one of them.

Realizing he still held his empty wineglass in his fist, he swore, threw it against the stone steps, and turned for home. The November air, already bitter with the first bite of winter, stung his cheeks like shards of crystal. The fog rolling in off Lake Michigan muffled sound, blotted out the stars. Nathan shoved his fists into the pockets of his coat and trudged into the thick of it.

Along the back side of the sprawling museum, shadows closed in on him from all sides. Cobblestone sidewalks deteriorated to cracked cement, and pruned holly shrubs gave way to gutter trash tumbling in the wind and the last scrappy weeds rebelling against the onset of winter.

No spotlights blazed a path back here. A single lonely street lamp stood sentry at a corner bordered by a high, turreted stone wall, its hazy light scattered by the icy mist in the air. Behind him the dark side of the museum rose into the night like Frankenstein's castle, black and foreboding.

Head down, he scuffed his heels along the cement, a yearning with the power of a thousand years of magic behind it twisting through his gut like a corkscrew. He'd just turned to cross the street when a scraping noise brought him up short. He stopped, looked over his shoulder. The night was silent and cold. Still.

At least on the surface.

Showing a deliberate lack of concern, Nathan kept walking. He made two steps before a figure in black leather pants and a black jacket jumped down from the shadows atop the stone wall beside him.

Nathan recognized the haircut first—it reminded him of a porcupine that'd stuck a paw in an electrical outlet—followed quickly by the familiar glint of a gold nose ring.

"Von, you forgot to yell 'Boo!' "

"If I was trying to scare you," Von Simeon answered, "you'd be the one yelling." He struck a match, held it to the tip of the cigarette hanging from one corner of his mouth, and drew deeply. The smell of tobacco mingled with the scent of cheap scotch that surrounded him like a soggy blanket. "Or maybe you've forgotten what one of us can do to a man alone on a dark street."

"I've forgotten nothing." He watched warily as Von circled him like a vulture. "And I'm no man, as you well know."

"All dressed up like Mr. Fancy Pants 'imself." Von fingered the soft lapel of Nathan's coat. "On your way out for a night on the town, hey?"

Nathan knocked his hand away. "I'm on my way home. It's nearly midnight."

"Just about time for the good parties to start."

"If by *party* you mean a hundred people crammed into a damp basement having their eardrums shattered by that infernal racket you call music and frying their brains on the drug du jour, then yes. I guess you're right."

Von smiled drunkenly. "Now you're talking. Want to tag along, eh?"

The wind shifted, and the sour smell of Von's breath hit

Nathan like a slap. He managed not to recoil. Barely. "No. Thanks."

"What'sa matter? Too good to hang with your old chums?"

"You're not my *chum*." He turned to go, but before he could take a step, the kid stood in his way again. Only he wasn't a kid anymore.

Von's eyes glowed with a green patina, warning that the Awakening was about to take him. His face shifted, the bone becoming heavier, the ringed nose blunting and tilting up like a pig's while his jaw protruded. His two lower incisors lengthened, jutting out like fangs. Saliva frothed in the corners of his mouth.

Nathan smiled, but pulled his fists out of his pockets and balanced his stance, just in case. "Well, if you're going to act like a bore, you may as well look like one, too, I suppose."

Standing upright like a man, but wearing the face of a wild swine, Von grunted and took a step toward Nathan.

"Leave him be, Von."

Never turning his head from Von, Nathan rolled a glance upward. On the ledge above him another man rose, a black trench coat swirling around his long body as he jumped to the sidewalk. A third, similarly clad figure leaped down next to him.

"Rhys." Nathan nodded toward the first man, the one he'd called his closest—only—friend for seven lifetimes before they'd set off on different paths, then turned to the man accompanying him. "Connor."

Von took a drag off his cigarette. "He thinks he's better'n us 'cuz he lives uptown and wears fancy clothes."

Nathan spun slowly on the balls of his feet as the three circled him. "I chose to make a new life for myself." He swung his head toward the darkness. "You chose this."

"You should be crushed for your disloyalty. Teryn is a weak old fool for allowing you to break from the congregation."

Nathan smiled wickedly. "Say that to his face and we'll see how *weak* Teryn is."

Von snorted.

"Get over it, Von." Connor shoved a hank of black hair in need of a trim out of his eyes. "Teryn is our Wizenot. His decisions, and those of the Council, are law. Let him hear you questioning him, and you're the one he'll crush."

Von pinned his ears like the angry animal he was and raised his face, staring into the reflective mist to test the tunnel of Second Sight. "He is not watching."

"Or he's blocking you so that you can't see that he's watching," Rhys said. Then he turned to Nathan, his lips curving downward to frame his black goatee. "Von has a point, though. Don't run us down because you're not one of us anymore. You made your choice."

"Choice? Since when were any of us given a choice?"

"You decided you were too good for our laws."

"Can you honestly say you like living as you do? Look at what you're becoming." He glanced aside at Von. Centuries ago his people had been an honorable breed, revered by humans. Now . . .

"Hey—" Von snarled and swayed forward again. Connor lashed one arm to the side, stopped the kid with a fist wrapped in his shirt.

"Will you skulk in the alleys for another century?" Nathan continued. "Lurk in the shadows another millennium feeding on the world's violence? On humanity's predilection toward death and destruction?"

"Pre-dul . . . huh?" Von asked, and belched.

"Shut up," Rhys ordered the kid.

Connor tightened his hold on the boy's shirt.

"Or maybe you'll get tired of waiting for the humans to start trouble and cause a little pain and suffering on your own. Maybe some of you already have. Your young friend here doesn't look like he'd be too particular about who actually started a fight, as long as he gets to end it."

Rhys flinched. "We don't start trouble. We put a stop to it. We're *guardians.*"

"Are you?" Nathan's fists tightened at his side. His throat constricted so that he had to squeeze the words out.

"A thousand years ago when we were created, maybe. The world was a different place then. There were dragons and black wizards and all sorts of evil. The villagers were simple. Helpless. But who are you guarding now? People who've forgotten we exist?"

Nathan could hardly contain the emotion in his voice. "Do you really think humans would thank us if they knew? All they would care about is what we are. If they had any idea what monsters roamed their streets, they would hunt us down and kill us like rabid dogs."

Or kill themselves out of fear, he added silently, then shoved the thought away.

He locked gazes with Rhys, willing his old friend to see the truth.

Rhys's shoulders rose and fell with his short, rapid breaths. He shook his head faintly, almost as if he didn't realize he was doing it. "You can't turn your back on who you are, Nathan," he finally said. "You're one of *Les Gargouillen,* created to protect the innocent from all that would harm them, whether they want your protection or not, as I am. You're a Gargoyle. You can't forget that."

Nathan rammed his fists back into his coat pockets and took a step forward, surrounded or not. "I can damn well try."

"Not tonight, you can't," Von snorted gleefully. Dropping to all fours, his body bulged, expanded at the shoulders, and contracted at the waist. His hands and feet clubbed into hooves, his neck thickened, and his fangs lengthened, sharpened wickedly, completing his transformation from man to boar.

Nathan stepped back, anticipating Von's charge, but Von made no move at him. Instead he reared and thrashed at the air with his front hooves.

Nathan's gaze was drawn to the reflective surface of a black puddle at Von's feet. Like an old-fashioned looking glass, his Second Sight tunneled back to the steps of the gothic museum. A group of men trod down the stone stairs to the street, where a line of limos waited. Rachel was with

them, the wind tearing wisps of hair from the knot at the
back of her head and blushing her cheeks pink.

Even as his throat went dry at the untamed sensuality of
her, he felt another watching her from a distance. He felt
the man's heavy breath. His deadly intent.

Nathan snapped the door to the Second Sight closed,
swayed dizzily as his consciousness poured back into his
body. "What the hell is going on?"

Connor had already shifted into his Gargoyle form, a
flying reptile vaguely resembling a pterodactyl. He
swooped around them with lethal talons extended.

"Can't you smell it?" Rhys asked in answer. Horns
sprouted on each side of his head and curled around his
ears as he took on the shape of a ram with a human face.
He lifted his nose into the wind and snuffled like a hound
scenting game. "There's blood in the air."

THREE

The smell of blood hit Nathan's system like a shot of adrenaline. It sizzled in his veins. Jolted his heart into a race with his lungs to pull in oxygen, pump it to his cells.

He recognized the biological signs of his body preparing for the Awakening as clearly as he recognized the Calling, the ultrasonic whistle *Les Gargouillen* emitted to draw others to the scene of trouble the way vultures called their friends to share a fresh kill. The Calling vibrated through him, well above the frequency audible to human ears, scraping his nerves. Raising his rage.

Von bolted toward the museum, still in his Gargoyle form of the wild boar. His hooves clattered on the pavement as he ran, concealing himself in the shadows along the wall. Overhead, Connor swept through the dark sky like a wraith.

Rearing back on his haunches, Rhys, the ram, turned to follow his friends, then looked back over his shoulder. "You coming?"

Nathan broke a sweat, fighting the beast inside him. "I can't."

He almost wished he could. Wished he could turn back

the calendar to the heyday of their friendship, when he and
Rhys had attended the Rookery—the school where young
Gargoyles were reared—together.

It had been London, 1872. The two of them had thrived
then, weeding out evil from innocent in an era of violence
and decadence. They hunted their prey as a pair in the fog-
riddled alleys and shadowed streets. They were, perhaps,
the only two beings alive who knew the true identity of
Jack the Ripper.

And the reason for the sudden end to his murderous
spree.

For a man who killed with such flamboyancy, Jack had
died in pitiful style, begging for his life up until the moment the last of it ran into the gutter.

For many lifetimes Nathan and Rhys had reincarnated
within a few years and a few miles of each other. They'd
sought each other out, recognizing each other's souls, if
not their faces and names.

Once he and Rhys had been as close as brothers. Now a
thousand years of tradition separated them.

Rhys settled down on all four hooves, returning to a
mostly human form so that he could speak. His horns tilted
speculatively. "What if we all chose your way, Nathan?
What would happen to our people then?"

"What will happen to us if you don't, Rhys?" He swept
one arm in the direction the others had gone. "Is this the
future of our people? Is this the life you want for Patrick?"

"Leave my son out of this."

The weight of his beliefs crashed down on Nathan.
"We're not guardians anymore, Rhys. We haven't been for
a century. We're *scavengers,* thriving on the scraps of
human misery we happen upon."

Rhys's eyes narrowed, flat and dark at the insult. "A lot
of us agree that some things need to change, you know. But
this isn't the way to persuade us to follow you. Washing
your hands of the congregation."

"It was the congregation that washed its hands of me, if
you remember."

"Because you gave us no choice." He turned once again to follow the others. "You don't want to get your hands dirty, suit yourself. But she's in danger, you know. The woman who has you so intrigued."

Nathan's lip curled. "You were spying on me?" Gargoyles weren't supposed to intrude on each other's minds. It was unwritten law, but law nonetheless.

"I didn't have to touch your thoughts to know what you were thinking. Lust was written all over your face." The ram lifted the corners of his mouth in something akin to a smile. "And hers."

The urge to Awaken the beast slammed through Nathan's system anew. Energy hummed through his body. His fingers tingled, the bones remaking themselves, nails sharpening. The skin on his back prickled, wings preparing to sprout, while the warning growl of a big cat crawled up his throat as he struggled to contain himself. "Stay away from her, Rhys."

"You should have taken what she offered. You could be home in bed with her by now, with those long legs of hers wrapped around you, instead of freezing your nuts off out here in the cold."

His talons dug into his palms until they drew blood. "Back off."

But Rhys pushed on. "Let go," he said in a low voice, almost a whisper. "Stop fighting your nature."

"Don't . . . push me."

"It's not too late. You can be the one to save her if you hurry. I'm sure she'll want to show her gratitude—"

Nathan sprang across the sidewalk to Rhys before his *old friend* could see him coming. He snatched Rhys's shirtfront. The hell with restraint. Rhys was the last person Nathan wanted to hurt, but the fury was on him. The beast was loose.

Rhys's face turned red. The chords of his neck stood out as he gasped for air. "You've got to quit blaming yourself for Marabella, Nathan. It's time to move on."

"I have moved on. To a new way of life."

"And a lonely life it'll be, never truly a part of either world, human or Gargoyle. And when it's over, it'll really be over. You won't reincarnate. Eternity is a mighty long time to punish yourself, don't you think, my friend?"

"Eternity is nothing compared to the length of each day I live with her blood on my hands, *my friend*." Nathan shoved him away before he killed him, and squeezed his eyes shut.

"Rhys—" he said when he opened them again, searching for words to bridge the gulf between him and the man he considered a brother.

But the ram was gone, disappeared into the dark.

Damn it.

He sucked in a deep breath of icy air, steeling himself against the transformation the millennium-old spell still tried to force on him. He would not do this, even for Rhys. He could not do this. He'd sworn to himself . . . never again.

But neither could he leave the night to end as it may. Blood had been spilled. The air was thick with its scent. More would follow, he was certain of it.

What he wasn't certain of was who that blood would belong to.

Nathan wanted nothing more than to leave, but even in human form he was too much the guardian to walk away from innocent lives in danger, especially with the image of Rachel Vandermere, moonlight smelting the gold strands of her hair to a thousand shades of silver, shining in his mind. And with the hot breath of the other, the one who was watching her, heavy on his own neck.

He caught up with Rhys outside the parking garage a block over from the museum. Rhys strode forward without reacting when Nathan appeared at his side. His face was still stonily set, but at least it was a human face.

Out of necessity, *Les Gargouillen* took great care in when and where they traveled in guardian form. If even one of them was seen, it could start a chain reaction of rumors and gossip that would lead to mass hysteria the likes of which hadn't been realized since the Salem Witch Trials. A single photograph could be disastrous, and there were cameras everywhere these days. Rhys and his friends' shenanigans behind the museum had been risky enough—they didn't need to take a chance on the busier street out front.

A police car sat at the entrance to the parking garage, the driver slumped against the window. Rhys used the tail of his shirt to make sure he left no prints and opened the door, gently catching the officer's body as it slid out. He looked at Nathan and shook his head, but Nathan already knew the man was dead.

Voices echoed from high in the parking garage. Nathan looked up to see shadows scrawl along the concrete backdrop of the third level, and ran for the stairs, Rhys at his side. By the time the two of them had pounded up three flights and burst through the stairwell door, they were both breathing hard and loud.

Von and Connor turned to stare at them. A third man, dressed in a black jumpsuit and wearing a ski mask, took advantage of their distraction to back warily away. On the floor just beyond his reach, the blue steel barrel of a rifle with a large sighting scope gleamed under the mercury lights.

"Well, well," Von mocked in his singsong voice, "look who decided to come out and play after all."

Rhys stepped between them. "This isn't a game, Von."

"It's all a game! He spills the cop's blood, we spill his. Tit for tat." Von shuffled along the concrete in a drunken tap dance. "Tat for tit. Tit for tat. We're gonna kill. Him for that."

Dread trickled down Nathan's spine like ice water. "You don't have to kill him, Von."

"Now, what am I supposed to do with 'im? Pinch 'is ear and drag him home to 'is momma?"

"You could turn him over to the police."

"The police!" Von flung his arms wide. "What do we look like, a bunch of freaking Boy Scouts?"

"Vengeance isn't ours to dole out anymore. These people have their own ways of dealing with men like him. They have laws."

"He's a murderer."

"He's unarmed."

"Not yet he's not." Von turned so that the masked man couldn't see his face. His nose blunted and tilted again. His incisors sprung up. Foam dripped from the corner of the boar's mouth. His eyes bulged. "But he's gonna be when I rip his limbs off one by one." Laughter erupted between a series of snorts. "Get it? Un-armed?"

The gunman edged back another step. "What the hell? That guy is nuts."

Connor flicked his wrist and a dagger sprung into his hand. Nathan wasn't surprised to see the knife. Many of *Les Gargouillen* carried weapons for those occasions when they couldn't fight in Gargoyle form for fear of being seen by innocent humans.

"Don't move," Connor ordered, his blade reflecting the harsh fluorescent light.

"That's right. I'm nuts. But at least I'm not a paid assassin." Von laughed and looked over his shoulder. "I just kill for *fun!*"

"You're so eager to get a taste of blood, Von, you come see me after this is all over," Nathan warned. "I'll give you something to sink your teeth into. If you think you're able."

"Oh, now, there's an invitation I can't refuse. But why wait until later?"

Von took a step forward. Rhys stepped between him and Nathan. "Knock it off! Both of you."

Nathan's pulse bulged in his veins. "You see what I mean, Rhys?" He nodded almost imperceptibly at Von. "Is this what our people are destined to become?"

Rhys visibly slowed his breath. Unclenched his fists. "You're asking us to go against a thousand years of tradition."

"I'm asking you not to kill a man in cold blood."

Rhys's eyes softened. For a moment it was as if Nathan looked at an old photograph, a faded portrait of the friend Rhys once had been. Then the stony countenance returned. "You ask too much."

Rhys turned on his heel and snapped out commands like a general on the battlefield. "Von, get the rifle, and be careful not to leave any prints. We'll have to take him somewhere else to finish it. There are humans coming."

Von bent, mumbling but compliant and once again wholly human looking. The man in the jumpsuit used the momentary distraction to slide a pistol from the sleeve of his jacket. He raised the snubbed steel muzzle toward Von.

Nathan yelled, but it was too late. In his drunken state Von could only stumble backward.

Rhys screamed, "No!" and leaped. A *pop* reverberated off the concrete walls, and Rhys and Von landed in a heap.

Shocked silence held them all in place for a heartbeat, maybe two. Von moved first, sliding out from under Rhys, turning him over. Shaking his friend's slack body by the lapels.

The smell of fresh blood hit Nathan like a second concussion, flipping his stomach. Bile burned the back of his throat.

"No. Goddammit, no!" Lashes wet and heavy, Von let go of Rhys and looked up at the stranger. "You son of a bitch! You killed him!" He stood, picked up the rifle next to him.

"Back off," the man said, pistol still stretched in front of him. "You haven't got a chance."

Von slammed the rifle into a concrete pillar like a home-run hitter swinging for a round trip. "No. *You* haven't got a chance."

The boar reappeared. Eyes feral, foam slinging from the corners of his mouth, Von dropped to all four cloven hooves.

"What the hell?" The pistol shook in the man's hand as he tried to take aim, stumbling backward. "Jesus H. Christ, what the *hell?*"

"Von, no." Nathan took a step forward to stop Von before he got himself shot, too, but Connor swooped out of nowhere, leathery wings blinding Nathan and talons raking three deep furrows in his chest.

Claws extended before him like a hawk ready to scoop its unsuspecting prey from a grassy field, the massive bird shrieked and banked toward the man with the gun as Von grunted, put his head down, and charged. The man's eyes rounded until they looked like two white china platters. He fired wildly, falling backward.

Then flipped over the steel safety-cable railing and tumbled three stories to land with a sickening thud on the cold, black pavement below.

FOUR

If the body had landed any closer to the government sedan Rachel had been riding in, it would have left a dent in the hood. As it was, the French secretary's driver had to lock up the brakes to keep from running over it. Him.

Or what was left of him.

Even without a picture to compare to it hadn't taken long to ID the man—the bulbous forehead, sunken eyes, and seven fingers on his left hand finally explained his nickname. He was William "The Freak" Bishop, the hit man she'd been looking for, and though he had some interesting genetic anomalies, he was no more a monster than your average circus sideshow.

The case would have been a total bust if not for the fact that a French diplomat's life had been saved—albeit not by her—and her chance acquaintance with Mr. I'm-late-for-another-engagement.

He'd neglected to tell her that his "other engagement" had been with a hit man. Of course, he claimed he didn't know anything about Secretary DuBois's motorcade. Or the fact that the secretary—and Rachel, who'd been in the backseat with him—would have been sitting ducks as they passed by the garage. He claimed he'd just been in the right place at the right time, seen a man with a gun, and tried to stop him.

Now if the do-gooder just had an excuse for being in the garage to begin with, she'd pin a medal on him and send him on home, where she could put him and his ridiculously broad shoulders out of her mind.

Unfortunately, he had no reason to be anywhere near the garage, third level or otherwise. What he did have was a curious unexplained injury, a very bad attitude, and a dead friend. Given the dead friend, she could let the bad attitude pass, but the lacerations on his chest intrigued her. Until she figured out exactly what had happened tonight and why, she had to at least consider the possibility he might have been involved in the conspiracy to commit murder, even if her gut told her otherwise.

When she could hear her gut at all over the clamoring of other body parts immediately south of that region with a much more personal interest in Mr. Just-happened-to-be-in-the-right-place-at-the-right-time, that is.

Taking a deep breath, she stepped off the curb and headed toward the ambulance down the street, laying a palm low on her abdomen. "Settle down in there, guys. He is definitely not our type."

Not that she had a type. She'd been too busy chasing monsters all of her life to spend much time chasing men.

She shivered as a cold wind cut through her stylish, but not very practical, wrap. Red, blue, and yellow emergency lights lit up the mist like a laser show.

Then again, she thought as she stepped up to the open back of the ambulance and was greeted by hair black as a crow's feathers, eyes so dark she couldn't distinguish iris from pupil and a wide swath of swarthy bare chest made to look even darker by the stark white bandage taped across it, maybe she was developing a type.

Nathan Cross sat on the bumper of the ambulance. A heavyset female paramedic leaned over him, taping the last corner of the bandage in place with gloved hands. He scowled, seemingly oblivious to the enormous breasts bobbing just inches from his face.

One point for him.

"You sure you won't go to the hospital?" the paramedic asked. "You really ought to have those cuts looked at."

"I'm sure."

"You'll have to sign a release." She straightened up, grabbed a clipboard from the bin behind her, and shoved it at him.

He bent his head, and a lock of raven hair fell over his forehead, ruining the illusion of perfect control he'd maintained earlier that night. Whatever he scribbled couldn't have been legible, given the way his hand jerked across the page, but the paramedic seemed satisfied.

Cross picked up his coat and lurched off the ambulance, nearly running Rachel over. Her pulse kicked up a notch and she had to clear her throat before she could ask, "Going somewhere?"

He whipped his head up, his dark hair flying, eyes cold as black ice. "Where is Rhys?"

"They've taken him to the hospital." She steered him toward the curb without adding that they'd be taking him straight to the morgue. There was such a thing as too much information.

"Has his father been told?"

"Chicago PD is on the way to his house now."

He raked his hand over a jaw beginning to show the first shadow of stubble. And eyes where shadow had taken hold hours ago. "I should be the one to tell him."

"The police are trained—"

"Fuck trained! Rhys and I grew up together. His old man helped raise me. I should be the one. . . ."

He turned away, looked up at the shrouded sky. His words trailed off in a surge of hurt so strong even Rachel felt it. The wave of pain buffeted her, and she swayed, surprised to realize what an effect his suffering could have on her. She'd felt compassion for crime victims before, the families and friends they left behind. But this was different. It was like she was inside him, feeling what he felt.

"God, he has a son. A little boy."

She took a deep breath, willed away the goose bumps that rose on her arms, and gathered her composure. She couldn't let herself think about a child who'd just lost his father. She wouldn't. "I'm sure his family will appreciate having you with them later. So why don't you answer a few questions for me so I can cut you loose?"

He looked back at her, his eyes wary as a big cat sensing a trap. "What questions?"

"Let's start with your name."

"I told you already. Nathan Cross."

"Just checking my facts."

His lip curled like a feral dog. "Maybe you should write it down this time. Shouldn't you have a little notebook or something?"

Reminding herself she was going to cut him some slack for the attitude tonight, she held her arms out to the sides of the green dress she'd bought for this evening's event. The thin wrap dangled over her elbows. "Sorry. No pockets."

He paused long enough to give her a lingering look up and down. Heat flooded her face and other areas. Damn him, how did he do that?

Focus. She needed to focus. "Tell me again what you were doing at the garage."

"I was waiting for Rhys. We were going . . . to a party. I told you I had another engagement."

"So you did. It's not exactly the kind of neighborhood I'd want to stand around in alone at midnight, but you were waiting, and when he got there the two of you saw a man with a gun on the third level and went to see what he was up to, at which point he attacked you. In the following fight Rhys was shot and the man with the gun fell over the restraining barrier."

She tilted her head and arched one eyebrow.

He nodded.

Bingo. She didn't need no stinkin' notebook.

"Why didn't you call the police when you saw the gunman?"

"No cell phone."

"Did Rhys arrive at the garage alone?"

"Yes."

"So it was just the two of you and the gunman up there?"

"Yes."

She paused, purposely giving him time to wonder what she was thinking, and then circled back to her original point. "Where was this other engagement?"

He hesitated just long enough to give away the fact that he was going to lie. "I don't know. The hosts were friends of Rhys's."

"What're their names?"

"I don't know."

"Who else was planning on going to this party?"

"I don't know."

"Why don't you give me the names of some of Rhys's friends who might have been going? I'll find out."

"Why don't you ask me what you really want to know?"

The rapid-fire repartee ended with a bang. Nathan's nostrils flared. He looked like he wanted to launch himself across the sidewalk at her, but he didn't so much as blink.

The man had self-control, she'd give him that. Besides, he was right. She was dodging the issue, and he was clearly a man who appreciated directness.

"How did you get those cuts on your chest?"

"What?"

She nodded toward the bandage. He looked down at the gauze beneath his open coat as if he'd forgotten it was there.

"I must have fallen on some glass during the fight." It was the same story he'd given earlier, and it still didn't ring true.

"Looks more like someone scratched you."

Nathan relaxed visibly, smiled a little too easily, sending her bullshit meter into a Klaxon frenzy. "Nobody could scratch that deep with their bare hands."

"No," she said. "No*body* could."

At least no human body.

On the other hand, that shadow she'd been trying for the last two hours to convince herself she'd only imagined seeing as it flew out the back of the parking garage just as she'd climbed out of the car and looked up at the third level had looked perfectly capable.

*Nathan tipped the cabbie twelve dollars on an eight-*dollar fare so he wouldn't have to wait for the man to make change for a twenty. The sun would rise in another hour, and the night was fast catching up with him.

Rachel Vandermere—God, he couldn't believe she was a cop; Interpol, no less—had kept him at the museum with her questions until he thought his control might snap. Then she'd insisted on having her driver take him home. With her in the car with them.

He'd had to practically bare his teeth at her to get her to back off and call him a cab. The last thing he wanted was to be alone in the backseat of a car with her. The beast within him was hungry.

For revenge and for a woman.

Inside his apartment he didn't bother to turn on the lights. The dark suited his mood. His hands shook as he stripped off his bloody tuxedo and crammed it in the trash bin. His teeth chattered as he uncorked a bottle of wine and poured himself a full tumbler, then chugged down the merlot like cheap beer and wiped his mouth with the back of his hand.

Not sure what to do next, too much energy pulsing through him to sit, too tired to make his way to the shower, he wandered through the dim recesses of his apartment the way a wild creature might prowl its den.

His place was large and airy, a studio-type floor plan,

sectioned off into kitchen, dining room, bedroom, and living area only by décor, and he'd never felt so lost in it before. The "library," a leather easy chair tucked into a shadowed corner between two floor-to-ceiling bookcases, had never appeared so cold and uninviting. The king-size bed covered in Egyptian sheets against the far wall never seemed so empty.

He considered sitting down with the books lying on the dining room table, texts on ancient spells and rituals. He spent most of his free time in this life studying, looking for a way to reverse the magic that cursed him and all like him.

Before he'd been banished from his people, his home, he and his mentor had learned the craft of their ancestors. They'd harnessed the power of the god and goddess and been granted many insights, including the ability to see the future from time to time, but they'd never found a way to counteract the evil that had been done a thousand years ago.

He wasn't sure there was a way.

A pit of hopelessness opened in his stomach. Like an ulcer, the sickness grew, consumed him until he swept the books off the polished cherrywood table and stalked to the window that covered the whole east wall of his condo, called by the night. The dark sky.

Naked save for the bandage covering half his chest and the blood crusted on his hands, he studied his reflection in the glass. His eyes glowed with a faint green sheen, a sign of the turbulence within him and his shaky control, but other than that, he looked like a normal human male. Better than many he knew who didn't take care of their bodies.

Only the vain gave importance to their appearance, he realized, yet Nathan prized his. He cherished the sinew and bone, the hard flesh, not out of vanity, but because it represented the one part of himself he considered good and valuable: his humanity.

But where had his humanity gotten him tonight? Where had it gotten Rhys?

On a cold slab at the morgue, that's where.

Unable to keep looking at the reflection in the window glass, Nathan tipped back his head and choked out an angry laugh. How did the old saying go—"It's what's on the inside that matters"?

Well, what was on the inside of Nathan was decidedly nonhuman. It was monstrous. A thing to be feared and hated by humans, even the ones who said they loved—

No. He would not go there. He was already raw and bleeding, figuratively and literally, tonight. And spending an hour being interrogated by Rachel Vandermere had been like rubbing salt over the wounds. She suspected something, though she hadn't let on what.

Her suspicions didn't concern him much. He'd dealt with cops before, although few had been as smart and none as attractive as her. What bothered him was the way she made him feel—as if he should know her. As if he *did* know her, but couldn't quite place her.

Restlessness gnawing at him, he looked out again on the city. Icy raindrops plinked against the window. Tiny rivulets shivered down the glass, refracting the red stop-lights, white streetlights, the yellow neon bar sign thirty stories below. Shapes and colors blurred into an odd abstract. A fuzzy Christmas tree against the distant, black background of Lake Michigan.

It was the lake that drew him. The black matte surface of the water. Sometimes he longed for a place like that. Eternal dark. Everlasting quiet.

If he closed his eyes, he could feel the rhythm of the water, the way the waves sucked at the shore, but always Rachel's face was in the forefront of his mind, her green eyes challenging him and her spun-gold hair enticing him.

His body humming like an electrical conductor, he let his vision blur even further. His reflection and the distorted city lights merged into one strong beam of light, opened into a bright tunnel. The tunnel of Second Sight. He reached through it, searching for porcelain skin, ripe-berry lips.

He caught the scent of rosemary, her scent, a heartbeat before he located her in her bed, her smooth skin and satin nightgown in stark contrast with scratchy hotel sheets. She'd left the bathroom light on and the door slightly open. An arrow of light angled across the bed, bathing her in burnished gold and gloom.

She moaned and writhed in her sleep. She seemed to be caught in a nightmare—something about firelight and shadow puppets. Her fear coursed through his veins as she thrashed, smooth legs tangling in the rough sheets. Her horror filled his chest with ice water.

Nathan frowned, reluctant to delve deeper into her mind than he already had, but knowing he couldn't stand by and watch her suffer. Unlike Gargoyles, whose minds could only be viewed, not influenced, through the Second Sight, humans were open to suggestion, especially in their sleep, when their thoughts were most unguarded. He could help her. He needed to help her, since God knew he couldn't help himself.

He tried to drop the curtain on the scene playing out in her dream by cocooning her in a telepathic sense of safety. He touched her mind with his, just a feathery stroke meant to comfort. "Shhh," he whispered in her ear, but she didn't seem to hear him. She twisted her fists in the sheets. He felt her whimper in his throat.

Stomach lurching on the taste of her fear, he pushed his mind, his will, deeper into hers, gasping softly in the dark as her thoughts folded around him. With some humans, making a connection this deep required force. The merge was as unmatched as square peg in a round hole. But not with Rachel. Her mind took him inside as if he belonged there. A perfect fit.

Breaking a sweat in concentration—not to mention arousal at being so intimately joined with her, her unconscious mind greedily clasping his—he focused his thoughts on her dream. He held her mentally. Rocked her and smoothed her hair. In seconds the troubling images evaporated like mist at sunrise.

Her thrashing quieted. Her body warmed, warming his as well. She turned on her side, and the covers slipped down, taking the thin strap of her satin gown with them. The smooth curve of her shoulder glowed like marble under a full moon.

Nathan should leave her now, only he couldn't pull away. He wasn't just in her mind anymore. He'd dissolved in her blood, spread to every cell. He was the breath in her lungs, the coil of desire in her belly.

She was hot now. Color bloomed on her pale cheeks. With his mind he held her tighter. Closer. She writhed again, not from fear this time, but as if under a lover's hands. Her lips pursed. Her back bowed. The covers slid down another few inches to the top of her full breast.

Nathan's breath came quicker as he traced the scalloped edge of her gown with his gaze, measured the full mound still hidden beneath the blanket. A thought built in his mind and drove into hers: nudge the blanket farther down.

She flailed her arms weakly.

His mouth went dry. His pulse pounded like a drum. He'd never used the Second Sight like this before—well, not since the teenage years of a previous life when he and Rhys had been enamored with a busty barmaid who lived two doors down. He wasn't a hormone-crazed teenager anymore, though. He was old enough to know it was wrong and it was perverted and still he wanted more. Craved more.

He'd already established he was a monster, right?

Brows drawn together, he thrust the thought deeper. Gathered himself and thrust again. The desire to roll over, onto her back, spewed out of his mind and into hers.

Her legs kicked. Her hips lifted. The bedsheets shifted to her waist, and she rolled to her back, exposing one plump, satin-covered breast to his view. She was perfect. Full and firm, her nipple already hardened in arousal.

Helpless to deny her, to deny himself, he reached out with his thoughts and gently, oh, so softly, strummed the pointed peak with his palm.

FIVE

"You look like hell." Balancing a wireless laptop on his thighs, the tech guy, Otto, pushed with his feet and sent his rolling chair wheeling across the Chicago PD conference room Rachel's team had been using as a command center during the French secretary's visit.

"Your powers of observation astound me, Otto." But not so much that she was too awed to dive for the last jelly doughnut in the cardboard box on the table. "Not to mention the extents to which you'll go in order to avoid physical exercise of any kind."

Otto added a file folder to an already-hefty stack at the end of the table, then put his chair in reverse, winding up where he'd started without ever getting off his duff. "Hey," he said, pushing his glasses up his skinny nose. "I resemble that remark."

One of the local detectives stood, seemingly absorbed in a folder of his own, and slung an arm around her waist as he edged his way around her toward the door. He smelled like Polo cologne and toothpaste. Far too fresh for her spoiled mood. "Don't worry, sweetheart. Otto wouldn't know a good-looking wom—" He gave her an empathetic glance, then did a double take at her and winced. "Geez, you do look like hell."

"Thanks." She pointed her doughnut at him, barely resisting the urge to squirt strawberry jelly all over his crisp white shirt. "Now get outta my way before I have to hurt you. You're between me and the coffee."

The detective threw his hands up in surrender and pressed his back against the wall. "For God's sake somebody get the woman a cup of coffee before she uses that thing!"

Otto rolled to the stained pot in the corner, tilted the carafe until a blob of black sludge plopped into a foam cup, then wheeled over and handed it to her.

Sighing, she slumped into a chair.

"So what gives with you today, Blondie?" The hostage she'd just held at doughnut-point crammed his lanky body into the seat next to her. "You okay?

Ordinarily she would have resented his assumption that something had to be wrong for her to show up at work looking like death warmed over. If one of the guys came in bleary-eyed and muzzy-headed after closing a big case, everyone would have assumed he'd been out celebrating. They would have clapped him on the back and made bawdy jokes about "the morning after."

Ordinarily that kind of sexist attitude would have put her dander up, but not today. She was too tired to fight.

"Didn't sleep well," she mumbled into her coffee.

In truth she hadn't slept at all other than the first fitful minutes after her head hit the pillow. Her mind just wouldn't shut down. The sights and sounds of a demanding day had swirled and mixed with older, darker memories from her past. She hadn't dreamed like that in months.

Correction. She had *never* dreamed like that.

Night terrors she was used to. Waking up bathed in sweat, heart pounding, breath coming sharp and deep was no surprise. But jolting awake with her skin tingling, breasts heavy, a coiling ache between her legs—that was definitely a new experience. Not to mention that in the in-

stant before she'd come fully back to consciousness she'd
seen—not imagined, but *seen*, as clearly as she saw Otto in
the chair across from her now—a man standing naked before a massive window, his impressive body lit only by a
hazy moon. Nathan Cross's eyes had been dark and turbu-
lent as a winter storm, his body taut with frustration, yet
his touch had been as gentle as a lover's—

His *touch?*

She couldn't really have felt his fingers on her breast.

Geez, she was really losing it. It had only been a dream,
and an embarrassing one at that. She hardly knew the man.
She certainly had no business dreaming about him naked.
Or wondering where he got the little moon-shaped scar on
his right thigh. No business at all reacting physically to the
memory—*dream*, since it couldn't be a memory; it had
never happened—of his thumb and forefinger tweaking
her nipple until she felt the touch in her womb, as if an
electrical wire ran between the two intimate locations.

"Let's get a move on, boys and girls." Carter Laisson
strode into the room looking very dapper with a diamond
stud twinkling from his left ear. He clapped once and
rubbed his palms together. "Get those statements signed.
Get the files packed up. My flight back to D.C. leaves in
two hours and forty-three minutes, and I don't plan to miss
it. I've got a hot date with my wife tonight."

Wishing she'd worn more than an unpadded bra and
thin T-shirt today, Rachel forced last night's erotic images
to the back of her mind, crossed her arms over her chest
and twirled her chair to face her temporary boss. "Prelim
autopsy reports in already?"

"Our suspect splattered on the concrete right in front of
us after a three-story fall; our Good Samaritan took a bullet through the heart. I don't need a medical examiner to
tell me how they died."

"What about CSI? Crime scene investigators find
anything?"

"Like what? Jimmy Hoffa's body?" Carter hefted a file
box labeled BISHOP in thick, black marker off the table and

sat it by the door. "The secretary is on a plane back to France, and William Bishop won't be assassinating any more politicians. Chicago PD can follow up on the forensics report when it's ready, so quit worrying. Life is good."

Rachel picked up a pencil and rolled it between her fingers. "I suppose you're right." Except her gut told her there was more to this case than they knew. Then again, her various body parts had been lying to her all morning and most of the night. Ever since she'd met Nathan Cross.

Nathan Cross. Refusing to allow the heat his name evoked in her to reach her cheeks, she let her mind wander over what she knew about him: Aside from the fact that he looked even better out of a tux than in one, he liked art so much that he made a career out of teaching its history, and he didn't pick up women who hit on him at museums.

Maybe he was married. What a crime that would be. All that man and only one woman could enjoy him.

She lost the battle to stem her rising blush and felt the blood fill her face.

No, Nathan Cross wasn't married. Besides the fact that he didn't wear a ring, she'd seen the appreciation in his eyes. He hadn't been thinking about another woman when he'd turned her down at the gala.

Which made her wonder why he'd been desperate to the point of rudeness to get away from her only to walk two blocks in the bitter cold and happen upon an assassination about to occur.

She chewed on her jelly doughnut, pondering, then tossed the uneaten half in the trash and helped her teammates pack up. They had flights to catch.

She, on the other hand, felt some vacation time coming on. She had plenty of unused days, and she planned to take a few of them.

In Chicago.

Nathan felt Rachel's presence a full second before she opened the door to the bar where he was nursing an empty shot glass. He smelled her signature rosemary scent. Who made perfume out of rosemary, anyway?

He lifted his glass toward the bartender. "Make it two."

"A double?"

"No. Two glasses."

The realization that he'd smelled her before he'd seen her, before she'd even come inside, grated his nerves. He didn't understand it; he shouldn't be able to feel a human this way. He shouldn't have been able to slide so deeply into her mind three nights ago. And when he had, she sure as hell shouldn't have been aware of him there.

Yet she'd snapped herself awake when he'd touched her, as if she'd actually felt his hand. Sitting stark upright in bed with the sheet clutched to her chest, she'd stared into the darkness as if she could see him.

Impossible.

She'd been having a bad dream, that's all. She'd frightened herself awake and seen only the nightmare images in the seconds before they faded, not him.

But if she had looked back at him, seen him standing before his window, she'd gotten an eyeful. And if his body had reacted to the impact of her imagined gaze, jumping to life as if she'd been the one to touch him so intimately, that was only wishful thinking on his part.

It had been a long time since he'd been with a woman.

It would be a lot longer yet, he reminded himself as she strolled toward the bar. He planned to live the rest of this life, his last life, in celibacy.

Sure, he could have a woman if he wanted one. Use a condom so that he wouldn't have to worry about stealing another baby from its mother's arms. He'd gained a little relief from the craving that drove him to reproduce that way in the past. These days he could even have a vasectomy if he wanted. Then he could be with as many women as he cared to, whenever he cared to.

But he wouldn't, because he didn't want just sex.

He wanted a mate. Someone to kiss good night and cook breakfast for.

If he shared his life with a woman, sooner or later she was bound to find out about him. She'd see something she shouldn't see.

Then . . .

He wouldn't let himself think about what happened then. It was enough knowing that a relationship with Rachel Vandermere would come at too high a price. For both of them.

She dropped a black leather clutch bag on the counter, hiked up the hem of a modest black dress that fell to knee-length, and swung herself onto the stool next to his. The bartender dropped two whiskeys in front of him, and he pushed one to her with the back of his hand, then downed his in one gulp.

Surprisingly, she followed suit, swallowing the drink without so much as a sputter.

"Thanks," she said, and slapped the glass down on the bar. "I needed that."

He took out his wallet, flipped a twenty on the bar, and turned to leave.

"I missed you at the funeral," she said, stopping him cold. "Rhys Keller was your friend. I assumed you'd want to pay your respects."

He turned, the whiskey burning in his gut. Something else burning a few inches lower. "There you go assuming things again. I would've thought a cop would deal more in facts than supposition."

"Which part did I get wrong? Rhys wasn't your friend, or you don't want to pay your respects?"

"I don't have to stand beside his grave to say good-bye to him. He isn't there. He's dead."

God, it hurt to say it. Hurt like a hole right through him where his friendship used to be. Nathan didn't know where *Les Gargouillen* went between lives; none of them did. But he knew it was a cold and empty place. Dark and silent. It wasn't as if Rhys was sitting on some cloud watching his family and friends mourn him below.

"He might not have been there," Rachel conceded. "But

his father was, and his little boy, Patrick. I'm sure it would have comforted them—"

He snatched his jacket off the bar. "You don't know what the hell you're talking about, lady." Patrick might have been happy to see him, but he was just a child. Too young to understand. "I have to go."

She stopped him with a firm grip on his arm. He could easily have jerked away from her, but the contact surprised him so much that he went perfectly still. People didn't touch him often. Something to do with his sunny disposition, he supposed. He'd once had a student tell him he was about as approachable as a Rottweiler with a T-bone.

Rachel Vandermere, however, did not look intimidated. When he finally pulled his gaze away from the spot where her hand rested on his arm, she hooked her off-kilter eyebrow, making her face even more uneven, and more interesting, than usual.

Curse him for noticing.

"Let me guess." She smiled at him. The look was casual, almost friendly, but there was something less affable just beneath the surface of the expression. "You're late for another engagement."

"As a matter of fact—"

"This isn't a social call, Professor Cross."

"I told you everything the other night. I have nothing else to say."

"Oh, there are plenty more things you can tell me." She let go of his arm, dug in the pocket of her coat, and pulled out a 4 x 6 photograph. "Like whether or not you know this man."

Reluctantly he took the picture. Looked at it much longer than necessary, his blood chilling. *Von.*

"He looks familiar." Nathan hunched his shoulders and handed the black-and-white mug shot back to her. He didn't lie well. Half-truths and evasion suited him better.

"He should," Rachel said. "His name is Von Simeon. The two of you went to the same school. St. Michael's, I believe."

"Unless that picture is very old, he was years behind me."

"Yeah, but St. Michael's is small, even for a private school. Only twenty or thirty kids across all twelve grades, right? Seems like you'd run into each other."

"We might have, years ago. I said he looked familiar. Now that we're all grown up, I don't tend to associate with his type."

Her green eyes gleamed. "And what type would that be?"

"A thug, judging by that picture."

"He's spent a few nights in Cook County Jail. Petty stuff mostly—stealing cigarettes, public intoxication. Are you sure you haven't seen him recently?"

The hairs stood up on the back of Nathan's neck. "Why would you ask?"

"His prints were found on the rifle we recovered at the garage the other night. William Bishop never worked with locals, certainly never with anyone as small-time as Von Simeon. If Von wasn't connected to him, I'm guessing he's connected to you. He was there last night, wasn't he?"

"I told you it was just me and Rhys."

"I know what you told me. Now I want to know the truth."

"You got your killer. The case is closed."

"Yeah, but I'm a cop. I have a fetish about leaving messy little details hanging, like unreported witnesses." She leveled her gaze on his chest. "And wounds that can't be explained."

He rolled his eyes. "That again?"

"We can talk about it here, or we can talk about it at the police station. Could take hours if we go down there, though. The other cops, you know, they'll start talking about conspiracies and accomplices. Might take all night to clear it all up."

She was bluffing. He knew she was bluffing. He could feel it around the edges of her consciousness.

Unfortunately, he could also feel an unflagging sense of determination.

He had to give her credit. He towered over her. They both knew he was physically stronger than she, and yet she tipped her chin up and met his maximum-intimidation glare with eyes as green and serene as a summer meadow.

"What do you really want from me?" he growled.

She smiled. "Let's take a ride. I'll show you."

"You'd think an outfit like Interpol could afford to put its people up someplace nicer than this." Nathan's voice rumbled close to her ear as he hovered behind her, his nearness sending a shiver rippling down her spine.

"Contrary to popular belief, Interpol is not a centralized organization whose agents jet around the world on the trails of hit men and jewel thieves. It's a consortium of eighty-four sponsoring countries who've agreed to share intelligence, each of whom funds its own National Bureau and works the cases within its borders. So although my ID says INTERPOL, I basically work for the U.S. government. Ergo, the dumpy hotel room."

Rachel's hand trembled slightly as she slid the key card into the slot on the door to said dumpy hotel room. Had she lost her ever-lovin' mind, bringing Nathan Cross here?

The door swung open and she stepped inside with a quick glance over her shoulder at the man behind her. She had nothing to worry about, she told herself. She prided herself on being a good judge of character. Nathan was hurt. She could understand that; he'd lost a friend. He was angry, too, that much was obvious, but she couldn't blame him for that, either. She'd practically blackmailed him into coming here. He was probably even a little bit dangerous, judging by his tumultuous eyes and shuttered expressions. But he wasn't evil, despite the fact she'd practically accused him of being in on the attempted assassination of a foreign diplomat.

He hadn't been in on it; she'd bet her life on that.

She might *be* betting her life on it.

He followed her into the room the way he'd ridden here

in her rental car—without a word. Throwing his leather jacket across the back of a chair, he went straight to the vanity sink outside the bathroom where he splashed water on his face and dried himself with a hand towel. On his way back into the room, he stopped to dig through the mini-fridge for a cold soda that would probably add five dollars to her hotel bill.

"Make yourself at home," she said sarcastically.

The can popped and fizzed when he opened it. He tipped it back and downed a slug, then wiped his mouth with the back of his hand. Gone was the sophisticated museum patron, the learned college professor.

The man who had taken their places oozed conscious conceit. He exuded power. Control.

Virility.

His voice slipped over her like crushed velvet. "You wanted me here," he said. "You got me. Now, what is it you're so eager to show me?"

He kicked back in the chair by the window, pulled at the knot of his tie, and opened two buttons on the front of his rumpled dress shirt, exposing a matte of fine chest hair. Her mind pictured what lay beyond the open vee, the triangle pointing down to a set of flat abs, the narrow arrow that led beyond. Suddenly she wished she were anywhere but here—preferably all the way back in her own apartment in D.C.

With the air-conditioning turned up and the ceiling fan on high.

He studied her appraisingly over the rim of his Coke, and her internal mercury rose another notch. Flames climbed her neck. What was it about this man that made her feel like he could see her thoughts, as if his mind and hers were opposite ends of the same bridge?

"Well?" he asked, and she swallowed hard.

Whether he was a mind-reading swami or not, she'd passed the point of no return. She was about to share a part of herself no human being had ever seen. He would either call her crazy and have her committed to the nearest institution or he would recognize what he saw, understand that it was okay. Then he could share what really happened at the parking garage the other night. Then she would believe whatever he told her, no matter how unbelievable the story might seem.

And in the telling, maybe, just maybe, he would help her understand what had happened to *her* all those years ago.

Inhaling a deep breath of musty hotel room air, she leaned over, opened her suitcase on the stand at the end of the bed, and pulled out a tattered manuscript box. Her hands shook as she balanced it on her knees. "I joined Interpol six years ago because it gave me access to case files from all over the world," she said, twiddling with the rubber bands that held the lid on the overstuffed box.

"There's not enough crime in the United States for you?"

"I'm interested in a particular type of case. One with . . . unexplained elements."

"What, like *The X-Files*? You believe in UFOs?"

She snapped the rubber bands off the box and pulled out the picture on top before he started making clucking sounds and digging through the phone book under *M* for *Men in White Coats*.

Handing him the picture, she explained, "This is from a double murder in Germany, 1980."

He took the picture, but his eyes never left her. The heat of his gaze softened her to the point of melting. "The dead men were later proven to be serial rapists working in tandem, but here, look at this." She scooted to the corner of the mattress where she could lean closer and pointed at the black-and-white print. "Those tracks in the blood around the bodies."

Finally he glanced down, but only for a fraction of a second, then his gaze jumped back to hers, focused on her with an intensity that scattered her thoughts.

"What about them?" he asked.

"They're hoofprints," she answered, making herself concentrate. Telling herself she moved from the bed to the edge of his chair only so that he could see better, not because she was drawn by his earthy scent.

"So?"

She tapped the picture. "This is Munich. How many hoofed animals do you think roam the streets of Munich?"

Before he could answer, she took the picture and handed him another. The explanation of this one came in a rush. "See the body in the top of this tree? It belonged to a wife beater who went a little too far one day and killed the woman. How did he get up there? He couldn't have climbed. He weighed a good two-eighty, three hundred pounds, and the lowest branch is twenty feet off the ground. Plus the coroner's report says he was placed in the tree postmortem. It's like something carried his carcass off, then dropped it."

Nathan was looking this time, studying, but she was on a roll and plopped another photo in his hands. "San Francisco, 1999. A banker who'd embezzled millions from his own company, leaving his retirees without a pension, is apparently mauled to death by wild dogs in his own home. Only all the doors and windows in the house are closed. How did the dogs get in? How did they get out?"

Without pause she flipped more papers into his hands, this time a sworn deposition. "Paris, 2002. This woman says she saw a snake strangle her husband and then slither into the sewer."

Another sheaf. "Dublin, 1994. An eight-year-old boy tells his mother he saw a creature that was half man, half mountain goat butt his father off a cliff." The words tumbled out faster with every file. She was babbling, but she couldn't seem to help it. "Boston, 2001. An amateur photographer gets a shot of something that looks like a giant bat flying over the harbor."

Nathan shoved her hands away when she pushed another picture toward him. "Stop," he said.

The picture fell to the floor. She grabbed another, feeling feverish, shaky with the truth erupting at last. "New York City, last month—"

"I said *stop*."

He stood. The papers and pictures she'd collected so diligently over the years fluttered to his feet. She fell to her knees on the carpet, scooping them up. They were her life. Her quest. "There are more. Hundreds more. All the major cities—"

She hadn't seen him stoop, but his hands were under her elbows, lifting. "What's wrong with you? Why are you doing this?"

"I—I have to do it." Her strength was fading fast, leaving her standing on rubbery knees.

"Why?" His hands cupped her face. His voice was passionate, silky.

She bent to the box for one last picture, lifted it in shaking hands.

"No." He pushed it away.

"Please. Just this last one."

He scanned the sheet. She didn't have to look. The image had been burned into her mind twenty-seven years ago.

"See those scrapes in the door to the cupboard above the body?" she asked, her eyes closed, seeing the prone figure on the floor through six-year-old eyes, remembering how it looked before the fire turned everything to ash, the puddle of blood around her father. Taking in a weak breath, she forced herself to focus on the grooves in the wood, not her daddy's pale face. "They're like . . . handprints, left by the killer. Only those weren't made by hands. They were left by claws."

She opened her eyes, looked into Nathan's, realizing she was standing so close that she could see the pulse leaping at the base of his neck.

She reached out and touched his shirt lightly, remembering exactly where his wounds lay beneath. "Three claws, exactly four inches apart. Just like the scrapes on your chest."

"Rachel—"

He reached for her hand. She pulled it back, spun away

from him. He rested his hands on her shoulders from behind.

"The man on the floor is my father," she choked out, futilely trying to stem her rising tears.

"Jesus."

"I can still smell the blood."

"You were there?" She heard the horror in his voice. The revulsion. She felt his hot breath on the back of her neck. His fingers searing her shoulders through her wool funeral dress.

Unable to speak, she nodded.

He turned her roughly toward him. His eyes were as hot as his breath, his hands. Hotter. "What do you want from me?"

"The truth." Her breath shuddered like an old dog's final gasp. Finally, after all these years, she could say it out loud. "I'm not chasing UFOs, Nathan. I'm chasing monsters."

SIX

Nathan knew he should let Rachel go, walk away.
Hell, he should push her away and run. Better yet, change
form and fly as fast and as far as his wings would carry him.

But he didn't move. Couldn't. It was as if his feet were
rooted in the threadbare hotel carpet. His hands frozen on
her trembling shoulders. He could only stare at her in mute
shock. In horror at the collection of data she held in her
hands. The havoc she could wreak with it.

Slowly she lifted her head. Her frantic green gaze
jumped, collided with his, jolting him out of the deep
pocket of his thoughts and drawing him into hers.

He knew the way through her mind, now, after his visit
into her dream. The pathways that wound through her
hopes, her dreams, her fears, were as familiar to him as the
last mile on the road home was to a weary traveler.

For a human, Rachel Vandermere possessed a startling
clarity of thought. She made no pretenses about who she
was, or what she wanted. Her whole being vibrated with
the energy she poured into a single mission: to find the
monsters she believed roamed the shadows and the dark
nights, and to kill them.

And she expected him to help.

Nathan recoiled. He tried to pull back, to retreat from her mind, but he found himself ensnared in her memories of the night her parents died. Her terror.

Through six-year-old eyes he saw the snapping tongue of flame spread across a wall hung with photos of a happy young family. He felt the heat. Heard explosions that might have been gunfire and saw a misshapen shadow rise in the eerie glow of firelight.

Again he tried to wrench himself free. He gained enough mental distance to be aware of not only the child Rachel, but of the woman. Her skin was hot where he still touched her shoulders. Her eyes stared up at him sightlessly, wide black discs surrounded by a sliver of green as she held him inside her long enough to let him feel the shock and cold rage settle into her young heart. Long enough to show him her father's lifeless body on the floor.

Show him. Christ, he wasn't just in her mind. She was in his!

While he'd been probing her thoughts, she'd slipped inside him like fog through a crack in a door, silently, stealthily. And like fog, she wandered, spread, tentacles reaching into the darkest recesses of his mind.

Humans weren't supposed to be able to initiate the mental connection, or even be aware of it when a Gargoyle formed a link with them. Yet there Rachel was in his every thought, and she was definitely aware. He saw it in her glazed eyes. He felt it in the way her pulse leaped, knew she felt his own jump in response, and the redoubled pounding added to the throbbing headache at the base of his skull. He felt her turn and twist through his present, his past. Another moment and she'd see everything. Know all that he was.

The whiskey he'd drunk earlier soured in his stomach.

With a great gathering of strength, he shoved her away. The mental connection between them broke with a white-hot flash, like a lightbulb burning out.

Rachel stumbled backward. The bed caught her behind

the knees and she sat heavily. Her green eyes were glassy now, but still full of questions.

Breathing hard, Nathan turned away, raked a hand through unkempt hair. When he noticed his fingers were trembling, he clenched them into a fist and shoved it into the pocket of his jeans. "This is a joke, right?" He didn't feel like laughing. "There's a camera hidden somewhere, and you're going to jump up and tell me to smile."

"You know it isn't."

He glanced over his shoulder at her. "You can't believe all this."

"I've spent my life trying to prove it."

Steadier now, but not by much, he turned to face her. "Because you saw your parents die."

"I saw them *murdered*. By something that wasn't human."

"You were a child. You were traumatized. Your imagination—"

"Don't! Don't tell me I imagined it. I know what I saw." Her eyes narrowed, still glazed. Her lower lip both trembled and jutted. "And don't you tell me I'm crazy. Don't."

She wasn't crazy.

Dangerous, yes, but not crazy.

She was an international cop. That gave her access to information and it gave her credibility. She'd already amassed enough evidence for the existence of monsters to make those who lived on the fringes of paranoia believe. How much more would it take to convince the mainstream? To have every housewife looking for the bogeyman under the bed, and husbands sleeping with loaded pistols in the nightstand?

How long before the streets of Chicago became hunting grounds, with his people the prey?

A sweat broke on Nathan's palms. *Jesus,* he had to get out of here.

He paused, though, to watch as Rachel stood and walked away from him, pressed her palm on the window. Without even reaching out to her mentally, he felt the cool glass beneath her palm. Outside, the lights of the city sparkled in the night like diamonds on black velvet.

"What are you afraid of, Nathan?"

He opened his mouth, but there was no sense denying it. She'd felt his fear, just as he'd felt hers.

"Is it the idea that monsters exist in the world that scares you? Or is it what people will think about you, say about you, if you tell them you saw one?"

"Neither." His voice was rough.

She turned and looked up at him expectantly, her green eyes back to normal. She wanted an answer, but how could he give her one? How could he tell her it was *her* he was afraid of? What she could do with what she knew.

"Maybe I just don't believe in getting involved in fools' quests."

"Is that what you think I am? A fool?"

"I think you're a beautiful, intelligent woman who's built a great life for herself despite a difficult beginning." Her hands stilled and she looked up at him, surprised. He blew out a breath. "And I think you need to let the past go and start living that life."

A shadow of disappointment fell across her face just before she looked back down. She finished gathering her files, straightened them, and set them back in their box in silence.

Nathan took that as his cue to leave and headed for the door. He paused with his hand on the knob when she spoke again behind him.

"I thought I saw something in you," she said softly. "With all your education and your travels and your appreciation of art, I thought I saw brains and open-mindedness. But more than that, after what happened to your friend in the parking garage, I thought I saw fury. Outrage at the injustice of it. The same kind of outrage I feel when I think about my parents."

Nathan squeezed the doorknob until the brass warmed beneath his touch. "Don't use Rhys to try to blackmail me into helping you."

"Are you telling me you can just walk away? Let your friend's death go unchallenged?"

"Unchallenged? The son of a bitch—the *man*—who shot him is dead. You call that unchallenged?"

"Look at the pictures. There are worse than him out there. Much worse."

"They're not my problem." He yanked the door open and stepped out without looking back.

"If you believe that, then you really aren't the man I thought you were," she called across the threshold.

She had that right, he thought as he closed the door behind him. He wasn't the man she thought he was.

He wasn't a man at all.

Rachel thought she'd gotten over being disappointed every time someone pooh-poohed her theories on monsters a long time ago. The first social worker she'd told what she'd seen the night her parents were killed had laughed at first, thinking she was making up stories. When Rachel insisted she was telling the truth, Child Protective Services had brought in a counselor to talk to her. Eventually they sent her to a shrink.

A child who'd never thought to lie, she remained steadfast in her story. As time passed, she was alternately patronized, ridiculed, and finally pitied by those charged with her care.

"Poor thing," they'd whisper when they thought she couldn't hear, and make little spinning motions with their fingers by their ears. "She's not quite right."

After a while she didn't care what *they* thought. She didn't care if they believed her. She knew what she'd seen. Every night she saw it anew, lying in her narrow bed in the orphanage, the covers pulled up tight under her chin. She'd squeeze her eyes shut tight and think hard about her mommy and daddy's faces. The sound of their voices. The way Mommy's hands were so soft, rubbing her back when she had a cold, and Daddy's hands were so strong and rough when he pushed her—not too high—on the swing set.

But after a few years, it was hard to remember exactly what Mommy and Daddy had looked like. Was his hair dark brown or light? What color lipstick did she wear?

She watched other kids get adopted from the children's center. Saw how they smiled when they walked out with new moms and dads holding their hands. Being a baby, and free of the psychological issues she supposedly suffered as a result of seeing her parents murdered, Levi had been adopted quickly, while Rachel languished in the public welfare system. Eventually she started thinking how much she wanted a new family. Maybe even with some other kids to play with her, a mom who would teach her how to make chocolate chip cookies.

A dad to check under the bed when he tucked her in at night.

She'd never get adopted if she didn't quit talking about monsters, the social worker said. If she didn't quit drawing pictures of ugly things with glowing green eyes and leathery wings.

And so she stopped—drawing pictures and talking, that is; not believing.

She'd always believed.

She kept everything she remembered about that awful night deep inside her, where no one would see. She made nice with a couple from upstate New York and got herself adopted. She went to school, studied criminal justice, and wound up at Interpol, where, her rookie year, when the most important task they assigned her to was organizing boxes in "the morgue"—the cold-case storage room—she came across a file that unearthed all the memories.

An elderly couple witnessed their son, a twenty-year-old crack addict who'd returned to their home to steal their Social Security checks, dragged off into the woods by a two-headed wolf with ram's horns and green eyes.

Glowing green eyes.

Police discounted the couple as hysterical, yet when the

young man's remains were found four days later, there wasn't an ounce of his flesh left and there were gnaw marks on the bones.

Rachel spent lots of time in the morgue after that. Lunch hours, nights. Weekends. She found other cases. Other witnesses, but none as credible as the couple who'd lost their son twice—first to drugs and then to a monster.

Having learned her lesson in childhood, she was careful who she told about her quest. Her obsession.

For two years she'd had a partner, Cash Sawyer. Cash knew. As many hours as she spent mulling over her growing file collection, it would have been hard to keep it from him. She figured she could trust him; he was her partner.

He was also her lover. Until she'd figured out that mixing work and sex made about as much sense as tap-dancing in a room with marbles spilled all over the floor.

Too bad Cash had never quite gotten that. But at least his hope that she'd fall back into his sack someday made it less likely he'd spill her secrets around the water cooler.

Unlike Nathan Cross, who wanted nothing from her.

What if he went to her superiors, filed a complaint? She was supposed to be on vacation. Working unofficial cases was strictly verboten.

"Idiot," she mumbled.

She'd meant it when she said she thought she'd seen something in him. She'd thought he was different.

God.

He *was* different. Just not in any way she'd expected.

When he'd touched her, it felt like she'd stuck her finger in a light socket.

What the hell *was* that?

She looked in his eyes and felt like she'd fallen inside him. She felt his blood pouring through his veins, the beat of his heart. Then, as if she'd suddenly been transported inside a European bullet train, she'd felt the floor move beneath her feet, heard the roar of the wind outside. She sensed landscape passing by in a blur in her peripheral vision. Then she had a feeling it wasn't landscape rushing by, but time.

She heard angry shouts and mingled laughter. Smelled sea air and mountain pine and smoke, saw birth and death flash by so quickly they were almost indistinguishable.

The farther she traveled, the darker it got and the louder the wind roared, until it wasn't just a wind, but a cyclone swirling in a black chasm, roiling, spinning, drowning out all thought, leaving only feeling. Pain and suffering, joy and hope, pride, shame, *regret*.

The tempest had dragged her nearer, an emotional vortex sucking in everything in its path. Rachel realized too late that she was being pulled inside. She tried to resist, suddenly afraid of losing herself in the storm of emotion, but the sheer power of it overwhelmed her.

She tumbled and turned in the gale, battered by sensation, hammered by uninhibited emotion. There was no defense. Every feeling was outside her . . . and inside her. She squeezed her eyes shut and drifted with the current, spiraling ever closer to the eye of the storm, a void darker than night, emptier than a black hole in space.

The strongest feeling of all emanated from that place. It pulsed as if it were alive. Roared as if it was suffering.

It was . . . a yearning like Rachel had never known. Never imagined. Craving to the point of insanity, like a big cat, a lion or a panther, chained without food day after day with a herd of sheep in sight but just out of reach. It snorted, its breath hot and moist, its eyes glowing, and charged her.

Then Nathan had let her go. The darkness, the wind, the feelings all disappeared as if a door had been slammed in her face. She had opened her eyes and felt cool trails of tears evaporating on her cheeks.

Rachel had never, ever been the type to swoon, but her knees had threatened to buckle. Lord only knew how she had managed to conduct a more-or-less coherent conversation with him until he left.

Now that he was gone, she sank to the bed, lowered her head to her hands, and scrubbed her face vigorously.

Okay, so asking Nathan Cross for help hadn't been a good idea. Being on the same continent as a man that had that kind of effect on her wasn't a good idea. There were other ways to find out what had happened in that parking garage. There were other witnesses. If she couldn't get what she needed from Nathan Cross, she'd find this kid Von.

Feeling steadier now, she drew in a slow, cleansing breath and reached to the floor for one of the pictures she'd dropped—the crime scene photo from the other night. It was a long shot of the body in the street, showing the perspective to the parking garage.

In the background Nathan Cross sat on the bumper of an ambulance, his white shirt smeared dark and hanging open. He was looking back to the street. Back at her. It was as if the photo itself were looking at her.

A shiver passed down her spine.

She would pick up Von's trail in the morning.

And if she was lucky, the trail wouldn't lead anywhere near Nathan Cross.

SEVEN

Nathan punched his fists into the pockets of his jacket and snugged the black leather tighter around his torso. A sharp wind bit at the skin left exposed, his neck and his cheeks. The first flurries of winter sifted down from the night sky, just tiny flakes, catching the moonlight like glitter, then disappearing as soon as they hit the sidewalk.

It was too early for real snow, the kind that drifted up to the doorknob on the front porch and overflowed the gutters onto the sidewalk, but the air already had that thin winter feel to it. By the time Nathan's mind settled after his encounter in the hotel with Rachel Vandermere and he became aware how far he'd walked—where he'd walked to—he was laboring for breath.

He stamped his feet under the streetlight at the corner of Madison and Cherry and looked across the street to the place that had been his childhood home in this lifetime. St. Michael's School for Boys towered like a medieval castle over the lower west side's blue-collar homes. Steam curled out of open manholes on the sidewalk to twine around the bars of its wrought-iron gates. The thick granite walls were pitted by time and weather, yet still stood strong, incorruptible by man or nature.

It was the civilization within that had eroded to the point of collapse.

Maybe the magic that created *Les Gargouillen* almost a thousand years ago was weakening. Or maybe it was their souls that couldn't stand the test of time. All Nathan knew was that things had changed. They weren't the saviors of Rouen any longer, slaying dragons and basking in the adulation of the townsfolk.

They weren't heroes in this age. They were antiques, as out of place as St. Michael's, with its crude monolithic architecture in a city of elegant glass skyscrapers like Chicago. Worse, they were monstrosities. Abominations of human nature.

And they'd begun to act like it.

They'd been men once. Could they not live as men again?

Nathan had to believe they could. He had to believe he had a choice, or he'd go insane. He chose to live as a man, in the light of higher education, studying art and passing on his knowledge to a new generation of mankind, not skulking in the alleys and shadows, following the scent of blood like the rest of his kind.

When his time came, he would choose to die as a man, without the promise of rebirth.

And for that he'd been turned out, banished from St. Michael's, forbidden to see his friends and family there.

So why had he come tonight?

To warn his people that an Interpol cop had her sights set on exposing them? Or because that cop had given him a big dose of reality, and made him realize that he wasn't human, no matter how badly he wished himself so?

When he was with her, the beast inside him rose close to the surface. The blood that beat in his veins was more animal than human. The drive to take her, by force if necessary, to make her his mate, was primitive and urgent.

She'd touched his mind, for God's sake, something no

woman, no human, should be able to do, and when she'd done it, she'd left herself wide open, exposed her heart to him, with all its beauty and its scars. The need she had to find the monsters that killed her parents was as deep and abiding as his need to find his humanity.

She'd shared her secrets with him, and he'd turned his back on her.

What else could he have done? To help her would be to betray his people. Just as to tell his people about her would be to betray her.

His breath whistled out of him and clouded before his face. He glanced up at the warm light glowing through the leaded glass in the north turret—the Wizenot's quarters.

The hell with them. The hell with all of them, including Rachel Vandermere. He wouldn't be driven by lust, scars, or thousand-year-old curses.

Hunching his shoulders against the cold, he turned toward home, determined to put them all out of his mind.

He was still trying the next afternoon when he finished his art history class. His thoughts absorbed so much of his attention that he didn't notice he was being stalked—again—until he drew up short on the sidewalk outside the Fine Arts building in order to avoid being mowed down by a city bus pulling away from the curb.

Instead he was mowed down by the girl on his heels. "Professor Cross? Oh, uh, sorry. You must not have heard me calling you."

Wincing, Nathan hitched the strap of his canvas book bag up his shoulder and turned. Melanie Something-or-other flashed her brilliant nineteen-year-old smile, tucked a strand of brassy red hair behind her ear, then clutched her notebooks with both arms across her stomach so that the tops lifted and plumped her already-generous nineteen-year-old breasts.

Nathan sighed silently. "Guess I was . . . preoccupied."

"Yeah, well." She wet her lower lip with the tip of her tongue. Slowly. "I just wanted to tell you how awesome today's lecture was."

"Thank you." He turned to go, doubting he would really get off that easily. He'd had students pursue him romantically before. They were usually put off easily enough, but this year's freshman class was especially bold. And especially determined.

"And," Melanie said, the I'm-not-finished note in her voice pulling him back, "you know what you were saying about the Chinese making pottery a thousand years ago of a quality that we still can't reproduce today? I mean, who'd've thought?"

"The Chinese, perhaps?"

"Well, hey, *duh,* I guess." A nervous laugh tittered out of her. Then she tilted her head and flashed a pair of big doe eyes at him. "It's just so cool that you know so much about all that old stuff, you know?"

"That's why they call me an art *history* professor."

"But you make it come alive. It's like you don't just look at the art, you taste it and smell it. You *feel* it."

He would have rolled his eyes, but she'd hit a nerve. He did experience art on a deeper level than just the visual. Maybe because, unlike her, he'd actually been around when most of it was created.

Melanie batted her heavily coated lashes at him, breaking the spell. "Just hearing you talk about art gets me . . . excited."

"Yes," he said, and stopped to clear his throat, check his watch. "Well. Miss, uh—"

"Melanie. Melanie Solvane. I was wondering if we could get together and you tell me some more about the imperial kiln at Jingdezhen. I'm not sure I understood what you were saying about how they used bamboo barriers to keep the kiln temperature steady through the firing process."

"My office hours are posted."

"I was thinking something more intimate—"

"I don't give private lessons, Miss Solvane." He arced one eyebrow. "In art, or anything else."

Her eyes narrowed. Her arms tightened around the

books still clutched to her chest. With an audible huff, she jutted her chin, wheeled, and strode off, hips swinging and heels clacking on the cement.

Letting his shoulders slump, Nathan turned down Ninth Street for the trek to his condo. A familiar chuckle stopped him.

"There was a day when you wouldn't have turned away such a pretty girl so quickly." A silver-haired man on the bus stop bench looked over his shoulder toward Nathan. The man's eyebrows were thick and darker than his silver hair, matching a streak of black that swept back from his temples like wings.

Pain lanced through Nathan's chest. His gaze automatically slammed to the pavement. "There has never been a day when I dated my students."

He'd intended to put an edge on the words, but they came out even sharper than he'd meant them to. He hadn't started this day in a good mood, and his temper had grown steadily shorter since breakfast.

Nathan heard the man rise. Soft footsteps shuffled across the sidewalk. A pair of expensive black wingtips came into Nathan's view beneath fine dark wool slacks. The hem of a gray cashmere coat swirled around the man's calves like a cat twining his ankles.

"Can you not bear to even look at me?"

Nathan's jaw hardened. He purposely kept his voice low so the pedestrians passing by wouldn't hear. The dangerous edge to his rumbling retort manifested without conscious thought. "You yourself commanded that I not look upon you again. Or have you forgotten?"

"I have forgotten nothing. When I said you would not look upon me, I meant in the Council Hall, before our people." A hand landed on Nathan's shoulder, squeezed. "Look at me, Nathan. This is a public street. Do not subjugate yourself before me here."

Anger surged, hot in Nathan's blood. He gritted his teeth and raised his gaze. "No, I am not your subject any longer, am I?"

Teryn Carnegie, anointed leader of the Chicago congregation of *Les Gargouillen*, neither smiled nor frowned. He simply was, as always, returning Nathan's stare from a timeless face. Teryn could have been forty or he could have been seventy. His smooth features and deep-set eyes gave few clues.

"Not my subject," he said, giving Nathan's shoulder a gentle squeeze. "But still my friend, I hope."

"Such a good friend that you had to sneak away from your own minions to come see me?"

The Wizenot never traveled without bodyguards. Their leader's safety was too important to the congregation. That he'd ventured out alone today spoke volumes about the kind of *friend* Teryn considered Nathan to be.

The old man didn't want to be seen with him, even by the chosen inner circle he trusted with his life.

When he got no response, Nathan marched away. The Wizenot quickly caught up and kept pace at his side.

"I do not sneak," he said, sounding slightly offended, but when he caught Nathan's sideways glance, amusement twinkled in his gray eyes. "And I did not come alone."

Nathan automatically glanced over each shoulder. He didn't see any familiar faces in the sea of pedestrians behind him, but that didn't mean they weren't there. He felt like a coward for it, but he was glad that whoever accompanied Teryn hung back. He'd had a bad week. The last thing he needed was another condemning look from one of his brethren.

Former brethren.

His jaw hardened, ticked. "You banned me from our church, Teryn, made me an outcast among our people. You *excommunicated* me."

"It was necessary. Your views, your beliefs, caused too much upheaval."

"My beliefs are realistic. Theirs are archaic."

"You ask them to change too much, too quickly."

"I didn't ask anyone to change. My choices are just that. Mine. No one else has to follow."

"But others would have. You aren't the only one who
sees what you see in the world. Feels what you feel. If you
had stayed, you would have taken my place as Wizenot
someday, as is your blood right. Some of the congregation
would have accepted your ways, perhaps even embraced
them as the new order, but others would not. The congregation would have been divided, and divided we cannot
survive."

He hunched his shoulders and picked up his pace. He'd
never wanted to be his people's leader anyway. Never
wanted to be responsible for their souls. Not when he
couldn't even save his own. "Then it's best that I'm gone,
isn't it?"

"Yet you came back last night."

Disbelief drew Nathan up short. "You were watching
me?" He hadn't thought to block his mind. Hadn't thought
he needed to.

"I was looking out my window."

Teryn's arched eyebrow was as effective as a scolding
at dousing Nathan's irritation. No matter what stood
between them, he couldn't help but respect the old man
for the burden he carried. It wasn't easy to lead a dying
civilization, much less to do it with dignity, the way
Teryn did.

"I thought you might want to talk," Teryn said as they
walked on in a companionable gait. "You looked like a
man with a lot on his mind, and I know I've a few things
on mine after all that's happened these last few days."

Memories of the days he used to open his soul to Teryn
pulled at the edges of Nathan's consciousness. They'd
once been able to tell each other anything. With steaming
mugs of lemongrass tea gripped in both hands, they'd dug
in before crackling fires and debated politics and religion,
pondered the course of human history, and envisaged a future without the curse of *Les Gargouillen* on their heads.
The day he'd lost that right had been one of the saddest
days of his life.

All of his lives.

His shoulders pinched inward, squeezing the air from his chest. "What's on my mind is none of your concern anymore, and I'm long past the day of caring what's on yours."

"Even if it concerns Rachel Vandermere?"

Nathan tripped over a drunk stretched out on the stairs to the L-train platform, caught himself, and stared back at Teryn. "What do you know about her?"

"I know she didn't leave town with her colleagues." Teryn bent over and slipped a hundred-dollar bill into the indigent's up-stretched hand. "And I know she's asking questions."

"She's an investigator. It's what she does."

"What is she investigating? Her assassin is dead."

Nathan's thoughts swirled like fallen leaves in a winter gale. How much did Teryn already know? How much did he suspect?

Nathan couldn't betray an innocent woman, possibly even put her in danger from the more extreme Gargoyles who wouldn't be happy that a cop had her mind set on proving the existence of monsters, by telling Teryn the truth. But neither could he betray his people by lying, even if it sometimes felt as if they'd betrayed him.

He'd made his own choices, he told himself, pressing his lips together in a thin, cold line. He alone decided to break from the traditions of his kind, deny both the first tenet of his congregation—to protect humans—and the second, to propagate the species. He had no one to blame for his loneliness but himself.

So rather than choose between Teryn and Rachel, his people and the truth that longed to be discovered by the world, he hedged. "She has her reasons for staying."

Teryn showed a rare frown. "And what might those be?"

The question gave him pause. He studied Teryn's expressionless face as his train pulled up to the platform. With each clack of metal wheels on rails, he was more sure that the Wizenot hadn't sought him out to lend a friendly ear while Nathan poured out his troubles.

The doors whooshed open, and Nathan climbed aboard with Teryn at his side. "What are you really doing here?"

Teryn slid into a hard plastic seat and held the chrome rail while the train jerked into motion. "Our people are in danger, Nathan. The god and goddess have warned me in the ritual visions. Our very existence is at risk."

"Our culture has been decaying for at least two hundred years. There is nothing you can do to stop it."

Teryn jerked his head to the side once. "This threat comes from a new direction, and it comes swift and deadly. I must find it, and stop it. You must help me. I have seen it."

"Me? What have I got to do with it?" Nathan snapped his jaw shut to stop it from gaping. The old man had had some wild ideas before, but Nathan hadn't heard anything about him losing his mind. It had come on so suddenly. . . .

"Look," Teryn commanded, swaying ever so slightly on his feet as he stared at a window on the train car. The setting sun glanced off the glass in a blinding blur. Nathan felt the pull of the Second Sight.

"You know her mind. You have connected with her. Seek the bond again and see what she is about."

Teryn was right. Rachel's mind was familiar to him. Too familiar. Too comfortable for his peace of mind.

He stared at the window glass until his vision blurred, became a tunnel. He found her easily, picking up first on the faraway tendrils of her thoughts floating, gently waving in the air like silk threads in an underwater current and following them back to her consciousness.

She was outside a bar on Seventh Street. A rusted Buick with the wheels removed sat jacked up on cement blocks at the curb next to her. Litter danced down the street on a cold wind like tumbleweeds in the Old West. A couple of hoods in skull caps and gang colors sagged against the building, passing a cigarette back and forth. Even in the stench of the ghetto, a soft scent, feminine and alluring, curled around him, seeped into his blood. Rosemary. Her scent.

Nathan sank deeper into the sights, the sounds, the smell of the street, holding just enough of himself back to be aware of Teryn next to him. "What is she doing there?"

"She looks for Von."

"Von?" Nathan's lip curled. "What could she—" *possibly want from him?* Nathan started to ask, but he already knew the answer.

Rachel couldn't get the answers she wanted from her assassin, wouldn't get them from Nathan, so she was following her only other lead—the mysterious fingerprints on William Bishop's rifle.

"The boy is brash and undisciplined," Teryn said. "And Rhys's death troubles him. He is more unpredictable now than ever. Who knows what he will say if he is pressured."

"Then you'd best keep him under wraps. Keep him away from her."

Teryn's sigh sounded very much like an expression of exasperation. The last time Nathan had heard that sound, it was because the Wizenot had found all of his shoes nailed to the floor of his closet in neat order, courtesy of Rhys and Nathan at the height of their adolescence.

Von was troubled by Rhys's death?

The boy had no idea . . .

"I would," Teryn said, yanking Nathan's thoughts back to the present. "If I could find him."

Nathan frowned at the Wizenot, who explained. "He took off on his own after he and Connor escaped the parking garage near the museum the other night. We've had people looking for him, but I'm sad to say we haven't been able to catch up to him. He's blocking our attempts to trace his mind."

Still focused more on the scene on Seventh Street than his present location, Nathan jerked his head once to the side. "Damn kid. Probably out drinking himself into a stupor."

"Probably," Teryn agreed. "Perhaps in that bar. We've got to keep her away from him."

Nathan watched as Rachel strode toward the door as if she belonged there. But she definitely did not belong there, especially not alone. What the hell was she thinking, even walking in a neighborhood like that, let alone going into the bar without backup?

The last of the physical world surrounding Nathan fell away like skin shed by a snake as he delved deeper into Rachel's mind. The clacking rails of the L train faded to quiet. The vibration of the floor beneath his feet went still. The scent of coffee from the mug the woman behind him held dissipated.

As if he were adjusting the range on a pair of binoculars, Nathan narrowed the focus of his attention from the street outside the bar, the boys in the stoop, the doorway, to her. Only her.

He felt the chill wind on her face, the way her bangs tickled her eyelashes, her soft palm as she swept them away. He felt the swish of blood in her veins, the rush of air in her lungs. He pushed past these surface perceptions, delved deeper inside her, as close as he could get to her conscious mind.

As always, her actual thoughts were just out of reach to him, hidden behind a mental bank of shimmering, shifting fog that none of his kind could penetrate. But the feelings, the emotions—her intent—were available for him if he concentrated hard enough.

She was determined to go inside. Despite the thugs in the doorway, the disreputable neighborhood, she intended to ask her questions, to find Von.

Damn it, didn't the woman have the sense God gave a snail? Just watching the boys watching her was enough to make his skin crawl.

Nathan gathered his will and tried to force it on her. He tried to force her to leave. But she fought him. He felt the core of justice inside her, firmly rooted and sturdy as an oak tree. She wanted justice. But beyond the bright banner of justice lay something darker. Something uglier, fiercer. Something savage.

While justice trumpeted her cause, revenge hissed and spat in the shadows of her mind. The woman and cop inside her wanted justice, but the frightened child wanted revenge for what had been done to her parents. What had been done to her.

Nathan's heart surged as she took the first step toward the bar, reached for the door, the boys eyeing her sideways. Their intent was as clear as hers—and it scared the hell out of him.

Damn it, get out of there!

Nathan sharpened his will to a pinpoint and forced himself deeper into her. He focused on that scared child she had been the night her parents died. He amplified those feelings and nearly choked himself as he felt the fear well up into her throat. He felt her limbs go stiff with it. Her fingers go numb and her breath rattle like old chains in her chest.

Then, incredibly, he felt her swallow hard, lift her chin, and shake it off. She marched up the last two steps, opened the door and walked inside like she owned the place.

Nathan pulled himself back in time to see the boys outside grin, gold-capped teeth sparkling in the cold sunlight. Two more hoods joined the two already outside from across the street.

They paused in the doorway, the four of them, heads together, and chuckled. The one with the dregs of the cigarette tossed the butt to the cement and crushed it with the toe of a pair of hundred-dollar athletic shoes.

Shoulders hunched, pants drooping, and eyes gleaming with anticipation, all four of them slunk through the door after Rachel.

Nathan blinked, closing the tunnel of Second Sight. While he reoriented himself, the train screeched to a stop at the Wacker Drive platform.

Seven blocks.

Jesus, she was seven blocks away. Without a thought

for courtesy, he shoved Teryn out of the way and dived out
the door. Two seconds later he was off the platform and
running down the sidewalk, the leather soles of his Rock-
ports slapping the pavement in time with his pounding
heart.

   Seven blocks.

EIGHT

*Connor Rihyad tucked the newspaper he'd been hid-*ing behind beneath his arm and strolled to Teryn's side. With a respectful bow of his head, he followed the Wizenot's gaze to the tall figure sprinting through the rush-hour pedestrian crowd as if hell were on his heels.

"You didn't tell me this meeting that was so important was with *him.*" He couldn't even bring himself to say the name. Nathan Cross hadn't just turned his back on his people. He was actively trying to destroy them with his ideas of reversing the magic that made them what they were. Not that that was possible. But even talk of it created strife among the congregation. It divided them.

If it were up to Connor, he'd let Nathan die his death without the promise of reincarnation and be done with him. Maybe he'd even help the process along. . . .

But it wasn't up to Connor. Teryn had forbidden his people to interfere in Nathan's life, and no matter how outrageous the man's choices, how sacrilegious his beliefs, none dared challenge the Wizenot's wishes on this.

Yet.

"Why did you warn him?" he asked, unable to read the

old man's face. No one read the old man's face unless he
wanted them to.

"She is in danger."

"If she finds what she's looking for, we'll all be in
danger."

"She is human," Teryn snapped. The look he flashed
made Connor feel like he was nine years old again, and
had just knocked a baseball through a stained-glass window—right after being told that batting practice was not a
suitable activity for the rectory yard. "We are guardians.
We have an obligation. Or have you forgotten?"

"Nathan is the one who has forgotten."

Teryn's gaze trailed off in the direction Nathan had
gone. He sighed softly. "Then perhaps Rachel Vandermere
will remind him."

Rachel paused just inside the door to the bar to let
her eyes adjust to the dim light. She wasn't afraid; she'd
been in worse places than this. Yet goose bumps pebbled
her upper arms. Her pulse thrummed in her veins and her
heart raced.

For some weird reason, she'd nearly had a panic attack
outside. As she'd reached for the door, the images she usually saw only in nightmares had flashed through her mind:
her daddy putting her in the cupboard under the stairs.
Shadows on the wall. Flames and eyes burning with green
fire. In the light of day she'd heard the *whump, whump*
of heavy wings that had previously only haunted her
nights.

The fear had paralyzed her for a moment. She had the
oddest urge to turn away. To run. But she didn't give in.

Over the years, Rachel had learned to transform the
rush of adrenaline and heightened senses that came with
the nightmares into energy. She'd learned to focus fear into
a sharp point of determination and use it for her own
purposes.

Fear was her friend. Fear drove her. Because she knew

that only by understanding what she'd seen and heard that night, by finding it and facing it, could she make it go away.

Could she find justice for her parents.

She'd become so used to accepting and harnessing her fear that Rachel was shocked when she stepped inside the bar and reached up to pull her sunglasses from her face to find her cheeks damp with tears brought on by the terror of her childhood memories. Horrified, she had hurriedly brushed the wet streaks away with the heel of her hand, and now stood scoping out the joint with what she hoped was a steely, don't-mess-with-me, bitch-face on, and not an expression of tear-stained vulnerability.

Luckily, most of the bar's patrons—those who were sober enough to pick their heads up out of their beers at five-fifteen on a payday Friday evening—had yet to notice her.

She took advantage of the unobserved moment to shore up her control. Her breathing had evened out, but her heart was still pounding. It felt as if it were beating double time . . . or as if there were a phantom organ inside her, shadowing her own, but heavier somehow. Bigger and more powerful.

Even more disconcerting was the new picture that formed in her mind when she tried to wipe the vestiges of the nightmare from her mind the way one might wipe condensation from a mirror: Nathan.

She felt his scowl more than visualized it. It was as if he were there, and she was tracing her fingers over his square, stubbled jaw, across the softness of his down-turned lips. His moist breath warmed her palm, and she realized he was breathing hard. The cords of his neck strained under her touch as she slid her hand down his throat. His carotid leaped angrily against her fingertips.

She could feel his anger as clearly as she could feel his skin, the muscle and bone beneath. And she could feel his fear. The fear she'd felt outside the bar had been his, she realized, somehow amplifying her own, twined as intimately as their heartbeats.

She wasn't sure how she knew—maybe she was just imagining all of this—but she felt sure that at that moment, wherever he was, Nathan Cross was afraid.

For her.

And Porky Pig can whistle Dixie, *too.*

A shudder wracked Rachel from head to toe as she yanked herself back from the brink of insanity. She'd been called crazy often enough, chasing after monsters the way she did. All she needed was to claim she was telepathic now, too, and they'd send the men in the white truck after her for sure.

She took a deep breath and pushed everything out of her mind except the bar. The place smelled like stale smoke, sweat, and cheap perfume. Pool balls clacked on a table under the circle of light from a single naked bulb hung in the far corner. Highlights from last night's Bulls game played without sound on a TV mounted above the bar. The bartender, a short guy with a shaved head, meaty, pocked face, and fingers and forearms as plump as pork sausages spared her a disinterested glance before he went back to wiping glasses with the dingy towel thrown over his shoulder.

A half-dozen men sat across from him, working men in dirty blue jeans, boots, and T-shirts with armpit stains that went to their waistlines. A couple of working women wearing short skirts and long hair extensions hung over the men's shoulders hoping to wheedle a drink and a trick. A couple of loners sat in the dark booths along the right wall nursing longnecks.

She didn't see Von—that would have been too easy. But she'd been told he hung out here, among eight or nine other watering holes in the hood, from time to time, so maybe someone here knew how to find him.

With a deep breath she started toward the bartender.

He looked up as she approached, his eyes narrowed. "Whoever you're looking for, I ain't seen him," he said before she had a chance to ask.

Behind her back, the hookers sidled toward the exit.

"Hold on, girls," she said without turning her head. She riveted her gaze on the bartender. "Only one kind of people can make a cop that fast. The kind of people that have reason to avoid them. So what are you hiding, Fred?"

"Name's Al," he sneered, and then cursed himself for telling her.

She smiled. "Works every time. You got a last name, Al?"

"Go fuck yourself."

"Unusual. Is that Polish?"

He turned his back to her and fidgeted with the bottles behind the bar.

"I'm looking for a kid, Al. Eighteen, blond. He has kind of an unusual name, too. It's Von."

"Nobody under twenty-one allowed in here." Al glanced over his shoulder, his lips twisted into a sick grin. "It's the law, ain't it?"

Rachel gave Al a long look, then turned to the hookers huddled together halfway to the door. "That true, ladies? Is Al here religious about carding his customers?"

The skinny black girl fluttered her lashes over wide eyes. "I—I've never really been in here before."

The guy in the first booth snorted and smacked his shot glass onto the table.

The girl glared at him, then turned back to Rachel. "I never really paid attention."

"What about you?" Rachel asked the other woman, who was trying to look bored with the whole scene and only succeeding in looking nervous.

"What about what?" she asked, her ruby red lips pouty.

"Al careful to keep the minors out of here?"

"Sheila . . ." Al growled.

"Careful," Rachel warned the woman. "Al might be able to keep you from working in this bar again, but Chicago Vice can keep you from working in this city."

"Well, you know." She shrugged. "It's hard to tell 'xactly how old anyone is these days."

Before the prostitute could come up with another

appropriately vague answer, the door swung open behind her, and with it, the balance of power in the room swung out of Rachel's grasp. Four guys sauntered in, pants sagging, gold chains glittering around their necks, and mouths streaming one obscenity after another. Rachel didn't have to understand all the words to know that most of them referred to her.

She resisted the urge to take a step back, not wanting them to see they intimidated her. Instead she pulled out her identification, flashed it at them, and met them with a square look while she put the leather bi-fold back in her back pocket. "Come on in and join the party, boys."

The tallest of the four, a loose-limbed postadolescent with a silver marijuana leaf medallion hanging from the requisite gold chain on his neck, sauntered forward. "Don't mind if we does."

He passed too close in front of her, his elbow brushing her breasts, then put his butt on the bar and swung his legs smoothly to the other side. "Why don't you take a cigarette break, Al," he said, and then winked at Rachel, turning her stomach. "I got you covered."

Al slapped his towel down on the bar and made time toward the back door.

Now Rachel did take a step back. The other three boys had faded to the sides, effectively surrounding her. Haggard faces looked on from the barstools and dim booths. The pool players leaned on their cues to watch.

"What'll it be, ma'am?" the boy behind the bar asked.

The boys on her flanks closed in. "How about Sex on the Beach?" one of them called.

The other shouted back, "Man, it's too frickin' cold outside for sex on the beach."

"Yeah," the bartender boy said, leaning so far across the bar that his face was practically in her bra. "Wouldn't want me to freeze my ever-lovin' cock off, would you? So how 'bout we share a Screaming Orgasm right here, huh, Doll?"

Rachel very deliberately stuck her right hand out, palm

flat, intending to shove the cretin away from her, but he was faster than she anticipated. His hand shot out and he grabbed her wrist, pulling her in closer and taking a deep sniff behind her ear.

"Mmm, mmm. You do smell good."

She'd made a major tactical error and she knew it. The other three boys saw she was caught like a fox in a trap and closed in.

Suddenly her lungs couldn't draw in enough air. Her knees threatened to buckle. Her mind whirled, sorting through possible solutions, probable outcomes.

None of them looked good.

Nathan was winded by the time he found the bar and crashed through the door without slowing a step, but what he saw inside made breathing low priority.

Fists clenched, feet spread shoulder width, balanced on his toes, ready to move, he flicked a quick glance over Rachel and then locked gazes with her captor. "Let her go. Now." He spoke softly, but the deadly intent behind the words was clear.

"Ease up there, Pops," the boy to his right said. "There's enough of her to go around. Maybe we'll let you have some when we're done."

Nathan's head turned slowly toward the boy. He shot him a hard look, then beckoned him with a waggle of his fingertips.

The boy grinned, licked his lips, and rushed Nathan. A simple duck of the shoulder and he caught the kid in the midsection, flipped him neatly to the floor on his back, where he stayed.

Nathan had hardly straightened up before the second boy made his run. He went low, aiming for a tackle at the knees. Nathan waited until the split second before impact, then simply lifted his leg so that the boy's chin collided with his kneecap. A second later he rolled the boy's limp form aside and stepped down toward the bar.

He raised an eyebrow to the third boy, asking without words if he wanted to give it a try.

Bar Boy looked back to his friend, the youngest of the hoodlums, for help. "Take him, Dickey!"

Nathan sent young Dickey a menacing look. The kid stumbled backward and scrabbled toward the door, but the momentary distraction gave Bar Boy the chance to gain another advantage. Nathan cursed himself for not paying attention as he saw Rachel fly through the air. The boy behind the bar had literally pulled her off her feet. When they landed, he let go of her with his left hand long enough to fish a small knife from his back pocket. The blade pressed perilously close to her jugular. She instantly went still in his grasp.

Nathan hissed. "Big mistake, kid."

Rachel blinked. He willed her not to move. The knife at her throat wasn't large, just a tiny blade. But how much steel did it take to perforate an artery?

For God's sake, Rachel, don't move.

"Back off, Pops!" Knife Boy yelled.

Nathan held his ground, fists clenched and murder swirling in his mind. "You hurt her, I'm going to eat you for lunch."

"I'll kill her." The boy's hand trembled. The weapon edged away from her throat an inch, then a little more.

"Yeah?" Nathan said. "Then what's going to stop me from killing you?"

"Are you crazy, man? You don't think I'll do it? I will! Now back off."

One of the drunks that had been hiding in a shadowy corner stood and staggered into the light. His blond hair stood up in pointed clumps like a spiked dog collar. Gold hoops pierced both his ears and one nostril. Blue bags hung under his bloodshot eyes.

Rachel's head turned, pressing her flesh into the blade. "Von?"

"Rachel, be still! Goddamn it, Von," Nathan sputtered, then focused back on the boy with the knife. "So help me, if you draw so much as a drop of blood from her, I'll rip your heart out with my bare hands."

Von grinned drunkenly at Knife Boy. He swayed as he jerked his head toward Nathan and belched. "He's not kidding, you know. The man is deadly."

Nathan's jaw turned to stone. "Shut up, Von."

Rachel's captor shuffled nervously behind her. The knife moved another inch or two away from her throat. He waved the blade in the air around her ear. "Shut up, both of you! I said I'd kill her."

Von laughed. "With that little knife? Man, what're you doing waving around a stubby little pecker like that? You couldn't cut Jell-O with that thing." He wobbled a step closer. His voice got softer, conspiratorial. "But you know, you forget the knife, give the woman a shove, and make a run for the back door, you just might get away before the big guy can get across the bar after you. You're fast, aren't you? You look fast. You're gonna have to be to outrun a—"

Now Nathan cut Von a look. His lip curled. "If you don't shut your mouth, I'm going to forget about him and kick *your* ass."

Rachel rolled her eyes. "You three want to have a pissing contest? Take it out back. The rest of us would like to get on with our afternoons."

Nathan frowned. A fragile conduit opened between his mind and Rachel's. He sensed something from her. Some plan.

She was going to do something stupid. He just didn't know what.

Von put on a cheesy smile. "Uh-oh. Now the big man's really torqued. You'd better run." Feigning fear, he waved at Knife Boy. "If I were you, I'd hurry."

"I ain't running, man. Not from nobody." Knife Boy jabbed the air in Nathan's direction to punctuate his point.

Nathan felt Rachel's breath. Felt her start to move.

His heart kicked. Fear jolted through him. Admiration rode its coattails.

She was either the most courageous woman he knew, or the stupidest. He'd wait to see if she lived before deciding which.

He shouted, drawing the attention of the boy with the knife as she tucked her chin to her chest and dropped straight down, out of Knife Boy's hold, elbowing him in the crotch as she fell, then rolled away.

She came up with a gun in a two-handed grip, safety off and ready to fire.

She pointed the weapon at the boy on the floor holding his groin and moaning, then looked up. "Von Simeon, I'm—"

It was already too late. Von was hoofing it toward the door double time.

"Nathan, stop him!" she yelled, but he let the boy pass with nothing more than a murderous look.

"Damn it!" She kicked the fallen knife away from the boy on the floor and holstered her weapon. As she passed Nathan, she shot him a murderous look of her own. "Watch this guy. I'm going after—"

"No." He snagged her arm. He didn't jerk her, but brought her gently to a stop, his fingers tingling as the conduit between their minds expanded, pulsed with life.

She squirmed in his grasp. "He's getting away!"

"He's already gone."

"We can catch up." She tried to jerk away.

He held her back. Waves of anger, his and hers, crashed between them, inside them. He was angry at her for putting herself in this situation. She was angry at him for interfering.

But on the backside of the anger, there was something else. Something quieter, but just as powerful. The ultimate affirmation of life. Of survival.

Sexual awareness.

Desire.

Her pupils dilated. His nostrils flared.

Need ebbed and flowed between the waves of anger.

Swearing, though he wasn't sure if the curse was meant for her or for himself, he tugged her outside, where he backed her into a recessed stoop and hemmed her in with his body in front of her, the building behind her, and one arm planted on the brick wall on either side of her head. He towered over her, his senses reeling, full of her. Blood pounded in his groin until he thought he would burst the seam of his pants.

"What are you doing?" She looked up at him, her green eyes wary but unafraid.

Why wasn't she afraid of him?

He was sure as hell afraid of her. Of what she could do to him.

The fact that she wasn't afraid—of monsters, punks with knives, or men with raging hard-ons who dragged her into the street—infuriated him.

Made him so mad that there wasn't a damn thing he could do about it except kiss her.

NINE

If Nathan's previous touch had been electric, his kiss was a power surge on a cosmic scale. Whatever the anatomical equivalents to circuit breakers were, Rachel's blew in rapid succession. She could feel the switches popping down her spine, in her mind. In her nipples and the core of her sex.

She was angry at him, but she couldn't for the life of her remember why. Her short-term memory, conscious thought in general, had been overwhelmed by heat. By need.

He was so close she could see each individual whisker on his jaw. The texture was fascinating. She wanted to feel it against her cheek. Rub her lips over it.

She settled for a single stroke of her fingertips along his jaw.

God, what was it about this man that attracted her even when she was furious at him?

He lifted his head a millimeter and drew a deep breath. His Adam's apple bobbed once and the chords of his neck strained, as if her desire pulled through his body, strung him tight.

He captured her wandering hand with his, linked their fingers and brought her knuckles to his lips—his incredibly soft, sensuously curved, full lips.

For all his hardness—his body, his eyes, his mind—his lips felt like moist silk on her skin. The sight of them nibbling at her sent her spinning on a journey she wasn't ready to take. A path to oblivious pleasure. She had to close her eyes to ground herself in reality.

When she opened them again, he'd tucked their joined hands against his shoulder, but his eyes still blazed with the heat of the kiss.

"You have absolutely no sense of self-preservation, do you?" he asked.

She barely found enough breath to reply. "I've managed to keep myself more or less in one piece for thirty-three years."

"Pure luck, most likely."

"Well, thank you for that vote of confidence."

"You aren't going to let go of this, are you? You're going to keep looking for Von."

"Yes."

"Even if it means you're stuck with me for the duration."

"Even if I'm stuck—" She blinked, mentally rewinding his words and listening again to what he'd said. "I'm stuck with you?"

Geez, was that mouse squeak really her voice?

He nodded.

"You're going to help me?"

"God knows I can't leave you on your own the way you attract trouble. The city might not survive."

Her face started to burn. She was still two sentences behind in this conversation and was losing ground fast. "I attract trouble? You're the one who bumbled into an assassination attempt—"

He swung around to her side, took her by the elbow, and propelled her forward. She only caught a glance, but she could have sworn one corner of his mouth kicked up in a ferocious smirk.

"We'll get started first thing tomorrow," he promised, tucking her into a cab. He gave the driver directions to her hotel, closed the door behind her, and slapped the roof to send her off.

As the car pulled away, he gave her one long, last look that sent shivers of renewed awareness down her spine.

His dark hair was tousled and a swath had fallen over his eyes. His tanned cheeks were ruddy from the fight or the cold or the kiss or all three. The knuckles on the hand he braced against her window were bleeding, but he didn't seem to notice.

Art professor, her hind end. Here was the consummate warrior. The bad-boy playboy from all her favorite romance novels. The beast that every beauty dreamed of taming in her fantasies, but didn't dare encourage when they crossed paths in real life.

And his whole focus was on her. He stared at her with a look so intense that the heat of his gaze warmed her skin. When she looked back at him, wondering if he could feel the same warmth from her, it was as if more than their gazes connected. Their minds joined.

She saw into his thoughts. Saw images of the two of them naked, limbs tangled. She felt their heartbeats pound in synchrony to the erratic beat of an unheard drum. And she heard voices, so far away they were like the buzzing of an insect in her ear—her mind, rather. It was hard to tell, but she thought they were singing, maybe. Or chanting. The sound was low and melodious, yet somehow ominous, like the deep, reverberating music that preceded disaster in the movies.

She felt a change in Nathan—the imaginary Nathan. His dream kisses became harder, more desperate. His weight began to crush her, his caresses to bruise. A strange light glowed in his eyes, no longer desire, but something much more primitive. More dangerous.

His muscles bulged as if taken by spasm. His chest labored for breath. The chanting grew louder. Nathan's drumbeat pulse more frenetic.

"No, no, no, no, no!" the dream Nathan cried, a litany of denial. Then he shoved her away. He curled up into a ball, naked and shaking, his face buried in his arms. "No, no, no, no."

Rachel stumbled backward in the dream, and opened her eyes in reality. Nathan was still on the curb behind her, upright and fully clothed. She shook her head, trying to figure out what had just happened. A fantasy . . . that was the only explanation.

Except the fact that she was fantasizing about Nathan Cross was no explanation at all. She barely knew the man.

And it had been so intense. So *real*. Her body was still humming with a hunger for the man so ravenous that it rivaled her most erotic dreams. She was slick and aching and ready for him between her legs, and he hadn't even touched her, except in some weird fantasy.

Or was it more?

She was three blocks away before her body returned to normal enough that she realized she hadn't asked how he'd found her in the bar, or even how he'd known she was in trouble.

Nathan watched Rachel's taxi until it disappeared in traffic, then stalked down the sidewalk like a man possessed.

Or a man cursed.

His shoulders stiff and hunched, he shoved a startled pedestrian aside. The man's indignant shout barely registered in Nathan's stormy mind. Bolts of energy cracked in his head like whips. Electricity sizzled out to his extremities, making his muscles contract and convulse. The ancient chant roared in his ears.

> *E Unri Almasama*
> *E Unri Almasama*
> *Calli, Calli, Callio*
> *Somara altwunia paximi*

The Awakening was almost on him. Seeing a knife pressed to Rachel's throat had triggered his protective instincts and brought the beast to life. The kiss had started his blood boiling.

It had been difficult enough to fend off the change then, but when he'd stood close enough to catch her scent, loomed over her the way a lion established himself as alpha over his mate, and then looked down at her to see the same arousal in her eyes—and in her mind—it had been nearly impossible not to give in to the magic and drag her off to his lair.

The entwined bodies she'd seen while their minds were fused were nothing compared to the reality of what he wanted to do with her. To her.

A new wave of magic coursed through his veins. His cells pulsed, reshaped themselves.

Grinding his teeth, he forced Rachel Vandermere out of his thoughts, lowered his head, and plowed down the sidewalk with even more determination. His only thought was to get to his home, his sanctuary, though he knew he'd find no more peace there than on the street.

What had he done, offering to help her? He couldn't say he'd done it for Teryn. He wasn't Teryn's pawn.

No, he was honest enough with himself to admit that he'd been glad for the excuse to see her again, to spend time with her, even if every minute was pure torture.

Every time he looked at her, he was reminded of everything he couldn't have: a home, a wife, lifelong love. Foolish of him to desire these things, he knew. He was a Gargoyle.

But he was also human. He was born of human mother. He had human needs. A human love of beautiful things. Beautiful women.

Therein lay the problem.

The Gargoyle compulsion to mate, the magic that ensured the propagation of the species, ran deep and strong inside him, as it did with all his kind. How could he fight a curse that had entrapped his people for a thousand years?

How could he spend time with Rachel without taking her for his own? Breaking the vow he'd made to himself?

Nathan looked up and found himself outside his condo with no knowledge of how he'd gotten there. He let himself in and slammed the door behind him, conflict sparking and sizzling in his blood. Unable to quiet his riotous body, he paced in front of the large window. Across the room his books called. Researching a way to end this blasted curse once and for all would occupy his mind for a while, drown out the ritual chant, but he couldn't work now. Couldn't even stand still.

The energy inside him needed to be unleashed.

He gazed outside, feeling the call of the dark sky. Every fiber in his being wanted to Awaken the beast within, wanted to fly through the scattering of charcoal clouds. Every cell wanted to hunt.

Maybe even find the punk who'd held a knife to Rachel's throat and make sure he never did it again. He could almost taste the bastard's blood on his tongue.

His breath deepened. His fists clenched.

No. He would not.

The spell did *not* control him. He wouldn't allow it to.

Forcing his fingers to uncurl he opened the bottom drawer of his dresser, pulled out a broadsword he'd saved from ancient times, left where he could find it life after life. The weight felt good in his grip, solid. The cool brass handle absorbed some of the heat from his body.

He wet his thumb and grazed it lightly along the edge, then twirled the sword once, testing its balance. The blade sliced the air with an audible *whoosh.*

Balancing the weapon against his thigh, he shrugged out of his shirt and walked to open space in the center of the room.

He would not hunt tonight. He would not fight and he would not kill—at least not a human, no matter how much some of them might deserve it.

Instead he would unleash all his anger on the one who really deserved it. He would slice and slaughter the object of his hate until he'd sweated out the need for blood, until his muscles ached and his legs buckled from exhaustion. He would kill Romanus, slaughter the priest who'd cursed his townsmen a thousand years ago.

Or at least the image of him Nathan forever carried in his mind.

*Nathan's black Lincoln Town Car slid into a re-*served parking space in front of the hotel at exactly 12:58 and thirty seconds. He was right on time.

Rachel had figured he would be. Over the course of her career at Interpol, she'd learned to peg people pretty well. Some of her colleagues liked to swagger around and jaw about "cop's intuition," but it was really just logic.

As an art aficionado, Nathan would appreciate detail. As a university professor, he would be accustomed to keeping a regular schedule. He wouldn't have made tenure at a school as reputable as Chicago University at the age of thirty-four by not showing up for class on time.

And as the kind of man who charged into a barroom brawl like Prince Valiant on his dashing steed, defending her honor—whether she wanted his help or not—he had to be a bit of a control freak.

All that added up to punctual.

Not to mention intense, infuriatingly arrogant, and sexy as all get-out.

He slid out of the sleek sedan with the grace of a big cat, the commanding presence of an alpha male within his pride. The lobby of the hotel was fairly busy, but a path opened up before him like the Red Sea before Moses. Nathan was the kind of man that people—even other dominant males—stepped out of his way to let pass.

Rachel's breath hitched in her throat. His loose-limbed, long-legged gait made her heart skitter. She actually caught herself patting her hair, straightening her bangs before she got a grip.

Dang, she had to get a grip. Put this physical attraction

she had going for him out of her mind. She had a job to do. A lifelong mission to fulfill.

She couldn't afford to be distracted. She was closer to the answers she'd sought all of her life than she'd ever been, she could feel it. She wasn't going to blow her chance to catch up to a monster like the one that killed her mother and father because she couldn't keep her mind on track.

Or her eyes off the way his chest tapered nicely down to a tight waist and slim hips, the hard-muscled thighs that bulged against the material of his slacks with every ground-eating stride, or the body parts between them.

She jerked her gaze up to Nathan's eyes.

Dang, she had to get a grip.

Scratch that. She did not need to think about gripping. Anything.

"Are you okay?" Nathan stopped in front of her, his gaze running up and down her body.

"Fine," she squeaked, and cleared her throat. "Why?"

"You winced as if you were in pain when I walked up."

"Did I?" She hadn't been in pain. In lust maybe, but not in pain.

She put on a smile she hoped would hide the turmoil her riotous hormones stirred up inside her and made for his car. "Must be the crick in my neck. I swear the mattress in my room is made of concrete. Ready to get started? We're wasting daylight."

The Town Car beeped and its taillights flickered as she hurried along the passenger side to the door. She heard Nathan shuffling up behind her, but grabbed the handle and let herself in before he could open the door for her. He looked slightly offended when he climbed in the other side and started the car.

Add manners to the list, she thought, and held back a smile by biting her lower lip. The man's momma had raised him right, whoever she was. Which made Rachel wonder who she was.

Fumbling with her seat belt to avoid having to look at

that beautiful face, she asked, "You were born in Chicago, right?"

"Yes."

"Lived here all your life?"

"Yes."

"Your mom and dad still in the area?"

"What is this, twenty questions?"

She scrunched up one side of her face in mock derision. A little prickly on the subject of family, was he? "Just making conversation. We're going to be spending a lot of time together."

"Not that much time, I hope."

"Ouch." This time her frown wasn't a mockery. So much for manners.

He sighed and flexed his fingers on the steering wheel. "I didn't mean it that way. It's just . . . I'm busy. I have lessons to prepare and papers to grade."

She clucked. "I can see how you'd hate to miss out on all that excitement for a dull little thing like helping in an Interpol investigation."

He narrowed his eyes at her. "I'm supposed to be appraising a collection coming up soon in an estate sale in Michigan for a potential buyer."

She didn't bother to respond to that one.

He huffed out a breath. "Look, I have—"

"A life?" She raised her eyebrows and looked at him. He wasn't nearly as appealing now that he was telling her he didn't have time for her, and yet looking at him still started an ache pulsing low in her body. "And you think I don't?"

"I didn't say that."

"You didn't have to." She set her lips in a firm line and fixed her gaze out the windshield. "You think this is a wild-goose chase, don't you?"

"I'm here, aren't I?" Their gazes crashed together like a pair of brass cymbals.

She opened her mouth to tell him he didn't have to stay. If he was so interested in preparing his lessons or grading his papers, he could go on and do it. But she closed her mouth without saying a word.

She was too afraid he'd take her up on the offer.

A cold knot formed in her chest. Her crazy infatuation with him felt foolish now. He certainly didn't return the interest.

He hit the brakes a little too hard at the exit to the parking lot, sending her bobbing toward the dashboard. She put out a hand to steady herself.

"Where are we going, anyway?" he asked.

"Wherever Von might be. What do you suggest?"

"His apartment?"

She shook her head, feeling steadier now that they were back on a safe subject—work. She felt herself fall into the groove of investigation. "Been there already. His roommate said he hadn't seen Von in days, and the kid's room didn't look like anyone had been around."

"You went inside?"

She shook her head. "Not without a warrant. Peeked in the windows."

"Von lives on the third floor."

"I climbed the fire escape. And I thought you didn't know Von that well."

He shrugged, but it wasn't as careless a move as it should have been.

"I've also been to St. Michael's." That got a sharp look out of him. Interesting. She made another mental note and moved on, feeling it wasn't the right time to probe. "Headmaster there was polite enough, but didn't give me squat. He makes a nice cup of lemongrass tea, though. Did Von have a job?"

"He worked on and off, I think. Mostly manual-labor stuff, warehouses and construction when he could skate by the union rules."

"Mmm. Cash under the table then, I bet. Makes sense. According to the IRS, he's never filed a tax return. What about family?"

A car honked behind them and Nathan pulled out into

the traffic on Lower Wacker Drive to clear the way. "His dad died when Von was about twelve." He rolled his gaze sideways sardonically. "And I know that because I used to be on the board of trustees at St. Michael's. We make a point of knowing when one of our students is orphaned."

She nodded, lost in thought. "The headmaster at St. Michael's became his legal guardian. Where was his mother?"

Nathan shrugged again. Stiffly again. "I never heard him or his father talk about her. If she's still alive, I doubt she's in Chicago."

Rachel leaned back against the leather seat. "So we're reduced to flashing his picture around areas he might have frequented and hoping someone recognizes him."

"And that they're willing to give him up if they do."

It was her turn to sigh. How many places were there for an eighteen-year-old to hide in a city the size of Chicago?

Too many.

Then again, they just might get lucky.

"Guess we'll start around where he lives. Someone in that neighborhood has got to know him." She gave Nathan a speculative look. "This could take some time, though."

His jaw set. He drove on without comment. It wasn't until he'd pulled to the curb six or seven blocks away, near Von's apartment building, that he turned to her and spoke.

"Look, about before . . ." His voice was soft, conciliatory when he turned to her, but his eyes went chillingly blank, as if he'd shut a door between the outside world and his feelings. Shut her out.

"You don't have to exp—"

"I . . . never knew my own mom. My dad passed just before my ninth birthday."

A gush of empathy warmed her from the inside out, loosed that knot that had grown in her chest. She knew what it was like to lose parents.

"You took me off guard with your questions," he finished. "Family is a painful subject for me."

Given that he sounded sincere, and that every nerve in

her body seemed to be firing at once under his repentant gaze, Rachel let go of the caustic retort that had been on the tip of her tongue.

Her skin prickled. Her breasts seemed to swell, the nipples tightening. Warm liquid streamed to her core.

So much for putting aside her physical attraction to him. All it took was one sorrowful look from him and her resolve melted.

She couldn't set aside anything when it came to Nathan Cross, not her grudging respect, not her curiosity, and certainly not her attraction. Her reaction to him existed beyond her conscious control. The only question was, could she resist it long enough to get the job done, find the answers she needed here, and get the hell out of Dodge?

Figuring the odds weren't in her favor, but determined to try, she pulled a photograph of Von Simeon out of her pocket, gritted her teeth, and opened her car door.

"Apology accepted. Now let's get to work."

TEN

After a long day spent searching for something— someone—he didn't want to find, Nathan watched Rachel glide through the sliding glass doors of the Wyndham Hotel into the lobby. He didn't dare escort her farther. Just being near her in the car and on the sidewalk all afternoon had been hard enough. To walk her to the door of her room—and walk away—was too much to ask of any man. Much less one of *Les Gargouillen.*

Tearing his eyes away from the denim-cupped backside, he pulled a cell phone out of his pocket and dialed the number he knew by heart. Connor Rihyad answered on the first ring.

"Let me talk to the old man," he said without preamble.

"You're not a member of this congregation anymore. You're not supposed to—"

Nathan's hand tightened on the plastic casing. "He came to me first and you damn well know it. Put me through."

There was a moment's hesitation, then the sound of the line transferring.

"Talk to me." The old man never had been one for formality. Much like Nathan.

"Have you found Von yet?"

"No."

Nathan cursed. "I don't know how long I can keep her off his trail."

"We'll find him soon. We have people looking."

Nathan paused, then snorted. "Connor? He couldn't find his balls with both hands."

"Did she come up with anything we can use?"

"No," he admitted grudgingly, then found himself defending her. "I steered her off course."

Oddly, he'd found he didn't like lying to her, no matter the reason. He'd told her that he thought Von had friends in a neighborhood of tidy row houses a few miles away. They'd spent two hours canvassing the neighborhood and interrogating old ladies. Then, desperate, he'd said Von liked to bet on the ponies and driven her all the way out to Arlington to flash his picture around the racetrack.

She'd ended the day discouraged, and he'd felt more than a pang of guilt until she'd lifted her chin and proclaimed she'd be ready to start fresh the following afternoon when Nathan finished his classes. Until then, she'd boot up her laptop and keep scouring law-enforcement and Internet databases for leads.

"Maybe you should let her go, see if she picks up his scent."

"Let her lead us to Von?" A frisson of alarm trilled up his spine.

"You said she was a good investigator."

"She is," he replied automatically, then regretted it. He didn't quite know why, but he didn't like where this was leading.

"She has access to information we don't."

"What if she actually finds him?"

"You'll make sure she doesn't." His tone fell to the range of sweet coercion. "Or if she does, you'll deal with it."

Nathan knew what Teryn meant. He would replace the images of Von in her mind with something different. Something trivial.

A sweat broke out under the wool scarf around Nathan's neck. The wool prickled and scratched. Memory alteration—a form of hypnosis bolstered by the ancient magic of the Gargoyles—was tricky under the best of circumstances. With Rachel he wasn't sure it was possible. When he'd been in her mind, he'd had very little control over the images they shared. He'd found himself in a pool of sensuality, of tangled sheets and warm flesh. He'd found himself drowning in the softness of creamy breasts and the wetness of hot, slick, womanly flesh, unable to fight the currents of desire, to resist the lure of sex. Unable even to drag air into his lungs, so focused had he been on her, on having her—and he hadn't cared. If he'd never drawn another breath, it wouldn't have mattered in those moments.

It shouldn't be like that. It certainly never had been in the past. He'd merged his mind with other women. Planted a part of himself other than his penis in them and seeded them with his thoughts.

Never had he been as helpless to maintain control of the images forming between them as he had been with Rachel, and he hadn't even made love to her yet.

Yet?

Ever. He had never, ever made love to her, and never would, he reminded himself, and shook off his reverie.

"This is a dangerous game you're playing, Teryn."

"These are dangerous times."

Nathan couldn't think of a response to that. In the background he heard the clink of china and knew Teryn was enjoying his evening snack.

"I miss your lemongrass tea," he admitted.

"I miss sharing it with you. Maybe when this is over—"

"Don't." Nathan wished he hadn't opened this particular wound. "Don't go there."

"Anything that is done can be undone, Nathan."

"Except this damned curse."

"Some consider it a blessing."

Nathan squeezed his eyes shut. "Just find Von. Quickly."

He stabbed the End Call button on his cell phone, hunched his coat tighter around his shoulders, and stared up at the light in the north tower of St. Michael's, Teryn's room. His gaze wandered to the buttresses, the crumbling statues adorning them, ghoulish creatures, mixtures of human and animal features with dead stone eyes.

He turned away, jammed his hands in his pockets, and headed for home.

Blessing, my ass.

Teryn settled the phone back in its cradle and took a moment to gather his strength before returning to the ritual preparations Nathan's call had interrupted. He was tired. It was as if the energy had been slowly draining out of him these past months. Years, really. Since Nathan had left.

Since he'd excommunicated him.

The decision weighed heavily on him, even if it had been for the good of the congregation. His people couldn't afford the division Nathan's beliefs were causing.

Maybe it was coincidence that this exhaustion had come not long after Nathan had left. Maybe he realized what a mistake he'd made. Or maybe he was just getting old.

Whatever the cause, Teryn could ill afford to be at anything less than full strength now, with the evil storm he sensed brewing in the distance growing ever more powerful. Ever closer.

With a sigh he hefted himself out of the armchair by the phone table. He crossed the thick Tibetan carpet to the antique bureau and studied himself in the mirror. His complexion looked chalky. Soon his skin would be as pale as his hair. His cheeks sagged and his shoulders stooped. His frail hands shook as he removed his modern clothes piece by piece, folding them carefully and placing them on top of the bureau to be laundered later.

Naked, he poured water from a chipped ceramic pitcher into a hand bowl and said a quick purification chant over the ceremonial bathwater. Tired or not, he must proceed with the ritual tonight as he had each of the last three nights.

Pulling his shoulders up as best he could—a pagan showed respect to his god and goddess during a ritual in every way, including proper posture—he dunked a square of sea sponge in the purified water and dabbed it at his forehead and then down his chest.

"Blessed be my mind," he said, his eyes closed, lips moving but hardly any sound coming out. "May it be filled with knowledge. Blessed be my heart. May it be filled with love."

His pulse began to quicken as he felt the ancient magic seep into him. He repeated the ritual cleansing at each wrist with another ceremonial phrase and then moved his hands to his genitals. "Blessed be my nature. May it be fertile and produce beauty."

His brow furrowed. He felt as if his lifeblood was no longer his own. It pumped to a rhythm set by another. By the god and goddess.

A moment of guilt pricked him as he finished the cleansing by dabbing at his knees and finally his feet. He and Nathan had once performed these rituals together. They'd studied the old texts, practiced, put together fragments of memory from their first lives, and rejuvenated their pagan magic.

And a powerful magic it had been.

Once they'd renewed their faith in the deities, they'd found themselves able to perform amazing feats. They hadn't found a way to reverse the spell that made them what they were, as Nathan had hoped, but they had learned to conjure up wind and rain. They'd healed minor illnesses in each other, and they'd summoned visions.

They'd seen the past, the present, and even glimpsed the future.

So why couldn't Teryn see what evil approached?

Taking a plain white cotton robe from the top drawer and pulling the coarse fabric over his head, he wished Nathan were here to help him with this seeing ritual. They were stronger together.

But Nathan was lost to him. They couldn't risk meeting again so soon. If the congregation found out, they would lose faith in their leader.

If they realized he was performing pagan rituals in violation of their Christian vows, they would banish him . . . or worse. Teryn had heard tell of other congregations whose devotees defied their legacy. They weren't all so lucky as to have been banished.

Some had been burned.

Teryn belted his robe with a black cord, opened the bottom drawer of the bureau, and slid aside a folded square of white silk to pull out a wooden box. His feet bare, his body clothed in nothing but thin cotton, he carried the box up two flights of stairs to the roof of the north tower.

The stone up here was part of the original structure built in the 1890s. It was so cold beneath his bare feet that it seemed to burn. A gust of wind bit into his unprotected skin, and a shiver slid down his spine.

Determined not to turn back, he locked the door to the stairwell behind him lest he should be discovered, set the box on a stone bench, and walked to the far wall to open the pigeon hut.

"Hello, my friends."

A dozen gray-and-black birds squawked and flapped their wings, startled, then settled at the familiar, soothing voice. He took a moment to throw them some seed, and then, turning back to the bench, he knelt before the makeshift altar and opened the box. The rough granite abraded his knees and the wind continued to whip his body, but he paid no attention. Just the anticipation of the ceremony to come raised his energy level.

He set his altar with candles and incense, a chalice of red wine, water in a stone bowl, a pouch of salt, a feather from one of the birds, his ritual knife, and small statues of the god and goddess. Holding the salt above his head, he bowed before the moon, then pinched out enough to cast a circle around his place of worship before opening his arms before him to call the first quarter.

"Oh, Guardian of the north, spirit of earth, I ask your presence here this night. Be you welcomed in peace. Blessed be!"

Next he turned south, and welcomed the spirit of fire, then east and west and their associated elements before kneeling again for the business of the ritual at hand. Already he could feel the heightened energy pulsing within him. His body shivered, but his mind was on fire. Magic lived and breathed—roared—inside him. He would have rejoiced to have the weariness which had cloaked him lifted, except along with the positive energy of the magic, a dark force crept up on him. He could feel it at the outer edges of his consciousness, but he couldn't see it.

Damn it, how could he fight an enemy he couldn't see?

Hands shaking from frustration and the bitter cold that his body knew even as his mind rejected it, he pulled his final token, a piece of lapis lazuli, from the box and dropped it carefully in the bowl of water.

"Oh, beloved god and goddess, lend me your eyes that I might see the danger that threatens us. Lend me your wisdom that I might recognize it. Lend me your strength that I might defeat it. All that is yours is pure and good. Tonight I seek that which is not of you. Show me the unclean. Reveal to me your evil enemies that I might protect your children from that which approaches. Blessed be!"

Moonlight, the gift of the goddess, glinted off the rippling surface of the liquid. The blue stone beneath shimmered as if lit from within. Almost immediately Teryn's vision began to change. His perspective shifted until he felt as if he were looking at his city from a great altitude, so high that the gentle curve of the earth's surface was visible to him. He could see the black water of Lake Michigan and the shore beyond. His gaze traveled across hundreds of miles to the north where a black mass of malevolence swarmed.

A band tightened around Teryn's chest. Suddenly the cold wind had teeth. It tore at his skin while the energy that had surged through him only moments before flickered, fighting for life like a candle in the wind.

Teryn struggled for breath. Again he wished Nathan were here to add his strength to Teryn's own, but he had to force that thought out of his mind. Nathan was gone. Teryn was alone.

Alone against an evil he intuitively knew would destroy him if it had the chance.

He pressed his lips together to stop the moan that threatened to escape. He clamped his eyes shut against the pain, squeezing out two tears that left a frozen trail down his cheeks.

In his mind he continued his quest for sight, continued his chant. He spat out each word in a staccato rhythm, concentrating on getting the pronunciations just right, the order perfect.

"Oh, god and goddess, lend me your eyes that I might see the danger that threatens your children. Lend me your wisdom."

He drew a ragged, frozen breath. The wind battered him. Even the pigeons squawked in discomfort, but still Teryn continued. The dark cloud to the east bubbled and boiled, but grew no more distinct. Teryn still couldn't put a face to his nemesis, a name.

He would stay here until he could, he vowed. He would search until sunrise, if need be, and then again the next night, and the next. If the effort drained the last of his strength and left him nothing but a carcass on the stone, so be the will of the god and goddess.

Either he would know his enemy or he would die.

• • •

Rachel heard Nathan's voice before she opened the door to auditorium 411-B in the Chicago University Fine Arts Building. The low tenor vibrated inside her like a tightly strung wire in a high wind. It hummed in her solar plexus.

Squaring her shoulders, she pulled on the brass door handle and slipped into the top row unseen.

She wasn't supposed to be here. He had promised to pick her up in the lobby of her hotel after his last class at noon, as he had each of the past two days.

But she was tired of being cooped up in the bland room with its stock curtains and blah bedspread. She was tired of the bad Renoir prints on the walls, the *Seinfeld* reruns on TV, the laptop that had, until this morning, refused to give her any clues to the whereabouts of Von Simeon, no matter how many databases she searched.

Today she'd made a breakthrough. She'd found her first concrete lead in a file of obscure state records, and she was ready to follow it.

She'd almost left to pursue the information on her own, but why go alone when she could share her glory? This nut had been a tough one to crack, and she deserved a little recognition. She wanted to thump her chest, sing the "Tarzan" cry, and have someone congratulate her on her superb investigative skill.

Not just any someone—Nathan.

With Nathan, even this small victory would seem larger. Everything seemed somehow . . . richer when she was with him. Happy was happier, funny was funnier, and sexy was definitely sexier. He was stimulating. Exciting. He titillated her every sense.

She crooked her lips in a wry grin. *Titillated?*

Geez, she had it bad.

Now if she could only figure out what "it" was.

To say she was curious about the man would be one of the great understatements of all time. To say she had the hots for him too shallow, too crude.

What she had was something she'd never felt before.

Some kind of deep connection. She had never met him before the night of the museum gala, yet she felt as if she'd known him all her life. She recognized him . . . but from where?

The feeling was unsettling. It left her restless. Edgy. Her mind wouldn't stop thinking about him, and her nerves wouldn't let her sit still.

So she'd given up. Given in.

She wasn't quite sure what kept her sitting in an art history lecture when she had a hot lead to follow, but sit she did, feeling a bit like a voyeur for watching him unawares. The auditorium was large enough and dim enough, and he was intent enough on his lecture that he didn't seem to have noticed her entry. Lord, she was practically stalking the man.

Except she was a cop, so she could call it investigating and get away with it. Satisfied, she sank deep into the hard plastic chair to watch.

He was wearing navy blue Dockers and a light blue shirt that might have been crisp four or five hours ago. Now the rumpled sleeves were rolled up to his elbows, and the knot of his tie hung down to the third open button beneath his collar. He was lecturing on pottery, the fine ceramics of the Jingdezhen kiln in Japan, circa A.D. 800. He stepped into the light of a slide projector splashing oversize images of vases and teacups on the wall behind him, and the light washed out his complexion but only seemed to make his dark eyes darker. More piercing.

A prickly shiver of awareness ran up her spine, and she rested her head on the back of the chair behind her and closed her eyes. His voice poured through her like lava through a mountain crevice, thick, slow, and hot.

She sighed quietly. On top of everything else—the face, the body, the sharp mind—he had to have a great voice, too.

The tension seeping out of her, she let go of the meaning of the words and just listened to the rhythm and tone. He was a good teacher. He varied the speed of his delivery

and his pitch to hold his audience's attention. He fielded
questions with rapid-fire answers and occasionally shot
back questions of his own. At this point she wasn't surprised to realize that his voice was as curiously familiar to
her as everything else about him.

Sighing at the mystery she couldn't quite unravel, she
quit trying to place the voice and just listened. Maybe the
guy was a long-lost relative or something?

Unbidden, an image of her father formed in her mind.
Through her six-year-old eyes she watched him watching
her as she picked a seashell out of the surf on their last vacation together, a few months before Levi had been born.
She scrunched her toes in the wet sand as she pelted him
with questions.

"Why does the inside of a shell sound like the ocean?
What happens to the animals that live inside when the
shells come to the beach? Do seashells have babies the
way Mommy's going to have a baby? How many seashells
are there in the ocean?"

With his jeans cuffed up around his ankles and the summer breeze ruffling his hair, Daddy strolled down the
beach hand in hand with her and patiently answered every
question. She could feel the waves break over her toes,
hear the raucous call of gulls overhead. Feel her little fingers snug in his big, warm palm.

The memory was startling in its clarity—and gut
wrenching in the sense of loss it created, knowing that it
was the last summer of her life that she'd felt completely
safe. Her last summer of innocence before she'd learned
the truth about the world, and the monsters that roamed
it.

Rachel startled at a touch on her arm. Her eyes jolted
open.

Nathan Cross squatted next to her chair, his dark eyes
both amused and alluring. "You know, when my students
fall asleep in my lectures, I make them come to class in
their jammies for a week."

Rachel scrubbed her face with the back of one hand, sat

upright, and swallowed hard. Heat rushed up her neck as she pictured her skimpy cotton nightgown. "I—I wasn't asleep."

"Mm-hmm." He tucked her collar down where one corner had turned up. She gritted her teeth against the trail of fire his fingertips laid across the sensitive skin at the back of her neck. "What are you doing here?" he finished, seemingly oblivious to her reaction to him. Except for that little glint of satisfaction in his eyes.

Or was that her imagination?

She groped for an answer to his question. *What was she doing here?* Hadn't she wondered the same thing herself just a few minutes ago?

The answer came to her in a gush of feminine awareness, of coiling arousal in her core, as her discomfiture raised a rare smile in him. His teeth flashed at her, straight and white, and his earthy scent bloomed in her nostrils, seeped into her blood, reminding her of the smell of the clean, wet sand she'd scrunched between her toes that summer at the beach with her dad.

She knew why she'd come here—because she couldn't stay away. She was drawn to him in a way she'd never been drawn to a man before.

She'd had lovers. She'd even fancied herself "in love" a time or two. Comparing the attraction she felt toward those men to what she felt for Nathan was like comparing pastel to neon.

Not that she was in love with Nathan Cross. She couldn't even claim it was a simple case of lust.

What she felt was much more primitive. An instinctive need to see him, to hear him, to taste him prowled low in her belly whenever they were apart. It rumbled and roared and gnawed at her bones like some wild, half-starved beast until all she could think about was raking her fingers through his flowing black hair and rubbing her body up against his until sparks flew between them.

"Hello." He waved a hand in front of her face. "Are you sure you're awake?"

She realized he was staring at her bemusedly, and even that mild expression made her womb quiver like a bowstring.

"I—Yes, I'm awake." Sitting up straighter, she dragged a hand through her hair and righted her clothes. Heat climbed her neck.

What the hell was wrong with her?

She wasn't some randy teenager. She had a case to work—a case she'd devoted her life to, and she was closer now to solving it than she had ever been before. She didn't have time to moon after her star witness.

But she also had questions. Questions she couldn't ignore much longer, like why all of her senses seemed heightened when she was around him. Even now she smelled the fumes of the city bus unloading outside, heard the whisper of water pipes beneath the floor. She could almost taste the spearmint gum the coed who'd sat next to her during the lecture—and left ten minutes ago—had been popping.

And most of all, she wanted to know why she didn't feel alone with her own thoughts when he was near. He was there, not just beside her, but in her mind, like a distant echo.

But how?

Ignoring him for a moment, she relaxed her shoulders and opened her mind to the intrusion. It was a frightening sensation, like letting a dangerous stranger into the house late at night. Her natural instinct was to fight it, but she forced her breathing to stay steady, and gazed into his eyes, as shiny and impenetrable as polished obsidian. In their reflection, images of herself formed. Naked and flushed with passion, she was in Nathan's arms, her back to his chest. Their skin glistened with sweat and her hair hung in limp curls over her shoulders. His swung like a curtain before his eyes as his big body curved protectively, commandingly, around her. With his palm in the small of her back, he bent her forward. Her spine arched. Her face pulled taut in deep pleasure as she threw a heavy gaze over her shoulder at him. Her tongue traced her lips in anticipation.

In the image his hips pistoned into her buttocks while his hands spanned her waist, holding her close.

In her corporeal body a strangled *O* formed in her throat as she realized he was . . . they were . . .

Oh.

ELEVEN

Nathan jerked his hand away from Rachel as if she'd bitten him. His smile fell like the cage door on a wild animal, slamming down on the howling beast inside him that longed to drag a willing mate into his lair.

It wouldn't take much persuasion and Rachel would be willing, he had no doubt about that. Damn but her mind was open, unprotected. The mental bridge had formed between them without him even consciously deciding to make the connection. It was almost as if she had initiated the link, as she seemed to have done before, reached out to him somehow with her thoughts.

Her desire.

But that was impossible. She was human. No way could she initiate the link.

Not unless she was telepathic, or psychic.

Shit. He didn't even believe in ESP.

Did he?

He blew out a breath and backed another step away from her.

Something had certainly passed between them. For an instant their minds had been on the same wavelength.

A highly erotic wavelength.

Realizing he'd broken into a sweat, he resisted the urge to tug at his collar and tried to figure out what had just happened.

With a single penetrating look, it was as if a veil had been lifted between them—the veil of pretense. She'd offered him the opportunity to drop the façade of indifference between them. To end the charade of dogged cop on a case and the reluctant, but resigned, good citizen helping her. She'd given them a chance to be just a man and a woman doing what came naturally to men and women.

Except he wasn't a man. And no woman, especially Rachel Vandermere, would want him if she knew what he really was.

Given a choice, he'd walk away right now. He'd turn his back and forget he'd ever met her. But he had no choice. His course had been charted a thousand years ago and he had to follow it, however rough the seas may be. His people's existence might depend on it.

He cursed himself for caring about the ones who had cast him out, but their rejection didn't squash his obligation. He wouldn't allow his congregation to be persecuted when they'd been given no say in what had been done to them. What they'd become.

The son of a bitch Romanus was the one who deserved to be punished, not the innocent villagers of Rouen—or their souls reincarnate.

He'd told Teryn he would keep an eye on Rachel. Keep an eye on her he would.

But only an eye. Not his hands, his mouth, or the assorted other body parts he longed to press against and inside her, flesh to flesh.

He was not going to touch her.

Even if it cost him his sanity.

She lurched out of her seat, her green-eyed gaze darting everywhere but at him. "I have a lead on Von," she said, sounding as uncomfortable about what had passed between them as she looked. "I thought you might want to tag along while I checked it out."

She fumbled with her purse, stepping into the aisle. Getting the hell away from him. He should have been happy about that, but instead it rankled.

"But you're busy," she said. "I shouldn't have—"

He capped her shoulder with his hand, stopping her. The tremble in her slight frame nearly undid him. "I'll go."

"You really don't have to."

"I said I'll go."

She looked like she might insist he stay. Before she had the chance, he hooked her coat out of her grasp and held it for her while she slid her arms into the sleeves. Their hands accidentally brushed at her collar and he gritted his teeth against the pleasure of the sensation.

If he had any sense at all, he'd run the opposite direction, obligation to his people or no obligation. But he couldn't. He was trapped by a skittish green gaze and a shaky smile.

Walking out of the auditorium behind her, trying hard not to notice the gentle sway of her hips, like waves lapping at a shore, he had a sinking feeling this woman was going to be the death of him.

But, oh . . . what a sweet death it would be.

"Do you recognize this girl?" A thrill of awareness skittered up the back of Rachel's neck. *Nathan was watching her.* Even though he was behind her, standing in the doorway to the Prime Time video store, she was certain of it.

No surprise there. Those unfathomable black eyes of his had been glowering at her all afternoon. Something had gotten under his skin, that was for sure. And whatever it was had made him about as sociable as a rabid badger.

She almost glanced over her shoulder to confirm that he was still scowling at her, but she caught herself. After the incident in his classroom, when she'd almost had an orgasm just from looking at him, she didn't want to risk making eye contact again.

Besides, confirmation wasn't necessary. She didn't know how she knew he was watching her when she couldn't see him, but she knew. His gaze was as palpable as a caress. Fingertips sliding up the bumpy ridge of her spine.

Stop it, she commanded herself. *Just stop.*

At least his standoffishness and her staunch refusal to think about anything remotely sexual between them—when she could control it—made it easier to focus on the job at hand.

Turning her attention back to the heavyset Asian woman behind the counter, Rachel handed her the picture for a closer look. "Have you seen her?"

The woman squinted at the grainy Polaroid. "Maybe she come in store sometime," she said in heavily accented English. "Buy movie."

"Do you know her name?"

The woman shook her head. The wooden needles holding a bun of gray hair to the back of her head wavered precariously. "Just face. And movie. She like chick flick."

"Is there anyone else who works here who might know her?"

The woman turned her head and let out a spate of Japanese. A moment later a man about her same age but a hundred pounds lighter pushed through the swinging door to the back room that appeared to double as warehouse and office. Rachel held her breath, hardly daring to hope that the man could ID the girl in the picture. All week long she'd been flashing a similar picture of Von to anyone who would spare it a glance with no luck. Discouragement had set in despite the fact that she knew, as an investigator, that even the most hopeless-seeming case could break at any time, without any warning.

All it took was luck.

Despite her determination not to, she glanced back at Nathan. Was he her good-luck charm or her curse?

For all his attempts to help, he'd provided more distraction than assistance the last few days. At times she'd wondered if he was purposely trying to misdirect her. To keep her from finding Von.

She still wondered, though she kept her suspicions to herself. She'd find Von with or without Nathan's help. She could ditch him any time, but if he was trying to sabotage her attempts, she didn't want him off doing it behind her back. She wanted him where she could keep an eye on him.

She rather enjoyed keeping an eye on him.

Sighing at the way her mind kept slipping into the gutter when she thought about Nathan, she forced herself to show an encouraging smile for the shop owner, who was still studying the picture she'd given him. He and his wife held a running conversation in Japanese.

Rachel's heart beat faster. She could practically feel Von's cold trail warming beneath her feet. Soon she would have him, thanks to an old rejected Workman's Compensation claim. Leave it to the government to save every scrap of information they ever collected on a person.

Apparently Von had worked at the car wash down the street a while back, where he'd had the misfortune of having an SUV roll over his foot. The manager had taken him to the emergency room for X rays, and some back office bureaucrat had found it necessary to file a claim with the state. The claim had been rejected because Von wasn't officially an employee. He'd been working for cash under the table to avoid paying taxes.

Still the record of the bogus claim was there, and it had led Rachel to his employer, who had been happy to identify him when threatened with federal tax-evasion charges and labor-law violations for failing to pay Social Security taxes on undocumented employees. The man even offered up a picture that had been pinned to the bulletin board in the back office. In the photo Von and a young woman the manager said used to visit the kid frequently at the car wash mugged it up behind the wheel of a Lamborghini that had come in for a hot-wax job last summer.

The manager didn't know where Von was now, or who the girl was, but Rachel had what she'd been looking for—a lead to follow. Someone in Chicago had to know this girl—her name, where she lived, where she went to school. Rachel would find her, and she had a feeling that when she did, she'd find Von soon after.

Unfortunately, it wouldn't be right now. The shopkeeper shook his head and handed the picture back to Rachel with a half bow. He responded in Japanese, which his wife interpreted. "We sorry. No know name or where find. Just girl come in sometime."

"Has she been in recently?"

"No." The woman shrugged. "Two week. Maybe three."

Disappointed but undaunted, Rachel bowed her head and thanked the couple for their help. The picture was still a solid clue, and she would play it out.

The bell above the door tinkled as Nathan pushed it open for her and followed her out. She was so deep in thought that her mind hardly registered the electrical jolt of her shoulder brushing his chest.

"Convenience stores, video stores, liquor stores, fast-food joints," she said, sucking in her cheeks as she thought. They'd checked all of them in the area. "Where else would a young girlfriend/boyfriend running a little on the wild side hang out?"

Nathan snorted derisively. "Drug dealers, flop houses, cheap motels."

She grimaced. "We'll scrape the bottom of the neighborhood barrel if we have to, but I don't know. . . ." She stared hard at the picture and cocked her head. "She looks like a nice girl."

"Nice girls don't hang out with boys like Von."

"Oh, come on, haven't you ever read a romance novel?"

"No." He cocked on eyebrow. "Have you?"

"Thousands. And trust me. Nice girls always fall for bad boys."

"In books, maybe."

"Art mirrors life." She gave him a cheeky grin, then held up the photograph of Von and his girlfriend again. "You know where I want to go?"

He didn't bother to answer. His expression made it plain he was sure she was going to tell him whether he wanted to hear or not.

"To St. Michael's. The man in charge there—"

Nathan came to a dead stop, pulling Rachel back to him when she kept moving. "The headmaster?"

"Teryn Carnegie."

"I know his name."

Rachel lost her train of thought a moment, looking at the sour expression the mere mention of the headmaster had put on Nathan's face. "Obviously it isn't associated with happy memories."

Scowling, he strode into the intersection in front of the video store, toward the garage where he'd parked his car.

She hurried to catch up. "What is it with you and that place?"

"What makes you think Teryn can help you?"

She grated her teeth. Mr. Enigmatic and his habit of answering questions with questions was starting to get on her nerves. "You're responsible for the welfare of a school full of boys, you're bound to have a few run-ins with the neighborhood girls."

Nathan checked his watch. "It's after five."

"It's a boarding school. Someone will be there."

"I have a better idea."

"Like what?"

Muttering to himself, Nathan fumbled with his car keys, then sighed and opened the passenger door for her. His jaw set hard as granite, his back straight and his shoulders tense, he shot her an impenetrable look.

"Like dinner," he said in a tone that dared her to argue.

Ten minutes later Rachel's eyes widened in horror as Nathan swung his Town Car to the curb and handed the keys to a valet. She was speechless as he got out, lifted the trunk, and pulled out a perfectly pressed dinner jacket.

When he tried to lead her toward the entrance to Olivetto's, she finally found her voice. "Oh, no. No way!"

"I told you we were going to eat."

"I thought you were going to pull over at the nearest hot-dog stand, not . . . not *this*." It annoyed her that she couldn't think of a word to describe the place.

She stared at the red carpet leading from the curb to the restaurant, the marble entranceway lit by fluted glass sconces, the uniformed doorman waiting to admit her.

Or throw her out on her bum.

Nathan might have pulled a jacket out of his trunk like a rabbit from a hat, but she didn't happen to have an evening gown in her back pocket. "I'm really not that hungry."

"You haven't eaten all day."

She planted her fists on her hips. And her feet on the sidewalk. He got the message and turned to look at her. "I'm not dressed, okay?"

He narrowed a gaze full of male appreciation up and down her body. Her skin heated under the perusal. Geez, if she kept reacting to him this way, she was going to have a heat rash before the week was out.

He still looked angry, but now it mingled with a kind of predatory arousal that set her back on her heels. "Just keep your coat on until we're seated," he said, passing the doorman a twenty. "No one will notice what you're wearing."

Catching her breath when he finally turned his mesmerizing gaze away from her, she stared morosely down at the corduroy bell-bottoms and clunky boots poking out beneath the hem of her Navy peacoat. "Yeah, right." But they were already inside before she could argue further, and her mind was otherwise occupied.

She'd heard about the famous Olivetto's restaurant on North State Parkway, but she'd never had a chance to see it for herself. The carpet felt like a bed of thick moss beneath the soles of her boots. Rich mahogany paneling covered most of the walls, dimly lit with the same brass sconces that adorned the entranceway outside. Lush greenery spilled off discreet privacy barriers, which gave every setting a secluded feel. From somewhere unseen, a string quartet played so softly that it was almost below her hearing range, muting the clink of silver on china.

And the smells . . . Seafood and pasta. Rich Parmesan cheese and flaming cherries.

Nathan leaned to whisper to the maître d' and passed the man yet another bill, one she suspected was quite a bit larger than the bonus the doorman had received. He stepped back to her just as her traitorous stomach let out a loud rumble.

"Glad you're not really hungry." He hooked her elbow in his and guided her after the waiter.

Ever so discreetly, she jabbed him in the ribs with the elbow he held.

Before she could spell *opulent,* they were seated at a table next to a stone fireplace. Low flames crackled in the hearth, adding that much more warmth to the aura of the room. Candlelight glimmered from a votive in the center of the table, its light flickering and twinkling in the crystal chandeliers overhead.

Nathan stood by while the waiter scooted her chair in and unfolded the linen napkin to her lap, then took his own seat and ordered without waiting to be asked. "I'll have a Manhattan. Make it a double."

He slashed an eyebrow toward her.

She glared at him for his rudeness, and then smiled apologetically at the waiter. "Wine, please. The house—"

"Give me the list." Nathan held out his hand. A wine menu appeared from nowhere. He scowled over it. "Red or white?"

"White," she answered, surprised he'd bothered to ask in his rapidly fouling mood.

"Sweet or dry?"

"Dry."

He folded the menu and slid it across the table. *"Le parfait coup du banois. Château du Golvie, 1905."*

She almost gasped. Her French wasn't as perfect as his, but she knew what he'd ordered—and what it cost. Apparently he realized that she knew. He gave her a look that threatened violence if she even tried to override the order.

What was with him? He'd been about as cuddly as a cockroach all day, but now he'd sunk to downright surly. His prickliness had her nerves jangling, her body ready to jump out of her skin. And she didn't even know why.

She tilted her head and studied him. The skin pulled tight over high cheekbones and the ornery lock of hair fallen over his forehead raised her internal threat monitor from yellow to red. But it was the way his lips, normally full and sensual, had thinned and twisted down at each corner of his mouth that truly alarmed her.

He looked like a man spoiling for a fight.

By damn, she was in a mood to give him one.

He was the one who had dragged her to an intimate table for two in the most exclusive—and romantic—restaurant in Chicago. If he wasn't happy with the company, that was his problem. He could just deal with it.

She wasn't going to cater to his temper. She was too edgy herself. Too off-balance, too . . .

Hot. Horny. So full of lust that she itched with it. She longed to rub her body up and down the length of him, dip her tongue into the shadowy hollow of his throat, wrap her arms and legs around him, pull him close, and make him fill the empty, aching well of desire he created inside her.

She groaned in frustration. Nathan cocked one eyebrow in a *What?* expression, though he didn't say the word. Ignoring him, she dropped her gaze to her fists, which lay clenched in her lap.

The force of her need for him shocked her. She'd never been an aggressive lover, preferring instead to let the guy take the lead. What was it about Nathan that made her daydream of giving up her inhibitions, throwing herself away to wild abandon?

And how was she going to keep her dreams from making her do something in reality that she would be mortified over later?

Her frustration rose until it rang in her ears like the whine of an engine turning a thousand RPMs over the redline.

It was obvious he didn't feel the same way. He didn't even like her . . .

Unless his testy mood and hers sprang from the same source.

Her heart kicked. Her gaze leaped up to his on a hitched breath. He stared at her darkly over the rim of his empty tumbler, then waved at the waiter to bring him another.

Was the attraction between them all one-sided?

She needed to think about this.

With a nod she excused herself to the ladies' room. Standing in front of the huge beveled mirror, she ignored the evil eye she was getting from the primly uniformed attendant, who looked with dismay at the unbuttoned shirt she wore over her plain turtleneck sweater, her warm, if not elegantly stylish, corduroy pants, and the clunky boots on her feet. Well, she hadn't been planning on dinner at a five-star restaurant, had she?

She might not be dressed for a fancy meal, but that didn't mean she had to look like something that ought to be thrown out with the spoiled cabbage, either. Blowing out a breath, she pulled the scrunchy out of her hair and finger-combed the thick locks until they fell over her shoulders in soft, blond waves. Digging in her purse, she sighed in relief when she found an old mascara and a lipstick pen under her service weapon. The mascara made her eyes look larger, deeper set, and the lip color highlighted her full mouth and suited her complexion perfectly.

She washed her hands and dabbed a little lotion from the complimentary supply across her wrists and behind her ears. It would have to do; she didn't carry perfume on the job. Finally she pulled a five-dollar bill from her pocket, shoved it in the jar for the attendant, who smiled at last, then squared her shoulders and pushed through the door, ready to do battle.

Rachel had never been the flirtatious type. She didn't do coy. But one way or another, tonight she was going to find out if Nathan Cross wanted her as badly as she wanted him.

TWELVE

"Tell me something about yourself."

Nathan's stomach quivered at the suggestive gleam in Rachel's green eyes. Dinner had gone better than he'd expected. When she made her trip to the ladies' room, he half thought she might bolt out a window or rear door and leave him waiting all night long. He deserved no better, the way he'd been stomping around and growling at her all day.

She'd come back, though, and made quite an impression when she had. Gone was the purposeful cop with the no-nonsense ponytail and down-to-business clean face. In her place a nubile goddess with a halo of golden hair and ripe raspberry lips sauntered back to the table in a hip-swinging, man-maddening gait. Just remembering it made his groin tighten so forcefully he winced.

He'd resisted her enchantment at first, gulping down another drink in an attempt to deaden the nerve endings that all seemed hypersensitive to her presence. Then he'd ordered the biggest steak on the menu, demanded it so rare it couldn't have been cooked, just waved over the grill once or twice, and attacked the bloody meat like a lion on a kill when the plate was set before him.

He'd been at war with himself—and her—all evening, unable to decide if he'd brought her here to seduce her or to scare her away once and for all.

He'd brought her here to keep her from going to St. Michael's tonight, he reminded himself firmly, though he wasn't sure why the thought of her at the school bothered him so much.

No one there would help her find Von. Yet the thought of her stepping inside the crumbling old castle of a cathedral he wasn't allowed to enter, walking the narrow halls he wasn't allowed to walk, trailing her fingers along the stone he wasn't allowed to touch fueled a fire inside him. Looking deep into her curious eyes, the flames leaped, burning bright but cold, like a distant star on a winter night.

Remembering she'd asked him to tell her about himself, he shook himself out of his reverie. "What do you want to know?"

"Were you born in Chicago?"

"Yes." *Twice.*

"You told me about your mom and dad. I'm sorry," she added quickly. "Do you have any other family here?"

"No."

"No one?"

"None."

She frowned. "Do you ever answer questions about yourself with more than one word?"

"Yes."

She waited, and when no more was forthcoming, she made a face at him. "Very funny."

He pushed his plate to the side and a busboy instantly appeared to remove it. "I'm the only child of an only child," he told her, having no idea why. He never talked about this. Especially with a woman. "I never knew my mother. I have no idea if she's dead or alive, or what family she might have had."

"I'm sorry," she said, her face swept with sadness.

"Don't be." Uncomfortable with the emotions she raised in him, the memories, he resisted the urge to squirm.

"I know what it's like to be alone at such an early age."

"I suppose you do." He no longer felt like squirming. Now he had to resist the urge to brush his knuckles across her cheek, to comfort.

Damn her, how could he stay mad at her when she made him want to tug that full lower lip of hers between his and kiss it until it turned from a frown to a smile.

"I spent a few years bouncing around the foster care system myself, then got lucky. I was adopted by a nice couple."

"I grew up at St. Michael's. My father left a trust to cover the tuition, and Teryn, the headmaster there, became my legal guardian."

"Was he . . . good to you?"

He didn't know what to say to that. Teryn had been more than good to him. He'd loved him.

Right up until the day he threw him out.

"I had a good childhood," he finally said. "Better than most."

That seemed to satisfy her. The worry eased from her face, and he was touched that she cared enough to be concerned.

His head was swimming from two before-dinner aperitifs and a coffee liqueur after the meal. His belly was so full he was afraid he wouldn't fit behind the wheel of his car, and yet certain parts of his anatomy were decidedly awake, alive, twitching every time she moved her head and the candlelight played across her face in a different pattern. Every time her breath lifted her high, firm breasts against her soft sweater.

How he'd like to reach across the table and lay his hands there, feel the tight peaks push against his palms.

Feeling his breath deepen and his blood stir, he decided he needed to move. But, masochist that he was, he wasn't ready to let her go yet.

He felt as if he were being drawn and quartered by indecision. He was trapped in a purgatory designed just for him. He couldn't leave her, and he couldn't take her home, to bed, either.

Lurching forward, he reached for his wallet with a curse and dropped a stack of bills on the table. "We're only a block from Navy Pier," he said, catching her hand. "Let's walk."

Her fingers clenched around his. Out of resistance? Or awareness? He had no idea.

"Are you kidding? It's freezing out there."

"I'll keep you warm." The words slipped out before he realized what he was saying. Damn. This was just a little walk. A little time to think. To gather the strength to push her away again.

Touching was not a good idea.

The wind off Lake Michigan blew crisp and clean and startlingly cold after the cozy warmth of the restaurant. Scattered flakes of lake-effect snow sparkled in the lights over the famed pier. The scents of popcorn and cotton candy mingled with the sounds of waves slapping against wooden piling and flags crackling on the breeze.

Within seconds the wind had ruddied Rachel's cheeks. She turned up the collar on her coat and sidled up closer to him as they walked. For a moment Nathan let himself believe they were no more than a pair of average tourists gawking at the glittering lights of the giant Ferris wheel while anticipation of the ride they would share back in their hotel room when the sightseeing was done slowly built.

"Can I ask you a question?" She rubbed her cheek on his shoulder.

He latched his arm around her back and snugged her up closer.

She stiffened for a moment against him, then relaxed. "Why don't you want me to find Von?"

He watched the moonlight flash on the tips of the waves

in the distance. His jaw set against the chill wind. The spinning lights of the Ferris wheel were suddenly dizzying, the carnival-style organ music blaring from the end of the pier a sickening dirge, like a recording played at the wrong speed. His stomach went queasy.

He jerked to a stop and turned Rachel to him. "Let me ask you a question. If you find your monsters, what then? What will you do?"

Her wide eyes told him he was holding her arms too tightly, and he forced himself to lighten his grip, but emotion still charged his voice. "Will you cage them and put them on display somewhere for children to gawk at like animals in the zoo? Or will you hunt them down and kill them until all trace they ever existed is gone?"

"I thought you didn't believe in monsters." Her breath exploded in a cloud of vapor.

He released her, practically shoving her away from him, and strode away down the boardwalk.

She caught up to him quickly. "You *know* they exist, don't you?"

"Let it go."

"I can't."

He warned her off with a dark look at her hand wrapped around his sleeve. He could easily have pulled away from her, but his feet felt as if someone had nailed his shoes to the boardwalk. Her crystalline eyes went soft and misty, and despite the fact that his feet were stuck, he felt like he was falling. Falling into her.

"Then let *me* go," he said.

"I can't. I need you." Her eyes shifted away from his. "I need your help," she corrected softly.

A cloud shifted over the moon, making the dark sky darker overhead. The lights and music of the pier seemed to fade into the distance. He thought he heard drums until he realized it was the pounding of his own heart. The ancient chants echoed along with the beat.

He shook his head. "What if I said I can't help you any longer?"

"Then I'd go on alone."

"And what if there were others out there who tried to stop you? To make sure you never found what you're looking for?"

A small shudder shook her, and he wondered if the cold caused it, or the direction of her thoughts. "I'd keep looking anyway."

"Even if it cost you your life?" *Les Gargouillen* were supposed to protect humans, but if the survival of the congregation were at stake, Nathan couldn't guarantee how his people would react.

"Even if," she said solemnly. She raised her gaze to his slowly, and his stomach clenched. He saw his mistake reflected in her hard, green eyes. A cop's eyes once again. "Who would kill me to keep me from finding Von, and why?"

He shook his head and shrugged. "He runs with a tough crowd. Who knows what they do and why?" he lied, even as he admired the hell out of her courage for asking.

His heart knocked against his ribs. Now was the time to make a strategic retreat, but once again he found he couldn't move. Couldn't pull away from her.

Damn it, this wasn't just Romanus's magic at work, driving him to take a mate. This was more. This was him, the man he used to be, looking at a woman he wanted. For the first time in many years his reasons for wanting went far beyond the physical. He liked Rachel. He respected her. In another place and time he could see himself loving her.

And that scared the hell out of him.

Reining in his galloping libido, he reached to her temple to tuck a yellow curl behind her ear. She leaned into him, lightly at first, turning her cheek against his chest. He banded his arms around her, allowing himself this one moment of feeling. One moment of humanity. Then he would push her away.

"How do you do it?" He pressed his mouth against her hair, inhaled her scent. "How do you keep chasing your dream day after day, year after year, no matter who tries to stop you? No matter what it costs?"

Desperation made the words ragged, harsher than he meant them to be. He didn't just mean her dream, he realized. He was asking about his own. How could he hold on to his dream of being human again when it had already cost him his friends, his family? When it would cost him the chance to ever be with a woman again? To love and be loved?

He clutched Rachel tighter. Her body felt small against his. Feminine and vulnerable. She wriggled, pushing against his chest, and he thought she'd finally come to her senses and decided to be afraid of him.

Quite to the contrary; when he released her, she stepped back only far enough to be able to look up at him without wrenching her neck. She turned his head to face her, holding him steady with her thumb in the cleft of his chin and her fingers along his jaw.

"It's all about desire," she said huskily. Her breasts brushed his chest, causing him to jerk, suck in a deep breath like a dead man suddenly brought back to life. His cock stretched and lifted, pressed into her thigh.

She inched closer to him, lifting her mouth until it was only millimeters from his. Her lower body pushed against the part of him where he most wanted the pressure, needed it. Their breaths clouded the scant space between them, merged soundlessly, seamlessly, like colliding banks of fog.

"Haven't you ever wanted anything so bad that you couldn't think about anything else?" she whispered.

Oh, yeah.

The blood pounded so hard between his legs that it felt like his heart had fallen to his groin.

Her nose brushed his jaw, like a flower petal on sandpaper. He stood like a stone statue, trying not to react, and failing.

"Haven't you ever known the kind of craving that eats you from the inside out? That wakes you up in the middle of the night, has you reaching for something that isn't there?"

He'd reached out plenty of nights and found nothing but air beside him. Damn her for reminding him.

A snowflake landed on her lower lip, its unique pattern distinct against her red lipstick, one of a kind resting on one of a kind.

Without warning, he slammed his mouth down over hers. The icy flake on her lip melted instantly, seared away by the heat of their joining.

He'd thought he understood need before. He thought he knew about desire. Tonight he'd discovered how woefully lacking his education had been. She'd brought whole new meanings to the words.

Now he had a thing or two to teach her. Starting with how a man with a thousand years of experience kissed a woman.

The force of Nathan's sensual assault shocked Rachel from the roots of her hair to the tips of her toes. This wasn't a kiss—it was a possession. He wasn't just holding her, touching her, he was inside her. She felt him in her blood, in the air that she breathed—when he let her breathe—in the electrical impulses leaping up her nerves to the pleasure center of her brain.

His thoughts mingled with hers. Even before the tip of his tongue probed the seam of her lips, she heard his command to open for him. She felt his satisfaction at her surrender. The erection pressed against her abdomen like a steel rod grew harder, thicker.

His fingers were in her hair, his thumbs at her temples, gently massaging, easing her head back to give him greater access. He slanted his mouth over hers, plundering and yet giving. Giving so much.

His thoughts rioted in her head. Behind the thin veil of his enjoyment, she felt a hunger bordering on violence inside him. A darkness so complete she could imagine it swallowing them both. A loneliness so devastating she couldn't imagine enduring it.

And yet he gave her tenderness. He gave her light.

He gave her the warmth of another human being to stave off the cold on a blustery winter's night.

Nathan jerked as if he'd been struck. His head snapped back, breaking the contact between them. Rachel gasped in pain at the loss of the connection between them. Their minds had been so merged that it felt like losing a part of herself.

Her knees threatened to fold. How was that possible? How could they so easily become so fully a part of one another that separating was like having a limb abruptly severed?

Nathan steadied her, his hands beneath her elbows the only place he touched her. Their breaths sawed the air like two jagged, rusty blades.

"Wh—what just happened?" she asked, surprised she had enough strength to vocalize the words.

"I believe I answered your question."

She looked up into dark eyes that glittered like cold, distant stars. *Question?* Her head was still muzzy. Had she asked a question? Oh, yes.

About desire.

Her cheeks flamed. Nathan Cross was no stranger to desire. He wanted many things, herself among them.

She cleared her throat. "I believe you did."

He let go of her, turned on his heel, and stalked back down the pier the way they'd come.

With the loss of his body heat and the fire they'd stirred between them, the night seemed even colder than it had before. Shivering, she pulled her coat closer and went after him. Fear clenched in her stomach, though she couldn't say what she was afraid of, him or herself.

At least she no longer had to ask herself whether he wanted her or not. But with one answer had come two new questions:

One, if she could feel not only her own emotions and reactions, physical sensations, but his during a simple kiss, what would it be like to make love? Would she experience both sides of the equation there as well?

And two, how long would it be before they gave into temptation and found out?

THIRTEEN

After dropping Rachel off at her hotel, his grip threatening to snap the steering wheel in two as he watched her walk inside and fought the urge to follow her, Nathan drove back to his condominium like a hell-demon, slammed the Town Car into park in the underground garage, stormed into the elevator, the hem of his coat billowing in his wake, and punched the button for the top, bypassing his own floor.

Alone in the lift, he stared at the red numbers over the door, willing the blasted hydraulic coffin to move faster. The drums were pounding in his head again. His veins bulged and his muscles stretched and contracted painfully as the magic tried to take him.

He slammed a fist against the wood-grained paneling and bowed his head, fighting the change. Fighting the primitive impulses that threatened to send him back to the garage, back into his car, and to Rachel's hotel.

Why shouldn't he take her? Why shouldn't he pound out his frustration inside her willing body? She wanted him, and he could do it gently, once the initial edge was taken off his mating drive. With all he'd learned about women in his many lifetimes, he could show her pleasure like she'd never known.

Sweat trickled down his temples and beneath his collar. Swearing, he ripped off his coat and threw it to the floor. Rage shook him. Bright bolts of lightning flashed behind his eyes, huge, jagged currents of electricity sizzled down his nerves. He could smell the ozone. Hear the crackle of flames.

God, he couldn't control it. If he wouldn't let the mating urge take him, the magic would force itself on him in other ways. His jaw splintered, lengthened. His fingers curled and hardened, sharpened into talons that left a three-pronged scrape in the wall when he pulled his hand away.

The security camera. He had to stop. He couldn't change here, but it was too late. It took all his strength to turn and face the wall, bury his head in his arms and tuck his hands—claws now—across his chest.

Damn her for doing this to him.

But even as he finished laying the curse on her head, he knew he was wrong. This wasn't her fault. It was his. He'd known he was playing with dynamite by being around her; he shouldn't be surprised that it had blown up in his face.

Blessedly the elevator bell dinged, bringing an end to his captivity. Careful to shield his face from the camera and keep his hands out of sight, he rushed to the maintenance stairwell and fumbled with the lock on the door to the roof. For security reasons, residents weren't allowed on the deck, but it hadn't taken much to pilfer a key.

His shaking hands finally getting the lock opened, he ran into the night. The fire door slammed shut behind him with a reverberating clang, but he didn't care.

He was free. He lifted his beak into the wind, inhaling the thousand scents, each unique and identifiable to his animal senses. He smelled joy and fear. Hatred and forgiveness. Doubt and bravado. Human emotion, his human memory of what they felt like, what they meant, fading with each passing second.

He stripped off what was left of his clothes, though he

didn't have to. The Awakening of the beast inside him was magical, not subject to the laws of physics. Had he left them on, they would have become part of the matter and energy making up his new form, and reverted to their initial state when he changed back.

Naked, he stepped to the edge of the roof and dived.

The last of the transformation occurred in midair. Skin changed to hide and fur even as the roaring wind rushed over it. His eyesight sharpened, focused on the fast-approaching ground. Even as he fell he felt the emergence of wings split the skin over his shoulder blades. Feathers plumed and his bones lightened, hollowed.

Almost wishing he could just keep falling, give himself over to gravity, he lifted his wings and flapped them down in one strong surge. Immediately his descent slowed. A wind current buoyed him.

No longer able to vocalize human speech, he screeched out his fury and turned toward the lake. Normally he would head out over the water, where he was less likely to be seen, but tonight he turned into the city, listening, scenting.

The freedom of flight alone would not be enough to calm his raging blood tonight.

He needed to hunt.

It didn't take him long to find his prey. With his eagle's eyesight, he spotted a man in tattered clothes holding a knife and bending over a woman's unconscious form.

Satisfied, Nathan swooped, sharp beak protruding, talons fully extended, the smells of blood and vengeance going to his head like a bottle of fine wine.

Lying on her uninteresting bed in her uninteresting hotel room, sleep eluded Rachel even though exhaustion had her flopped out spread-eagle like a limp noodle. She'd tried paging through her notes on Von, flipping channels on the TV, even reading the complimentary magazine in the nightstand drawer, but nothing could keep her mind from replaying The Kiss.

It was silly, really. She almost giggled when she found herself reaching up, touching her lips like a teenage girl with a crush as she relived the press of Nathan's mouth to hers. Except there was nothing juvenile about the things she wanted to do with, and to, Nathan Cross. The scenes her imagination conjured up were definitely NC-17 material.

She'd never thought of herself as a particularly sexual creature. Her job, her mission, always came first. Men and relationships were those things she crammed into the little crevices of time her career and her search for monsters left her.

What man wanted a woman who believed in monsters, anyway?

Nathan's chiseled features swam before her tired eyes.

He wanted her. He hadn't laughed at her crazy ideas.

A pang of sadness pulling at her gut, she wondered if he'd ever laughed, even as a little boy.

Resigned to a sleepless night, she reached over the side of the bed for her files. With all the lights off save the bed-side lamp, she scanned the pictures and reports she knew by heart.

Humans couldn't have committed these crimes. Didn't anyone else see that?

The gruesome images would have been enough to give any normal person nightmares, but when Rachel finally nodded off, curled on her side with her knees drawn up and one hand under the pillow, the other beneath her cheek, it wasn't bloody crime scenes she saw.

It was a giant creature with the massive body of a lion and the head and wings of an eagle swooping through the darkness over Chicago, blood dripping from its claws, its shriek of victory and vengeance splitting the night air.

Connor Rihyad plodded up the old stone stairs to the top of the north tower cursing the early hour. The beam of his flashlight cut through the dank darkness before him. He hated this part of the school. The slippery rock steps were treacherous even in the light—which was only during the day, since there was no electricity up here. The narrow passage smelled like old socks, with the only ventilation coming from the slits that served as poor excuses for windows, and it was cold as a witch's tit, since naturally, where there was no electricity, there was no heat.

No, Connor didn't like it here. He liked his modern conveniences—microwave ovens and high-speed Internet connections and digital sound.

The Wizenot seemed to like this place just fine, though. Whenever the old man couldn't be found, this was usually where he was hiding. Made Connor wonder what he did up here at all hours, with the door locked from the outside so no one could intrude unannounced.

Talking to his pigeons, or so Teryn claimed.

As long as he didn't claim they talked back, Connor guessed there was no harm in it.

Crazy old man.

Let him have his birds. He wouldn't live forever, and when he was gone, his people would need a new Wizenot. With Nathan out of the way, Connor was next in line for the position.

There would be some changes in the congregation, then. He wouldn't tolerate dissenters the way Teryn had. Banishment was too good for the likes of Cross. He was still able to influence the weaker among the people.

Connor wouldn't tolerate Nathan's insurgence. He'd bring him back into the fold.

Or else.

The wooden door at the top of the stairs crashed open, banging against the wall behind it. A gust of wind nearly blew Connor backward. Footsteps slapped frantically down the stone stairs, accompanied by cursing and flapping wings. Connor jerked the flashlight up to see who—or what—rushed toward him.

"Ach!" Teryn skidded to a stop and threw an arm up to shield his eyes. His complexion was gray as ash, his lips blue. His white hair swirled around his head in wild disarray. "Get that blasted light out of my eyes!"

"Teryn? Are you all right? What's wrong?"

"You're blinding me, that's what's wrong! Get out of my way!"

Before Connor could lower the beam, Teryn had pushed past him and was pounding toward the dormitory. Somehow in the blur as the Wizenot passed, Connor noted that his feet were bare and he wore only a thin cotton robe belted with a black cord.

What had he been thinking? It couldn't be thirty degrees out there this time of the morning.

Crazy old man.

Sighing, he followed his leader through the open door and found him in the youngest boys' room, kneeling over the bed of little Patrick, just six years old and still grieving the loss of his dad.

Teryn brushed his knuckles against one of the boy's pink cheeks.

The old man heaved out a giant breath. His shoulders sagged.

"Sir?"

"What is it, Connor?" Teryn answered without turning.

It wasn't what the old man said that gave him pause, but the way he said it. He'd never heard him sound so weary. So old.

Maybe he would be Wizenot sooner than he thought.

The possibility brought him no pleasure. Damn it, he wasn't a jackal, waiting for his prey to die so he could leech the flesh from its bones. He would earn his right to lead his people. He would be patient.

"There is someone waiting to see you. The woman."

He didn't have to say what woman. There weren't a great many women in their lives.

"Is Nathan with her?"

A feral growl rose in his throat. He swallowed it. He would show no disrespect to the Wizenot.

"No," he managed to say pleasantly. "Do you want me to get rid of her?"

Teryn placed a feathery kiss on Patrick's forehead, then frowned and rose stiffly. "Show her into my office," he said. "I'll be there in a moment."

Teryn stood before the pedestal sink in his utilitarian washroom and pressed a warm, wet cloth to his face, not only in an attempt to warm himself after a full night—far longer than he'd planned—in ritual on the roof, but to buy himself time to pull himself together before he sat across a desk from Rachel Vandermere. He'd already raised Connor's concern, storming down the embattlement steps this morning like a wild man. He had no desire to pique an Interpol investigator's curiosity, too.

Finally regaining some feeling in his frostbitten fingers and toes, he combed his hair and replaced the ceremonial robe he wore with a pair of gray slacks and a charcoal turtleneck. When he finally felt human again, he glanced in the mirror one last time and headed toward his office.

"Ms. Vandermere, how nice to see you again."

He smiled genuinely and held out both hands as he crossed the room. She rose and smoothed the wrinkles from the thighs of a pair of worn jeans that hugged the gentle flair of her hips and tugged at the sleeves of her thick Irish wool sweater that hugged parts of her a man his age shouldn't even be thinking about.

She really was a lovely woman. He could see why Nathan was interested in her.

"Thank you, Mr. Carnegie. Or should I call you Headmaster?"

"It's Teryn. Please." He clasped her small hands in his in a two-handed shake.

Her miraculous green eyes widened. "Your hands are freezing, Teryn. Are you all right?"

She turned his hands in hers until her palms covered them, warming him. The simple gesture of kindness squeezed his heart. He could definitely see why Nathan was interested.

"Quite. I've just been up feeding my birds. I have a covey of pigeons on the roof, and I always seem to forget my gloves. Bad habit," he said, allowing himself another moment to soak up her warmth before pulling away and waving at the overstuffed chair in front of his desk. "Please have a seat, Connor," he said to the man who stood in the shadows by the door, "bring us some of my homemade tea. Strong and hot."

He needed something hot, though the tea could only warm his flesh. It would take something much stronger to break the chill on his heart. More than the temperature had shaken him during his hours on the roof. It was what he'd seen. . . .

Fire and Ice. Death, both human and Gargoyle. The destruction of his people.

And the children. Dear God, the children.

The vision had sent him rushing pell-mell into Patrick's room. He'd had to see for himself that the boy was all right. The devastation he'd seen was the future. It hadn't happened yet.

And if it hadn't happened yet, he could change it.

He *would* change it.

Teryn burrowed into the soft leather of his chair and took comfort from the familiar room around him. This was his space, his domain, from the cluttered desktop and bookcases on the far wall overflowing with everything from leather-bound textbook first editions to popular fiction paperbacks, to the old-world globe standing in the corner with its fanciful sea monsters depicted in the oceans, to the tabletop of herbs under the grow light in the corner.

He inhaled the familiar scents of lemongrass, basil, and rosemary. He needed familiarity right now. It helped him forget about the strange sights he'd seen in his vision.

"Perhaps you'd rather have coffee, Ms. Vandermere,"

he said to the young woman following his gaze around the room, taking in the same details, "but I grow the herbs myself, and I do love to show off my botanical skills."

"Tea is perfect."

He smiled. "So, what brings you here so early this morning?" he asked.

She looked over his shoulders at the pictures that lined the wall behind him. He knew the moment her gaze landed on the gilt-framed 8 x 10 of him and Nathan tacking a two-man catamaran in a charity regatta out on the lake several summers ago. The trophy they'd won sat on a shelf next to the photograph.

Looking at them, her green eyes softened from emeralds to moss and a wistful smile played across her lips. "You're a sailor."

"I used to be."

"Why did you give it up?"

He shrugged. *Because sailing was what he and Nathan did together. It was their time. They worked as a team. Without him, their was no joy in the glide of a hull over water, the power of the wind.* "Sailing is a young man's sport."

"A man like Nathan Cross?"

"No, racing was my passion, not Nathan's. He only went along to humor an old man. I doubt he's been on a boat since the summer we won that." He jerked his head over his shoulder toward the trophy.

"You two are close."

"We were." He'd paused a heartbeat too long, and he knew it.

"But not anymore?"

He sighed, laid the letter opener flat on his desk blotter, tracing the intricately carved lion's head on the handle once in remembrance. "Nathan isn't involved with the school any longer. He has his own life."

"How much do you know about that life?"

That Nathan was determined to live it his own way, no matter what the cost. To himself or anyone else.

Teryn's heart beat sluggishly as he thought about his own role in Nathan's decisions. "May I ask why you're interested in Nathan? I thought it was Von you were looking for."

"I am. It's just that Nathan has been helping me, showing me around the neighborhood, and I, well, I was just curious about him."

Teryn eased back in his leather chair, noting her blush. "He can be a curious man."

She avoided his gaze and dug a photograph out of her purse. "I was able to locate this picture of Von with a girl. I wondered if you might know who she is."

He took the picture of the young couple and did his best to mask his surprise. Several of the boys at St. Michael's had shown interest in Jenny Lovell, but he hadn't realized Von had been seeing her. She didn't seem his type.

He handed the picture back. "Her name is Jenny. She lives in one of the old blue-collar neighborhoods south of Jefferson."

"Address? Street name, at least?"

"I'm afraid I don't have it."

"How about her last name?"

"Lovern, Loveless, Lovejoy. Something like that." He lifted his gaze meaningfully. "Nathan might know." He didn't want her finding Jenny on her own.

"If he does, he's not telling me."

He tilted his head, wondering what that meant.

She chewed on the inside of her cheek. "I'll try the phone book. Maybe I'll get lucky."

She stood, gathered up her purse, moved toward the door, and said good-bye.

Teryn watched her go, then shut the door softly behind her.

This wasn't good. Nathan had to take a mate, to procreate, in order to be brought back into the fold, and if Teryn was going to save their people, he needed Nathan at his side. He didn't know why, or how, but he knew Nathan was key to their survival.

By the grace of the god and goddess, he'd seen it.
He just didn't know what to do about it.

Connor stepped into the office with two mugs of lemongrass tea just as the woman breezed out the door. "Where is she going?"

Teryn came to stand beside him, took one of the cups, and drank deeply. "She has a lead on Von," he said, sounding far too calm.

"How? Where the hell is Cross? I thought he was supposed to be watching her."

"Watch your language. This is a school. I gave her the lead. And I don't know where Nathan is."

"If she finds Von before we do—"

"She won't."

Damn the crazy old man. How could he be so sure?

He took a slow breath to steady himself. It wouldn't do any good to tick off the Wizenot. "You want me to follow her?"

"No. I want you to find Nathan. Tell him Rachel Vandermere is on her way to Buchanan Street. She may find Von there."

Fighting back a scowl, Connor nodded stiffly and took his leave. What kind of game was Carnegie playing? And why?

He threw on his coat and stepped outside. The cold morning air had him sucking in his breath. If it was this cold so early in the year, it was going to be a bitch of a winter.

Down the street the Interpol lady fumbled to unlock a car with mittens on her hands. His scowl deepening, he turned the other direction to retrieve his own car, then paused.

Why should he go running to Nathan? The Headmaster's pet was out of this. Out of it all. He'd been excommunicated.

Nathan was a radical, his ideas destined to drive his people to ruin.

Connor, on the other hand, had always been loyal to the congregation. He had only his people's best interests at heart.

Slowly he turned back to Rachel Vandermere, then hurried toward her, his decision made. He reached her car just before she pulled away from the curb, and knocked on the window. When she rolled it down courteously, he forced a smile. "Headmaster Carnegie suggested I go with you. I know the neighborhood where the girl lives. I can help you find her."

There would be hell to pay later if Teryn found out his orders had been disobeyed, but by then, with any luck, the idiot Von would be safely under wraps, thanks to Connor.

And Nathan Cross could rot in hell for all he cared.

FOURTEEN

Jenny Lovell lived in a neat little two-story, redbrick home fronted by a cement stoop with a wrought-iron rail on a street lined by neat little two-story, redbrick homes fronted by cement stoops with wrought-iron railings. The small patch of grass out front, though already brown with fall hibernation, had been neatly edged, the walkway swept, and the flowerbeds mulched for winter. The only thing remotely untidy about the place was the string of last year's Christmas lights still drooping from the gutter. The red and white bulbs framed the lines of the roof and then twined around the porch post in a candy-cane pattern.

Far from being in a mood to appreciate jolly old elves and flying reindeer, Nathan leaned against the side of an identical house across the street and two identical houses down, watching the Lovells' door for signs of life. His feet hurt from standing on the cold ground. His eyes ached from lack of sleep. And despite the cold, his side burned from the knife blade the whacked-out junkie he'd killed last night had managed to scrape across his ribs before he died.

His eyelids fluttered shut. *He'd sworn to himself he was through killing.*

The man had deserved to die. He'd beaten an old woman into a coma for the eight dollars and thirty-two cents she carried in her pocketbook. Still Nathan suffered for his actions. He wasn't a guardian anymore; it wasn't his place.

He'd given the fool a chance to run. It didn't matter that he'd seen Nathan in guardian form—he'd been so high, no one would have believed the wild tale of a beast, half eagle, half lion, that had torn him off the woman, thrown him against a wall more than fifteen feet away. But the drugs had control of the man. They made him irrational. Instead of hightailing it out of there, he'd pulled a knife and rushed Nathan.

He'd had no choice but to kill him.

Or so he told himself.

Swallowing the memory like a bitter pill, he opened his eyes. A blue Honda pulled up in front of the Lovell house. His breath hitched. It was Rachel's rental car.

He'd known she'd track Jenny down sooner or later. He'd just hoped it would be later.

An invisible fist tightened around his heart as she got out of the car. She had on blue jeans, the clunky boots, and wool peacoat she was so fond of, and the mittens that seemed childishly incongruous with the sensual woman he knew her to be. His imagination conjured images of her bending over and scooping up a handful of snow in those mittens, firing the powdery missile at his chest while he laughed at her attack.

But there was no snow, and he certainly wasn't laughing.

It hurt to watch her and not be able to talk to her. To touch her. It was for the best, though. He couldn't be around her. Last night on the pier had been proof enough of that.

He turned and rested his back against the wall so that he didn't have to look at her. It was safer that way, for both of them. He heard her car door *thunk* shut . . . and then another.

He swung his head to check over his shoulder.

Son of a bitch!

What was Connor doing with her?

Rage roared to life inside him. He was no longer Nathan Cross, but the male lion protecting his pride. The eagle defending his mate. A growl rose low in his throat. His pulse thundered and his veins bulged.

Turning all of that energy inward, he focused his mind and sent an ultrasonic blast, the high-frequency whistle that only another Gargoyle could hear, right at Connor.

The Calling.

And this time, a challenge.

Stone-faced, he watched as Connor said something to Rachel, then turned and walked toward him. As soon as he'd cleared the corner of the house, Nathan grabbed him by the collar and threw him against the wall. The wound on his side protested the movement, but he ignored it. He threw a glance back down the street to make sure Rachel hadn't followed.

"What did you tell her?" he demanded, turning back to Connor.

"That I had to take a leak," he spat. "Now back the fuck off!"

Nathan adjusted his hold from the collar of Connor's coat to the man's throat and tightened his grip. "What are you doing with her?"

"Keeping an eye on her in case she actually manages to find Von. A job you were supposed to be doing, I believe."

Nathan would have liked to argue. He would have liked to tear Connor's head off. But Connor was right. He'd let his attraction toward Rachel—and his determination to fight it—get in the way of his duty.

He gave Connor one last shove for good measure, then let go and swept a hand through his hair, tugging at the roots. "I didn't think she'd find the girl so fast."

"You were wrong." Connor circled Nathan slowly. He sniffed the air, stopped and smiled sardonically. "You've been hunting. I can smell the blood on you."

He shook his head, ignoring the taunts. He still didn't understand how Rachel had caught up to the girl . . . unless she'd had help. "No way she could have traced Jenny this quick on her own."

Connor lolled his tongue in his cheek. "I thought you didn't like turning yourself into the beastie anymore. Didn't want human blood on your hands."

"Goddamn it, Connor. Who told her about this place? Was it you?" he said, although this time Connor's accusation hadn't gone unnoticed. It rang in his ears. *Blood on his hands. Human blood.*

"So much for your *principles,* huh?" Connor sneered. "So much for your *sacred vows.*"

Connor laughed. Nathan had killed a man, taken a life, and he laughed, and the sound boiled in Nathan's blood like acid. It ate at him.

"Guess the memory of your dear, departed wife wasn't enough to make you forget what you really are, after all."

Nathan lowered his head and rushed Connor, catching him in the face with the top of his head. He felt the crunch of cartilage, the warm spurt of blood. Heard the surprised grunt, the quick intake of a painful breath as Connor flew back into the side of the house.

Then claws more powerful than any man's hands gripped Nathan's biceps with bruising force. He was lifted off his feet, swung through the air like a rag doll, and slammed to the ground.

The impact with the frozen turf knocked the breath out of him. Wheezing and holding his injured side under his jacket, feeling fresh, warm blood oozing from the wound, he raised his head.

Connor loomed over him, partially changed into Gargoyle form. He stood on two legs, but his skin had transformed to scales. A bony point protruded from his skull and angled backward. A long, narrow tongue, forked on the end, flicked out to lick the blood draining from his beak. His eyes glowed with an unearthly green light.

He held a dagger to Nathan's throat.

"You want to fight, Nathan?" His voice sounded unnatural. Nasal. He backed away a step, flicked his right wrist, and his spring-loaded knife retracted into his sleeve. "Fight like the big boys. Awaken the beast."

Nathan propped himself up on one arm. "Are you crazy? It's broad daylight!"

Connor kicked his arm out from under him. "Awaken!"

"No!" He rolled with the blow, wincing as the laceration on his side tore open.

"Connor, are you there?"

Rachel's voice doused the sallow light in Connor's eyes. "Uh, yeah. Here." His skin bulged once, like a living creature writhed beneath it, then returned to human flesh. His skull rounded to normal shape. "Hold on, I'm not decent."

Her laugh tinkled like crystals, growing closer. "How much of Teryn's tea did you drink this morning? This has got to be the longest leak in history."

"I'll be there in a minute."

Get out of here, Nathan mouthed to him.

Connor jerked his thumb over his shoulder in a *you go* motion.

Standing up, Nathan shook his head furiously.

"Are you sure you're okay?" Rachel asked. "It really has been a long time."

"I'm fine." He wiped his bloody nose with the back of his hand. "Just give me another second."

"You don't sound all right." She wasn't laughing now. A heartbeat passed with Nathan and Connor staring each other down. Snarling, Connor blinked.

"Zip it up, mister," she said in her cop's voice. "I'm coming back there at the count of three. One."

Connor turned to leave, conceding, but stopped and spoke close to Nathan's ear, where Rachel couldn't hear. "Teryn told her how to find Jenny. He's playing you."

"Two."

Nathan refused to give up a millimeter to the hot, angry breath on his face. "Get lost."

"The old man wants you to break a few more of those vows of yours. Like the one about taking a mate. He's using you."

"Three." Rachel's footsteps were audible now, just around the corner.

Connor ducked his head toward the sound. "He's using her."

And then he was gone. He crossed the backyard and jumped the fence so fast the movement was hardly visible.

Rachel stopped at the front of the vacant house. If Connor was indeed relieving himself, she didn't want to intrude. But she thought she'd heard voices. Of course, a few minutes ago she'd thought she'd heard the most ear-splitting whistle she'd ever experienced—except it had been coming from inside her head, not outside, so maybe she was coming down with an ear infection or something. That was better than thinking she'd just imagined it.

She heard another whisper, and knew this time she hadn't imagined anything. Squaring her shoulders, she walked around the corner of the house and was stopped in her tracks by what she saw.

"Nathan?" Her stomach fluttered as if a flock of startled geese had suddenly taken flight inside her. His presence hit her like a physical jolt, bringing every nerve to life. "Where's Connor?"

"Gone." The grating timbre of his usually smooth voice rasped over her skin like a horsehair blanket, making her flinch.

"Gone where?"

"How should I know? Back to whatever hole he slithered out of, I guess. What the hell were you doing with him?"

Now that the surprise of finding him here was wearing off, she took stock of him. Something wasn't right. He wasn't himself.

The hair he usually combed back neatly now fell over

his forehead in a dark curtain. Shadows hung under his eyes like two pale blue crescent moons, and a day's stubble darkened his jaw. His black jeans were rumpled and had a few twigs and leaves stuck to them. A scarred leather jacket replaced the elegant cashmere coat he usually wore. His hands were dirty and . . . was that blood on his sleeve?

He looked rugged and more than a little bit dangerous.

Except for the night his friend had been killed, she'd never seen him look so out of sorts. There was a deep-set pain in the way he held himself, the rhythmic clenching and unclenching of his fists that had the most unsettling effect of making her want to lay his head on her shoulder and stroke his hair in comfort.

Then his words sank in, and indignation cleared the stupor of physical attraction that had clouded her judgment. "Since when is it your concern who I'm with?"

"Since you don't have the good sense not to get in a car with a man you don't even know."

"I know him. He works at the school. He—" She stumbled over her words, realizing how little she really knew about the man who'd introduced himself only as Connor. Stubbornly she jutted her chin. "The headmaster asked him to help me."

"Did he?" Nathan's eyes glittered devilishly. He advanced on her until her senses were filled with the earthy smell she associated only with him. She couldn't quite place the scent. The closest description she could come up with was wet stone. Granite heated by the summer sun, then cooled by a sudden shower.

"Do you know that for sure, or is that just what he told you?" Nathan finished.

"He said . . . ." She crossed her arms over her chest. Nathan was right, and she could see he knew it. Dark victory glistened in his eyes.

Damn him for making her question her every move. What difference did it make if the headmaster had sent Connor, or if he'd acted on his own?

"He delivered me to the front door of the best lead I've had on Von yet. Which is more than you've managed to do." She narrowed her eyes, turning the tables on him. "What are you doing here, anyway? I thought you didn't know Jenny Lovell."

He took a step back—a symbolic retreat. "I made a few calls."

"Calls you couldn't have made yesterday?" It was her turn to advance on him. "You knew who she was all along, didn't you? You knew exactly where to find her."

Anger seethed in her voice as she stepped up under his chin. He flinched, but to his credit, held his ground. Also to his credit, he didn't deny what she was sure was the truth.

She glared up at him. "I should have you arrested for obstruction of justice."

"You don't have that authority."

"But the local cops do. I can have them here before you can click your heels and say 'bail bondsman' three times."

"And tell them what? That I won't help you prove the existence of monsters? You'll be the one they lock up."

Gasping, Rachel spun away from him. The pain was as sudden and as intense as if he'd socked her in the solar plexus. Her eyes misted. She had to bite her lip to keep from doubling over.

"Ah, Rachel," he said on a sigh behind her. His hand brushed the hair off her neck, landed on her shoulder in what she supposed was meant to be a reassuring gesture. A peace offering, now that he'd won and he knew it.

She whirled again, gritting her teeth to keep her voice even, and planted both her hands in the center of his chest with a solid *thunk*. The impact ricocheted up her arms, but he didn't move. It was like shoving an armored tank. "Don't patronize me. And don't you ever. *Ever.* Call me crazy."

"You want to slap me for lying to you? Slap me." He held his hands low and out to the side, palms facing her in a defenseless position.

She made a fist. She just wasn't the slapping kind of girl. "Why don't you want me to find Von?"

"Did it ever occur to you that maybe I couldn't care less whether you find Von or not? That maybe I just don't like to see you torturing yourself like this, chasing shadows you saw in a nightmare more than twenty years ago?"

Tears welled in her eyes. Her clenched fingers unfolded and then gathered again in a fist. She didn't want to hit him. She wanted to hug that stoic body. To kiss that rugged, sincere face. To bury her face against that strong chest and forget all about monsters.

And that made her mad.

It hadn't been a nightmare. She knew what she'd seen. And she couldn't forget; she wouldn't, for her parents' sakes.

She pulled in a slow breath, uncurled her stiff fingers one more time, lowered her head, and marched back the way she'd come.

He followed. "Where are you going?"

"To interview Jenny Lovell."

"Alone?"

"I don't need you there."

"I know." He reached out to her again, and this time she didn't push him away. His hand cupped the back of her neck, lifted her hair. "But I need to be there."

He massaged her scalp gently and a shudder of pleasurable awareness rippled down her spine. She relaxed, letting her head fall back into his palm. Her skin tingled with a million tiny electrified pinpricks, and despite the fact that every cop instinct she possessed screamed in opposition, she knew she couldn't deny him.

Anything.

"Did Connor really leave?" She raised her head, opened one eye, albeit reluctantly, before she lost herself forever in the languorous warmth of his arms. "Or do I need to help you bury the body?"

"Funny girl," he said, but eased himself away from her as if he understood that she needed the space. "You want to work on that standup routine some more, or go do this interview?"

"How long have you been watching the house?" Rachel asked as they reached the Lovells' door.

Nathan shoved his hands in his pockets. At least she was talking to him again. "Since daybreak."

"Did you see anything?"

"Mr. Lovell came out to get the morning paper, kicked a stray cat out of the way. A little while later Mrs. Lovell snuck out the side door with a bowl of milk for the poor thing. That's it."

"Snuck out the side door?" Emphasis on *snuck.*

He shrugged. "That's the way it looked to me. Guess Mr. Lovell is not an animal lover." *And Mrs. Lovell wasn't willing to confront him on the issue.*

The interior of the Lovell home was as tidy as the exterior. Nathan settled deep in a tufted wingback chair to let Rachel handle the interview while he absorbed the details of the place and the people. The furniture was worn, but spotless, and the living room smelled of Lemon Pledge. Mrs. Lovell insisted on bringing out coffee and a plate of cookies. She was a waif of a woman, dressed in flat shoes and a cotton-print shift that appeared older than the furniture. Mr. Lovell watched her every move, but never lifted a finger to help. Mrs. Lovell's gaze jumped nervously when she sloshed a drop of coffee over the rim of his cup when she handed it to him.

After checking her credentials twice, Mr. Lovell agreed to let Rachel talk to Jenny, but insisted on being in the room while she did it. Dressed in loose jeans, white Keds, and a gray Chicago Bears sweatshirt, the girl sat with her knees pressed together and her hands clamped together over them.

"Do you know a young man named Von Simeon?" Rachel asked.

Mr. Lovell answered for his daughter. "We don't allow Jenny to date. She's only seventeen."

Rachel smiled at Jenny. "Maybe you're just friends with him. Hang out once in a while?"

"My girl don't hang out with the likes of him."

Nathan smiled inwardly as Rachel steadied herself with a deep but subtle breath. "You know Von, Mr. Lovell?"

"I've seen him around. Punk kid. Always up to no good."

Nathan couldn't disagree with that assessment.

Rachel turned back to Jenny. "Have you seen Von around, too?"

Jenny's fingers twined nervously. "Sometimes."

"Maybe at the car wash on Jefferson?"

She didn't pull out the picture. That would set Mr. Lovell off and end the interview. Smart lady.

The girl's big blue eyes widened. Mr. Lovell sat his cup down on the coffee table a little too hard, sending a wave of hot liquid over the rim. Mrs. Lovell was there in an instant, blotting it up with a linen napkin. Her hands shook as she mopped up the mess.

"Jennifer," Mr. Lovell said. "You talked to this punk?"

"No, Daddy," she said quickly. Too quickly. Her gaze fell to her hands, where she chipped at the edge of her thumbnail.

"Have you seen him anywhere, honey?" Rachel asked gently. "The last week or so?"

Jenny's blue gaze leaped from Rachel to her father and then back. "No. I'm sorry."

"That's okay. Thanks anyway."

Rachel stood and started toward the door. Nathan and Mr. and Mrs. Lovell followed. On her way past she patted Jenny on the knee and handed her a business card. "If you think of anything else, or if you see him, give me a call, okay?"

Mr. Lovell plucked the card from his daughter's hand. "We will."

Rachel was silent until she and Nathan reached her car.

Once she took her place behind the wheel and he'd folded himself into the passenger seat, she turned to him, her expression thoughtful. "What do you think?"

"I think Daddy dearest rules the Lovell household with an iron fist." He slammed the car door behind him and pulled on his seatbelt. "And I don't think he has a clue who his daughter does or doesn't hang out with."

She started the engine. "You should have been a cop."

He snorted. "Fat chance. What next?"

"Next we drive away and give them some time to forget about us."

"Then we come back and watch the girl?"

"Then we come back and watch the girl."

Nathan settled back into his seat and smiled. The beast inside him growled and paced in anticipation. Long hours trapped in a confined space with Rachel, nothing to do but look at her, listen to her, inhale her heady scent. It would either kill him or drive him stark-raving mad.

He could hardly wait.

FIFTEEN

❧

"*I can't feel my feet.*" *Nathan leaned over to touch* the lead blocks on the floorboard to see if they were, indeed, still attached to his legs.

"I'll run the heater for a while," Rachel said.

"It's not the cold." He sat up, bumping his head on the glove compartment in the process and cursing the inventor of compact cars. "It's this blasted matchbox you rented. A man would have to be a pretzel to sit comfortably in this thing."

She arched one eyebrow at him. "Are you whining?"

"Just stating fact. We should have used mine."

"Your Town Car would stand out like a sore thumb in this neighborhood."

"Like two people sitting in the cold in a parked car for eight straight hours blend right in?"

They hadn't moved from their position in front of the vacant house two doors down and across the street from the Lovells' since nine o'clock that morning. They'd gotten curious looks from a few of the neighbors, but so far no one had gone in or out of Jenny's house. He was beginning not to like this surveillance business.

He shifted, trying in vain to gain another inch to

straighten his legs and restore circulation before gangrene set in. Twisting the other way, he glanced behind him, at the house with the For Sale sign out front, and frowned.

"Something wrong?" Rachel asked.

"That light in the window. It wasn't there before."

"It's just now getting dark. Maybe whoever lives there didn't need a light until now."

"No one's living there."

"Just because it's for sale doesn't mean no one is living there."

"It doesn't look lived in." He could hardly tell her that he hadn't smelled any human scent fresher than a week old when he'd been in the yard. "No one's gone in or out, and I haven't seen any movement inside all day."

"Maybe the lights are on a timer, then. Make the burglars and vandals think it's still occupied."

"Maybe." He rolled that thought around in his mind. "We could help them out with that a bit."

"What?"

"Keeping the burglars and vandals away. We could go inside, watch the Lovells from there." He put on his most charming face. "There's a lovely view from the bay window in front."

"Are you nuts? What if someone called the police?"

"You'd show them your badge and explain everything." She scowled at him.

"Okay," he amended. "We'll make sure no one knows we're inside."

"How do you propose we do that?"

"We'll go in through the back door. I think I can handle the lock. The living room is dark. No one will see us."

"Forget it."

"It'll be warmer in there. We can stretch out."

"You're dreaming."

"We can get some water, maybe there's even some food in the cabinets." He saved the best for last. "Not to mention, we can use the facilities."

"Facilities?"

"The bathroom."

She gave the empty house a lustful look, and he knew she was intrigued. "What if the owners really are still living there, and they've just been out all day?"

"Then we'll run like hell when they come home."

"A bathroom, huh?"

"Maybe two. One for each of us."

She rolled her lower lip between her bottom teeth the way she always did when she was trying to make a decision, then spit it out. "I don't like the possibility of civilians walking in on us, but hey, the hundred-yard dash was my best event in school. How 'bout you?"

Five minutes later they were standing inside a house not unlike the Lovells', except the furniture was newer. Rachel went to use the facilities while he checked the furnace.

"Bad news," he said when she came out.

Her eyes went huge. "Someone's coming?"

"No." He laughed. "The gas has been turned off. No heat."

She expelled a noisy breath. "Don't scare me like that. You were right about no one living here. There were no personal things in the bathroom, not even any soap."

"No food in the refrigerator, either." One couldn't have everything, he guessed. Maybe he could talk Rachel into ordering a pizza later.

"It's just set up with some furniture so it shows better to buyers, I guess."

"And so it's more comfortable for intrepid investigators."

"Investigators?"

"Investigator," he corrected. "And sidekick."

He turned the couch so that it faced the bay window while Rachel gathered a couple of blankets and checked the timer to make sure the lights wouldn't come on and expose them. With nothing else to do but wait, they settled in, she at one end of the camelback sofa, he at the other.

To Nathan, the scant three feet between them seemed at once like the other side of the moon, and far too close for comfort.

•   •   •

"Did something happen between you and Teryn Carnegie to drive you apart?" Rachel asked, unable to stand the silence a second longer. Shivering, she pulled her borrowed blanket up under her chin and tucked her shoeless feet into the seam between the two cushions in the middle of the couch. Darkness had taken hold of the quiet neighborhood hours ago, and with it, the temperature had dropped another ten or twelve degrees.

"What makes you ask?"

He could have been a statue, he'd been so still all night. The little bit of light that filtered into the room from the street cast his face in beveled shadows. They made the angles look sharper, the hollows deeper.

"You said he raised you. He has a picture of the two of you sailing on the wall in his office, you know. You looked so close. And he seemed so sad when he said that you didn't see each other anymore."

In his usual reticence to talk about himself, he asked her a question instead of answering. "Do you stay in touch with your adoptive parents?"

"Not so much anymore."

She shivered again, harder, and he pulled her feet from between the sofa cushions, massaging and warming them with his hands. "Let me guess. They don't know you believe in monsters."

She shook her head. "I learned to keep that little tidbit to myself after the first four sets of foster parents sent me back."

"They sent you back?"

"They thought I was nuts. Guess they were afraid I'd totally flip out and butcher the whole family in their sleep or something." She shrugged. "Can't say I blame them. I didn't just tell them I believed in monsters. I told them I'd seen one. The first family thought it was just stress and ignored it until I started scaring my foster brothers and sisters. A couple of nights of six kids waking up screaming from nightmares, and they sent me packing."

His lip curled in disgust. "How compassionate of them."

"The next three called me 'troubled.' They sent me to social workers, psychiatrists, psychologists, the whole gamut." She looked down at her little feet in his big hands. He was surprisingly tender with her. And the effect was surprisingly erotic. She was starting to think about those big hands on other parts of her body.

What was she talking about again? Oh, yeah. The drugs.

Shame dulled some of the sensory overload he was causing her nervous system. "When I was ten, they decided meds would solve the problem. They gave me drugs that whacked me out for days at a time. Sometimes I would hold them under my tongue and spit them out later, so they started giving me shots instead. They call—called me—" She was so cold now that her teeth chattered. "They called me crazy."

She looked up at him from under eyelashes apologetically. "That's why I freaked out on you today. I get a little defensive about that word."

His hands stilled on his feet. Angry fire burned in his eyes, but somehow she knew it wasn't directed at her, but at those who had hurt her.

She decided to finish it. He may as well know everything. "They talked about putting me in a . . . hospital. A mental ward. That's when I finally decided not to talk about it anymore. I let them win."

When he let go of her feet and gathered her body in his arms, she went without resistance. She went gladly.

"They didn't win," he said, hugging her fiercely. She tilted her head back and looked up into the face of a warrior. He was fighting. For her.

"You won." His hands dug into her upper arms hard enough to bruise. "Do you hear me? You survived, and you stuck by your beliefs, whether you talked about them or not. No one beat you. You beat them. All of them."

Rachel inhaled the damp granite smell in the curve of his neck. Her fingers spanned the hard muscle of his back, tracing the lines, measuring the bulk. Against her breasts his heart beat out a staccato rhythm, and she burrowed closer to it. To him. His body burned hot, and she was so cold.

He hadn't laughed at her. He hadn't pushed her away when he learned she'd nearly been sent to the loony bin before she'd reached her twelfth birthday.

He hadn't called her crazy.

Okay, so he hadn't said he believed her about the monsters. But he actually sounded proud of her for standing up for what she believed for so long, against such antagonism.

Wonder bloomed in her heart, her mind. He pushed her hair out of her face, and she looked at him and smiled despite the tears running down her face. He looked back, not retreating, unafraid.

He didn't care that she believed in monsters.

He didn't strike her as a man given to doling out fanciful displays of affection, but she couldn't think of a nicer gift he could have given her.

She reached out and touched his lips with trembling fingers. It was amazing. The human mouth was capable of such cruelty and such kindness, and he'd chosen kindness.

"Be careful," he warned, but he took her hand in his and kissed each fingertip so tenderly she thought her heart might break from it. Only she didn't want him to hold her hand. He already held her heart.

"Let me touch you," she whispered, easing her fingers out of his grasp and grazing his stubbled cheek with her palm, teasing the sensitive skin below his ear with her nails.

He shuddered and closed his eyes.

"Mmm." She nuzzled his jaw, inhaled deeply, and smiled against the pulse leaping and dancing under the thin skin of his neck. "What is that cologne you wear?"

"I don't wear cologne."

A whetstone, that was the description she'd been looking for. Her father used to have one. He sharpened his pocketknife on it, with a thin trickle of water running over the smooth rock. That's how Nathan smelled: earthy and clean. Male.

She twined her arms around his neck and threaded her hands through the silky fall of his hair while she spoke against his lips. "I seem to be doing all the work here."

He sat perfectly still. If it hadn't been for his breath, hot and moist on her eyelids, and the feel of his heart crashing around his chest against her breasts, she wouldn't have known if he was alive or dead.

"If we start this," he said in a haggard voice, "I don't know if I'll be able to stop."

She lifted her head until she could look straight into his obsidian eyes, and said, "Then don't stop."

On a groan that sounded like it had been torn from the bottom of his soul, he grabbed her hips and dragged her onto his lap. Had she just wondered whether or not he was alive? He was definitely alive. Long, hard, and throbbing with life.

He drew her head back by her hair. Their mouths met, fused, a union of mutual need. His hand found her breast, and she pushed against his palm, her nipple already painfully achy. The physical sensations swamped her, left her itchy and raw, but with Nathan she knew there could be more. So much more.

Leaving his hands and mouth to arouse her to a fever pitch, she sought out his mind. She visualized a door between them, and reached out only to have it flung wide before she touched the knob. A howling wind gusted through the opening, buffeting her, nearly knocking her back. On the other side was a dark place full of creature sounds and flashes of movement.

She called out to Nathan.

"I'm here," he answered, but she couldn't see him.

She stepped over the threshold and found herself in a dense forest. She whipped her head around to see the door slam shut behind her, then forward again to see something large and hairy vanish in the vegetation before her. Heavy wings flapped over her head, but she couldn't make out the species of bird. Surely it must be as large as a condor.

"Here," Nathan said again, more urgently, and she saw him then, standing naked in the shadows under a sycamore tree. She realized she was naked, too, and crossed her arms over her chest and crotch to cover herself until he held out his arms and she rushed into them, frightened by the scurrying sounds and the wails of wild things all around her. With clothes or without, in his arms she felt safe.

She skimmed her hands down his sides and stopped when he hissed, stiffened. She looked down to see a jagged tear in his side. A knife wound, it looked like.

Her fingers hovered over the swollen red edges. "My God. What happened?"

"Nothing. It's nothing," he murmured against the top of her head, and drew her hands up to his chest.

She used the inch of separation between them to draw back and look around, not so afraid of the dark noises of the forest with him near. "Where is this place?"

"My home." Even though they were only millimeters apart, he sounded strangely distant, as if he were speaking to her from the far end of a long tunnel. "This is where I come from."

The roar of a large cat rumbled like thunder in the distance, and scores of smaller animals shrieked in terror. The trees and the underbrush rattled with their frenzied escapes.

With the last shreds of her rational mind, she realized no man could live here. It couldn't be Nathan she was talking to, but some figment of her imagination. Only this figment had form and mass. It had satin-textured skin glazed with sweat and muscles like steel cables bunching and bulging throughout his body. It lay her back on the mossy ground and covered her with its heat.

"Wh—what are you?"

It circled her nipple with its tongue. "What do you want me to be?"

He—it—suckled on her, inciting pangs of pleasure so intense she nearly cried out. When it moved its head lower, it left a wet trail that chilled her, made her nipples tighten even further. It dived to her navel and below, then slid back up her body, lathing and nipping every inch of the way. With every movement the phantasm's hips gyrated against hers with delicious friction. She bucked and writhed, straining to increase the pressure, and the pleasure, for them both.

A part of her realized this wasn't right, that this dream wasn't like the others where she'd been fully connected with Nathan, able to hear what he heard, feel what he felt. This seemed more like an orchestrated fantasy, one-sided and staged.

A part of her knew she wasn't in the forest, but on a couch in the living room of a vacant house.

Most of her didn't care.

Need coiled so tightly inside her that she felt as if she might burst from her skin.

"I'm ready," she told the fantasy Nathan, the figment of her imagination. "Please, I'm ready now."

She reached for his erection. He hissed, and for a moment the fantasy skidded out of focus. She was back on the couch with the flesh-and-blood Nathan on top of her, breathing raggedly. His face was drawn taut and his eyes were closed. Sweat plastered his dark hair to his forehead. His lips moved, but no sound came out, as if he were mumbling or chanting to himself.

Then, like a scratched record that skipped over the flaw and found the groove again, she was back in the forest. She tried to reach across the dreamscape back to the living room. She groped for something tangible to hold on to, for Nathan, but it was like being trapped inside a gigantic balloon. The veil between reality and fantasy gave to her touch, but gently rebuffed her, also. The harder she pushed, the more oppressive, more all-encompassing the darkness of the forest became.

The trees were full of sound. Insects buzzed and sang. Birds warbled. A woodpecker tapped at the trunk of a tree and an owl hooted nearby. She recognized these noises. They calmed her.

The deeper growls and heavier footsteps she didn't want to think about.

A moment later she couldn't think at all. The dream Nathan knelt between her legs and slowly lowered his weight to her. The head of his shaft probed her entrance, circling and rubbing the sensitive folds until she felt as swollen as he was. He laid his palm on the damp skin above her heart and slid it down between her breasts, over her navel, leaving a trail of fire in his wake.

Locking her legs around his hips, she urged him home.

He opened her folds with his thumb and middle finger while the knuckle of his index finger pressed on the center of her desire.

She gasped and surged up against his hand. He clamped his mouth over hers and plunged into her in one swift stroke, taking her breath. Taking her body.

They danced together in an easy rhythm at first, dipping and tucking, gliding and swaying, then the tempo increased. The dream Nathan's hips heaved with the full force of his powerful body. Rachel gasped, opening herself and tilting her hips to take him all the way inside, then clenching tightly, trying to hold on to him when he retreated for another thrust.

The pace quickened again. Rachel's erratic attempts at breathing kept time with the slapping of their bodies and the grunts and moans of pleasure. She tried to think, to memorize the moment, the sensations, but found herself mindless. There was only heat and craving and the all-absorbing sensation of Nathan's penis plunging impossibly deep inside her. Caressing parts of her she never thought to expose to a man. Splitting her in two and making her feel whole.

She raked her fingers down his back. Arched beneath him, hungry for him, urging him on. His body quivered at her touch.

Her blood began to run into her core, like fluid swirling down a funnel. She stiffened, helpless to control the gathering power of orgasm. Not wanting to control it.

Time slowed. A second became an eon. Nathan moved above her in slow motion. She stared into his eyes, and the figment of her imagination and the flesh-and-blood man merged. She felt his need, tenfold the intensity of hers, and sensed his control, hanging by a tattered thread. She barely had time to acknowledge that something was wrong, that he wasn't lost in the throes of their lovemaking as she was, before she shattered.

The tidal wave of climax swept away all thought. All control. It blinded her. Deafened her. All she could do was hang on, and feel. Feel the spasms wracking her body like convulsions. Feel the thick spread of warmth between her legs. The gentle floating back to reality as the dream faded.

"Shit!"

Rachel's eyes jolted open, but for a moment, her mind wouldn't process what she saw because it didn't jive with what she expected to see.

She was on the couch again, and except for the boots she'd toed off earlier, she was fully clothed, as was Nathan. He leaned over her, but was propped on one arm to hold his weight off her. His other arm . . . She gasped for air and choked. His other arm reached down inside the un-snapped waistband of her jeans. His fingers were inside her, three of them. The last vestiges of her orgasm rippled softly around his digits. His sex, though bulging boldly at the fly of his black jeans, was safely tucked away out of sight. And definitely out of her body. Her right hand was caught between his two powerful thighs, cupping his testicles through rough denim.

She jerked her hand away. A flush screamed up her neck to her face.

It had all been in her mind? She'd been dreaming of making love while he'd administered her a hand job?

And a first-rate hand job it had been, too.

Confused how that could be, she opened her mouth to ask him, but couldn't find her voice.

He stared out the window, oblivious to her distress. His back was rigid, his shoulders tense. He was breathing in giant gulps, like a man who'd been under water too long and only just come up for air. The chords of his neck strained with each gasp. A vein bulged in his neck, and despite the lack of heat in the room, sweat dribbled from his temples down the side of his face in a steady flow. Though he didn't move, his muscles bunched and released randomly, as if a living thing were crawling under his skin. Trying to find a way out.

But it was his eyes that made her heart stop and brought back the memory of the beady eyes glowing from the underbrush in the dream forest. For a moment his eyes caught the glare of some sallow light outside. They glowed a dull green.

Then he blinked, and the effect was gone.

"Goddamn it," he grated between heaving breaths. He pulled his fingers from her and left her feeling as hollow as a cored apple.

She scrubbed her hands over her face. The clock on the mantel read one a.m. "What is it? What's wrong?"

"Jenny Lovell just climbed out her bedroom window. She's on the move."

SIXTEEN

Nathan knew he needed to get off of Rachel—quickly—but he wasn't sure he could move. His legs had turned to rubber, and no matter how hard he breathed, he couldn't get enough air. Maintaining control of the images he had planted in her mind had drained him.

Maintaining control of his own impulse to strip her clothes off and plant more than just dreams inside her had nearly killed him.

Was still killing him. A slow, tortured death.

Just breathe, he told himself. In and out.

No, not a good image.

Just breathe.

Rachel pushed against his chest and rolled from beneath him. "We have to go."

The animal inside him sprang to life, reaching out to snatch her wrist and hold her back. Drag her back, if he had to. He barely suppressed the roar that rose in his throat.

"Nathan!" She tugged against his grasp. "She'll get away. We have to go!"

Her words sounded far away. The drums beating in his

head drowned them out. Above the din rose the echo of the ancient chant, calling him to his obligation. Procreate. Populate the species.

He squeezed the delicate bones of her wrist with crushing force, saw her wince, and flung her away with the last ounce of his willpower.

No! He would not give in to magic that had been done to him against his will. He would resist.

Legs trembling like those of a newborn fawn, he stood.

Rubbing her arm, Rachel watched him with huge, luminous eyes. "Are you all right?"

His laugh was weak and shaky to his ears, but genuine. He glanced down at his aching dick, then raised his gaze to hers, somehow finding the strength to wrench up one corner of his mouth. "Give me ten minutes and a bucket of cold water, then ask me again."

They followed Von's girlfriend four blocks into a low-rent business district, hanging back and dodging from shadow to shadow, as Jenny had a habit of checking over her shoulder frequently, and they didn't want to spook her. She turned south at the red light on Delta Drive and walked another half mile into progressively worse territory.

Businesses protected by burglar bars gave way to boarded-up storefronts. The streets narrowed and grew darker while the stench of rotting garbage from the alleyways grew stronger. Rachel jumped when a pile of newspapers on the sidewalk at her feet rustled, and the stocking-capped head of a man popped out.

"Watch where yer walkin', bitch." The vagrant swatted the air, his fingers poking through holes in the ends of a pair of filthy knit gloves.

Nathan stood in front of Rachel instantly, pushing her behind him. "No harm done, old man. Let it go."

The man grumbled and pulled the papers back over his head, and they moved on.

At the next corner they slowed. Jenny picked her way across a vacant lot piled with rubbish to pry back the corner of a sheet of corrugated tin tacked over a ground-floor window of an abandoned tenement. When she disappeared from sight, they nodded to each other and followed.

Crouched outside Jenny's bolt-hole, they peered down the dim corridor. The slap of her Keds against the cement floor was clearly audible, but even Nathan, with his exceptional eyesight, could barely make out the girl's thin figure making her way slowly down the hall. He wondered if Rachel, with her human eyes, could see anything at all.

He got his answer when a second figure stepped out of the shadows and pulled the girl into his arms. It was Von.

Rachel turned her head to Nathan. A satisfied smile lit her face.

"Got him," she mouthed silently.

When the couple strolled down a perpendicular hallway, Rachel held the tin out of her way and lifted one leg through the window.

"What are you doing?" Nathan hissed.

"Going after them. Are you coming?"

"You have no idea how many drug addicts and homeless people are flopped in this place to get out of the cold. You can't go in there."

"I'm not letting him get away. And if this place is so dangerous, I'm certainly not leaving Jenny here." She pulled her other leg through the opening. "Come with me or not. Your choice."

As if he had a choice. He climbed in after her before she vanished in the dark.

Silently they followed the little sounds Jenny and Von made as they walked. A murmur. A light step. The swish of material. The click of a door.

Candlelight flickered in a few of the passages off the main hall. Dark shapes shifted over the peeling paint on the walls like macabre shadow puppets, giving the place an eerie feel. Snores rasped from behind a closed door, and somewhere above them a baby cried. Nathan had been right. Von wasn't the only person crashing here tonight. But, thankfully, no one bothered them. So far.

Nathan stayed close to Rachel, just in case.

The trail ended on the third floor, in a hallway of warped linoleum that curled at the corners like the pages of an old book. Von and Jenny lay chest to chest on a blanket at the end of the passage. Three votive candles dripped wax down the side of an old-fashioned radiator above them. One of Von's arms pillowed Jenny's head. The other was under her sweatshirt.

Before Nathan could stop her, Rachel stepped into the center of the hall about twenty feet from them. He held his position behind the wall, out of sight. If this came down to a fight, the element of surprise would work in his favor.

"She deserves better than a dirty blanket on the floor of a flophouse, don't you think, Von?" Rachel said.

Jenny startled and flayed her arms, pushing Von away from her and pulling her shirt down. Von leaped to his feet and crouched, ready to fight. He squinted into the darkness, and recognition flared into his eyes. At least he had the grace to look almost as embarrassed as the red-cheeked girl peeking over his shoulder. "Who the fuck are you, lady? What do you want with me?"

"Rachel Vandermere, and I just want to ask you some questions."

Von straightened a little, but the way his gaze darted around, Nathan figured he was looking for a place to bolt. Silently slipping out of his coat, he readied himself for the chase.

"Questions about what?" Von asked, nudging a frightened Jenny behind him when she stood.

"William Bishop, and the shooting at the museum last week."

"I don't know no William Bishop. And I don't know nothing about no shooting."

"Then maybe you can explain to me why your fingerprints were all over his gun."

That was it. Von panicked, as Nathan had expected. He flung himself at a door halfway between him and Rachel. The door rattled in its frame, but held. Rachel started forward. Jenny looked from her, to Von and back, tears welling. "Don't hurt him, please." She clung to Von's back.

"I'm not—"

Von hit the door again with a grunt. The jamb splintered, and the idiot kid almost tumbled headfirst down the stairwell. In the time it took to catch his balance, Rachel was on him. Nathan charged. Rachel reached out, managed to snag Von by his collar, but he shoved Jenny at her and pulled away, clattering down the stairs in a headlong rush.

Rachel caught Jenny, and Nathan caught Rachel. She turned, pushing the girl into his arms and starting down the stairs in one smooth move. He set Jenny aside and jumped the first three steps in one stride after her.

Rachel paused below him and looked up. "Stay with the girl," she said, then hurried on.

Nathan looked back to the doorway. Jenny stood with her hands twisted in the hem of her sweatshirt. Her face was blanched and her chin trembled.

Swearing, he reached up and grabbed her wrist, pulled her after him. "Come on. We've got to go catch lover-boy before he does something even stupider than usual."

Tugging Jenny along slowed him, but he could hear the chase below. Doors slammed and floorboards groaned. Vagrants shouted, "Git outta here!"

He worried for Rachel, and considered cutting Jenny loose, but Rachel had been right. This was no place to leave a seventeen-year-old girl alone.

He barreled down a second-floor hall only to hear Rachel shout above him. Cursing, he found another set of stairs and stormed up them, his young charge in tow.

The silence that greeted his emergence from the stairwell scared him more than the violent noise of the chase.

"Rachel?" he called, and didn't breathe again until she answered, "Here."

He found her at the intersection of the main hall with a side passage. "Where?" he asked.

She nodded toward a door at the end of the short hall. "Dead end," she said.

Nathan's heart did a slow roll. Von was cornered, and like any cornered beast, that made him dangerous. Unpredictable. He was young, too young to be in full control of his powers, and yet the raw energy of the guardian race flowed in his blood. The savage instinct to hunt. To kill.

He wouldn't go down without a fight, and if he was going to fight, he was going to use every advantage he had to win. He would fight as a Gargoyle, and Rachel was standing between him and freedom.

"I'm going after him," she said.

Nathan grabbed her jacket. "Give him a minute to think about it. Let him calm down."

Desperately he sought out Von's mind and pushed images to the boy. Serene pictures. Calm.

In return he got a blast of rage that nearly knocked him on his butt. The kid was strong, Nathan had to give him that.

"That's enough time. Let's end this before someone gets hurt."

That was exactly what Nathan was trying to do, only he didn't think her way was going to work. She crept forward, one slow step at a time.

Damn, this was going to get ugly.

He had to get her out of there. Now. He'd carry her bodily if he had to. His people would take care of Von. With a fresh scent trail to follow, they'd find him.

He turned to Jenny, backed her up to the far end of the hall, and pinned her shoulders to the wall. "Stay here."

"Von?" he heard Rachel call. By the time he got back, she was nearly at the door. "I just want to talk."

Willing her to wait a few more seconds, Nathan focused his energy and sent out the Calling. Now all he could do was hope his people answered, given that he was banished.

Rachel stood beside the door—not in front of it—as she'd been trained. Carefully she reached out and tried the knob. Unlocked! She readied herself to jump in case Von tried to rush by her, and pushed it open.

She heard heavy breathing inside, then a couple of snuffles, almost grunts. Was he all right? Had he been hurt?

"Von, did you hear me? I'm not going to hurt you. I just want to talk."

The only answer she got was a gruff snort and a shuffling sound, as if he were scuffing something hard on the floor. The snorting grew louder, more agitated. She risked a peek around the doorframe, lurching back when two beady green eyes gleamed at her from the far side of the room. Something snarled and growled.

Some kind of feral animal was in there with Von!

She took a deep breath, ready to jump to the boy's defense, but as she started forward, the same earsplitting whistle she'd heard at the Lovells' house the day before stopped her in her tracks. The shrill blare momentarily immobilized her. It overloaded her senses for about three seconds, then died as abruptly as it had started, but it was too late. She heard the scrabble of hooves toward the doorway where she stood. She saw the unearthly eyes coming right at her, the silhouette of serrated horns sprouting from the creature's skull. She felt the slimy flesh of a snout hit her above the knee, then the rub of coarse hair. She saw the fangs, gleaming white in the dim light, just before she felt the teeth rip through her jeans and sink into her calf, gnashing through flesh. The rest of the animal's body scraped by, changing from fur to scales as a sharp reptilian tail sliced her open with a single lash. Pain flared, white

8

CARVED IN STONE   181

hot, a second after the initial attack, and she felt blood
pooling in her sock.

Finally she felt herself falling, her body numb with
shock. Then Nathan was there, catching her. He kicked at
the beast and it ran off, squealing. She tried to get a better
look at it, but her eyes were blurry. The ceiling seemed to
be spinning above her as she fell.

Her mind whirled with the world around her, but she
managed to cling to one thought as she hit the floor: She'd
seen a monster.

Now Nathan had to believe her.

Nathan tapped his fingers on the steering wheel of
Rachel's rented Honda as he watched Jenny Lovell tiptoe
to her bedroom window and climb inside. The lights of the
house stayed dark. Apparently her parents would remain
unaware of her little foray onto the wild side tonight. Even
though he felt guilty about helping her sneak in, he was re-
lieved. He didn't think Mr. Lovell would take the news of
her nocturnal adventures well.

As he started the car, he glanced over at Rachel. Her
eyes were open and her head was up, but she looked out of
it. He'd practically carried her all the way from the tenement back to Buchanan Street, and her car. By unspoken
agreement, neither of them had said a word, not in front of
Jenny. But now that the girl was safe in her own home,
Nathan had a feeling the discussion he dreaded wasn't far
off.

He was right.

Three blocks down the road she rolled her head toward
him and said, "I can't believe you let Von get away.
Again."

"I was more concerned about you. You passed out on
me."

"You saw it, didn't you?"

His jaw hardened involuntarily. "Saw what?"

She sat up. Her face was pale in the moonlight, her

pupils large and dark. She pointed to her leg. He'd wrapped his coat around it to slow the bleeding. "The thing that did this!"

"The wild dog?"

"That was no dog!"

He turned back to the dark road in front of him. "We need to get you to a hospital. That wound needs to be cleaned and stitched."

"I don't want to go to a hospital. I want you to tell me what you saw."

He tightened his fingers on the wheel. What now? "It was dark," he hedged.

She flopped back in her seat and stared at the roof. She traced idle patterns on the window next to her. At least he thought they were idle until he glanced over and saw it was his reflection in the glass she was tracing.

"Coward," she said.

The quiet accusation twisted his gut like an old dishrag. "You'll feel better in the morning, when you've had time to think about this and realize that it was just the commotion and the adrenaline and that weird place that made it seem—"

"Don't patronize me, Nathan. It had yellow-green eyes, cloven hooves, and a snout."

"Maybe there was some kind of wild boar in there."

"In Chicago?"

"Could've been a pet, or a zoo animal that got away."

She crossed her arms over her chest and turned to look at him again. "It had horns. And a tail like a lizard."

His mouth went dry. Damn observant woman. She'd gotten a good look. He hoped she hadn't seen the nose ring and ear studs Von was fond of keeping visible, even in Gargoyle form, or she'd put two and two together and they'd be in big trouble. Big*ger* trouble. As it was, any hopes of her ever giving up her hunt for Von were gone.

She sighed when she didn't get a reaction to her description. "You are the most stubborn man I know. More pigheaded than that pig thing that attacked me."

He tried not to smile, but he couldn't help it. "Now, there's something we can agree on."

"I don't care if you admit it or not. I know you saw it. And I'm going to find it again. I won't leave until I do."

Which was exactly what Nathan was afraid of.

The truth of what he had to do settled into his bones like a numbing cold. He thought she was unbelievably courageous for sticking by her guns. She didn't let anyone talk her out of what she knew to be true. She faced shame and humiliation for what she believed. Fought back against coercion and downright strong-arming, yet she never let them break her, or her spirit.

She stood by the vow she'd made on the graves of those she loved, her parents, and she never bowed to the pressure to break it.

But she'd seen one of his kind. He couldn't let her keep that memory.

The thought of stealing something so precious to her, the proof that she'd been right all these years, sickened him. But if he didn't do it, and the other Gargoyles learned what she had seen, one of them would.

He forced himself to relax the death grip he had on the steering wheel. "You sure you don't want to go to a hospital?"

"Positive. I'm fine." She tried to lift her foot and winced. "Really."

A sweat broke under his collar as he swung the Honda back toward Lake Shore Drive and his condominium.

His people had long covered their tracks with the few innocent humans who had caught a glimpse of them by replacing the image with a manufactured memory. It wasn't particularly difficult to do.

With most humans.

But Rachel's mind worked differently. She seemed to have as much access to his feelings and sensory stimulation as he had to hers when the connection formed. He'd used the technique to create the lovemaking experience for her so that he could bring her pleasure, *have* her, in a way, without *taking* her, and his control over the fantasy had been tenuous at best. She'd drawn the forest setting out of his mind—he'd been unable to bring her back. Throughout the fantasy she'd pushed at the barrier he'd created between their minds.

If he tried to influence her again, and she ruptured that barrier, she could slip deep into his mind, where there would be no hiding. No secrets.

She would see exactly who—and what—he really was.

SEVENTEEN

Balancing a bamboo dinner tray loaded with the cup of tea and medical supplies he'd gathered for Rachel, Nathan tread carefully across the deep pile carpeting between his kitchen and living room, where he'd left her on the couch with her foot propped on a stack of pillows.

She wasn't there. .

"Rachel?"

"Over here." She hobbled over from the dining room area.

"Is something wrong?"

"I was looking for the, uh, facilities, I believe you called them earlier."

He set the tray down and laid the clean kitchen towel he'd slung over his arm down next to it. "Do you need help?"

"Only if you want to save my leg but have me die of mortification."

That was his girl. Never let 'em see you sweat.

He nodded at the double doors to the left of the bed in his loft-style condo. "That way. And take your pants off while you're in there."

She blinked.

"So I can clean your leg," he said. "There's a robe on the back of the bathroom door. Put that on."

He waited on the couch, steeling himself for the night ahead. The closer the time came to actually try to alter her memory, the more unsure of himself he became. He didn't know if he could pull it off.

When their minds connected, the sexual attraction between them overpowered them both. And the further he went with her, the closer they came to making love—for real, not in a fantasy—the closer he needed to be. He was like a junkie, always needing a bigger fix. She was his drug.

He looked up to find her watching him from across the room. She dug her toes in the carpet and took in her surroundings. "It's cozier than I expected."

He followed her gaze over the warm cream leather sofa with brown and gold upholstered throw pillows stacked on each end, across the neutral beige carpet. Neat rows in the nap showed that his housekeeper had vacuumed recently.

Rachel lingered in her perusal of the floor-to-ceiling bookcases that lined each side of the marble fireplace, the healthy green ferns on the hearth.

The huge iron bed stacked with pillows against the far wall.

Turning back to him, she arched one eyebrow. "Did you hire a decorator?"

"No." He'd picked out every piece himself, buying for comfort as much as aesthetics. He patted the cushion beside him. "Come on. Let's get this over with."

She limped to him, and he pushed aside a pile of art magazines so he could put her foot up on the raw pine coffee table with wrought-iron legs, then handed her the tea he'd brewed her. "Drink this. It'll take your mind off what I'm going to do."

Everything he was going to do, he hoped.

She sipped silently while he wet the kitchen towel and

dabbed at her leg. Her calf was smooth and cool, firm without being overly muscled, and tapered nicely to a delicate ankle. As he wiped the crusted blood away, he felt like a master restorationist refurbishing a priceless piece of art. Each millimeter of ivory skin he uncovered was flawless. Perfect.

Except for the two large gashes.

A hot surge of protectiveness gushed through him. He could kill Von for this.

Anger made him daub a little too hard at her leg, and she winced.

"Sorry."

The worst of the two cuts oozed clear fluid, but the bleeding had stopped. There didn't seem to be any dirt or debris in the wound, but he flushed it, putting the dishtowel beneath her and pouring a thin stream of water from the glass on the tray over it just to be sure. She didn't seem to be in pain. The muscles of her face had relaxed, giving her a look of childlike innocence. Her eyes had taken on a glassy sheen.

"Will you tell me something, Nathan? Honestly?"

He bent over her leg to inspect his work. "If you want me to tell you I saw a monster, no."

"Why didn't you make love to me earlier tonight?"

He caught himself before he looked up, before he had to look into those glassy, innocent green eyes and lie, but he couldn't stop the reflexive tightening of his groin.

He wrung the water out of his washcloth and dabbed at her leg again. "Because you would have regretted it later."

"You can't know that."

"I do."

He leaned over and picked up the stone apothecary jar from the tray of supplies.

She wrinkled her nose. "What is that?"

"Just some herbs ground into a paste. It'll help the swelling."

"It smells like sewage."

He hoped the odor wasn't strong enough to clear her

head. He needed her a little fuzzy. "No sewage, I promise. Just a little comfrey, myrrh, and garlic juice."

"Well, at least I'm safe from vampires for the night." She watched him warily but didn't pull her leg away. "Teryn had a grow light over herbs in his office. Did he teach you about them?"

"I taught him."

She cocked her head curiously, but didn't reply.

Reminding himself firmly to think of the object he held in his hands as a task, not a long, sexy leg attached to a long, sexy lady, he smoothed the paste around the edges of the wounds in slow, careful circles. He looked up to make sure he wasn't hurting her, and found her face dewy soft. She closed her eyes and stretched like a cat on a sunny windowsill.

Now was his chance, while she was relaxed. Now was the time to reshape her memory.

By damn, he didn't want to do it. Hated the thought of the invasion, the manipulation. But what he wanted didn't matter. It had to be done.

He searched his mind for a way to bring her chase after Von to the forefront of her thoughts. To take her mind back to the tenement.

He needn't have bothered. She was already there.

A giddy smile, full of glee, slowly spread across her face. "Deny it all you want, Nathan, but I know what I saw tonight. I know what *you* saw."

His fingers tightened on the delicate bones of her ankle. His heart struck low and deep, like a kettle drum in his chest. "What did we see?"

"A monster. After all these years I finally saw another monster." Her glazed green eyes flickered open, but her eyelids hung sleepily.

Ever so gently he probed with his mind and found the wispy edges of the memory. She was standing outside the doorway Von had rushed through. Her heart was pounding furiously—he could feel it in his own chest. He saw the green glow of feral eyes with her. Heard the animal snuffles and snorts. Fear coursed through her like a bullet train trying to make up time, but with the fear there was another emotion. Elation. The sweet taste of victory.

She smiled like the proverbial cat that got the pet canary. "Too bad all those social workers and psychologists couldn't have been there. I'd liked to have seen them call me crazy then."

His stomach turned. She wasn't just looking for monsters in order to avenge her parents' deaths, he realized. She was trying to prove to herself that she wasn't crazy.

Now that she finally had the proof she'd sought so long, he had to take it away.

Pushing back the sickness in his gut, he delved deeper into her mind, focusing his thoughts to a sharper point. He tried to drown out the glowing eyes with remembered darkness, the sounds with silence. She frowned, but the gauzy fabric of her memory held. He had to take her back, to before she'd seen Von in Gargoyle form.

"You believe me, don't you?" she said dreamily. "You have to believe me this time."

"Tell me what you saw. All of it, from the time you left me and Jenny."

He visualized her memory as a glass ball with the events playing out inside, and cupped it in his palms. He felt it warming to his touch, molding to the shape of his hands so that he could manipulate it.

She rubbed her forehead absently. "I chased him down the stairwell and into a long hall. It was dark. There were faces in the shadows. They leered at me, a few yelled at me. I was gaining on Von and then I tripped, and when I looked down I realized an old man had hold of my ankle. I was breathing so hard I couldn't scream."

He felt the deep drag of air in her lungs. Heard the rasp.

"But he let go. He was just some vagrant we'd woken up with all the running. Von turned and went up another stairwell."

"You followed him to the third floor. At least, you thought that's what floor he went to," Nathan suggested.

He pictured an empty corridor and tried to force that image over the one of Von running down that hall. The malleable memory hardened, resisted his view of what had happened.

Her forehead furrowed. "I'm sure he went to the third floor. I mean . . . I saw him. I think I saw him."

"You were mistaken. You lost him, but you decided to check out that floor anyway. You walked down the hall."

"I stopped at the last room," she said, sounding less certain now.

"But you didn't see anything. The room was empty."

He squeezed the imaginary memory in his hands. She whimpered. Her back arched as if she was in pain. "I saw . . . That is, I thought . . . It was dark."

His shoulders ached with strain, tension. He mopped the sweat off his forehead with his sleeve. "The window was broken. The moon was shining in. You could clearly see there was no one in the room."

Her head thrashed left and right. Her chest heaved as she breathed in desperate little pants. "No, it was dark. The window was boarded over. I peeked around the door-frame."

"But you didn't *see* anything. You didn't *hear* anything."

He focused all his energy into her mind, into the memory, but again she resisted his attempts to alter what she'd seen. Recollections of other moments in her life assailed him—her father steadying her while she rode a grocery store mechanical rocking horse, her mother spreading a picnic blanket beneath a maple tree in a green meadow. Each time he thrust aside one of those family moments, a bolt of pain lanced through his skull. She wasn't just resisting now; she was fighting back.

How the hell could a human, a woman, do that?

Gritting his teeth, he held steadfast to the memory of the tenement hallway. The room.

The empty room.

"Not at first," she said, rubbing her temples in earnest.

Apparently the war they waged took its toll on her, too, even if she wasn't aware of fighting it. "I was about to go inside when that god-awful whistle started."

Nathan lost his mental grasp on Rachel's memory as if it were a bar of soap he'd squeezed too tightly with wet hands. "What whistle?"

"Didn't you hear it? That earsplitting screech a minute or two before you came out of the stairwell after me. Everybody within two blocks must have heard it. I thought Von had pulled a fire alarm or something for a minute. It only lasted a few seconds, but it was so loud it sounded like it was coming from inside my head, not outside."

His body temperature dropped from overheat to subarctic in the span of a heartbeat. The sweat he'd been mopping only moments before felt like ice water on his skin now. He knew exactly what she'd heard, and it wasn't a fire alarm.

She'd heard the Calling.

This time it wasn't her heart he felt thundering in his chest, but his own. This wasn't possible!

"Then I looked in the room, only it wasn't Von that looked back at me. It was some kind of creature with queer, beady green eyes and a snout. I froze. I couldn't believe it, couldn't move, then the . . . thing, the monster, rushed me. I don't know how Von could have been in there with it all that time unless . . ."

Their minds were still connected. Nathan had lost all control over her thoughts, but he could still feel her. Her excitement grew. Passion for her quest swelled inside her. She was drunk on the thrill of her discovery.

"Unless they're shape-shifters. Unless that wild, snarling pig-thing *was* Von." She threw her forearm over her eyes and laughed out loud. "My God, it sounds crazy, even to me. I never thought—I mean, I suspected. How else could they move around, how could they live without anyone seeing them? I just never had any proof. But now . . ."

"You call this proof? What are you going to do with it?"

An angry fire kindled in his blood. "Are you going to hold a press conference? Tell your story to *Newsweek*?" He shook his head in disgust. "I doubt even the grocery store tabloids would buy drivel like that."

He felt her exhilaration wane a bit and was forced to pull back mentally, lest he forget that with their minds connected she could feel his emotions, see the images in his mind as clearly as he saw hers, if she thought to look. His true nature was vulnerable to her. Exposed.

She lifted her arm and squinted at him as if she could barely hold her eyes open. "I don't need headlines to validate what I saw with my own eyes. And you know I'm not looking for publicity."

"Then what are you looking for?"

"The truth, Nathan. Just the truth."

How could he argue with that?

She sat up and scrubbed her hands over her face. "God, I'm so tired all of a sudden."

He took her feet from his lap and set them on the floor a little too roughly. "It's late. You should get some sleep."

One of them should, and it wouldn't be him. He had too much to think about. And he couldn't take her back to her hotel. He couldn't let her go while she still had ideas of men changing into monsters running around in her head.

Jesus, what was he going to do with her?

"You can have my bed for the night." He scrubbed his hands over his face and tried not to think about carrying her there himself, climbing in beside her, on top of her. It could never happen, especially not tonight, when she wasn't responsible for her own actions.

She sighed, and swiveled her body around so that her legs stretched away from him curled up against his side. One of her hands threaded the hair at the back of his neck. Her other palm splayed across his chest. His heart reached for her fingertips with every beat.

With her head resting on his shoulder, she looked up. Their gazes connected, and the fire raging inside him warmed to a mellow glow. Damn, she was beautiful, all soft and weary and righteous.

"It's okay," she whispered. "You don't have to admit you saw it, too. Not tonight."

"Rachel—"

"I know it's a lot to accept." She snuggled her face into the curve of his neck. Soft lips skimmed the cords of his neck. "But you'll come to terms with it eventually."

That simple acceptance, simple forgiveness—even if it was brought on as much by the tea as real sentiment—brought a monster of another kind roaring to life within him.

He should have pushed her away, but it was all he could manage not to crush her closer. The swell of her breast against his side was a siren song, calling him to touch. Her warm breath on his skin was the breath of life, reviving him from the living death of his existence.

She wedged her hand between his back and the sofa cushion, skimmed the length of his spine and caused his nerves to sizzle and crackle like a Fourth of July sparkler. She kissed the line of his jaw, gentle nibbles that had him turning his head, seeking her lips with his.

He made one last grasp for sanity. "You're hurt," he mumbled against her lips.

"My leg feels much better, thanks to your magic potion." Her fingers traced along the skin just above his belt, lingering at the buckle. Her lips curved into a smile against his cheek. "Are you some kind of shaman, Nathan Cross? A witch doctor or wizard or warlock or something?"

It was all he could do to breathe, much less think, but some part of his brain still realized her question came from more than wild imagination. He'd left his research materials spread across the dining room table. He should have guessed she hadn't just been looking for the facilities earlier. She'd been snooping. "You saw the books."

"*Druidic Magic, Paganism Through the Ages, Ancient Rites, Spells, and Enchantments*." She tickled his ear with the tip of her tongue. "Should I be worried about you turning me into a frog or something?"

He shifted his legs apart to make room for his growing erection. One of his hands found its way under her sweater and toyed with the lacy edge of her bra. "Only if you pull a harebrained stunt like chasing a fugitive through a condemned building again."

Her neck arched back, baring her throat to his pilfering lips. "I think you've already put some kind of spell on me."

Curious, he glanced down at her.

Her eyes opened, such a dreamy green that he half-expected her to float right off the couch. Good. She was almost gone, and not a minute too soon.

"I have the most wicked daydreams when I look into your eyes."

Not so good. The hot, hard shaft between his legs began to throb.

"They're so real," she said. "It's like I'm me, but I'm you, too. I'm inside your skin. I can feel the tension and power in you, all coiled and ready to spring, like a racehorse in the starting gate. I can feel how much you want me."

"It's just a dream, Rachel."

"It doesn't have to be."

"I can't," he moaned.

She drew her hand along his thigh until she cupped his pulsing cock. She squeezed lightly, and he thought he might burst from even that slight pressure. The buzz of a colony—a hundred colonies—of bees swarmed in his head. His eyes went blind.

"You can't tell me you don't want me," she said.

"I'm telling you I can't make love to you." He closed his eyes as her fingers trailed upward.

She found the tab to his zipper and tugged. "Then let me make love to you."

EIGHTEEN

Nathan's arms jerked reflexively to stop her, but Rachel was too fast. By the time she'd had her first taste of him, the hands he'd raised to push her away were twined in her hair, drawing her closer instead.

As always when she was with him, she was aware of her own actions, her own body and sensations, and yet was a part of him, too. His power, the overwhelming strength of him, surged in her veins, as did his lust, his craving for the contact she gave. But she also sensed the collar of his control. She felt the weight of the chain that restrained him, kept him from giving himself completely to her.

And she vowed to break it.

She nibbled and sucked, massaged and molded, feeding the wild side of him that struggled against his bonds. She taunted him with her lips, her teeth, her devilish tongue until his hips lifted on a groan. He thrust and she parried, teasing him into pursuing her.

Her mind spun, filled with the whetstone scent of him, musky and male, his salty-sweet taste, and with his sensations of her, all soft skin and curves, the slippery friction of her wet mouth.

He surged toward her again, and Rachel felt the tether that bound him stretching, straining.

She pulled the hem of his shirt from his waistband and slid her hands beneath, running her palms over the crisp fur of his chest, finding his stiff male nipples and pressing down with the heels of her hands before sliding lower. His ribs heaved upward, into her touch. She grazed his sides with her fingernails heightening his—

Pain?

She felt the sting her touch caused him.

He sucked in a breath and flinched. She raised her head, peeled up his shirt, and exposed the wound. It was just like she'd seen it in the fantasy at the vacant house.

"It wasn't a dream." He really did have a knife wound in his side, not deep but raw and tender-looking, just as it had been then.

"What?" His head rested on the back of the couch. His breath was ragged as a battle flag after heavy fighting.

She traced around the edges of the injury with her index finger, careful not to hurt him. If she hadn't been dreaming when she'd first seen this cut, then what had happened? He'd been fully clothed when she woke up. She couldn't have seen this. They certainly hadn't been making love— at least not in the biblical sense.

Or maybe they had. Not with their bodies, but with their minds. Lord knew, their thoughts weren't their own when they were with each other. Something magic happened between them. Something mystical.

Using only his hand, he'd brought her to a climax more intense than any she'd experienced during honest-to-goodness genital-to-genital sex. He'd made her feel loved, cherished, lost in the throes of mutual passion—and she had no doubt it really was his doing.

He'd given her a gift. The mental expression of the love act he couldn't give her physically for reasons he wouldn't explain.

If he could make her think she was buck-naked in a forest, panting beneath his naked body with his flesh inside her, loving her, could she do the same to him?

She could damn well try. He might not be willing to make love to her in the real world, but he didn't seem to have any problem with it in their shared fantasies.

She slid to the floor, kneeling between his legs.

He grasped her shoulders. "Rachel, please."

She wasn't sure if he was pleading with her to stop, or to keep going. It didn't matter.

He groaned again as she lowered her head, took him all the way to the back of her throat and beyond. Even as he swelled and thickened inside her, she concentrated on the mental image of the forest, only this time no beady eyes spied on them from the darkness. No bestial roars echoed in the woods. Nothing more than the occasional flutter of bird's wings in the trees broke the quiet.

She stood alone in a small clearing for a moment, resisting the urge to cross her arms over her naked body. She worried that she couldn't do it. That she couldn't project the dream to Nathan and bring him here.

Then a twig snapped. Brush rattled behind her. She spun around as he stepped into the open circle of grass.

He made a fine specimen of a man, she thought. His legs were long and muscular, his shoulders wide. Dark hair cascaded over a brooding forehead and slashing lips gave him a dangerous air. His sex, proudly erect and flushed with color, still sparkling damp from her attention, arced toward his flat belly.

Fury darkened his face. "How could this be? How can you bring me here?"

Light-headed from the rush of success, she sauntered toward him, no longer interested in covering herself. She wanted him to see her. Loved watching the way his pupils dilated and his nostrils flared when he looked at her.

"The same way you brought me," she said, and on reaching him, took one flat copper nipple between her teeth and drew on it. She pulled for a second, then released him and looked up. "With my mind."

"Why?"

"So you can make love to me."

"I told you I can't."

She grazed her hand down his hip to his erection. "You seem to be a bit conflicted on that point."

Pumping and squeezing, she relished the feeling of him expanding in her grasp. She was the powerful one now. The one with the strength.

"Besides," she said, and then laid a trail along his collarbone with her tongue, "it's just a dream, remember?"

"It's no damn dream, and you know it."

"What is it, then?" She thought she should know, but she couldn't think. The light-headedness had worsened to dizziness. Her brain felt disconnected from her body.

She was sure it wasn't a dream. Pretty sure. The hot, hard shaft pulsing in her palm felt real enough. But a part of her also knew she wasn't in a forest at all, but on the floor of Nathan's condo with her head in his lap, getting carpet burns on her knees. She was two people, the forest Rachel and the condominium version, then four as she gathered the sensations of the Nathan images from both places, too.

Her head began to swirl in earnest. The forest, the room, even Nathan himself became a kaleidoscope of color constantly shifting and reshaping.

Her muscles quivered. Her legs threatened to collapse. She wasn't sure she could keep standing—or kneeling, as the case may be—then Nathan took the problem out of her hands. He hooked a foot behind her knee and tumbled her to the grass, breaking her fall with his own body by twisting so that she landed on top.

Her head still threatened to snap off and roll away, but she decided she didn't need it now anyway, at least not in the fantasy.

It was playing a crucial role in the condominium scene, however.

Nathan palmed her tingling breasts and she quit worrying about it. All she needed was her body. Her stomach, contracting as the stubble of his beard grated across her midsection, raising her nerve endings to new levels of sensitivity. Her hands, which guided the mushroom cap of his arousal to her body's slick entrance.

He plunged inside without hesitation, taking her by surprise. She gasped and bowed, hung for a moment between pleasure and pain, and then falling fast and hard to the pleasure side.

His touch gentled. He set an easy rhythm for them, raising and lowering himself in long, lazy strokes. She hooked her legs around the back of his thighs and with her body let him know it was okay to take her deeper. She needed him to take her deeper. Faster.

He seemed happy to oblige.

Their labored breathing deteriorated to irregular wheezes. Rachel locked her arms around his shoulders and hung on for the ride, throwing her hips up to his, savoring the feel of him so deep inside her he almost touched her heart.

He did touch her heart. Not physically, but emotionally. The intensity of the connection she felt with him amazed her. Surely what they experienced together wasn't of the natural world. Normal people couldn't see each other's thoughts, play out a shared fantasy.

Yet her feelings stemmed from more than the sexual side of their relationship. She knew him as a lover, but she'd seen the teacher, the neighbor, the protector in him as well. He loved art, had great taste in wine, and spoke French like a native.

Most of all, he believed in monsters.

Whether he admitted it or not, she'd seen the truth in his mind.

The thought bloomed inside her like a hibiscus in the sun. He believed her.

Her eyes snapped open. Overhead, the sun peeked through breaks in the tree cover. The edge of a cotton-ball cloud drifted softly by. A finch sang in the boughs beneath. And still dread dragged a cold fingernail up her spine.

Something was wrong.

Her corporeal body moaned even as she continued to bob over him. She felt a responsive rumble roll up her chest, and knew it was his groan, and not her own.

Her dream body clutched his shoulders as she felt him tense, felt the storm and the power gather in him, ready to fling a lightning bolt into his blood.

A dark place drew her gaze over his shoulder. She ducked her chin against him, but she couldn't stop herself from looking. Through the trees she saw it—a cave. It was cold; she could feel its chill from here. It was a pit of sorrow and despair. Cursed. Evil lurked there.

Despite her fear, she tried to see inside. She lifted her head, just a little, but with a roar, Nathan's full weight came down on her, crushing her. His haunches bunched, drove as he plunged into her one final time, and then his back stiffened and his neck craned as he pulled out of her, shoved himself away.

In the real world Rachel was flung back. She hit her elbow on the coffee table and hissed while Nathan grabbed the kitchen towel he'd used to clean her leg. Holding it against himself, he fell to the side and buried his face in the sofa cushion as his body convulsed.

She tried to stand, to go to him, and when that didn't work, to crawl. She tried to move at all, but found her legs were like a rag doll's limbs stuffed with cotton. The room blurred in and out of focus. When her eyelids sagged despite her best efforts to hold them open, it hit her.

The bastard.

"You put something in the tea!" she cried, her speech slurred.

He didn't answer. He simply watched her slump to the carpet with dark, ravaged eyes.

For a long time after he'd carried Rachel to his bed, Nathan sat on the brocade ottoman in a shadowed corner and watched over her. He'd known mystics in his time. He'd seen magical deeds and met creatures of mythic invention. Hell, his own immortal soul was created by a spell cast a thousand years ago.

But he'd never seen anyone like Rachel Vandermere.

As beautiful as she was intelligent, more stubborn than a mule in a pasture full of clover, kind and self-sacrificing, she intrigued him. She also vexed him and pushed his self-control beyond restraint.

In a thousand years he'd never let another woman do what she'd done tonight. Couldn't imagine ever letting another.

Her sensual nature wasn't her only special ability. She not only resisted the images he tried to seed into her mind, but pushed visions of her own back at him. She'd seduced him, yet she took no pleasure for herself. She only gave. She let him make love to her mind, while she took care of his body.

Unable to sit still, he paced the length of the dark room and dragged his hand through the tangle of his hair. His bare feet swished over the thick carpet. Outside his window, Lake Michigan absorbed the city lights. Mist rose from the water, swirling and twirling in the cooler air. He paused a moment to watch the ghostly dance, then paced on.

She'd heard the Calling.

It wasn't possible. Humans didn't have the capability to do any of the things she'd done. And yet she'd done it. There had to be some explanation. Some precedence for her ability.

Maybe she really was psychic. He'd never met a human with supernatural aptitude before. To his knowledge, none of his congregation had.

If they had, though, the story would be in the ancient texts at St. Michael's. His people were nothing if not great record keepers. Nathan thought he vaguely remembered the tale of a woman with some powers, but he couldn't recall the details.

Teryn might, though. The Wizenot had studied the medieval volumes longer than Nathan. Perhaps he'd come across the information.

He paused in his aimless roaming again, this time by the bed. Her face soft with sleep and her long lashes curled against her cheeks, she almost looked like a child. But there was nothing childish about what she'd done tonight. Just looking at her made his body burn again.

He hadn't been inside St. Michael's since his banishment. Only the most extreme circumstances could make him go now. He wasn't welcome there, but he was beyond politics and protocol now.

He had questions, the answers to which might help him understand what had happened between him and Rachel. If the old man didn't want to see him, he could just be damned.

The sedative he'd put in Rachel's tea would keep her sleeping a few hours yet. He had time.

Pausing only to brush a golden curl back behind her ear and press a silent kiss to her forehead, he left her and headed for the roof, his muscles already bunching and bones bending in preparation for the Awakening.

He had too much energy pent up tonight for the Town Car. Too much torment. He needed air and exercise. The freedom of a more primitive mode of transportation—

His own wings.

NINETEEN

Teryn felt the presence in his quarters as soon as he put his hand on the doorknob. The ritual he'd spent most of the night performing had heightened his senses, left his mind open to the energies of the universe.

He sensed no danger from the intruder, no threat, and still his fingers closed instinctively over the gold hilt of the ceremonial dagger sheathed at his belt. The visions of death and destruction creeping toward his people without shape or form, like fog rolling along the gutter, had him edgy enough that he wasn't taking any chances.

Slowly he opened the door to the darkened room, trying to remember how long it had been since he'd oiled the squeaky hinges. Mental turmoil washed across the threshold, buffeted him, swirled and eddied with anger and hurt. Resentment.

And guilt, as if the man who waited in the shadows sometimes thought the torture inflicted on him was justified. As if he deserved to be outcast from his people. To spend his life in exile.

Teryn's fingers uncurled from the handle of his knife. Shoulders sagging, he stepped into the room on a sigh.

"It's good to see you, Nathan. I was hoping you would come."

Nathan stood in silhouette before the narrow window that admitted the only sliver of light in the room. His mind might be a cauldron of roiling thought and emotion, but his body was as still as one of the statues hanging from the old stone edifice in front of him.

Teryn stowed his ceremonial tools in his dresser. "How did you get in?"

"The window to the sixth-floor bathroom was open. It smelled like one of the boys had been smoking in there again."

"Collin Waverly," Teryn said, and sighed. "You'd think he could at least be more creative in his choice of locations."

"All fifteen-year-old boys have to smoke in the bathroom at least once. It's a rite of passage."

Teryn heard a note of the old Nathan in the voice, and arched one eyebrow, hoping to hold the light mood. "Including you?"

"Especially me. I was the headmaster's *paytreán*. The teacher's pet, so to speak."

Teryn could have wept for what they'd had together once. What they'd lost.

No one could say he showed Nathan favor now.

"Did you get Von?" Nathan asked, breaking Teryn's reverie.

"We lost his trail about a mile from the tenement. Do you mind if I turn on a light?" He pulled out matches to light the candles on his desk. He preferred natural light over the harsh modern bulbs.

Nathan swore. "How could you lose a fresh trail?"

"He went into the river. We couldn't find where he came out. Sonjay and Christian are still looking." He didn't add that if his two best trackers hadn't picked up the trail by now, they weren't likely to.

"Damn it, I should have tracked him myself."

"Why didn't you?"

"Rachel was with me." He hesitated. "She saw Von."

"Did she, now?" Teryn struck his match. A sulphurous scent curled into his nostrils. Light leaped from his hands, and the sight of Nathan's face hit him like a blow to the stomach.

He looked pale. His dark eyes stood out against his chalky complexion like black buttons on a white waistcoat. He hadn't shaved; his hair was mussed. His lips turned down in a grimace of misery that Teryn suspected stemmed from more than Von's exasperating penchant for escape and evasion.

Guilt smothered the joy he'd felt at finding Nathan here. He'd done this. At a time in the endless series of Nathan's lives when he had been questioning everything he was, when he most needed the support of the only people in the world who could understand what he was going through—those who shared his legacy—Teryn had turned him out.

He'd abandoned the one who meant the most to him, and that was a knowledge he'd have to live with for innumerable lifetimes.

Maybe Nathan had the right idea about not allowing himself to be reincarnated again, after all. Immortality wasn't all it was cracked up to be.

But he was the Wizenot. He had a responsibility to his people. He couldn't abandon them, too. Not even for Nathan. Especially not now, with a mysterious cloud of evil lurking on the horizon.

He sat down heavily on the thin mattress of his twin bed. The cold of the roof had made him stiff. What he'd seen there had made him tired. "And have you made her forget what she's seen?"

Nathan paced the long, narrow room and dragged a hand through his hair and over the back of his neck, rubbing. Teryn leaned back and waited for him to come out with whatever troubled him.

"Teryn," he finally said, "have you ever met a human who was . . . psychic?"

"Not that I'm aware of."

"Ever come across any records of our kind interacting with humans with any kind of . . . supernatural abilities?"

"Not that I recall." He took a shot at where this was going. "Do you think Rachel Vandermere is psychic?"

That brought Nathan's relentless pacing to an abrupt halt. He narrowed his eyes a moment, then scrubbed his face. "You know me too well for your own good, old man."

Teryn chuckled. He knew him so well because he saw so much of himself in Nathan. "So what makes you think our beautiful and intrepid investigator has more than visions of sugarplums dancing in her head?"

Nathan shot him a fierce glance. "Her mind is unusually strong. I can read her easily enough, but when I try to send visuals, I have trouble controlling the images. They seem to take on a life of their own, or else she's influencing them."

Teryn frowned. Some humans were harder to influence than others, but Nathan had an exceptionally powerful mind. His soul was one of the oldest of the congregation. The woman shouldn't have been able to resist the thoughts he tried to implant.

Nathan stopped across the room and stared into the cold moonlight again. "Then tonight, when I looked into her mind, there was this moment when I could swear she looked back. She saw everything. Or was about to when I broke the connection." He shoved his hands in his pockets, turned to face Teryn, his expression equal parts concern and wonder. "She heard the Calling, Teryn."

Teryn whistled, low and soft. "Did she, now?"

"How can that be? I didn't think it was possible."

"It shouldn't be."

"She has to be . . . gifted. Psychic. A gypsy stolen from her wagon at birth—hell, I don't know. There must be some explanation."

"Why don't you sit down before you wear a trench in my floor?"

she couldn't quite remember how she'd gotten it, she tried to ignore the ruckus and go back to sleep, but she found the sound oddly compelling . . . once she got used to feeling like someone had stuck an ice pick in her ear.

The sound drew her. It called to her in a language she couldn't quite understand, but couldn't ignore, either.

Slowly she lifted the pillow. Sunlight streamed through a high window on a white wall. She squinted.

This wasn't her bedroom. Or her hotel.

Nathan.

Groaning, she fell back to the mattress, arms spread eagle. It came back to her in a rush. Von and the tenement. The cut on her leg. The herbal salve.

The couch.

He'd drugged her tea, the bastard, but somehow even that seemed unimportant. Overshadowed by the insistent whistle in her mind.

She got out of bed and dressed quickly, not sure where she was going, knowing only that she had to go. A quick search proved Nathan wasn't in the condominium. She didn't bother to leave him a note. The whistle had become more urgent. By the time she reached the sidewalk in front of Nathan's building, she was running, clutching her coat at her throat and her pistol in her pocket.

At the corner of Rush Street and Limmerman Drive she stopped, swiveled her head left and right, then knew she needed to go straight ahead, and that she needed to hurry. She had no idea how she knew. She just did.

The pedestrian light in the intersection blinked red. She crossed anyway, dodging honking taxis and a belching Chicago Transit Authority bus.

She'd jogged nearly a mile north when the sound pulled her down the stairs into one of the underground train stations. She took the steps three at a time, and saw them at the end of the platform—two men in jeans, dirty canvas coats, and hard hats holding a third man up by the arms while two others punched him in the face and body. Between them and Rachel, a clump of bleary-eyed businessmen read their papers, sipped coffee from cardboard cups, and ignored the violence as if it happened every day.

Maybe it did.

The man strung between two captors jerked as another blow landed at his temple. The whistling noise went silent. The victim's head snapped to the side, then lolled forward. Rachel got a look at curly blond hair and caught a flash of gold among the blood spewing from his nose. Two diamond studs glittered in his ear.

Von Simeon! The version without the snout and razor tail.

Fear paralyzed her. For a moment she was six years old, watching the shadow of a monster hover over the spot where her father lay dead. She heard the *whump, whump* of wings, and a whimper worked its way up her throat.

What the hell was wrong with her? She'd been searching for monsters for years, and now that she'd found one, it was all she could do not to run away.

She stood and watched the men beat the blond-haired boy. With each blow her terror subsided, like a high tide ebbing a little farther out to sea on each wave. He couldn't hurt her; she wasn't a helpless little girl anymore.

But she remembered that little girl. She remembered tickle fights and gap-toothed giggles. Stuffed rabbits and the smell of Mommy's flowers outside her window. She remembered the day she'd lost all that. The day she lost her youth. Her innocence.

She remembered what a monster like Von had done to her parents.

A part of her wanted to join in the beating. Wanted vengeance for what had been done to her family. Wanted to hurt him for all the hurt one of his kind had caused her.

Then he lifted his head and seemed to look right at her. His back hunched as if he couldn't quite stand straight, he watched her watching the men hit him again and again. His lower lip split. Blood dripped out one corner of his mouth and stained his chin. His face was red and already swelling from the repeated blows, and yet his eyes didn't plead with her. They didn't cry for help, or even forgiveness.

His eyes simply watched, until the men hit him again, doubling him over, then driving him to the ground with a chop to the back of the neck, and still she did nothing, and then he craned his head back for one more look at her, and the look condemned her.

A chill crawled up Rachel's spine. They were killing him before her eyes. Not a monster, but a boy. A boy clutching his middle and coughing blood as four grown men took turns kicking him while he writhed on the ground and tried to curl up to protect himself.

The human being inside her wanted to cry. The cop in her roared to life.

"What the hell do you think you're doing?" she yelled, breathing hard as she wondered what the hell *she* had been doing, letting this happen without intervention. Shame flooded her cheeks with heat. "Let him go!"

One man delivered a final kick to Von's kidneys, then turned to Rachel. It was Mr. Lovell, Jenny's father. "This isn't none of your business, *little lady.*"

She pulled her Interpol credentials from her coat pocket and flashed the badge. Lovell knew who she was and obviously didn't care, but maybe the others would be more impressed. "I'm making it my business, *little man.*"

His partners snickered.

"Shut up," Mr. Lovell snapped at them, then turned back to Rachel. "I told this punk to stay away from my daughter."

"Fuck you," Von mumbled through swollen lips. Lovell kicked him in the face with enough force to snap the boy's head back again. Von spit blood on the man's pant leg in return. The man with what looked like a knife scar across the bridge of his nose standing next to Lovell pulled back a foot.

"Touch that boy and you'll be lucky to ever use that leg again," Rachel warned, pulling out her weapon. The few early-morning commuters who had been pretending not to see anything wrong on the platform made for the exits.

Scar Face lowered his foot.

Rachel advanced carefully, watching them all.

"He touched my daughter." Lovell spat on the concrete. "He put his filthy hands all over her. She admitted it."

And Jenny would pay for that admission, Rachel was sure. But right now she was worried about Von. She jumped the ticket turnstyle in the unattended station. "That doesn't give you the right to beat a boy half to death."

At his side she nudged one of his captors out of the way with her elbow and bent down, lifting Von with one shoulder. His weight sagged back, nearly pulling her down with him.

She shifted him for better balance and hefted him to his feet. He winced and coughed, a wet, racking sound that made her wonder how many ribs these goons had broken while she stood by and did nothing.

"Gentlemen, it's been interesting." She backed away, dragging Von along with her with one arm and keeping her Sig trained on the four men with the other. "But we'll be leaving now."

She didn't say that she hoped to be seeing them all again real soon . . . in jail. She'd have arrest warrants out for them five minutes after she got this poor kid to a hospital, but she was hoping to get at least a mile or two away before they figured that out.

She didn't make it ten feet.

Lovell and Scar Face circled in front of her. The other two kept her from making a getaway toward the rear.

Von lifted his head. Except for the red welts and rising bruises, his complexion was ashen. He coughed and spat blood and mucous on the pavement at her feet. "You shoulda just stayed out of it."

"Shut up, kid." She glanced around the platform, looking for options. They were alone now. No one to see, no one to help. The only way out was up the stairs, and that wasn't going to be easy, lugging Von along. Even if she managed to dodge between the men who surrounded her, she sure wasn't going to outrun anyone.

A train clattered down the tracks in the distance, but it didn't look like it was going to get here in time, the way the four men were closing in on her.

She shuffled a step toward the stairs, brandishing her pistol at the closing circle of men. Lovell and Scar Face cut her off, forcing her backward. She raised the gun in earnest this time. She'd never fired her weapon at anything but a paper target; she wasn't sure she could.

It looked like she was about to find out.

A humorless chuckle rumbled in her chest. Where was Nathan—her knight in shining armor—when she really needed him?

As if his name were a talisman, he was there. Not physically, but in thought. He was in her mind. She blinked and shook her head, dizzy with the merge of his feelings and hers.

That momentary distraction cost her dearly. One of the men behind her moved.

"Look out!" Von lunged out of her grasp and half-tackled, half-fell on her attacker as the man was about to put her in a choke hold.

While she spun out of the way, the other man grabbed her wrist and twisted. Pain spiraled up her arm. Her hand went numb and the gun clattered to the pavement at the edge of the platform. She wrenched herself free and instinctively sprung after it.

Unfortunately, she turned directly into the fist of Von's man, who'd gotten away from the injured kid.

Even as pain exploded in her left cheek, she felt the change in Nathan's mind, instantaneous and violent. Gone was the veneer of sophistication, of culture, so familiar to her. In its place she felt a savagery so primitive, it was impossible for the civilized mind to comprehend.

Bright lights exploded behind her eyelids. She swayed in midair as if suspended by a string for a long second, swamped by her own dizziness and Nathan's rage, and then began falling forward. The air over the tracks was hotter. Oilier. She swam through it, then landed with a thud that took her breath away.

The bright fluorescent bulbs above her dimmed. Her world went muzzy and gray. Sick to her stomach, she closed her eyes, but that didn't stop her from feeling the vibration in the steel rail bruising her hip. Or the hot gush of air rushing down the tunnel.

Wryly she realized she might have been wrong about that train being so far away.

Suddenly it sounded perilously close.

Trying to move, to pull herself out of the pit before the train arrived, and failing, she reached out to Nathan's mind for reassurance. For comfort.

Instead she found rage. Blood lust.

She heard the angry screech of a bird of prey, felt the wind beneath her wings. Her wings?

Trembling, she looked down and saw talons extended in front of her where her hands should be. She tried to speak, to call Nathan, but found her vocal cords incapable of producing human speech.

With her last moment of coherence, she opened her eyes to slits, saw the streets of Chicago, the entrance to the underground section of the L train, from high above, as if she were flying, and knew without a doubt that she was seeing the city through the eyes of a monster.

Nathan's eyes.

TWENTY

Nathan cursed the masses of people on the sidewalks beneath him. He couldn't risk being seen, so he had to divert down the alleyways, and even that was dangerous. All the while he turned and twisted along narrow brick walls and dodged Dumpsters, a sense of impending doom settled over him like snowfall on a park statue.

It wasn't just Von's Calling that had his heart sitting like a cold rock in his chest where his heart should have been. Another weaker cry had joined Von's voice.

Rachel.

There wasn't time to question how, but he knew it was her.

He felt it in every cell of his body, and sensing the danger she was in brought the beast inside him roaring to life, bursting forth in an explosion of fear and outrage.

At the corner across from the train station, he had to land and change back to human form. Teryn, the owl, swooped in behind him, winded, but Nathan didn't wait. He took the stairs three at a time and hopped the ticket turnstile.

Three men nearly ran over him on their way out of the

tunnel. They were part of whatever had happened, he sensed, but he didn't spare them a thought. He had to get to Rachel. Had to get there in time.

Only Lovell and a half-conscious Von remained on the platform. Already scanning the area for Rachel, Nathan simply grabbed him by the collar and threw him twenty feet against a tiled wall.

Lovell slumped to the floor, unconscious.

Teryn clumped down the steps behind him, breathing hard. The Wizenot sized up the situation quickly and knelt at Von's side. "I'll take care of him," he said. "Where's Rachel?"

Nathan found her. She lay sprawled across the tracks below, her blond curls spread around her like a halo, her pale, scratched arms flung straight out to the sides. Her eyes were closed. She was so still he couldn't even tell if she was breathing.

Please, be breathing.

A single, bright light broke the darkness in the tunnel behind her, and the sweat on Nathan's brow turned to ice water. The train must be an express. It was coming fast, not slowing for the stop.

He closed his eyes and Awakened the beast again in a single flare of mental energy that threatened to tear his body apart, cell by cell. He groaned in agony, his spine popping, teeth enlarging, cracking his jaw, and talons splitting the ends of his fingers to erupt in a bloody mess.

Out of time, he leaped off the platform before he'd completed the change, and thought he might fall to the tracks to be torn apart alongside Rachel as air sifted through wings not yet fully formed. But he gained lift at the last second and snatched her by the collar of her coat.

The air turbulence caused by the approaching train buffeted him. He couldn't make the turn quickly enough to circle back to the platform. The warm breath of the train washed over his tail, and the headlight glared at him like the eye of a Cyclops when he glanced over his shoulder to see how close it was.

He banked as sharply as he could and headed down the tracks, just feet in front of the speeding commuter line. He dug deep for the strength, the speed to stay ahead of it until he came to a service tunnel coming in from the side, and angled sharply into the narrower passageway.

The train passed so close behind him that he felt the brush of steel on his haunches.

He glided to the end of the service tunnel, where he eased Rachel to the ground and retook his human form. Iron steps led to the street above. He pulled Rachel up, opened the manhole cover, and lay her out in the alley.

Her face was chalky, her lips thin and trembling. Her hands were clenched across her waist, and her eyes were squeezed tightly shut.

Too tightly for her to be unconscious.

She knew.

He lurched to his feet and backed away. He didn't want to look at her when she opened her eyes. Her eyes had fascinated and enchanted him when she'd looked at him as a man. That was the way he wanted to remember them. Not full of horror and fear as they would be now.

He didn't want to see the hatred in them when she looked upon him as a monster for the first time, so he turned his back to her and crossed his arms over his chest as if to hold himself together when he felt like he might splinter into a million pieces.

What the hell was he going to do now?

She knew about Von. She knew about him.

He couldn't alter her memory.

He couldn't let her go.

He couldn't let her go.

Something crashed behind him and he turned to find Rachel scrabbling backward, away from him, like a crab. She bumped into a Dumpster and flinched as if she expected it to grab her and carry her off.

As he had.

Her eyes were too big for her face. She was breathing

in rapid little pants, and he doubted she even realized she'd clenched a rock in her hand. A weapon.

She stopped, swallowed hard. "Are you the one?" She swallowed hard. "The one who killed my parents?"

His stomach twisted. "No."

"But it was one like you. One with wings."

The revulsion on her face laid him open like a knife in the gut as much as her words. "I don't know what—*who*— killed your parents, Rachel."

She looked him up and down, as if expecting to still see a few feathers sticking out under his collar. "Wh—what are you?"

"Not what you think."

"I figured out that much."

"Not a monster," he corrected. But he was, both in her eyes and in his own.

She waved her hand—the one without the rock—at him. "You changed into something." Her voice was nearly hysterical and rising with every syllable. "Something with wings, and claws, and—"

"A griffin. The head and wings of an eagle, the body of a lion, it's—"

"I know what a griffin is."

"In most societies it's considered a symbol of courage and wisdom. A protector of man."

She laughed harshly. Madly. "Is that what you were doing in the train station? Protecting Lovell?"

His voice rose despite himself. "I was protecting you!"

She stood, leaning heavily on the garbage container. "Thank you very much. Now please, don't ever come near me again."

Nathan watched her limp away, bitterness rising in him like steam up a geyser. "That's not what you were saying last night." God help him, he couldn't quash the image of her taking him in her mouth. Driving him to the brink of insanity.

Loving him the way no other woman ever had.

Blood pooled in his groin just thinking about it.

He didn't mean to project the image, but he saw her eyes widen, her breath hitch. "You lied to me," she said. "You lied to me about everything!"

"No," he said, defeated. Deflated. "I told you the truth about one thing."

She waited for his explanation.

He raised his head. "I told you that you would regret it in the morning."

To his horror, her eyes filled with tears. She stifled a sob as she turned to hobble away.

Swearing, he caught up easily.

"Get away from me!" She brushed his hand away when he tried to help her.

"I can't." How he wished he could. How he wished he could forget her, forget what he was. Forget that he could never be the *man* she wished him to be.

She'd almost made it to the street. Cars whipped by, oblivious to the drama in the alley, but if she stepped out and called for help . . .

She lunged for the sidewalk, stumbled.

He caught her, pulled her back to his chest. She trembled in his grasp, her eyes huge, and he called down a thousand curses on his own head for what he was about to do. What he had to do.

And what he couldn't do.

"I can't let you go," he said.

Steeling himself as her green eyes filled with shock and disbelief, he put his hand in his coat pocket, pressed the barrel of the gun he'd retrieved when he'd scooped her off the tracks against her side, and turned her toward St. Michael's.

The council room smelled of soft wax, old wood, and older men. The assembly of elders, cloaked in heavy velvet robes of maroon, navy blue, and forest green belted with gold cord, stood in a semicircle on a long, curved dais, each behind an ornately carved pulpit depicting its owner's Gargoyle form. Some of the lecterns portrayed graphic scenes of guardian vengeance, with the Gargoyle poised over a cowering human with blood on the perpetrator's hands and the body of an innocent at his feet. Others were studies in character, capturing the fiery passion of a dragon-beast or the stealth of a big cat.

Connor stood before them, as did the rest of the congregation. Standing during council was more than a tradition, more than a sign of respect for the elders. It was a matter of efficiency. Decisions tended to get made a lot more quickly when all parties had to stand during the debate.

"If this woman has seen one of us, why didn't he who exposed himself alter the memory?" Elder Dane asked from his position at the far right of the dais, the position held by the most junior of elders. And at just forty-five years of age, without a gray whisker in his black beard or on his head, Dane was indeed junior, for a leader of the congregation. Not so many lifetimes ago, it was rare for one of the congregation to ascend to the council before seventy years of age.

Those days were long gone. If the congregation continued to dwindle, soon fledglings and teenage hoodlums, like Von, would be all that were left to lead their people.

Murmurs rippled through the assembly. Heads nodded, wanting an answer to Dane's challenge.

"He tried," the Wizenot said from the center of the dais, but his words were nearly lost among the whispered conversations from the floor.

Teryn held his hands up, palms out, for quiet, his position mocking that of the owl that seemed to leap from his podium into the crowd, claws out, talons extended.

Silence descended slowly. Conversations trailed off one by one, like fall leaves drifting to the forest floor to lie still. Hushed.

"He tried," Teryn repeated, more softly this time.

Connor worked to keep from sneering. *He.* Even the

Wizenot wouldn't say his name. None looked at him, save Connor, who glared openly.

Nathan Cross was excommunicated. He shouldn't even be here. This was the congregation's sanctuary. The inner sanctum of a world to which he no longer belonged—by his own choice.

He had decided he didn't need his people. Didn't need their tenets or their traditions.

His people damned sure didn't need him, either.

"What do you mean, *he tried*?" Elder Dane asked.

"She has some unusual . . . abilities," Teryn answered.

Congregation and elders alike fired questions at the Wizenot.

"What kind of abilities?"

"I heard she was psychic."

"Is it true she can hear the Calling?"

"Hear it, be damned. She Called us herself!"

"How can that be?"

"Where did this woman come from?"

"Why the hell did he show himself to her, anyway?"

"He saved her life!" Teryn said, defending Cross, as always.

"What are we going to do about her?"

"About them both!"

All hint of decorum disintegrated, and conversations erupted around the room. Voices raised as tempers flared. Connor had never seen anything like it in a council room. Not in all his lifetimes.

He glared at Nathan, standing still and silent across the room. This was his fault. He was responsible for the division among the congregation. The unrest. If something wasn't done, he might be their destruction.

Or maybe he already was, Connor thought, watching as the discord rose in the room. Bile climbed his throat. This couldn't continue. He had to do something.

The council couldn't. The Wizenot wouldn't, not when it meant standing against his precious Nathan.

That left it up to him.

Turning quietly, he slid out the door unnoticed and headed upstairs to find Rachel Vandermere.

"You're . . . one of them?" Rachel asked.

The man who'd introduced himself as Evan Cain nodded, still bent over the bandage he'd just applied to her wrist.

He was a thin, wiry man, with round, wire-rimmed glasses and quick eyes that never landed too long in any one spot. Even his hands were quick, working in sharp, nervous little jerks. His anxiety was so palpable, so human, that it was hard to imagine he was a monster.

"And you're a doctor," she asked, as much to divert her imagination from the path it was headed down as anything.

"University of Illinois," he said. He straightened and gathered his supplies—stethoscope, antiseptic, gauze, bandage scissors—back into his black bag. "Two years' residency in the ER at Chicago Medical Center. Three in pediatrics at Pearland Children's Hospital."

She wondered if they had a vet, too, to take care of their alternate personas. Or if the good doctor just studied up on nonhuman anatomy for the occasional animal emergency. She didn't quite have the courage to ask, so instead she said, "Did you take care of Von? He was hurt much worse than me."

"Not as much as he deserves."

"He's just a boy." A boy who could turn into a boar at will, and still she couldn't get the image of his poor, abused, *human* face out of her mind.

The doctor sighed. "He'll live. As will you," he said, and closed his bag.

She tested her aching wrist, had to admit it did feel better, and turned her attention back to the doctor, her mind working. He stood, but she wasn't ready for him to leave. Wasn't ready to be alone, even if the only company available was a self-admitted monster.

"Must come in handy here," she said, "having a doctor around that's one of your own."

He turned his back to her, didn't answer, but the tense set to his shoulders told her plenty.

"How many of you are there in Chicago?"

"Take it easy for a couple of days," he said, the words as stiff as his back. "Change the bandage on that wrist. Put some Neosporin on those scrapes. Take a couple of Tylenol if you need it, but have Nathan call me if you have any serious pain."

He didn't bother to say good-bye, and Rachel felt a moment of pinching guilt that she'd offended him, which annoyed her, since she was the one being held her against her will. It took her a moment to realize that he also hadn't closed the door.

Surely her escape wouldn't come so easily.

She tiptoed across the room. As she was about to peek around the corner and look for guards, a big body filled the doorway.

She jumped back, her hand automatically covering her heart before she recognized the man who'd driven her to the Lovell house and then disappeared yesterday. "Connor?"

He scowled down at her, his face dark, and then without a word, he closed the door behind him.

And locked it.

It took Teryn a good ten minutes to bring order to the council chamber. For a few moments he hadn't been entirely sure order would be restored. This had once been a body of dignity, of honor, unified for the greater good against all that opposed them.

How quickly they'd degenerated into factions and cliques, like boys in a schoolyard. Maybe Nathan was right. Maybe the magic that had held them together for so many centuries was weakening.

Or maybe they were all just tired.

Teryn was tired. Too many hours spent in ritual on the rooftop left him deprived of sleep. Too many nightmares, repeats of his ritual visions, left him edgy.

He let his gaze meet Nathan's. Nathan, who should be here next to him, his right hand. He studied Nathan's stony expression. The hard eyes that gave away nothing of the hurt Teryn knew he felt inside at being back amongst his people, and yet not here, a shadow no one spoke to, no one saw. The distance, emotional and physical, between them tightened his chest, weighted his shoulders.

He thought he understood—finally—a little of what Nathan felt. Nathan was the one who'd been excommunicated, and yet, standing apart from the others at his center podium, with no one to share the responsibility, no one with whom to share the prophecies of destruction he'd been given in his visions, Teryn felt isolated. Alone.

With the room finally quiet, he turned back to the assembly. "The woman is aware of *Les Gargouillen*. But even if she were to tell anyone, none would believe her. The worst that could happen is that she would draw unwanted attention to us." He held up his hand before another outburst could even begin. "We have survived worse. What is more important is that we understand how she is able to resist the touch of our minds. What she knows of the Calling. If one human can do such things, there may be others. We must be prepared."

A dead stillness fell upon the room. Teryn let his gaze travel from man to man, locking gazes with each one. When their eyes fell to their feet or hands or the floor, he moved on.

"What about him?" Christian, the tracker, said, jerking his shoulder toward Nathan.

"Nathan is the only one who has spent time with this woman." He purposely used Nathan's name, though it was forbidden, giving him existence again. Giving him some measure of acceptance, no matter how slim. "To learn more about her, we're going to need her trust. He stays until we have it."

Nathan took one clipped step forward, surprising Teryn. The fool shouldn't push his luck.

"I won't allow you to hurt her," he said.

"No one is going to hurt her, Nathan." Teryn looked him in the eye, tried to say with his expression what was forbidden with words.

At the top of the stairs he and Nathan had trudged up in silence when the council meeting ended, in the small room that quartered Rachel Vandermere, he found out how wrong he'd been.

TWENTY-ONE

❦

Rachel couldn't breathe, but not because of the hands on her throat. Connor held her in place, but he wasn't choking her.

Yet her vision had gone stark white with fuzzy black dots dancing around the edges. The dots were *him*. His thoughts. His vision, trying to get in.

She felt the invasion to her mental processes the way she had felt it when Nathan created false images in her mind, only this time it hurt. Where Nathan's intrusion had been soft, stealthy, Connor was trying to force himself on her. To take her mind by brute strength.

The images from his mind tried to pierce the mental barrier she'd put up between them. She felt each jab like a knife through the eye.

Panicked, she pummeled him with her fists. He straddled her on the twin bed and held her arms down with his knees. His hands tightened on her throat.

"Easy," he said. "I'm not going to hurt you. Just relax. Let me in."

Relax? *Relax?*

Who the hell was he kidding? She'd die fighting first.

Revitalized, she bucked, trying to throw him off, but succeeding only in losing more air when she dislodged him a few inches and he landed hard back down on her chest. She tried to cough, but there was no passageway for the air to squeeze through, so it turned into a swallowed hiccup.

At least she'd gotten one hand free. She turned her claws on him, gouged at his eyes, but couldn't quite reach.

A knock sounded on the door. The knob rattled.

"Ms. Vandermere?" *Teryn.*

Connor turned his head and her index finger found his eye socket. She drew blood.

"Shit!" he cried, and let go of her neck to swipe his hand over the wound.

Dragging in a quick breath, she tried to scream, but her voice wouldn't work. She must have managed some small sound, though, because the next thing she knew, the door burst inward and Nathan tumbled through, Teryn on his heels.

"What the fuck?" The look of fury on Nathan's face would have sent the devil himself scurrying for the nearest pit of fire. He dragged Connor off her and slammed him into the wall so hard the room shook. But Connor seemed unfazed. In the blink of an eye his arm had changed to a claw. Talons reached out and razed Nathan's neck. The shape of his head changed to some dark, leathery-skinned bird with a single horn sloped back from his forehead.

Nathan began to change, too. His jaw lengthened. His shoulders bulged with muscle. He opened his mouth and the sound that came out wasn't human, but an unmistakable animal challenge.

Rachel curled up in a ball on the thin mattress and squeezed her eyes shut. *Now I lay me down to sleep . . .*

"Stop it, both of you!"

Despite her fear, Rachel's eyes snapped open. Teryn stood in front of her bed, arms out to his sides, one extended toward each of the other two men—who, thankfully, looked like men again—like stop signals. When neither one tried to dive past toward the other, he slowly lowered his arms.

"Connor," he said. "What are you doing?"

"What *he* should have done already. Making her forget what she saw. What she knows."

Nathan took an aggressive step forward, held on a look from Teryn. "By holding her down and choking her?"

Interestingly, Rachel thought, Connor's gaze fell. "She was resisting."

Nathan's jaw ticked. He looked at and spoke to Teryn, and Teryn only. "I told you she couldn't be manipulated."

"I did not order this."

Suspicion flickered across Nathan's dark expression, then grudging acceptance. He pulled back his shoulders and squared off with Connor. "Touch her again, with your hands or your mind, and we'll finish what you started here." He spared a glance at Teryn, then looked back at Connor, his dark eyes glittering with malice. "Without a referee."

Teryn put a hand on Connor's shoulder and nudged him toward the door. "Go downstairs. We'll talk about this later."

Rachel uncurled herself and stood up cautiously. Silence reigned in the room, none of them seeming to know what came next. Nathan stared at Rachel. Rachel stared at the wall over his shoulder.

Teryn finally broke the deadlock. "You've had a difficult day, my dear. Why don't you rest? Nathan will stay with you. I'll send up some tea."

Rachel let her gaze slide slowly over Nathan, his taut shoulders, hard jaw. The agony in his eyes. "What makes you think I'll be any safer with him than I was with Connor?"

Teryn smiled, an endearingly human smile that made her stomach twist in confusion. "Perhaps the fact that he outran a speeding train and very nearly did battle with one of his own brethren in order to protect you?"

He nodded at Nathan, a gesture Rachel was sure meant something, and backed out of the room.

Nathan walked to the window, his fingers shoved in the pockets of his jeans. "Are you all right?"

"Besides being held against my will in a stone fortress

by a bunch of men who aren't human and nearly having my mind raped, you mean?"

He turned around. She stepped quickly back. Her knees hit the edge of the bed, and she sat to keep from falling. Better to be sitting, anyway. Makes her look calm, she thought. Keeps him from seeing that her knees were shaking.

"I mean, did he hurt you?"

"No, he didn't hurt me. At least he was honest about what he intended to do, and why." She looked up at Nathan, grieving for the innocence of yesterday. "What you did, lying to me, using me. That hurt."

"I only wanted to protect you."

"Bullshit." She pushed herself off the bed, walked right up to him, stood toe to toe. Fear razed her nerves like a butter knife scraped over dry toast, but it didn't stop her. Didn't paralyze her. If he was going to kill her, he could have done it a hundred times already.

Which made her wonder what the last week had been about. "You were protecting yourself, weren't you? Your secrets."

"There's a reason for those secrets, Rachel. Because some things people are better off not knowing."

"Like the fact that there're a bunch of vigilante bogeymen running around in Chicago and God knows where else, slaughtering people in the name of justice?"

"Is that what you think we do?"

"I've overheard a few conversations in this place. Are you telling me I misunderstood?"

He flinched. "I suppose some might see us that way."

"How do you see it?"

"I see a species on the edge of extinction. An ancient civilization struggling to survive in a modern world, and failing." He strode to the window, stared off into the distance, and shook his head. "A bunch of dinosaurs that can't go on living the way they are, and can't just lie down and die, either, even if they wanted to."

Her breath caught on his last few words. "Are you telling me you're . . . immortal?"

He turned, shoved his hands in his pockets, and rattled change while he considered her. "No. We're born just like everybody else, die just like everybody else—a good bit younger, actually. Our life expectancy isn't very long." He shrugged. "Occupational hazard when you're out rounding up the scum of the city every night. It's just that when we die, if we've been good little Gargoyles and produced a son and heir, we're born again. And die again, and are born again and so on, ad nauseam."

"You reincarnate?"

His smile didn't reach his eyes as he strolled around the little room, hands still in his pockets. "Even cats get to die after nine lives. Me? I'm on number fourteen."

She plunked down on the bed, chin in her hands to think, and shook her head at the enormity of it. Fourteen lives?

"You don't believe me?" he asked. "You wanted the truth. I'm giving it to you. I'll give it all to you, if you're ready to hear it."

"As opposed to the truth you gave me yesterday. Or the one you'll give me tomorrow. How do I know what to believe, Nathan?"

"Fine. Don't believe it. Just think of it as a story." He sat down beside her on the bed, not close enough to touch, but still too close. Too overwhelming, with his whetstone scent and the heat that always seemed to emanate from him. "The story of how monsters came to walk the world."

Teryn disapproved of eavesdropping, but he stayed by Rachel's door a while to make sure there would be no more bloodshed, then, satisfied, lit a candle to carry and crept down the stone stairs to the basement.

In the vault room, where the ancient volumes of his people's history, passed down from generation to generation, lifetime to lifetime within *Les Gargouillen*, were hermetically stored, Teryn carried a heavy manuscript to the desk. After flipping on the small lamp, he put on his reading glasses and began to turn the pages carefully, slowly scanning for the text Nathan had asked him to look for amidst the fading illustrations and scrolling, hand-penned letters.

He had a vague memory of the passage, something he'd seen years ago when he'd first become interested in the centuries-old illuminated manuscripts. Something he'd come across when he'd begun helping Nathan search for a way to reverse the curse that made *Les Gargouillen* what they were, and then forgotten. Or at least partially forgotten.

Something about a woman with the power of a Gargoyle.

Though he was several generations removed from the original *Gargouillen* of Rouen, Nathan described the scene of their transformation into beasts to Rachel from memory. Rouen was the foundation of Gargoyle history, not to be forgotten by any of his kind. The images were passed to each new soul in much the same way Nathan had tried to plant images in Rachel's mind, and were now part of his continuing consciousness, recoverable in each new life into which he was born.

With his eyes closed, the pictures formed in his mind now, a simple time, green land, kind people, days that passed much slower than they seemed to now. "It was about the turn of the millennium," he said, and opened one eye to check her understanding. "The first one."

She stared at her hands, twining in her lap, and he closed his eyes and settled back into the story.

"The people of Rouen were pagans. They worshipped the god of the hunt, and the forest. But Christianity was sweeping the land. Still, the people of Rouen held fast to their beliefs. At least until a dragon took up residence on a nearby mountain. La Gargouille raped and pillaged the town, burning the fields before harvest and swallowing ships from the port."

He could smell the acrid smoke. Hear the screams, and he knew Rachel picked up at least some of the impressions whether she wanted to or not. She shuddered so hard the bed shook.

"The villagers tried everything to get rid of the dragon, but the more they fought, the more destruction La Gargouille rained down on them. Until one day a priest named Romanus showed up. He said he would slay the dragon if the townspeople would promise to be baptized and build a Christian church. The people held out a while, but eventually were so desperate they agreed." He snorted. "They figured the white-haired old fool didn't have a chance, anyway, and maybe the meat on his bones would placate La Gargouille for a few days."

Rachel lifted her head. She was as caught in the story now as he; it was in her eyes, sparkling green and misty. "I take it he wasn't quite the fool everyone thought he was."

"No." Nathan fought the attraction he felt for her. The need to reach out and brush his knuckles across her soft cheek. To tell the story under cover of darkness, his body curled around hers.

He cleared his throat. "On the night he was to do the deed—kill the dragon—Romanus called the men of Rouen into the forest on the hill above town. They didn't realize they were standing in a pentagram inside a circle until it was too late."

A furrow formed on the bridge of her nose.

"Ritual symbols," he explained. "The bastard crusaded for Christianity, but he used my people's own pagan magic against them, and it was powerful magic."

Nathan's heart beat in time with the drums echoing in his head. The chanting. He couldn't make out the words, or didn't know their meaning if he did, but their rhythm was seductive.

> *E Unri almasama*
> *E Unri almasama*
> *Calli, Calli, Callio*
> *Somara altwunia paximi*

"He lit fires at the four cardinal directions of the circle and burned incense." Nathan's voice was rough, smoky.

His blood percolated in his veins as he relived the damnation of his forefathers and all their descendants.

"It was a clear night, but lightning flashed in the sky. A gale wind picked up and bent even the old trees double. Limbs cracked and popped."

E Unri almasama

A sweat broke out on Nathan's forehead. He didn't realize he'd fisted the bedcovers in his hands until his fingers cramped. By force of will, he uncurled his fingers and smoothed the comforter. "Some of the men cowered, but others rushed the edge of the circle, only to be thrown back by an unseen hand."

E Unri almasama

The leaves on the trees curled and died. They swirled in the wind now, brown and withered, rattling like bones. The cloying incense and the smoke stole Nathan's breath, burned his throat and eyes. "Romanus stood on the north side of the circle and raised a chalice. Blood ran down both sides of his mouth as he drank, and the warmth of the earth, the power, soaked through the leather soles of his boots, coursed up his legs."

Calli, Calli, Callio

He didn't intentionally project the image, but the force of the memory was too strong to contain. Its energy rippled in the air around him and Rachel. Between them. He felt her gasp at its strength. Felt it probe and prick and slither into her mind until she lived the nightmare he lived.

"He moved to the south, and the east, and the west, and each time he drank, the heat grew more intense until the men were breathing fire and snorting ash."

He couldn't speak above a whisper when he tried to continue, the hot air rushing in his ears, hot blood pumping in his veins. His muscles bulged and his skin thickened. His bones began to reshape.

Nathan didn't care; he was mindless to the pain, caught in the dream, the memory.

"Romanus called to the beasts of the forest," Nathan croaked. "And they came to the edge of the circle, enthralled by the light and power. He called the life from them; he called their souls, and then even as the animals fell dead in the trees, the men began to writhe. Their bodies stretched and bent. Their organs shifted. Their teeth broke through their jaws and their fingers merged into misshapen clubs, and then hooves. Some dropped to all fours and others fell to their bellies, their spines dissolving as they coiled like snakes."

He choked, swallowed dryly, and gathered his breath to continue. "The men took the beasts' souls inside them, in all manner of configurations, species combined, breeds merged. Then when Romanus drank the last bit of blood from his cup, the hillside exploded. Fire rained from the sky. The ground opened up in great crevices that swallowed some of the men. Charred tree trunks crashed, killing others.

"When it ended, those who were left looked down at themselves, at what they'd become, and knew they'd been tricked. The bastard Romanus had betrayed them."

Somara altwunia paximi

"What happened to them?" Rachel asked, as breathless as he.

He looked up, coming back to himself a bit, saw her red, watery eyes, and knew his must look as bad. "The dragon Gargouille appeared on the crest of the hill about then, angry at being woken by all the noise and shaking, and the men, overcome with revulsion at what they'd become, what Romanus had made them, filled with rage, terrified, and ashamed, they stormed the hill and tore the dragon apart with their teeth and horns and claws while the women and children of the village watched in horror."

"Le Combat de Rouen," she said. "The tapestry at the museum."

He inclined his head. *"Le Combat de Rouen."*

"My god."

"Even that wasn't the end of Romanus's treachery. He'd gotten what he wanted—La Gargouille was dead, and the people of Rouen were obligated to honor their promise and convert to Christianity. But Romanus was too enthralled with his new pets to give them up. He added to the spell he'd cast, telling them that they should forever be protectors of the human race, the way they'd protected the women and children of Rouen from the dragon. He proclaimed that they would always carry these beasts inside them, slumbering until they were needed. And that they should go forth and propagate. Produce sons that would be like them—guardians."

Rachel sat silently, taking it all in. At least she hadn't run away.

He took that as a sign he should finish the story. "For many years we were revered by humans. We kept them safe. Shielded them from the dangers of a dark time. They brought us their daughters to mate with, so that we could produce sons—it was considered an honor for a virgin to give herself to a Gargoyle, bear him a son before seeking her marriage to a human. They even carved our images into the walls of their buildings as signs that they were protected. Evil dare not lurk there. But as the centuries went by, they just . . . forgot. People evolved, they wrote laws and hired police to protect them. They didn't need us anymore, and we faded into legend."

He strolled to the window, looked out at the heavy stone walls. "Just grotesque statues hanging high above their streets. Interesting artifacts of a time long passed."

She drew in a shuddering breath, pulled her shoulders up, and shook her head as if to clear it. Seeming just to realize he held her hand in his, she pulled out of his grasp.

"We didn't choose what we are, Rachel, none of us, not even the Old Ones, the original Gargoyles of Rouen. We were cursed. Betrayed." He shrugged. "We've lived with it the best we know how."

Rachel rose, crossed her arms over her middle as she paced. "You can't really expect me to believe that."

"It's the truth. You saw it. You *felt* it."

"I also saw us making love in a forest when we were really on a couch in a vacant house. I felt . . ." She left the sentence dangling, a flush rising on her neck. "Who's to say this isn't another of your parlor tricks?"

Nathan's world fell from beneath him. He felt as if he were falling. Floating. He stared at her for a full second before the sensation passed, then he threw his head back and laughed, the first full belly laugh he'd enjoyed in several lifetimes.

Furrows plowed across her forehead. "What's so funny?"

"You." He swiped the back of his hand across his eyes to dry the tears of laughter. "You're the first human to hear that story in centuries, maybe the first human ever, and you—" Another chuckle rumbled up his gullet. "You don't believe it."

"That's funny?"

"It's ironic. Do you know the lengths we've gone to in order to keep our secrets? All this time we could have blabbed to anybody. What difference would it have made? If you, who actually believe in monsters, don't believe what I've told you, what do you think are the chances anyone else would?"

She still didn't seem to see the humor in the situation. Her silence dampened his own amusement. His smile fell flat.

"I didn't say I don't believe you, exactly," she said, "I just . . ."

"Don't trust me," he finished for her. Her lack of denial confirmed his suspicion. "Fine. You don't trust me, don't trust what you see in your mind, maybe you'll trust what you see with your own eyes."

Sighing, he opened the door and motioned her out. She made no move to join him.

"Where?" she asked.

"I can't prove to you how we came to be. But at least I can show you what we are now. Who we are. If you have the courage to see."

TWENTY-TWO

Rachel walked out of her room in stuttering steps, Nathan behind her, guiding her along with a hand in the small of her back. Her legs were as stiff as tree trunks. Her feet felt like cement blocks.

She'd been searching for monsters most of her life, and now that she'd found them, she was afraid to look.

"This way." Nathan turned her right, led her downstairs to a hallway lined with doors, and stopped outside the last room. Rachel stopped behind him, her heart turning cartwheels in her chest. Not knowing what to expect, what horrors she might see, she fixed her gaze in the center of his broad back.

"St. Michael's was a struggling church and seminary in the late 1800s. When the philanthropist who funded it decided to move west in 1898, it stood empty until my congregation purchased it in 1905. We've added on some since then, but the original structure is intact. The two towers here serve as dormitories. The older boys are in the north tower. The younger ones, ten or eleven years old and down, are here in the south tower. The ground floor of each tower is made up of a half-dozen classrooms." He checked over his shoulder, as if to make sure she hadn't vanished. Or died of fright. "There was a time when it would have been brimming with boys, but we only have eighteen students now. Most of the rooms upstairs are empty."

"Why so few children?"

His face darkened. "Let's just say the villagers aren't bringing us their virgins any longer."

He stepped to the side. Rachel automatically locked her eyes shut and clamped her teeth down on her lower lip. Her breath froze in her lungs, then puffed out of her in a soft explosion of air when she saw what lay inside the room.

No torture chambers. No savage beasts tearing each other apart with terrible claws. No glowing, feral eyes.

It was a schoolroom, full of boys ranging from five or six years old to ten or so. The stoop-shouldered man with gray hair and a goatee in the front of the room spun a globe on a table. "Who can tell me how many oceans there are in the world?"

A boy in the second row shot his hand into the air.

"Charles?"

"Five!"

"Correct. Five. Now, Paul, can you name one?"

A sleepy-eyed child in back straightened. "Umm, the Pacific?"

"Very good." The teacher turned to write *Pacific Ocean* on the chalkboard in round, even letters. A blond-haired kid with a cowlick quickly pulled out a paper football. The boy in the desk next to him made a goal with his fingers and Cowlick flicked it through. They smiled and high-fived each other across the aisle before the teacher turned back to the class.

Grinning, Nathan gave them a thumbs-up, and then nudged her past the door.

"You shouldn't encourage them," she said.

"Boys will be boys." He cast her a sideways look. "Human or otherwise."

The words plunked into her consciousness like stones

into a pond. She should have realized the boys were like Nathan. Of course they were.

But they'd looked so normal. So innocent.

She shook her head. "Is that what you wanted to show me? How civilized you all are? I never doubted your education, Nathan."

"No," he said without looking back as he shoved his way through a set of heavy double doors and gestured inside. "This is what I wanted to show you."

She followed him over the threshold into a cavernous room two, maybe three stories high. It looked like a gymnasium of sorts, with a blue sky and fluffy clouds painted around the skylights in the ceiling. Murals of green grass, bright flowers of every color, and trees stretched up three walls, while a vivid blue waterfall tumbled down the fourth. But it wasn't the setting that caught her attention, but the half-dozen children hooting and hollering as they chased each other around it.

At least, she guessed they were children.

"Between the two towers are the administrative offices, and this. We call it the aviary," Nathan said. "It's where the boys born to a winged form learn to fly."

What appeared to be a pair of young red hawks—except these hawks sported a line of bony finlike ridges down their backs and had leathery tails that forked like snakes' tongues, not to mention glowing green eyes—swooped out of the painted sky, the one behind nipping at the tail of the one in front, made a kamikaze dive for Nathan's head, then rocketed up into the rafters again.

Rachel watched them in wonder, a tingling mix of amazement and curiosity dissolving her fear. A bat with horns and oversize fangs performed a perfect barrel roll right in front of her.

"Very nice, Ellis," Nathan said.

One by one, the other creatures—boys?—in the room did loop-de-loops, dives, hammerhead stalls, and various other aerobatic feats. Nathan found a kind word and encouragement for each of them, and then turned to a

platform about ten feet off the floor against the wall to
their right decorated to look like a tree house.

"And how about you, Patrick? Aren't you going to
come out and say hello to me?"

"Patrick? Rhys's son?" She remembered the sad-eyed
child from the funeral. Her heart had gone out to him then,
as it did now. She'd lost her father at about the same age.

Nathan nodded, then turned back to the tree house.
"Aren't you going to show me what you've learned since
I've been away?"

A pair of dark eyes, almost covered by a shock of even
darker hair, peered out of the tree house cubbyhole. "Don't
wanna."

"Why not?"

One of the hawks, now transformed into a lanky preteen
boy with spiky red hair, laughed. "'Cause he can't do
nothin'!"

The other, also in human form and also redheaded, put
his hands in his armpits, flapped his elbows, and strutted
around bobbing his chin while the other children laughed.
"*Bawwwwk. Bawwwwwk.* When Patrick Awakens, he
ought to be a chicken, cuz he's too afraid to fly!"

Nathan scowled over his shoulder. "Aren't you boys
going to be late for your history lesson?"

The laughter gave way to a round of complaints, but the
boys filtered out of the room. Except for Patrick.

"It's all right. They're gone," Nathan said. His voice
was amazingly gentle for a monster. "Come on out."

Patrick eyeballed the room, just to be sure. He stared at
Rachel as if she were the strange one here. "Who's she?"

"This is Ms. Vandermere. She's a friend."

"She's a *girl.*"

Rachel felt Nathan suppress a chuckle. "Yes. She is.
Now come on out."

Patrick scanned the room once more, then crawled out
on the platform and sat with his sneakers dangling over the
edge. Rachel's throat clutched at the humiliated way his
lower lip poked out. He was just a baby.

"Now, what's this about you not flying?" Nathan asked, but his voice was light, not accusing.

Patrick swallowed. "I'm skeered."

"Everyone's afraid when they first learn. Even Jacen and Josh were, I bet."

He sniffed. A teardrop hung like a crystal ornament in his eyelashes. "Even you?"

Nathan glanced at Rachel, then shifted his feet and looked away. "Yes. Even me."

"But you flied anyway?"

"I did. All of us who Awaken with wings learn to fly, Patrick. The sky and the wind call us. It's our nature."

He made it sound like a grand and noble adventure, and her insides softened as she fell as much under his spell as the little boy. Until she wondered if being a Gargoyle would seem so glorious when Patrick learned he also had to kill people.

"Stand up now, and listen to the drumbeat of your heart. Hear the words *E Unri almasama.*"

"*E Unri almasama,*" Patrick repeated. Wiping his nose with the sleeve of his T-shirt, he stood on the edge of the platform. His eyes glazed over as if he'd fallen into a trance.

"*Calli, Calli, Callio,*" they chanted together. "*Somara altwunia paximi.*"

That quickly, the beautiful, sad little boy was gone, and a miniature dragon squatted in his place.

"Now lift your wings," Nathan said. "Feel the air beneath them. Feel how solid it is. How it can hold you up. Feel how you can push against it."

Patrick gave an experimental little flap of his iridescent wings, his feet—claws—still firmly planted on the edge of the platform.

"Good," Nathan encouraged. "Keep thinking about that. About pushing against the air. Now lean forward just a little bit."

The boy's wings beat irregularly. He swayed, panicked, and then righted himself before he took a header off his perch.

"That's okay," Nathan said quickly. "Just slow down. Just stand there and move your wings up and down. Feel the wind."

Patrick's rhythm evened out.

"Now lean forward a little bit. Arch your back and keep your head up. Keep flapping. Good. Very good. When you're ready, just lean forward a little more. Keep your head up and keep flapping, nice and steady.

The boy leaned forward until he teetered precariously on the edge of the platform. Rachel's heart lurched and she clutched at Nathan's arm, but he gave her hand a little squeeze she thought was meant to reassure her. Or keep her quiet.

"Are you ready?" he asked the boy.

Patrick squawked. Rachel took that as a no.

"Lean forward a little more," he crooned. "And come to me. Come and see me. It's been a long time since I've given you a big hug."

Her chest warmed at the soft look in Nathan's eyes, the gentle, longing tone in his voice.

The little boy-dragon blinked, then tipped slowly forward, wings beating, until he tumbled off the edge of his tree house.

Rachel's hand flew to her mouth. Patrick free-fell about four feet, then gained enough control to level out. Or sort of level out. He flopped through the air about ten feet off the ground, losing and gaining about three feet of altitude with each beat of his wings, lurching left and then right and then left again.

"Arch your back," Nathan called. "Head up. Use your tail like a rudder, use it to steer."

Apparently Patrick knew what a rudder was, because he steered, all right. Directly into Nathan's chest. The impact drove him back a step, but he caught the boy, who once again looked like a boy, and wrapped him up in a bear hug.

"I did it! I did it! You're squashing me!" Patrick said against Nathan's shoulder.

This time Patrick didn't need wings to fly. Nathan

tossed him over his head and caught him on his way down, then tickled him. Through the giggles, Patrick said, "I missed you, Un'ca Nate."

Nathan gathered him up in another long hug. "I missed you, too, Peanut."

Uncle? Rachel thought, but didn't want to interrupt the reunion to ask. Instead she stared at the rare sight of unadulterated joy lighting his face. Their gazes connected over Patrick's shoulder, and as always, a bridge formed between their minds. She saw inside him, all the way into his heart, and the warmth that had been stirring in her chest turned to liquid and drained down the center of her body to puddle in her core like molasses.

The images and feelings that passed between them weren't sexual in nature this time, but they were just as arousing. The love she felt in him for this boy who'd lost his father, Nathan's friend. The honor of family and friendship in him tugged on a line that seemed to run from her nipples to her womb. It made her breasts turn heavy and ache for a child to suckle them. A man to hold them, to hold her.

A man, not a monster.

Tears rose, hot and salty, behind her eyes. She broke the connection between herself and Nathan before he could see them and turned away, but knew she'd been too late. He'd felt her reaction. Her longing.

And her rejection.

His gaze meeting hers sadly, he set Patrick down and told him to scat. Again his gentleness with the child struck her, and then a new reality set in, its sharp point spearing through her.

She waited for the door to close behind Patrick, and then asked, "Where are all these boys' mothers? And why aren't there any girls here?"

"*Les Gargouillen* were created about a thousand years before Women's Lib was ever dreamed of. The magic that makes me what I am is only passed to males of my kind. Or at least it's supposed to be." He shrugged. "It probably never even occurred to Romanus to include women in his curse. France in the Dark Ages wasn't exactly an equal-opportunity-employment state."

"Then how . . . ?"

"How do we get women to mate with us in modern times?"

She felt a yawning chasm of despair open inside him. Anger skulked in the darkness. Fury turned inward.

His lips set in a hard line. His face had never seemed harsher, made up of more shadows and sharp angles. "Pretty much the same way as human men. Except once a male child is born, we take it."

Her throat pinched her voice. "What do you mean, 'take it'?"

He advanced until he towered over her. His dark eyes smoldered. His earthy, wet scent enveloped her. "There are lots of ways. Some of us pay women to have babies and give them up, no questions asked. Others prefer not to have to deal with negotiating agreements. They simply tell the woman the child is dead. Infant death certificates can be faked. We have doctors among us."

All of Rachel's blood drained to the ends of her fingers and her toes. Her limbs felt heavy, her heart sluggish. She opened her mouth to say something, but couldn't think of anything to fit the horror of what she was hearing.

She backed up a step. He followed.

"Does that repulse you, Rachel? I'm supposed to be making nice, helping you understand my people. But you can't understand us if you don't know it all. The bad and the good."

"Stop it."

She put her hands on his chest. He swiped them away.

"Sometimes we just make our sons disappear without explanation. Human children are abducted all the time. The Gargoyle will pretend to be the concerned father for a while, anxious for his boy's return. Then eventually he'll just . . . fade away."

"I said stop it."

He leaned forward. His breath was hot on her face. She couldn't understand why he was doing this. What demon was driving him.

"I know of at least one case where the babe was literally ripped from his mother's arms while she screamed and tried to hold on to her son."

She tried to turn away. He held her by the elbows.

"I can still hear her screams in my head."

In her mind Rachel saw a dark-haired woman before a window, holding a baby. She saw her eyes widen as a shadow fell over her. Felt her lunge backward, holding tight to the bundle in her arms as something tried to wrench the baby from her.

"My God!" Blinded by tears, Rachel fought to free herself, from the dream image, the pain, the horror, and from Nathan's grip.

She jerked one elbow free, then the other. Stumbling, she ran toward the exit, but before she got there, the big double doors to the aviary swung open.

A man with clear, fair skin and hair as light as Nathan's was dark stood on the other side. He looked from Rachel to Nathan and back, clearly curious.

"Mikkel," Nathan said. "What is it?"

The man pulled his gaze away from Nathan and looked at Rachel, who was wiping her eyes. "The Wizenot needs you in the kitchen," he told her.

"Me?" she asked.

"It's Jenny Lovell," the man Nathan had called Mikkel said. "She's been beaten and she's hysterical. We can't seem to calm her down."

"Where's Von?" Hiccup. "I just want to see Von!"

Rachel heard the crying before she reached the kitchen. Before she reached the hall that led to the kitchen. Everybody on the north side of Chicago probably heard it.

She was having a hard time getting over what Nathan had told her, but when she finally reached the wide entrance to the room filled with wide expanses of stainless-steel cabinets and granite countertops, the sight that greeted her pushed all other thoughts from her mind.

These guys might have no problem slaying dragons, but they clearly had no clue what to do with a hysterical teenage girl. Eight of them stood around Jenny Lovell, staring at her as if she were a two-headed cow.

Pushing past them, Rachel wrapped an arm around Jenny's trembling shoulders and guided the girl to a wooden chair. "It's okay, honey, everything's going to be all right."

Jenny's black-and-blue eyes widened. "You're the one who was chasing Von. Did you—Is he—"

"He's fine." She tilted Jenny's chin to the light to get a better look at the bruise on her temple and then shot a look at the men standing around doing the helpless two-shoe shuffle on the tile floor instead of doing something constructive. "Get the doctor," she ordered.

"I don't need a doctor," Jenny whined, trying to get up.

Rachel pushed her back down, but gently. Very gently, considering she felt like breaking something—or more accurately, like breaking some*one*. "Who did this to you?"

The girl sniffled, but said nothing.

Rachel glared at the men/monsters around the room. "If one of you—"

"No." The girl sniffled louder. "They didn't do it."

She brushed blond bangs off Jenny's forehead. "Your father?"

She didn't answer, but her expression caved, speaking volumes. Tears began to flow again. "Please. I just need to see Von. Just let me see Von."

"I'm here." Looking even more battered than his girlfriend, Von hobbled across the floor toward Jenny. The orange University of Illinois football jersey he wore swallowed his shoulders, and his navy blue sweatpants sagged on narrow hips. Gone were the ear studs and nose ring.

Funny, but Rachel hadn't noticed how gangly the boy was before. How immature.

This time when Jenny leaped up, there was no holding her back. She vaulted into Von's arms with a thud that had to hurt both of them, in their conditions.

"I'm so sorry," she sobbed. "I didn't mean to tell Daddy where you were hiding. I didn't want to. He—he made me."

"I know. I know," Von murmured in a very un-Von-like tone. "It's okay. I'm okay."

"I thought he killed you."

She hugged him so tightly that he winced, but he didn't let go. Didn't push her away. Everyone in the room suddenly found the ceiling exceedingly interesting to look at as he whispered in her ear and stroked her hair. Eventually the hiccups subsided, and he eased himself away a fraction of an inch.

Defiance gleamed in Von's swollen eyes. "I'm not sending her back to him."

"Von," Teryn started, sympathy in his voice. Calm.

"She's here." The boy jerked his chin toward Rachel, and Rachel suddenly felt like the duck in a game of Duck, Duck, Shoot. Every gaze in the room landed on her.

"Von, that's diff—"

"I heard what happened in Council."

Bewilderment snapped Rachel's chin up. "What happened? What Council?"

Von drew the attention back to center stage. "If she can stay, so can Jen."

Jenny pulled herself against Von's side and looked around the room with Barbie-doll eyes. "You guys, you could make him like, lay off me, right? My father, I mean. Make him leave me alone? Not like, hurt him or anything," she added quickly. "I mean, I hate him, but he is my father." She turned her gaze to the floor. "You guys could do that, couldn't you? Without hurting him? It's what you do, right?"

Tension crackled in the room. Spines stiffened. Jaws hardened.

"Vo-on," Teryn said, drawing the name out into multiple syllables.

Von swallowed and eased Jenny behind him, but she didn't stay there. Apparently living with an abusive father hadn't broken her spirit. The girl still had backbone.

She just didn't have a lot of sense.

"It's okay," she said. "Von told me all about you, all of you. He told me what you guys do. He's shown me what he is."

Nathan's eyes fell closed. One of the other men groaned.

"I'm cool with it," Jenny said. She didn't sound quite as confident now. Probably because the less-than-enthusiastic reaction she was getting had finally sunk in. "Really. I mean, you protect people, right? And Von is so sweet to me. He—he drinks too much sometimes, but he's tryin' to quit. And he's not mean when he's drunk like my dad. He's gentle and caring and—"

Silence. A few glares at Von, whose face—the parts not covered with bruises—reddened.

Jenny's voice started to squeak, but she was still passionate in her convictions. "Von would never hurt me the way my father hurts me and my mother," she said, lifting her chin. "So who is the real monster?"

TWENTY-THREE

It took another hour to get Jenny settled. Nathan stood by, watching as Rachel did the womanly thing: talked the girl down, patted her head and fixed her hair, and told her everything would be okay. Evan showed up, did the doctor thing, clucking as he looked Jenny over and pronounced her injuries superficial, if brutal.

Then they had the argument about what to do with the girl. She couldn't stay here. She was underage, not to mention human, and a female.

But they couldn't send her back to her abusive father, either. She claimed she'd just run away. They couldn't send her out to fend for herself on the street.

Even if they could, she knew about them.

Damn Von, anyway.

Now there were two women with the knowledge to destroy them. Maybe Jenny's memory could be altered, but it was doubtful. The technique worked well enough on fresh memories that covered short periods of time. Jenny, though, had known about them for a while. There was simply too much to erase. The knowledge of *Les Gargouillen* was too deeply rooted in her consciousness.

In the end they'd agreed to let her spend the night nursing Von—under supervision—until they could figure out what else to do.

Nathan pinched the bridge of his nose as Rachel ushered the girl down the hall toward Von's room. "He's too damn young," he muttered.

"Weren't we all, at that age?" Teryn sighed tiredly and pulled his reading glasses out of his pocket. "Well, it's back to work for me."

"Have you found it yet?"

"The passage?" He shook his head, looked around as if to make sure no one was in earshot. "Only vague references. But I've a good bit more reading to do."

"We're running out of time." They'd been exposed. Their long-buried secrets were rising, taking form and shape like mist off the lake on a chilly fall morn.

Teryn gave Nathan a speculative look. "It would go a lot quicker with two sets of eyes. Be just like old times, the two of us rummaging around the vault room at all hours."

Nathan heard the sadness in Teryn's voice. Felt the same yearning for better times in his own gut. The clock couldn't be turned back. What was done couldn't be undone. They both knew that.

But they could pretend, just for a little while.

For an old man's sake.

And for his own.

Rachel paced her narrow prison cell and chewed her thumbnail—a habit she hadn't indulged since she'd been thirteen. Jenny was off hovering over Von, but her words echoed in Rachel's head like a CD stuck on continual replay.

So who's the real monster?

Out of the mouths of babes, indeed.

As a cop, she'd seen plenty of monsters of the human variety. Serial killers, child molesters, rapists.

The . . . people . . . she'd met here bore them no comparison. With the exception of Connor—and she believed

he hadn't meant to physically hurt her—they'd treated her
with kindness and respect. Humanity. They'd taken in
Jenny, whose own father had beaten her, even though her
presence put them at risk.

She'd seen honor among them. Loyalty. Certainly
courage.

She also knew them to be killers and baby-stealers.

Yet they killed only to protect, or so she was told. And
they loved their sons and raised them well, judging from
what she'd seen. They took their boys out of necessity—
even she could see that. To isolate them from the human
populace who wouldn't accept them.

So did that make them more men, or monsters?

Les Gargouillen challenged her preconceptions about the
monsters she'd spent twenty-plus years searching for. Made
her realize that people . . . beings . . . don't always fit neatly
into a category. Human or animal. Man or monster.

Some men were true monsters.

Some monsters were true men.

If one wasn't inherently good, and the other innately
evil, then had she spent her adult life hunting the rabid
wolf only to find herself looking down the barrel at a fuzzy
puppy with a pink tongue and sad, brown eyes?

Could she avenge her parents' deaths at the ruin of an
entire race?

Embroiled in solving the conundrum, the unsolvable
puzzle, she paced, door to window, window to door. Minutes ticked into hours. It would be dawn soon, and still energy brewed inside her. It welled and surged. She needed
to move more than ten steps in one direction and ten back
the way she'd come. She needed air. She needed escape.

From this prison, and from her own doubts.

They'd posted a guard outside her door—they'd have
been foolish not to. Her eyes darted around the thick stone
walls. No way out, there.

The window offered her only chance. She stopped before it, flattened her palm on the cold glass. Seven stories
up. She'd have to be crazy to try it.

•

Or desperate.

Deciding there had to be a way, she opened the latch
and slid the glass up. Cold night air tumbled in, carrying
along traces of oil and exhaust fumes from the city and the
dank scent of the lake.

She leaned outside. A small balcony, just a plank with a
wrought-iron rail for plants and such, hung beneath the
sill, but there was nothing to climb down. No drain spout,
no ivy growing this high on the crumbling stone walls. The
street below was quiet and dark, no one to call for help,
even if she wanted to.

The situation looked hopeless, but it wasn't in her nature to give up. An L train clattered in the distance, and she
took hold of the railing and shook. The rusty wrought iron
rattled in its moorings.

Seven stories, she reminded herself. A long way to fall.
Then you'd best try not to fall.

Drawing in a chilly breath, she crawled onto the windowsill. Another window set beneath hers in the stone
wall, one that looked in on a dark and silent—and, she
hoped, unoccupied—room. Nathan had said most of the
rooms were empty. If she could swing down to it, she
could slip out the unguarded door on the floor below and
make her escape.

She edged one knee onto the warped plank that formed
the base of the balcony, holding firm to the window, ready
to yank herself back in if need be. After a moment she slid
her other leg out, then stood up gingerly, still maintaining
her death grip on the windowsill.

She worried for a moment about Jenny. She should take
the girl with her, but Jenny had made it clear she didn't want
to go. She'd have to send the authorities back for her later.

Assuming Rachel didn't break her neck before she got
to the authorities.

Letting out a long, slow breath, she let go of the window and climbed over the iron rail. Dust spilled from
around the bolts that attached it to the wall, but the platform held.

For a moment.

A small avalanche of crumbling mortar preceded disaster. Wrought iron groaned. Wood splintered, and Rachel suddenly found herself standing on air, then falling.

Instinctively she reached out, grasped a piece of twisted metal still anchored in the wall. When her weight hit the end of her reach, something snapped but the metal brace held, and it took her a moment to realize she wasn't falling.

But she was dangling.

Don't look down.

Of course, she did, and panicked. The ground looked as far away as the face of the moon. She whimpered and kicked—not too hard. She didn't dare kick too hard.

Despite the cold, her hand began to sweat. She slipped an inch down her iron lifeline. She swung her other arm up to clutch the bar in a two-handed grasp.

Think. Think.

The window below. Her toes dangled about a foot below the top, still two feet above another wrought-iron balcony. No way she was jumping. The impact of her landing would snap it off for sure.

She looked up. She had about another foot, maybe eighteen inches, of length on the iron bar she held. Inching carefully to the end, she felt the wall with her toes, searching for a foothold. Feeling nothing but rough stone, she risked a glance down. Still six inches short.

She would have to swing to get her legs in the window. She pushed weakly away from the wall with her elbows. More debris rained in her face.

She stifled a whimper. She hadn't gained enough momentum.

Breathing in tight little gasps and biting her lip, she swung harder. Metal scraped against the stone wall. Dirt and chips of cement blinded her. Her hand slipped and the bar pulled another inch out of the wall, then popped free just as her feet kicked out the glass window below.

She felt herself free-falling for an instant, then her hips hit the windowsill. The impact jolted up her back as she grabbed frantically for the window frame and pulled herself in before she could fall backward.

The adrenaline hit her system once the danger was over. She sat in a heap on the floor of a dark room, glass scattered around her, and fought back tears. That had to be the stupidest thing she'd ever done. And the bravest. But mostly the stupidest.

She shook for a good fifteen seconds, then realizing the noise of her escape must have been heard, and people would be looking for her, she stood on rubbery knees, dusted herself off, checked for cuts. Deciding she wouldn't bleed to death before she found her way outside, she headed for the door.

Her footsteps sounded like gunshots in the quiet hall to her ears. A few dim lights, nightlights, provided enough of a glow to keep her from tripping over the carpet runner that covered the bare wood floor and running into the corner of the table protruding from an alcove.

At an intersection of corridors, she paused. Light angled out of an open room to her left, so she turned right, looking for stairs. She found a door marked EXIT and had one hand on the pull, the other over the hinges, as if her touch could keep them from squeaking, when a high-pitched scream behind her made her heart flip and the hair stand on the back of her neck.

The anguished voice sounded young, much younger than Von or Jenny even. One of the children, and it sounded as if someone were torturing him.

Telling herself she had to go, she pulled the stairwell entrance open and leaned in like a sprinter about to spring from the blocks, but paused. The little boy's wails rose in pitch and decibel.

Gods, what were they doing to him?

Without consciously making the decision, she turned and ran down the hallway toward the din, the soles of her boots slapping on the smooth wood floors, and skidded to a halt when she saw Teryn had gotten there first.

Actually, Teryn had gotten there second. Inside a dimly

lit room identical to the one from which she'd just escaped except for the Chicago Cubs bedspread and the glow-in-the-dark stars and moons pasted to the ceiling, Nathan cradled Patrick, rocking him back and forth, smoothing his hair and cooing in his ear. She couldn't make out the words, but the language sounded foreign. French, maybe.

Rachel froze, watching, entranced at the sight of the tiny child pressed against Nathan's big body. At the gentleness behind each brush of his fingertips on translucent skin. It was a sight deserving of oil and canvas. A master painter.

Father and Son, it would be titled, even if Patrick had called Nathan his "un'ca," and it would draw sighs from every parent and would-be parent who looked upon it. It was a picture of pure magic. Pure love.

The little boy's cries gradually became less frantic. The little fingers bunched in Nathan's shirt relaxed, and still Nathan rocked.

"What happened?" Rachel whispered to Teryn.

"Just a nightmare. Nathan and I had been up talking. We were just checking on the little ones one last time before we turned in when we heard him." He pulled her back a step, away from the doorway. "Nathan has told you about us?"

Suddenly afraid, she hesitated a second before nodding. She had a feeling he was going to dump some more stuff she didn't want to know about monsters on her, and she wasn't sure she could absorb any more.

"In young Patrick's previous life, he died in the Great Chicago Fire. He burned trying to save an elderly woman from her apartment." He gave that a moment to sink in before continuing. "Patrick is at the age where he's beginning to recover memories of that life, but he isn't able to fully understand what happened, or why, yet. He just remembers the flames, and the pain. He dreams of it sometimes."

"My God. To live it over and over. He's just a little boy."

Teryn smiled tightly. "One of the disadvantages of

being reborn again and again. You get to enjoy the good times many times over. But you suffer the tragedies forever, as well." He gave Nathan another long look. "Some of us suffer more than others."

Then he patted her on the shoulder, and walked away.

Rachel stepped up to the doorway, leaned her shoulder against the jamb, and watched Nathan holding the child like precious cargo again, and wondered what tragedies he'd suffered. If he relived the moment he'd flashed into her mind, the screaming woman and child, every night of every life.

Since she'd been a child, she'd felt sorry for herself because she'd lost her parents and dreamed of a great winged beast.

Now she wondered how many loved ones he'd lost, how many women he'd cared for and had to let go.

Someday, maybe she'd have the courage to ask him, but it wouldn't be tonight.

Patrick's eyes finally drifted shut, and Nathan laid him back in his bed and tucked the covers under the little boy's chin. He stepped into the hallway looking more weary than she'd ever seen him. More disturbed.

He still wore the clothes he'd had on earlier in the night. His eyes were bleak and shuttered as they scanned the length of her, lingering at the scuffed knees of her jeans, the cut on the heel of her hand. "What are you doing down here?"

"I was on my way out." No sense lying about it. He'd already seen the evidence.

"Out, how, exactly?"

"Out the window."

His arm jerked up and he dragged a hand through his hair. "Jesus, your room is on the seventh floor."

She shrugged. "It wasn't one of my brighter ideas."

He ran his hand through his hair again, as if he didn't know what else to do with it. She'd never seen him so lost.

She felt his pain, his unease vibrating inside her, and it triggered an inexplicable need to comfort. To hold him and take away his hurt, to bury it in her body. To bury him in her body.

She tried to quash the rise of awareness inside herself and nodded toward Patrick's closed door. "You were good with him."

His eyes darkened. His nostrils flared, and she knew he'd caught the scent of her arousal.

Damn the way their libidos trusted each other, shared with each other, even when the rest of them didn't want to.

Nathan broke eye contact with her. "He's just a little boy."

And you're the monster who holds him when he cries.

"You were still good."

Suddenly she didn't want to leave this place. She wanted to talk. She wanted to understand. Him. His people. This crazy connection they shared.

She needed to know which he was—good or evil.

Man or monster.

She wanted to know why the attraction she felt toward him, the need to be near him so strong it bordered on pain, hadn't gone away even with all she knew.

"I need to talk to you," she said.

She had lots of questions to ask, of him, and of herself. Raising her hand to his cheek, she let the energy arc between them. Let the warmth of her body, her curiosity, her burgeoning desire flow into him, felt his eddy back into her. It was getting easier to control now, this whatever-it-was between them. Easier to give herself over to it.

Images of the two of them together, their slick bodies sliding against each other, flowed into her. She let the mind pictures, the heat of their joining, wash over her, through her, until the current between them stopped abruptly, as if the floodgates had been closed on a dam. Nathan wrapped his fingers around her wrist and lowered her hand.

Her heart withered as he looked over her shoulder at the man charging up behind her, the one who'd been outside her door before her escape.

"There she is," the man said between heaving breaths. "I've been looking all over. She—"

"Take her back to her room." Nathan handed her wrist over to the guard, his eyes hard. "This time keep her there. Nail the damned window shut if you have to."

Then he walked away from her without a backward glance.

Nathan leaned against the doorjamb in Teryn's quarters looking over the text the Wizenot had copied from one of the ancient tomes.

Teryn sipped a cup of lemongrass tea. "You'll tell her what we found?"

"Not tonight."

"She deserves to know."

"She's not ready."

How could anyone ever be ready, he wondered, to learn that their whole life had been a lie?

He shoved his hands in his pockets, shut the image of hurt draining the color from her face when he'd sent her back to her room—alone—from his mind. "You could send Connor to the congregation in New York."

Teryn smiled tiredly. "The two of you really need to stop this feud—"

Nathan cut off the lecture. "Most of the major cities in the U.S. house at least a small congregation of *Les Gargouillen*. New York's is the oldest. And one of the most conservative traditionalist. We might get more answers if someone went in person."

"I'm sure the Wizenot in Syracuse is familiar with the use of the telephone. I've already left him a message." He squeezed Nathan's shoulder. "Besides, I'd like to keep everyone close to home right now."

Nathan frowned. "The visions?"

Teryn hadn't told him exactly what he'd seen, but whatever insight the deities had granted, it troubled the old man. Nathan had never seen him so concerned over a precognition.

"Something is coming. I don't know what, or when, or

whether what I'm doing might stop it or is the catalyst that brings it on, but something is definitely coming."

He squeezed Nathan's shoulder again, and this time his smile didn't look quite so weary. "It's good to have you back, Nathan. We're going to need you soon. I can feel it. I'm going to need you."

"You know I can't stay."

"Can't, or won't?" The first hint of irritation rang in Teryn's voice.

"Can't, on my terms." He started out the doorway. "Won't, on yours."

He left without turning around, not wanting to see the shadow he knew would have fallen over Teryn's hopeful expression. In all the time he'd been away, been excommunicated, nothing had changed between them. He still hurt the old man without even trying.

He always hurt the people he loved most.

Like Rachel.

With the ache inside him spreading cell by cell through his body, Nathan clomped up the stairs to the seventh level, where he paused in the stairwell, leaning his forehead against the cool stone. It was this place, he realized. It brought everything back. Opened the wounds. Made him realize how alone he'd been.

He hadn't wanted to fall in love with her. God knew, he'd tried not to. He still didn't want to *be* in love with her.

His fist joined his forehead against the stone. It was her fault. She'd opened the door to all these emotions, sifting into his mind the way she did.

At least now he knew how she did it.

Lifting his head, he gave the stairs down to his own room one last look, and opened the door to the seventh floor. Outside her room, he sent the guard he'd posted away with a jerk of his head.

She bolted upright, clutching the sheet to her chest when he opened her door without knocking. The bedside lamp was off. Only the glow of the setting moon lit the room, giving her bare shoulders a mercurial sheen.

He closed the door behind him, leaned against it. This time when the connection flared between them, he opened the conduits full bore. He let her feel his frustration. The need that pounded all the blood in his body to one point. Hammered his cock into tempered steel.

Her eyes went wide and luminescent. "I thought you weren't coming." He heard anger mixed with the desire in her throaty growl.

"Did you want me to advertise to everyone in that hallway that I was?" Something else put the growl in his voice.

"No." She eased out of bed one long leg at a time, dropping the sheet.

His throat closed. His heart seized. She looked like a porcelain doll in the moonlight. Fragile. Priceless. And naked.

He crossed the room to her, and she looped her arms around his neck and balanced against him. Her breasts and hips pressed into him, searing impressions of her curves, her shape, on his skin.

"Just like I didn't want them to know that I needed to do more than just talk to you," she said, bringing her lips to his. "A lot more."

TWENTY-FOUR

Rachel closed her lips over the straining cords on the side of Nathan's neck. Her fingers threaded the silk of his hair.

"No mind games tonight," she said, needing to know this was reality, not fantasy. "No dream images."

"No." The word shimmied out of him roughly as she bit down on his neck.

"Just me and you. Here."

"God, yes."

He lifted his hands to her breasts, palmed the mounds, then tweaked her aching nipples into tight buds.

Throwing her head back, she dragged the hem of his shirt over his head, then reached for his belt buckle. He picked her up, pinning them chest to chest with her hands caught between them. She locked her legs around his waist, settling her crotch against the straining fabric of his slacks and the hardness beneath as he carried her to the bed. By the time they reached it, she had his belt undone, his fly down, and his erection in her hand.

She marveled at the length and breadth of him, even harder, even hotter than when she'd held him before. When she tightened her fingers around him, it was like closing a fist over her own heart. His reaction flooded her senses through the connection between their minds. His blood pounded in her ears. His breath stuttered in her chest.

He set her on the edge of the bed and hastily divested himself of his shoes, slacks, and underclothes to stand before her in all his fully aroused glory.

He started to climb onto the bed next to her, but she looked up quickly, pushed him back. "No. Let me look at you. I want to touch you."

She circled his knees with her fingertips, trailed her nails up the back of his thighs, stood, and felt his heavy gluteus muscles contract as she cupped an ass as fine as that on any Greek statue.

His shoulders lifted with each breath. His hands rested on her shoulders, kneading impatiently, but he let her finish her exploration. He gave her the time she needed.

She skimmed her palms up his back, the trail widening as she measured the expanse from trim waist to broad shoulders, then brought her hands to his front and retraced the path down his chest, across his six-pack abs to his groin. Avoiding the staff that called her like lightning to a rod, she cupped the soft sac beneath instead.

"You have a great body," she whispered under his chin. "It's very . . . human."

He tensed as if he'd been poked with a sharp stick. She grabbed him in the one hold a man couldn't break, no matter how strong he was, before he backed away.

"I want to see the other body." Fear and excitement zinged through her. She needed to see the other body, to know all of him. To understand what he was.

She felt a cold river of apprehension pour through his mind, and shivered. She raised and lowered her hand, warming them both, calling him back from the dark place he'd retreated to.

Change for me, she urged without words, using the feelings, images. She felt powerful—hell, invincible—communicating with him this way. She let go of his sex and wrapped her arms around him. With her cheek pressed flat against his navel, she thought the thoughts that would allow her to face her fears once and for all.

Change. Awaken the beast inside.

No.

E Unri almasama. She recalled the rhythm and the texture of the words, even if she didn't know what they meant.

Nathan gasped in pain, and for a moment she thought she'd done something terrible. Hurt him unimaginably.

Then the muscles of his back bunched and expanded beneath her touch. His shoulders broadened. The skin on his back rippled and became velvet fur.

E Unri almasama.

Power rushed through her, through them both. Her mind went native. There was only his powerful body, and hunger. For him.

Calli, Calli, Callio.

Groaning, he dropped to all fours, but lifted his head. "Please," he said, panting and looking up at her through haggard, avian eyes.

She knelt beside him, pulled him up to his knees. "I have to see. I need to see."

"No!" He sounded as if he were dying. "It's too much. You'll—"

Images rushed through her like a cyclone. A dark-haired woman in a print cotton dress that looked like something from the 1940s, holding a baby. Her eyes widening. Screaming.

"Please." The word sounded as if it had been dragged from Nathan's soul. He crouched on the floor, looking up at her, pleading with his mind, but she drove him forward. She took hold of the mind pictures and wouldn't let go. His face twisted in agony. Muscles seized and rippled beneath his furred shoulders.

The woman in his memory backed away, clutching the baby now, horror pouring off her, out of her.

"No," she heard a male voice say in the scene playing

out in her mind. She recognized the presence, the voice as Nathan, and yet not her Nathan, she realized. Nathan in a previous life.

"My God!" the woman cried. "What are you? What kind of monster are you?"

"I'm still the man who loves you. Please, just look at me. It's still *me.*"

The woman turned to run. Her way to the door blocked, she turned for the window, heaved it open, and tried to climb out.

Heavy footsteps chased after her. "Marabella, no! We're ten stories up. The fire escape is not safe!"

"Get away from me. Get away from my baby!"

She lurched out the window. Nathan made a grab for her, struggled with her, finally pried the baby out of her arms.

As Marabella fell.

Gulping for air like a fish out of water, Rachel opened her eyes. The vision dissolved, and she was back in her room at St. Michael's.

Nathan clung to her waist as if she were Marabella on the windowsill. "She couldn't stand it," he mumbled against her stomach. "I tried to tell her what I was, so she would know. So we could stay together, raise our son together. But she couldn't stand me. She chose to die rather than to look at me."

Trying to slow the crazed beating of her heart and his, she stroked his shoulder. "I *want* to see. Change for me, Nathan."

She did need to see. She also realized he needed her to see him. Needed to know she could stand the sight of him.

His back heaved.

She sat on the edge of the bed, lifted his head by the chin, and looked into his strangely shaped eyes. "I'm not her. I'm not Marabella. Change for me."

He paused so long she thought she'd lost. That he wouldn't do it. Couldn't. Then, trembling violently, he laid his head against her chest as if he were too tired to hold it up, pressed a kiss to her breast, and whispered, *"Somara altwunia paximi."*

The cool air of his words brushed over the breast still wet from his kiss and made her shiver with need, but what was happening to Nathan's body set off a quaking much deeper inside.

He easily doubled his weight and mass. His bones popped like a sack of microwave popcorn. He dropped back to all fours and his hands curled, his knuckles bulged into gnarly knots, then rounded and smoothed into razor-edged talons.

Rachel watched, fascinated and horrified, fighting back the demons of her past. She would see this. She'd waited all her life to see this. And it was Nathan. *Nathan.*

He needed her to see this.

He reared up and a triumphant shriek threatened to crumble the mortar between the stones in the old wall. It was a wild call, the call of a predator on the hunt.

As much as she tried to ready herself for the sight, Rachel couldn't help her reaction. He moved too fast. His mind shifted too suddenly. The ordered, disciplined thoughts of the art history professor, the man, were gone. What took their place was untamed. Savage.

She lurched onto the bed, scrabbling backward on her elbows and heels until she hit the wall. He rose up, spread his wings, and screeched again. The cry rang in her ears. Echoed in her soul. She'd heard a cry like that before.

The night her parents died.

Rachel had a beast inside her, too, and its name was terror. It ripped at her guts, set her lungs on fire, used her own heart to try to pound its way out of her, to escape into panic, but she drew her knees to her chest, held it inside. With nowhere to run, she pressed her back against the rough stone wall and stared at Nathan.

Slowly something changed inside her. Terror shrunk until it was more of an annoyance than a threat. The thread that still connected her mind to Nathan's grew broader, stronger. She knew he was behind the change in her. He was helping her see him—not the bizarre half-lion, half-eagle body, but the real him.

She felt his animal nature seep into her. The mating drive still ran hot and furious in his blood. She felt his hunger, and beneath it the capability for violence. The bloodlust.

She also began to feel the deeper emotions, if such a creature could have emotions. She sensed pride. A strong belief in justice. The fierce need to protect the things—the people—he loved.

Loved.

God, was it possible he loved her? And if he did, was it the man or the beast who felt that way? Was the beast even capable of such a complex emotion as love?

She pulled herself forward an inch, then another, edged toward the side of the bed and studied the powerful body in front of her. "You could kill me with the flick of a talon, couldn't you? Break my neck with a single swipe. You always could have."

He reached out, but not to lay her open with his claws, to crush her bones. But to very carefully, very gently, tuck a strand of hair behind her ear.

"Oh, God, Nathan." She threw herself at him. "Oh, God."

All Nathan could do was suck up a breath and take the hit when she launched herself at him. When she burrowed her fingers into the soft feathers of his neck, massaged the cartilage and sinew that connected his wings to his back.

He'd already been in a state of nearly unbearable readiness before the Awakening. Now his pulse screamed through his veins. Mating fever threatened to consume him.

It was hard enough for one of *Les Gargouillen* to control their baser instincts in human form, but as the griffin, a beast in every way, the urge to mate drove him savagely. Pushed him to the point of madness.

Worse, it wasn't just the magic driving him to take her. He could resist that. It was his human side.

He cared about her, not as an object to provide sexual relief, or to bear a child, but as a life companion. A lover in all senses of the word, physical and emotional.

She ran her hands everywhere, sending him flying without his feet—paws or claws—leaving the ground.

He whipped his lion's tail on the floor like the agitated cat he was, warning her, but dared do no more. He couldn't touch her, for fear he would cut her. Couldn't hold her for fear he would crush her. But when she finished her perusal and turned her face to him, and he saw something in her eyes that he hadn't seen in a woman for fourteen lifetimes—acceptance—he could stand the torture no longer.

He was already pushing her back on the bed, cupping her head to protect her as she fell, and coming down on top of her even as he shifted back to human form. There was still enough of the beast awake inside him that he nipped roughly at her throat, her lips, her cheeks. Just enough of the man that when he guided his erection to her hot, slick folds, he held himself back to give her time to adjust. To use his fingers to prepare her.

He gave her time to accept this, too, before easing himself all the way home.

Home.

Nathan felt like he belonged inside her. Like he'd always been inside her. They were a perfect fit, sex to sex, hip to hip, chest to chest. Lips to lips.

This time he kissed her with more finesse. Her hands came up to cup his face, and he took them in his and raised them over her head, their fingers linked, while his tongue danced along the seam of her mouth. Her lips parted and took him inside the same way she'd taken him in below.

He pushed an inch deeper. Her head thrashed to the side. She gulped down a needy breath. "More. I want more. All of it."

He pulled back until her moist heat encased just the tip

of him, checked to make sure the last of the beast lay sleeping inside him, and then gave her what she asked for.

She surged up to meet him, her mouth open, rounded, her eyes blind. He curled an arm behind her for support, and held himself still for what seemed like eons, but no one, man or beast, could have held out forever, not with Rachel Vandermere draped over his arm like a broken doll, her arms flung to the sides and her breasts jutting up, nipples stiff and puckered like berries just ripe for tasting. He circled one with his tongue, pulled his hips back, and thrust, grunting with the effort of going slow.

She ground her hips against him and moaned, but it seemed to be a sound of frustration rather than pain, so he pulled back, pushed forward again. Her inner walls glided over the sensitive head of his cock, gripped the shaft in exquisite torment. When she locked her legs behind him and pulled him deeper, it was his turn to moan.

He'd spent so long avoiding this, so long fighting it, and now look at him. He couldn't get enough. Couldn't get deep enough. Couldn't plunge fast enough or far enough.

Her mind was as open to him as her body, and still he wanted more. He didn't want to just take, he wanted to share. So he opened some of the locked doors in his mind, too. Images drifted between them, not fake settings or memories, meant to deceive, but pictures of their lives.

She showed him a dance recital. She'd been twelve and awkward, tall for her age. She'd fallen in the middle of her routine, and her teacher had taken her out for chili dogs afterward. He showed her a Moorish pony he'd ridden as a boy in 1640. He'd loved that horse.

They dodged around the difficult times, concentrated on the happy, the funny, and ended up smiling in a kiss and gasping for breath at the same time. Near the edge, Nathan rolled, taking her with him, raised his knees to support her back. "You ride, now," he ground out. "I'll be your pony."

"More like a bull moose," she panted. "Not that I'm complaining."

"No, Stephen is the moose, at least in Gargoyle form.

You haven't met him yet, and after that comment, I'll make sure you don't."

She paused for a second, hanging above him, and a laugh bubbled out of her, but it was a weak one. They were both too lost in the passion for laughter. Besides that, they were breathing too hard. Neither of them had enough air to laugh.

Nathan pushed the pictures out of his mind and focused on the feelings, his and hers. There was no trace of fear in her now, only joy and need. She was nearly as frantic for completion as he was. Every nerve sang. Her skin nearly crawled with need. Her heartbeat crashed like thunder and her blood roared like a swollen river, the current headed south, to the throbbing spot between her legs.

He squeezed a hand between them, lubricated his fingers with her moisture, and circled her clit. She tossed her head back. Her golden hair showered over his knees. Her fingers dug into his thighs.

"Oh, Nathan!" she cried.

He circled, circled the point above where their bodies slipped and crashed together, until he felt a vibration rumble through her, felt her muscles quiver, and then he pressed his thumb against her and held it.

"Oh. Oh, Nathan!"

Her muscles clamped down on him, contracted like a fist, released and contracted again. Wave after wave shuddered through her, into him. He held her until the last ripple faded, then rolled her to her back, jerked his hips two times, three, pushed himself in as far as he could go while she rested her head on his shoulder, boneless and still shaking, and let himself go.

A guttural roar rumbling out of him, he poured himself into her, not daring to think about the consequences, not yet, and then collapsed, barely managing to slide enough to the side to allow her to breathe.

"Rachel," he whispered, a prayer and a plea, and kissed the sweet underside of her breast, not so done in that he couldn't be fascinated by a full female breast two inches

from his face. "Damn, Rachel." The consequences were
creeping up on him. So much was still unsettled. "What am
I gonna do with you now?"

She didn't answer; she was already asleep.

It was dark. Daddy forgot to leave her bedroom door
open a crack so the hall light could get in. He never forgot.
Then Rachel remembered: She wasn't in her bedroom. She
was in the cupboard under the stairs. Mommy had given
her Levi to hold, and he was squirmy. She hoped he didn't
fuss. Mommy had told them to be quiet, but Levi was just
a baby. He didn't understand things like that.

Angry voices shouted outside, people pounded on the
door, they said bad things. Bad words. Mommy told Daddy
they had to leave; he said it was too late.

Rachel didn't understand why they'd put her in the cupboard. Why they'd left her with Levi to take care of, when
she didn't know how to take care of babies. She hadn't
even been able to take care of Mr. Mott, her stuffed bunny.
She'd cut off his ear with the sewing scissors last summer.
What if she cut off Levi's ear?

Tears dripped down her cheeks onto her pink nightgown. She felt them soak through, and even though they
were hot, they made her shiver.

She opened the cupboard door just a little. She needed
the light; she was afraid of the dark.

The mean voices were inside the house now. Shadows
splotched the living room wall she could see. One of the
bad men fought her dad. They fell, grunting and punching,
then there was a big bang and a terrible screech. The bad
man stood up, only he wasn't a man anymore. He was a
monster, with big wings and terrible, terrible claws. The
monster shadow killed the other shadow, her Daddy's
shadow, and then flew across the room.

She sat as still as she could and held Levi and prayed it
wouldn't find her. She sat a long time, until the smoke
made her cough. Finally she had to crawl out. Her eyes wa-

tered; she couldn't see. The smoke choked her; she couldn't breathe.

She clutched Levi, who was crying by then, his little face pinched and red, to her chest and ran. "Mommy? Daddy?"

The floor was hot underneath her feet. The heat from the flames burned her skin. She tripped and looked down to see her Daddy on the floor. He had blood on his face and his chest. It puddled underneath his shoulders. His eyes stared up at her lifelessly.

Screaming, she ran for the door, but she couldn't get through the fire so she went to the bay window and pounded on the glass until it shattered.

She had to get away before the monster got her.

Nathan ambled down the hallway toward the little room where he'd left Rachel sleeping, his hands in his pockets and his mind on what he and Teryn had learned from the Wizenot in Syracuse, and how he would tell her. If he should tell her.

The first scream yanked him out of his reverie like a hooked trout hauled out of the water on a fisherman's single mighty heave. He ran the last few feet to her room and threw the door open so hard it nearly came off its hinges.

She stood at the window, clutching a pillow to her chest with one hand and pounding on the glass with the other. He had no idea what she was doing, or why, but he knew he had to stop her before she hurt herself.

When he grabbed her, turned her, he understood. Her eyes were glazed, seeing, but not him. Not the room, or the cold winter sun that had risen while he'd been talking to Teryn. She continued to pound his chest as if it were the window.

"Have to get out," she chanted in a child's voice, caught in the nightmare of her past. "Fire. Have to get Levi out. Mommy? Daddy? *Daaa-deeeee?*"

He pulled her to him roughly, pinned her arms to her

sides, the pillow she'd held so gingerly flattened between them, and murmured in her hair the way he'd murmured to Patrick just hours ago. He ran his palms up and down her arms, soothing away the goose bumps, his and hers. "It's okay. You're okay. It was just a dream. You're okay."

After a few moments her sobs died. Her legs were still quaking, so he led her to the bed, sat her down, and pulled the comforter over her shoulders, tucked it in at her sides. He gave himself a moment to regret covering up such a beautiful body, but her skin was cold, as bump-covered as a frozen turkey. She needed to be warm. She didn't need him jumping her bones.

Yet.

He rubbed her hand, waited for her to come back to him.

"Feel better?" he asked when her eyes finally focused and she heaved out a gusty sigh.

"I—" She clutched the blanket tighter. "I had a nightmare."

"I noticed. Want to tell me about it?" He sat down next to her, pulled her close. Thankfully, she didn't push him away.

"It was the night my parents died."

"I figured."

"I guess all this"—she shrugged—"brought it back."

His fists clenched in the blanket at her sides, cursing himself for the pain he'd caused her. And the pain he was about to cause her. "Me, you mean. *I* brought it back."

She looked at her hands, sniffed back tears. All except one. That one left a shiny trail down her cheek and plopped onto the blanket. "You can't help what you are. You didn't choose it. You've lived with it the best way you can. I understand that now, really I do."

"But?"

She had the grace to look at him when she said goodbye, at least. "But I can't stay with you. I can't live with you. It hurts too much."

She stood, swirling the blanket around him as she pulled out of his grasp.

Growing up Gargoyle, Nathan hadn't known much fear in his life, not really. He'd had his powers to rely on. The beast. He'd had his congregation. He'd known pain and he'd known rage.

But not fear. Not until now.

Rachel was leaving him, and he was terrified he wouldn't be able to stop her. He could think of only one thing that might stop her.

Bile soured his stomach.

He had to tell her. Now, before it was too late.

Before he lost her.

"I didn't kill your father." He watched her reaction carefully, sick with the knowledge that he was about to shatter the memory of everything she held dear. "None—"

"I know you didn't do it," she cut in. "That . . . that one is probably long gone, but it's still too much. The memories are too raw."

"You didn't let me finish. I didn't kill your father," he repeated, *"and none of our kind did."*

She stiffened, confusion carving brackets beside her eyes, around her frown. "I saw it! I was just a kid, but I saw the thing that murdered my mother and father. Are you calling me a liar, or just telling me I'm delusional?"

"Shhh." Nathan got up and stood behind her, put his arms around her, though it was like holding a concrete pillar, she was so stiff. "You're not a liar and you're not crazy. You saw two shadows fall, two men. You couldn't tell which was which. One got up, only it wasn't a man anymore, it was a"—the word stuck on his tongue—"a monster."

He turned her around and opened his mind fully, hoping it would help if she could see the truth in his eyes, in his thoughts, as well as hear it from his mouth.

"The monster didn't kill your father, honey. The monster *was* your father."

TWENTY-FIVE

"No!" Rachel's father hadn't been a monster. He'd been a kind, loving man, and . . . and . . . a hardworking carpenter, a craftsman who always strove to improve his skills, though he never put work above his family. He'd been the most *human* person she'd ever known. She wouldn't have his memory desecrated. "You're wrong. You're wrong about him."

"It's the truth, Rachel. Look inside, remember that night, all of it, and you'll see."

"No!" She didn't want to remember that night. Didn't want to relive the nightmare, but even trying to shut out the memory, she heard the *whump, whump* of enormous wings, heard the monster's eerie cry.

Her throat closed and she coughed like she'd coughed on the acrid smoke, only it was her own words choking her. "No. No, you're wrong. Oh, God. You have to be wrong."

"I spoke to the Wizenot in Syracuse myself. Your father was one of us. *Les Gargouillen.*"

"He would have told me. I would have known if my own father wasn't human."

"Maybe he would have told you eventually. Maybe he

thought you were too young. Or maybe he never wanted you to find out. I don't know. I just know it's true. It makes sense."

"Makes sense?" Her voice rose to a grating shrill. She tried to pull out of his grasp, but Nathan held tight to her elbows. "How does my father being some godforsaken miscreant beast make sense?"

He blanched at her words, rocked back as if she'd taken a swing at him, and she realized Nathan was one of those miscreant beasts. Nathan, who'd made love to her with his beautiful body and his more beautiful mind.

Nathan shook her shoulders lightly. "You told me you heard a whistle in the condemned tenement the night we found Von and Jenny. That's the *Calling*, the way we let each other know when we need help, and it's well above the hearing range of humans."

"I have excellent hearing. I—"

"You heard Von calling for help from the train platform. Then, when you were in trouble, you didn't just hear it, you made it. You called *me,* honey."

"No!"

"Accept it. You know it's true."

She turned away. "But we were a family. They were married. You said Gargoyle's took their children . . . took their male children, and . . . and—"

An ugly possibility tried to invade her mind, but she pushed it out.

Until Nathan spoke what she hadn't allowed herself to think. "Your brother was just a baby. Maybe your father would have left your mother and you, taken him and returned to the congregation eventually."

Rachel felt like someone had stuck a fist into the center of her heart.

"Or maybe he'd broken with tradition. Maybe he was as tired of the lies and the grief as I am. Maybe he wanted to stay with you, and love you, forever." Nathan's voice gentled. His big, warm hands cupped her shoulders. "Like I want to."

It was too much. She couldn't absorb it all. Couldn't process it. Couldn't believe it.

Wouldn't let herself believe it.

Eyes wide, shaking her head in a soundless no, she backed away, ran for the tiny bathroom, and slammed the door behind her.

Nathan figured he'd give her five minutes to pull herself together before he went in after her, even if they would be five of the longest minutes of his life.

Her sorrow, her suffering radiated out of the 8 x 12 room like the shock waves of a nuclear blast. He tried to send back waves of calm, ripples of reassurance, but she'd shielded her mind.

Terrific. Now she'd figured out how to shield, as well.

Which left him standing there feeling every bit of the agony she felt, plus his own, and not able to do a damn thing to take the pain away.

Screw the five minutes; he was going in.

The drum of the shower drowned out his low, "Rachel?"

Steam banked and rolled across the narrow vanity, fogged the mirror. On the other side of the beveled-glass shower door, he could just make out her creamy shape. She leaned on the front wall, her palms flat against the tile, head hanging between her shoulders.

"Rachel?"

A sniff and a stifled cry were his only answer, barely audible beneath the sluice of water.

Without a word he peeled off his clothes, opened the door, and stepped in behind her. Her thin frame shook soundlessly as he ran his hands up either side of her spine, gathered her hair and lay the sopping ponytail over her shoulder, wrapped his arms around her waist, and pulled them together until the ivory curve of her butt nestled against his groin.

"You looked so familiar to me," she finally said. "From the moment I saw you, you were familiar."

"I thought the same about you."

"Not just physically, but everything about you. I knew when you were upset, when you were going to smile. I knew how much you loved this place."

"You were sensing my mind. We were connecting even before we realized it." Holding her against him with one hand, he lowered the other to the triangle of curls between her legs, parted the slick folds, and eased his middle finger inside her.

Within seconds the shower water wasn't the only lubricant easing his passage. Despite everything, she still wanted him, and that was his miracle for this day. This lifetime.

"You touched my mind," he told her, easing his finger in and out. "It's why I first suspected you were different. Humans shouldn't be able to do the things you and I have done. With our minds."

She swayed against him. "You said female children of Gargoyles were just plain humans. They weren't born really Gargoyles."

"They haven't been for centuries. But we've passed down old manuscripts that document the history of *Les Gargouillen* since our beginning. I remembered reading a passage once that alluded to some of the early females showing abilities from time to time. Teryn and I found the text again last night. Apparently the magic that created us runs stronger in the older souls than the newer ones."

"New souls?"

He shrugged. "Our numbers grew dramatically for several hundred years. There were only thirty-eight men in Rouen. As we continued to produce sons, new souls were created. Or at least the souls of the boys born to us became *Les Gargouillen* instead of human."

He slid the hand around her waist up to her breasts, cupped and measured them, then laid his palm flat between them as if he could quiet her fluttering heart. "Your father was one of the Old Ones, the original townsmen of Rouen."

With his thumb he rubbed the nub of flesh above the point where his finger glided in and out of her body. "Open your mind and let me show you. I can help you understand what it means to be a Gargoyle."

A sob tore out of her. "My father wasn't a . . . He wasn't like you."

Hope plummeting like deadweight in his chest, he dropped a sad kiss on each vertebrae down her back. She could accept him being a Gargoyle, but the nature of the beast was too ugly, too savage and primitive to associate with her saintly father.

What had he expected? That she'd believe his tale of pagans and dragons and rituals of magic, that she'd accept what she was, though she'd spent a lifetime believing otherwise, hating what he was, and move on?

That they'd live happily ever after?

He was a fool. She would never be his. Not entirely.

But he wasn't enough of a fool to give up the one part of her he had: her passion. Her body.

Her mind was still closed to him, but her body was wide open. She arched her back, pushed her buttocks against the erection nestled between her ass cheeks, and rode his hand, her breath coming faster and sharper, but it wasn't enough for her. He knew it wasn't enough.

"God, I feel so empty." Panting, she tossed her head back, let the spray hit her full in the face. "Like everything inside me leaked out and swirled down the drain." She gyrated against him, nearly sending him over the edge right there.

"Fill me up," she pleaded. "Fill me up to the hilt. I don't want to be empty anymore."

From behind, he thought. She wanted him to take her from behind like the animal she knew him to be.

So she wouldn't have to look at him.

And he wasn't enough of a man to refuse.

• • •

Rachel had known since she was six that something was missing from her life. She'd thought it was parents she lacked. Growing up in the security of a family home. A mother and father to usher her into adulthood, give her advice, nag about calling more often, and remind her to keep at least a half tank of gas in her car in case of emergency.

Now she realized how wrong she'd been.

She'd long since grown past the need for advice, a sympathetic voice on the other end of the phone, or even a place to come home to when life got rough.

This was what she needed: a man to stand with her, to fill the dark hollows and empty places inside her. To pull her from the grasp of nightmares and make her feel whole.

A man to chase away the shadows.

She'd thought Nathan was that man; she wanted him to be that man.

Except he wasn't a man at all, was he?

He felt like a man inside her, stretching her, pushing deeper into her than she'd believed possible. Driving her inexorably up the pleasure peak.

She was willing to pretend he was a man, just for a few minutes, to reach the oblivion of release. To hide from the possibilities he'd waved before her, the doubts in her own mind.

As long as she didn't have to look at him, to see the dark shock of hair that fell over his forehead, ruining his otherwise impeccable look, the dark eyes that saw so much more than what the rest of the world saw, she could pretend he was a man.

And for that, she was ashamed.

The water had cooled to tepid. She realized Nathan had bent over her, warming and shielding her, and the simple gesture tore at her pride. Ruined her self-respect.

Bracing one hand against his hip, she stepped forward, away from him, and shut the water off, then slowly turned and lifted her gaze to his face.

His own self-respect was more than a little worn, by the looks of him.

She'd done that, she realized. She'd hurt him, and he loved her anyway.

Afraid he'd change his mind now and push her away, she eased her arms around his neck and pulled herself up to stand nose to nose with him. She sucked in a breath when the hair on his chest razed her nipples. He gasped when his erection pressed against her belly.

"I think I'd like to finish it this way," she said, and reached up to smooth the harsh lines of regret from his face.

He captured her hand and kissed, then suckled each fingertip. "I can live with that."

He lifted her, pinned her against the cool tile, and surged into her again. And again. She threw herself back at him, using the wall for leverage. Their bodies slapped and slid and sucked. Their mouths devoured. Their hands mapped every nook and cranny of each others' bodies, found every erogenous zone, tweaked every jumping nerve as if they knew this would be their last time together.

The certainty of that crashed down on Rachel at the same time as a stupendous orgasm. The barrier she'd constructed around her mind crumbled and Nathan was there, all around her, inside her, and she was inside him. She couldn't stop it, didn't want to stop it. All she could do was dig her fingers into the heavy muscle of his back, bury her head against his shoulder, and try not to let him see her tears as she came. "Nathan!"

His name was still ringing in her ears when his back stiffened. His hips bucked once, twice more, heaving himself as far inside her as he could possibly get.

"Ah, god. I'm coming apart." His arms tightened around her until she could hardly breathe. "I can't—"

Whatever else he'd meant to say was lost in a gurgle, then a groan, as he came inside her in three long, shuddering spurts. She held his body while his consciousness drifted somewhere beyond her reach.

When his arms finally loosened around her and his breath evened out, she unwrapped herself from him and stood on her own rubbery legs.

He lifted his head and stared at her knowingly. He'd been in her mind. He knew everything she knew. "You're still leaving."

She resisted the urge to cross her arms over her chest even though she was cold. "I have to."

His brows drew together furiously. He pulled out of her, backed up until his shoulders rattled the glass door. "So this was a good-bye fuck? You could have just sent a card."

She shoved past him and into the bathroom.

He followed. "Did it ever occur to you that we might not let you leave? You know too much."

Snatching her clothes from the vanity, she pulled on her bikini-cut underwear and kicked her legs into her pants as she walked. "What are you going to do, lock me away in your tower here for the rest of my life? Or just kill me and be done with it?"

He blocked her march toward the door with his naked, dripping body. His very angry, naked, dripping body. "*Les Gargouillen* don't kill innocent people."

She sighed. Forced herself to unclench her fingers, touch his shoulder, and speak softly. "I know that. With all my heart I trust that you won't hurt me, Nathan." She pulled her shirt on, flipped her hair from beneath the collar, and wrung out the last of the chilled water with a nonchalance that was pure charade. "Which is why I know you won't stop me."

Check and mate.

She winced as she pushed past him.

Poor choice of words.

TWENTY-SIX

Rachel clomped down the stairs toward the ground
floor with Nathan on her heels.

He stumbled, stubbing a toe, and swore. "You want to
leave. Fine. Go anywhere you want. Just know that I'll be
right on your heels every step of the way."

"And if I said I don't want you on my heels?" She
glanced over her shoulder at him.

He smiled like a hungry wolf. "I'd ask what made you
think you had a choice."

Rachel frowned, figuring out what he was up to. She'd
guessed right when she'd said he couldn't stop her from
leaving, so he was doing what came natural to every male
on the planet when outwitted by a woman.

He bullied her.

Only Rachel Vandermere wouldn't be bullied.

She looked back at him as she turned the corner at
the bottom of the stairs. He'd thrown on a pair of jeans,
but hadn't taken the time to button them. His feet were
bare and he was tucking the tails of his shirt—very gingerly—into the front of his pants. If the man wasn't in
love with her, he was at least in lust. He'd watched her

dress with heavy-lidded eyes, and was already aroused again.

She clucked. "You might not want to follow so close with that thing sticking out in front of you. I'm liable to slam it in the first door you try to follow me through."

He curled his lip at her in response.

Too late, she realized she should have been watching where she was going instead of ogling the impressive specimen of manhood trying to break free of the captivity of Nathan's worn denim jeans.

She ran smack into Teryn, who grabbed her and just managed to keep her from taking a header down the next flight of stairs.

Heat leaped to her face in a nearly audible *whoosh* as she realized he had to have heard her taunting Nathan, but he made no comment. He frowned as if he had something more important on his mind. Something alarming.

"Come with me," he said. "Both of you."

He led them downward at an urgent clip.

Nathan nudged Rachel in the back, prodding her to keep up. "What is it?" he asked. "What's wrong?"

"Jenny Lovell's father is out front, looking for his daughter. He's carrying a baseball bat and making a scene." Without slowing a step, Teryn threw a look over his shoulder that had Rachel's stomach bouncing off the floor of her abdomen. "Him and about a dozen of his knuckle-dragging friends."

"Have you called the police?" she asked.

"I'd prefer not to draw that kind of attention."

Nathan nodded. "Cops show up and see her face, Daddy Dearest is going to blame the damage on us. I can't see him copping to hammering on his daughter in front of all his beer buddies."

"Jenny would tell them the truth," she argued.

"She's seventeen—jail bait, by the way, should her father try to make something of the fact that she spent the night in a school full of men and boys. Even if she tried to defend us, he'd just claim we threatened her or brainwashed her somehow."

"I'm a cop. They'll believe me."

Nathan smiled sardonically. "Yeah, especially when you tell them you were kidnapped by a monster and held here against your will."

Sucker-punched. Damn if the man hadn't suckerpunched her again. "I was thinking about leaving that part out, but now that you mention it—"

Teryn dragged a hand through his silver hair in a motion that looked so much like Nathan that her stomach pinched. "We don't have time for this."

She grabbed his sleeve. "You can't turn Jenny over to him. Not after what he did to her!"

He blew out a frustrated sigh. "I don't plan to. But I've got to tell him something before someone gets hurt out there. If I can reason with him—"

"Huh." Nathan snorted. "You might want to find yourself some body armor first, if that's your strategy."

"I have to try. I have no choice."

They met Connor and Mikkel on the first floor and turned as a unit toward the vestibule. The men on either side of the front entrance swung the double oak doors open on their approach.

The sight outside was straight out of *Frankenstein*—the villagers storming the castle.

Teryn stepped purposely out onto the polished granite stairs, his head high, his back straight. All wearing matching fierce expressions, Connor, Mikkel, and Nathan stood up shoulder-to-shoulder at his back.

Hanging off to the side just long enough to pull in one long, fortifying breath, Rachel joined them.

What the hell. Given how she'd felt about monsters at the time, she'd always cheered for the villagers when she'd watched the old black-and-white flick, but somehow a lynch mob didn't seem so heroic in real life.

Lovell raised his bat, pointed at them with the wide end.

"That's her. That's the bitch and her boyfriend that took my daughter.

A cold winter wind whipped Teryn's hair on end. He raised his hands, palms out. "Let's all calm down, here. No one took your daughter, Mr. Lovell."

"You telling me she's not in there? You tellin' me you're not hiding her, you and that freak boy that's been nosing around her?"

People from the neighborhood and passersby began to gather on the fringes of Lovell's crowd. "Freaks," a man in a poorly tailored business suit yelled. "I heard they're all freaks that live here."

Teryn ignored them, focused on Jenny's father. "If you'd just put the bat down, we could talk about this."

"I didn't come here to talk, old man. I came to get my daughter. Bring the little whore down here, or I'm going up to get her." Lovell slapped the bat in the palm of his hand.

"This is a school, Mr. Lovell," Teryn said in his headmaster's voice. "I won't have you prowling the halls and frightening my students."

"Just what kind of school are you running here, mister?" a man carrying a metal lunchbox and wearing repairman's coveralls shouted. "My wife cleans up in that office building across the way. I heard her tell of strange things going on on top of that tower over there all hours of the night."

Teryn's posture changed subtly. Most people wouldn't have noticed the rocking back on his heels, the curling of his fingers, but Rachel was a cop. She was trained to watch people's behavior. What they did usually meant more than what they said, and if she'd been in an interview room with a suspect, she would have known she was about to be lied to.

Teryn had plenty of reasons to lie, given he was the leader of a secret society, but what was so secret about the tower?

"I keep birds on the roof," he said. "Just pigeons. I care for them at night, after the children have gone to bed."

A man with a dirty blond beard stepped to the front of the crowd that was quickly becoming a mob. "How come we don't never see these *children* outside, playing or nothing? Where are all these kids that supposedly go to school here?"

"We have an indoor gymnasium. We prefer to keep our boys off the street."

The man turned to the gathering behind him. "I'm telling you, something ain't right about this place."

"Ain't nothing right about this place."

"Always thought it was strange, boys living in a school like that. Where's their mommas?"

The mass of people surged forward over the bottom step.

"What're you doing to them boys in there?"

Lovell led them halfway to the entrance. His face was puffy and red. "What're you doing to my daughter? Git her out here!"

A brick crashed through the stained glass window to the left of the main doors. Several people bent to the ground, presumably searching for their own missiles.

"Get her out!" someone demanded.

"Get 'em all out!"

"Freaks!"

Rachel stepped up to Teryn's side, pulled her identification out of her pocket, and flipped it open. "That's far enough."

The crowd settled, fell silent. Expectant.

Lovell sneered at her. "Aw, what's that? A toy badge?"

"Interpol," she said, meeting his eyes dead square. His gaze looked glassy, hollow. Like the lights were on, but nobody was home, as the saying went. She wouldn't have pegged him as a drug user, but he certainly didn't look like a man in full control of his faculties.

"You don't have any jurisdiction here," he said.

"No, but I have friends who do," she lied. She didn't know a soul on the Chicago PD except the couple of detectives who had worked the museum gala, and she didn't know them well. "You take one more step, I'll have so many charges piled on you, you won't be able to see over the stack of paper it's going to take just to write them all down."

He checked back over his shoulder to see if his supporters were still behind him. Or to make sure his audience was listening. "Well, then, at least I won't have to worry about having something to *wipe my ass* with for a long time."

Laughter rumbled up behind him, then more jeers toward the school. The horde swelled, took on a life of its own. Lovell swung his bat, shattering one of the ceramic planters lining the steps and ground the little holly bush it once held into the marble with the heel of his boot. The man next to him pulverized the wrought-iron handrail.

Teryn backed through the doorway, motioning the others inside, and bolted the door behind him. He sagged against the carved oak panel. "Mikkel, call the police."

"But Wise One—"

"Do it."

Mikkel spun on his heel and marched off.

Rachel jolted when a second stained-glass window burst in an explosion of brightly colored shards.

Nathan pulled her farther away from the windows. "If they find Jenny here, we're liable to be wearing handcuffs before anyone asks for our side of the story."

The oak doors shuddered, but held. Rachel shuddered to think what had been thrown against them.

Teryn took her by the shoulders. "You've got to take Jenny and get out of here. There's a tunnel that leads beneath the gates in back, comes out in the alley. Connor, you'll show her."

"I'll show her," Nathan said, scowling.

"No. I want you to take a couple of men and have them gather the children. Take them up into the towers, and then come back. I need you here. With me."

Connor didn't look happy about being sent away, but Rachel didn't have time to wonder about it.

She swiveled her gaze between the three men, her pulse leaping like a deer over fallen logs. "Where am I supposed to go? What do I do with her?"

Teryn turned her toward the back of the school. "Take her to the hospital. Child protective services. It doesn't matter. Just get the girl and go."

"The girl is already here."

"And she isn't going anywhere without me."

Jenny and Von stepped out of the doorway that led to the dining area. Between them, their faces sported more colors than a pair of peacocks in full plumage. Von still curved an arm protectively over his ribs, but he looked steady enough on his feet.

Teryn looked at Nathan, who nodded, then nudged Rachel toward Connor. "Take them both. Go."

Hardly ten minutes had passed since Rachel had left, and already Nathan wondered where she was.

If he would ever see her again.

It was ironic. He'd finally found a woman who could accept what he was, and he'd lost her.

Because she couldn't accept what *she* was.

Teryn lifted the blind on the window in his office and looked at the mayhem outside. The air crackled with the promise of violence. He could almost smell the blood in the air already.

"This isn't a natural madness. Some magic feeds their frenzy. Drives them like draft horses under the lash."

"Who? Or what?"

"I don't know, but he must have great power to turn even our friends and neighbors against us. We lived peacefully next to some of those people for decades."

"I saw Mrs. Millan from the dry cleaners throw a stone. Didn't you sit with her grandchildren last year when her husband had his heart surgery?"

"It's not her fault. Her mind isn't her own. Evil stands at our doorstep now. Soon it will find its way inside."

Not if Nathan could help it. Not with innocent children upstairs, and the only family he'd ever sworn to protect. "Is this what you saw in the visions?"

"This. And more."

As if this wasn't bad enough. Nathan paced, too sickened by what he saw to look out the window any longer. Unable to break in the doors, they'd taken to bashing the cars parked on the street. The cries of the mob rose and fell like an unholy symphony. "Where the hell are the police?"

"On more important business, I'm sure," Teryn said. "At the doughnut shop. You know I refuse to make the *donation* our local precinct asks for each year."

Another window broke, and this time someone in the hall outside Teryn's office screamed. "Molotov cocktail! Fire!"

Teryn's eyelids drifted shut. "And so it begins."

TWENTY-SEVEN

*Connor felt his way along the slimy wall of the tun-*nel that led under the back gates of St. Michael's. The single bare bulb that should have lit the way was burned out. The darkness reeked of mildew and rat feces. He didn't even want to think about what the goo he'd stepped in might have been.

The trio of deserters shuffled along behind him.

Why the hell had Teryn anointed him to play guide dog for two humans and a juvenile delinquent Gargoyle while a crazed mob threatened his school, his home?

Because Nathan Cross was back, that's why.

The toe of Connor's shoe hit something solid. "Stairs," he warned the group behind him.

Thank god. Almost out of this stink hole. He counted ten steps, then felt for the padlock that secured the door and fingered the keyhole until he figured out which way the key went. The lock snicked open. The door swung outward. Light flooded in, making him squint and those behind him lift their forearms to shield their eyes while they stumbled out of the passage like mummies from a tomb.

Connor dragged in a deep breath. Even the exhaust

fumes and rotting garbage at street level smelled better than the dank air in the tunnel.

Rachel stared over his shoulder at the rear of St. Michael's. "I don't hear any sirens."

He listened. Only the occasional shout or crash of something breaking was audible.

"Maybe I should stay," she said. "You might need help."

"Teryn wants you gone. You're going." No way was he messing up on a simple assignment to dump some excess baggage. One of these days Teryn would come to his senses and realize he was the best choice to succeed him as Wizenot. One of these days Cross would go too far. Betray the congregation one too many times.

Besides, he wanted the woman gone himself. Nathan would have no reason to stay without her.

He shoved some money in her hand, turned her by the shoulders, and physically pushed her down the alley. "Go."

Rachel clenched the bills in her fist. "Aren't you coming?"

"Like you said, they might need help."

He watched them until they were out of sight, then turned back to the school. The mortar between the old stones was crumbling in places. The steeple in the central cathedral needed a good cleaning. But the grounds were neat. The walkways edged, bushes trimmed. The windows sparkled in the pale winter sun.

It was home, the only one he'd ever known.

Damn Nathan for trying to take it away from him. He'd earned the right to lead this congregation. He'd stuck with his people while Nathan had abandoned them. He'd accepted the obligations of *Les Gargouillen* while Nathan denied his legacy.

If Teryn couldn't see that—wouldn't see that—then Connor would have to make sure the elders did. Several of them were already unhappy with the Wizenot's continuing support of Nathan. Cross had been excommunicated. He shouldn't even be here, much less be at Teryn's side during

a time of crisis, while Connor was sent outside with the
women and children.

He just needed to get the elders' attention, to gain their
support. To show everyone that he was the better man to
lead them. He was their future.

Growling in frustration, he slammed his shoulders into
the brick wall of the abandoned building behind him and
dug a cigarette from his shirt pocket. He'd just struck a
match and lifted it to the smoke when he froze, mid-puff.

On the other side of the wrought-iron gate across the
street, two men in black trench coats sneaked along the
back wall of his school, his home, testing windows until
they found one unlocked and slipped inside.

A sneak attack, under the diversion of the riot out front.

Connor's blood began to pound. The cigarette fell to the
sidewalk. The match fizzled out in the gutter. This time
when he stepped into the dark tunnel, he didn't curse the
burned-out light. The hot, green glow of his eyes lit his
way.

Nathan stuck close to Teryn as they moved quickly
from room to room, assessed the damage. At least three
separate fires burned already: the dining area, the vestibule,
and the library, God, Teryn's treasured library.

When the flames crossed the large living areas in the
front of the building and reached the smaller rooms in the
back where the floors were carpeted and the walls closer
together, the fire would be unstoppable.

The heat was already intense. Sweat plastered Nathan's
shirt to his back and rolled down his temples. His eyes
burned and his throat was raw.

In the sitting room off the vestibule, Teryn ripped a curtain engulfed in flame off the wall and stomped on the
heavy brocade.

Coughing, Nathan clapped a hand over the Wizenot's
shoulder. "Forget it! We have to evacuate!"

"This is our home!"

Nathan knew what he was feeling. The importance of this place to their people. Its history. The congregation had centered around St. Michael's since they'd built it more than a hundred years ago. Still, it was just a building, and buildings could be replaced.

"We have to get the children out!" he yelled over the crackle of the fire.

Nodding reluctantly, Teryn gave up on the curtain and let the fire have it. Red blotches marred his face. A soot checkmark scored one cheek. His chest heaved in defeat. "I'll take the south tower, you take the north. Make sure everyone gets out. Leave no one behind."

On Wabash Drive the city went about its business as if the city hadn't gone mad just a few miles away. A businessman checked his watch as he turned into the bank. A harried mother stopped her stroller in the crosswalk to retrieve her toddler's pacifier from the sidewalk, wiped it on her pants, and popped it back in the screaming child's mouth. A young couple in gothic dress strolled hand in hand on the sidewalk, chains jangling and studded collars gleaming in the sunlight.

They all looked so normal.

So blissfully unaware.

Of the riot a few miles away.

Of the monsters that roamed their city.

Rachel's wistfulness didn't make sense to her. She'd gotten what she wanted—her freedom. She didn't have to listen to crazy stories about pagan rituals or lies about her father anymore.

Funny how sometimes once a person got what they wanted, they suddenly realized it wasn't such a great thing after all.

She'd found the monsters she'd been looking for since she was six years old.

And fallen in love with one of them.

How was that for irony?

"Do you think they'll be all right?"

Yanked back to reality by Jenny's high, strained voice, Rachel looked over her shoulder at the couple in the back-seat of the taxi.

Von lifted his arm to drape it over Jenny's shoulders, winced, and pulled his hand down and patted her gingerly on the knee instead. "They can take care of themselves."

The girl sniffed. The tip of her nose was as red as a cherry. "My father's an asshole."

Rachel agreed, but she kept the thought to herself. "Sometimes when people get in crowds like that, they don't think. Mob mentality takes over."

Von's face pinched. "He's an asshole even in a crowd of one."

Rachel agreed with him, too, but still felt compelled to send him a quelling look.

Jenny's lips wobbled, then set in a hard line. "I'm not going home. I don't care what he says."

"No one's going to let him hurt you again, honey. We just have to—"

Rachel glanced out the back window of the taxi. In the distance a thin plume of smoke spiraled toward the clouds like a ghostly skyscraper, making her forget what she was going to say.

No. It couldn't be.

In her gut she had a terrible feeling it was.

"We have to what?" Von asked.

Jenny blinked her big wet eyes, waiting for an answer.

"Turn this car around," Rachel said, her heart going zero to sixty in less than a second. She shifted her gaze to the driver. "We have to turn this car around."

Connor stalked the two intruders up the north tower like a starving cheetah trailing the last antelope during a game-killing drought on the Serengeti. He could already feel the flesh of their necks giving way as it tore away from their spines, taste their blood on his tongue.

He didn't know who these men were, or what they wanted, but a sense of malice surrounded them. Dark magic pulsed in their wake. The realization that they navigated the narrow corridors and winding stairwells like they knew the place—or had studied the floor plan—chilled him despite the heat rising from the fire below, seeping through the walls.

What could they want up here, in the boys' dormitory?

Whatever their intent, they were going to die before they fulfilled it. Connor would make sure of it.

Above all else, *Les Gargouillen* protected their children.

Tuning out the pandemonium from the street below, the roar of fire, the moans of the old building shifting under the stress and heat, Connor listened for the smaller noises that would help him track his quarry: the creak of a floorboard, the snick of a door lock, the muted cough from a hallway filling with smoke.

On the seventh floor, behind the door of the common room where the older boys gathered to study or relax, the cat-and-mouse game ended. The sounds of stealth became sounds of a struggle. Young voices, the boys, cried out in alarm and then in fear. Furniture scraped the floor and toppled. Connor dragged in a smoky breath that left his eyes burning and his lungs raw, and burst into the room poised to kill.

In an instant, his eyes took in every detail of the room that was to be his battlefield. Chairs lay scattered around the room like fallen soldiers. A boom box dangled off the edge of a shelf by the electrical cord. Four boys huddled against the far wall, their eyes huge and faces milk white. At the window one of the trench coat men stood with the red-haired twins, Jacen and Joshua, in each arm.

One of the men. Which left one unaccounted f—

He felt the attack before the first blow landed. The whisper of air moving above his head. The weight of a thin shadow thrown over him. A lizard the size of an alligator dropped from a crossbeam on the ceiling overhead. Jaws open wide, the creature reached for Connor's throat with two rows of serrated teeth while its hooked claws flew toward his eyes.

Gargoyles! The sons of bitches were Gargoyles!

He ducked and rolled too slow, too late. One of the razor-sharp nails caught him beneath the ear and split his cheek to the bone from the corner of his jaw to the bridge of his nose. Blood spurted in his eyes and flooded his mouth. Blindly, choking on his own blood, he tried to scrabble away on his knees and elbows, but the creature sank its teeth deep into his calf to hold him. He tried to pull up the words that would bring on the Awakening, to fight on equal terms, but the snapping of bone and tearing of muscle as the monster dragged him back obliterated the chant that would bring on his alternate form.

Sliding in a pool of his own blood, being pulled backward toward the monster, toward death, shock and disbelief dulled Connor's pain. Numbness set in.

He'd always expected to die violently. Why should this life be any different than the last eight?

But he hadn't expected to be killed by one of his own kind.

Or to go down before he'd earned his right to return.

He hadn't had a son yet in this life. Why the hell had he waited so long? He'd gone soft, listening to Nathan preach about the wrongness of their ways. The injustice of stealing infants from their mothers' arms. Even as he'd decried Cross's fanatical ideals, the words had crept into his heart, rooted.

And now he was going to pay the price.

Anger lifted the chill that enveloped him like a death shroud. Feeling returned to his fingers. Pain returned everywhere. Seething, he strained to lift his head, to see the traitor who would send him to his final death.

The yellow-scaled lizard loomed over him, lips pulled back in a reptilian grin. Strings of drool hung from his jowls, dripped into Connor's open wounds. The stench of evil clung to him like flies to a dung pile.

Connor swallowed the blood in his throat, an inhuman

howl welling up inside him. If this was to be the end of his eternal soul, it would not be a quiet end.

He would go down fighting.

Fingers curling on the cold tile floor, he waited. His attacker snarled and snapped above him, taunting him. Still, he waited. Until the beast reared back like a baseball pitcher winding up, and then dived for his throat.

Connor flicked his wrist and brought the blade of the spring-activated dagger hidden under his sleeve up into the beast's soft belly.

The lizard slumped to one side, morphing back into human form, both hands clasped around the hilt of the knife stuck in his gut.

Shoving the man to the floor, Connor yanked his dagger from the corpse and rolled to face the Gargoyle by the door, who dropped Jacen and Josh and fell to all fours, already more animal than man.

"Run!" His shout prompted the stunned boys into action. They scrambled for the doorway.

Dragging himself to his knees with the last of his strength, the knife in his hand slack at his side, Connor put himself between the boys and the great, lumbering bear that charged them.

Rachel's stomach plummeted like a skydiver without a parachute when she jumped out of the cab in front of St. Michael's. The street was in chaos. Ugly words from the protesters greeted the soot-blackened children and men streaming from the school. Accusations were tossed back. Vehicles just trying to make their ways down the street nosed through the mayhem, drivers shouting and gesturing wildly out the windows.

In the distance sirens screamed. Finally.

Rachel fought her way to the bottom of the stairs that led to the front doors, elbowing and shoving unconcernedly in her haste. She told herself to take it easy, to be calm, but panic beat at her self-control like a wrecking ball on a condemned building. She reached out with her mind to Nathan, but couldn't find him in the storm of mental energy and emotions of the crowd.

Where are you, Nathan?

At the front door she stopped every man who stumbled out of the billowing smoke. She looked into bleary eyes and searched ash-covered faces. When she finally recognized one, it wasn't Nathan, but Teryn, a half-dozen little boys clinging tearfully to his pant legs.

Coughing, he pulled her away from the heat pouring out the doors behind him. His eyes looked wild. Panicked. "Have you seen Patrick? I can't find Patrick."

"No. Where is Nathan?" she shouted.

He rubbed each boy's back and ruffled their hair, his eyes scanning the street. Looking for one more lost little boy, she knew. "He was in the north tower. He should already be out."

"I can't find him."

He shook his head. "There are too many people. He could be anywhere." And she wondered if he was talking about Nathan or Patrick.

Rachel raised her head toward the north battlement seven stories up. What if Nathan wasn't out here? What if he hadn't made it out of the tower?

Choking back a fresh wave of terror, she spun away from Teryn and fought her way around to the side of the school. The windows on the lower floors were dark now, black pits of roiling smoke. On the upper floors, flames licked the glass.

He had to have gotten out.

Everyone had to have gotten out.

But they hadn't.

Rachel jolted as if she'd been slapped when a pair of tiny palms pressed against the glass of a window on the seventh floor. The hands pounded, then fumbled with the latches and raised the window.

Patrick leaned out and gulped in air between sobs, smoke wafting around his little head like a dingy halo.

Oh, God. Oh, God. *Patrick.* Who'd died in a fire once, and knew the terror. Knew the pain. Reliving it.

Tears scorched Rachel's throat. A tremor surged up her, shook her, and sent her spurting toward the burning building in a gush of fearless anguish.

Oh, God. He was just a little boy, with intelligent blue eyes and a cowlick.

A little boy who could turn into a dragon at will.

A little boy who flew for the first time before her eyes.

What did it matter what he was? What he would grow up to be?

He was just a little boy.

She shouldered open the door and stumbled through the murky kitchen to the sink, where she turned on the tap. Thankfully, the plumbing still worked, though the water burst out scalding hot.

She found two kitchen towels and soaked them both. One she draped over her head. The other she held to her mouth as she started up the back stairs.

The intensity of the heat on the first two flights of the stairwell shocked her. She could feel her skin blistering. Her lungs searing, even breathing through the dampened towel.

The next three flights were even worse. There was fire here, crackling over walls and at times under her feet. She had to stop twice and take the towel off her head to beat out the flames on the steps before she could continue.

The world tilted as the smoke made her light-headed. She couldn't see, so she felt her way along the hot walls. Her lips dried and split from the heat. She tried to moisten them with her tongue, but her mouth was just as parched.

By the time she made it to the seventh floor, she wasn't sure where she was anymore. Wasn't sure it mattered. She could hardly move. Hardly think. The fire had spread to her lungs. She couldn't breathe. Couldn't see.

She stumbled in a dark corridor, couldn't get up, so she crawled. The floor was so hot it burned her hands. She lost a shoe, turned around, and went back two steps for it before she realized it didn't matter.

She was lost. Lost and doomed. And she'd let Patrick down. And Nathan.

The ceiling crumbled above her. Embers fell on her neck, her shoulders, caught the ends of her hair on fire. She slapped her head and huddled against the wall, her knees up to her chest and her arms protecting her head, defeated.

Then she heard the keening, thin and frightened.

She raised her head. "Patrick?"

He didn't answer, but she zeroed in on the direction of the sound and started crawling again. "Patrick, can you hear me? I'm coming!"

She found him in the room at the corner of the building, curled up beneath the window like a fetus, rocking himself and sobbing. "Aieeeeeeeyyyaaa!"

The hardwood floor was so hot the finish was peeling and curling. Flames ran up the walls like the rivers of hell.

Quickly she pulled Patrick into her arms and wrapped the damp towels around him as best she could. She leaned over him, out the window, to call for help, but the smoke was so thick she couldn't even see the sidewalk below. No way they would see her. Or hear her, over the roar of the fire.

At least, they wouldn't hear her voice.

But they would hear the Calling.

She'd heard it, when Von had cried for help. Nathan said he'd heard her in the subway, though she had no conscious recollection of it.

Could she really send out the ultrasonic whistle that would let Nathan know she needed him?

If he was right about her father, her powers . . .

No. Her father wasn't a monster, no matter what Nathan said. She wasn't one of them.

Patrick whimpered, his eyes squeezed tightly shut and his fingers bunched in her shirt. She rocked him, stroking his hair. Suddenly it was all too much. The heat of the fire, the smell of smoke, the feel of a terrified baby in her arms—it was all too familiar. She was catapulted back in time to her little house in New York.

The cupboard under the stairs was dark. There were people outside, then in the house, yelling. Mommy was scared. Daddy fought with a bad man, and someone set off firecrackers.

No, not firecrackers, her adult mind realized. A gun. Someone shot a gun. Her father hadn't owned a gun.

Shadows rolled across the wall. Mommy's shadow fell and Daddy's jumped on another man. They rolled together and then the monster came.

Rachel squeezed her mind's eye shut. She couldn't look anymore. She wouldn't. Nathan was wrong, he had to be wrong.

Patrick gasped for breath in her arms. His arms went limp. A wail broke out of her chest. She shook him until his eyelids fluttered.

Still alive. He was still alive.

But not for long.

Tears scalded her throat. He was so little. So innocent. Dear God, she had to save him. She had to try, no matter how futile her efforts might be.

Clutching Patrick to her chest, Rachel closed her eyes, bit down on her lower lip, and focused her untrained mind, every fiber of her being, on the high-pitched plea that would let Nathan know she needed him.

And faced a truth about herself she wasn't sure she would be able to withstand when this was all over.

Assuming she survived.

TWENTY-EIGHT

❦

Each step up the stairs of the north tower was like a step deeper into a blast furnace. Hunched to protect his face, Nathan punched through the heat as if it was a physical barrier. He could hear the fire in the walls, climbing, devouring, looking for escape, for air, of which there was precious little left in the stairway.

The older boys who dormed on this side of the school fled past him, clomping down the stairs pell-mell while he fought his way up, stumbling into him in the murk.

"Get out!" he yelled at each sooty, terrified face. "Get outside."

Two, four, six boys, he'd counted. There should be eight. The twins—two boys, such a rare gift to his people—he hadn't seen Josh or Jacen. Had they found another way out, or were they still up there, trapped?

Fighting to claim enough oxygen from the smoke to climb another flight of stairs, he grabbed the banister and pulled himself up to the seventh floor.

As he reached for the doorknob on the stairwell exit, the door burst open. Josh and Jacen burst through, their eyes wild and feet scrabbling for purchase as they changed from human to hawk mid-stride.

Behind them a grizzly the size of a dump truck stood on its hind legs and roared, peeling its lips back over yellow fangs and clawing the air with deadly intent.

"Go!" He yelled to the twins. "Fly!"

He would have followed them, but his wingspan was too wide for the twisting stairway, and no way could he outrun the bear.

The bear swiped at him. Nathan ducked under the swing, rolled, and came up on the other side of the beast, but the sting on his back told him he hadn't come away unscathed. Blood and sweat trickled down his shoulder blade.

He'd been lucky. At least he could still use the arm. It could have been worse.

Looking through the open door to his left, he saw how much worse. On the floor inside the room, Connor lay unmoving against a backdrop of blood.

Nathan turned back to the bear, balancing for a fight. "Son of a bitch. Who are you?"

The creature dropped to all fours and charged. Nathan changed in an instant and met the attack in griffin form, pecking at the bear's eyes with his beak, ripping through fur and hide with his talons and lion's claws.

They grappled and rolled. Snarls and squawks mingled with blood and spittle. Embers flew through the air as a ceiling beam crashed to the floor beside them. Smoke roiled, choking both beasts.

The bear managed to get his mouth on Nathan's right wing, sank his teeth through feather to bone, and shook his great head. Flesh tore and sinew rent.

Nathan's back arched involuntarily. His muscles locked spasmodically. For a moment the pain threatened to throw him out of Gargoyle form, and he found his human voice and screamed.

The bear slung him to his back and went for his throat. Nathan beat his good wing in the monster's face to protect himself, but knew it wouldn't be enough. Not nearly enough.

He drew his powerful hind paws between him and the bear and tried to kick him off. When that didn't work, he extended his claws, felt for the soft flesh between the creature's legs, and when he found it, raked with all his might.

The grizzly stumbled back, no longer a bear, but a man in black slacks and an open black trench coat.

Blood spurted between his fingers where he cupped himself. He stumbled backward, landed hard on his butt.

Nathan followed him back and, without a second's hesitation, clenched the man's throat in his talons and ripped out his trachea with one swift yank.

Wiping the blood from his hands onto the thighs of his jeans, he knelt next to Connor. Surprisingly, Connor's blue eyes opened, stared up, unfocused, but knowing.

"Got one," he whispered, nodding almost imperceptibly toward the body lying on the other side of the room.

"I got the other," Nathan told him.

"Boys?"

"They all got out. Thanks to you."

Connor smiled through busted lips. His face was a smear of blood, his cheek laid open to the bone. His left leg was twisted beneath him, the flesh of his calf in tatters. But it was the wound on the abdomen that caused Nathan the most concern.

Connor had his arms folded over his middle as if they were the only things holding him together. Blood seeped from beneath his forearms, dripped steadily to the floor to puddle around his waist.

The bear could have killed him quickly, mercifully. Instead the bastard had eviscerated him and left him to burn.

For that alone, Nathan wanted to rip his throat out. Again.

A cough that wouldn't end racked Nathan's chest. The room creaked around him, studs warping and nails popping from the heat.

"You go," Connor gasped. "Before it's too late."

He scooped Connor up by the shoulders, wishing he could be gentle and knowing he didn't have time.

Connor slapped a bloody hand over Nathan's wrist. "No. I'll slow you down. No time. You have to hurry."

Nathan squinted at Connor through bleary eyes. The two of them had never been friends. They stood on opposite sides of many ideals. Connor had been a key player in the faction that had gotten him excommunicated. There had been days he hated him for that.

But not enough to leave him to die.

"Shut up," he said, and jerked his arm free to pull Connor over his shoulder.

Connor groaned in anguish. His blood soaked through Nathan's shirt, coursed down his chest and back in thick rivers. Ignoring it, Nathan ran from the room, took the stairs blindly, three at a time, grabbing the newel posts as anchors to swing around the turns in the winding stairwell.

The sixth and fifth floors were full of smoke. He held his breath and felt his way through the darkness. Fire formed a tunnel of flame on the third and fourth floors. He held his free hand up to shield his eyes, yelled for Connor to cover his face, and dived through.

When he reached the charred wood steps on the second floor, he thought he was home free.

Until he heard it. The high, distant whine that became a shaky whistle.

He knew that pitch, that tone. Knew the mind that made it.

Rachel!

Dredging up every ounce of speed he had inside him, he exploded out the front doors of the school, dumped Connor into Teryn's arms, and ran, searching for the source of the sound.

Searching for a place out of the sight of human eyes to change.

•   •   •

*Rachel crouched against the wall beneath the win-*dow, Patrick's head tucked beneath her chin and her body curled protectively over his.

His frail shoulders shook. "Don' wanna die," he choked. "Don' wanna burn up again!"

The old building grunted and moaned as the fire consumed it, joint by joist.

Her mind slipped back in time, to the little girl in the cupboard. *Now I lay me down to sleep.* Her lips moved silently against the little boy's hair, only it wasn't Levi. It wasn't her brother. It was Patrick, and she wasn't a scared, helpless child any longer. She hadn't been for a long time.

But the nightmare called to her, and she was lost. She opened the cupboard door to smell smoke and see the flickering light of a fire. Shadows scrolled across the wall. Men, fighting. Angry voices.

Her mother, screaming.

Gunshots.

Then the hideous screech. The shadow loomed larger, grew closer. She could smell her fear. Taste panic in her throat. The air vibrated with the heavy *whump, whump* of gigantic wings, and she saw it. The monster she'd feared for twenty years.

"Rachel?"

She opened her eyes, and found Nathan squatting beside her. He stood, lifting her by her elbows, and took the limp Patrick from her.

Tears rolled down her cheeks. "It was him. I looked out the cabinet door and saw the monster. It had leathery wings and scaly yellow claws and a beak like black obsidian, but when I looked into its eyes, I knew it was him. The monster was my father."

Shifting Patrick into one arm, he palmed the back of her head and pulled her to him. "I know."

For a moment, the comfort of his nearness, his understanding, obliterated the smoke, the heat, the hungry fire from her mind, but then the floor shuddered. The walls shifted and creaked. Dust and mortar crumbled from the ceiling.

The structural damage was too extensive. The old building couldn't take any more. Its guts were collapsing, the façade falling away, leaving its naked, charred skeleton exposed.

Nathan pushed her away. "We have to get out."

Rachel looked over his shoulder at the inferno that used to be the hallway. "How? There's no way out."

She'd been too late. She'd finally accepted the truth, but it was too late. For all of them.

Nathan shook his head. "We fly out, the way I came in. I can carry Patrick, but you'll have to hold on to my back."

He wanted to fly out? From a seventh-story window?

Her heart skittered across her chest like a drop of grease on a hot frying pan. "There're too many people. They'll see."

"Not in this smoke."

She blinked, and by the time she'd opened her eyes, he'd changed. He stood facing the open window and nudged her around to his back with one wing.

It was then she saw the blood. The score marks across one shoulder. The bite where his wing joined his back.

"You're hurt!" She reached out, but dared not touch the wounds for fear of causing him more pain.

The ceiling across the room caved in a shower of sparks and ash.

"Caw!" he cried, and nudged her harder with his good wing.

Swallowing hard, she leaned against his back, tucked her knees beneath his wings, careful to avoid the injured spot, and wrapped her arms around his neck.

Smooth as a silk ribbon floating on a warm summer breeze, he glided out the window.

Rachel twisted her fingers in the quills of his feathers and squeezed her eyes shut, but after a moment, she realized they weren't falling. They were riding a warm draft upward. The air was easier to breathe here. The heat not so intense.

She dared to open one eye. True to his word, the bubbling cloud of smoke below them obscured the view of the street. But the city around them sparkled like a snow globe village. The streets and buildings and water looked peaceful from up here. Clean. Quiet.

And the sense of calm wasn't just coming from outside, either. A sense of security spread inside her, relaxing her. She smiled in wonder at the bunching and stretching of the lion's powerful muscles beneath her, the heavy beat of its heart—Nathan's heart—between her thighs.

He made a quick stop on the roof to flip open the latches on a rack of birdcages, then soared into the air again.

She almost laughed. What kind of monster remembers amidst chaos to stop and free a flock of helpless pigeons before their roost goes up in flames?

None, that was what kind.

It was an act of purely human kindness.

With a soft sigh she unclenched her fingers, leaned forward, and rubbed her cheek on the luxurious down that circled Nathan's neck. The wind in her face was cool and cleansing, and she smiled.

After all this time, all these years of searching, she'd finally found what she'd been looking for.

The truth.

TWENTY-NINE

Six days had passed before the Gargoyles of St. Michael's had recovered enough, and felt secure enough, to hold Council in their temporary home, an old YMCA they'd leased. Even now four members of the congregation were absent, standing guard over the sleeping children. Four more were off on secret errands for Teryn.

Those who were present stood somber faced before the semicircle of elders in the front of the room. The flamboyant podiums were gone, as were the rich, colorful robes and velvet hoods, victims of the fire. The elders stood in full view of the congregation in plain slacks and sweaters, jackets and shirts with the sleeves rolled up to the elbows.

It seemed to Nathan he'd never attended a more honest council. As he had last time, he stood in the back of the room, there, and yet not there in the eyes of his brothers. That he'd been allowed to attend at all was nothing short of a miracle. Showed how deeply the congregation had been shaken by all that had transpired.

Now that he was here, he almost wished he hadn't come. It was hard to be part of the congregation and yet not. He felt like a traveler who'd made the long trek home

only to be forced to stand outside his cabin looking in
while his loved ones sat down to a family dinner.

From his position in the middle of the crescent of elders, Teryn scanned the faces of the men gathered before
him. "A great shadow has turned its dark eye on St.
Michael's. I believe the two who came here are not alone
in their quest."

He didn't say how he knew, and thankfully no one
asked. Nathan doubted Teryn would like to explain the
source of his knowledge.

Teryn lifted his chin, a small defiance to the evil they
faced. "A danger like we've never known is upon us, for
these are no mere thieves who tried to take our children, no
humans driven to ill by greed or pride or depravation. They
are *Les Gargouillen*."

"Bah!" Eric Stevers spit through his shaggy blond
beard. "*Les Gargouillen* do not kill their own. They do not
steal each other's children. These creatures are an abomi-
nation. A blight on our race!"

Heads nodded and mouths murmured assent around the
room. Teryn silenced them with a lift of his palm.

"These men are driven by an evil power, that I cannot
argue. They've shown they can use their abilities to turn
our friends and neighbors against us. To influence human
minds to commit acts I do not believe they would otherwise perpetrate."

Mr. Lovell and several of his friends had been arrested.
They all claimed they didn't remember setting the fire.

Mrs. Lovell had left her husband, taking her daughter
with her. She and Jenny were staying in a women's shelter
until they found a place of their own.

"I have sent some of our brothers to congregations
around the country to learn what we can of these men,"
Teryn continued. "Of where they come from and what
their purpose may be."

"We know what they want. They want our children!"
one of the listeners shouted.

"But we do not know why. Until we do, we don't know how to stop them."

"We'll kill the bastards, that's how we'll stop them," Connor said from his wheelchair up front. Just released from the hospital, his face—what Nathan could see of it—was sallow and drawn, but his voice was steady. The others rallied around him.

Teryn waited for the hubbub to die down. "We must be vigilant to keep our sons safe, that is certain. We'll need every pair of eyes, every able body. Which brings me to the next order of business tonight. A petition to the elders." He nodded respectfully to his right, then his left, then raised his chin.

"A petition to reinstate Nathan Cross to the congregation."

The flutter of a hummingbird's wings would have sounded like a jet engine in the silence of the room. A moment stretched into an eternity.

"Has he repented of his refusal to accept our ways?" Elder Price finally asked, his heavy white brows drawn together to form a single, unbroken line across his forehead.

Teryn turned to the elder on his far right. "He has taken a mate."

The crowd murmured again. A surge of adrenaline set a jackhammer to work in Nathan's chest, and it took him a moment to realize it was his heart trying to pound its way through his ribs.

"Leave Rachel out of this," he said. He shoved his way to the front of the crowd. Screw the rules. He didn't care if they *saw* him or not.

They were sure as hell going to hear him.

In the front of the room he faced the congregation. "I didn't ask for this petition. I don't want it."

"Is the woman willing to bear him a son?" Elder Price asked as if Nathan weren't there.

"I said leave her out of this. She—" Nathan started to wheel as he spoke, but a movement in the corner of the room caught his attention. A cloaked figure drew back a heavy hood, and Nathan's heart slammed to the pit of his stomach.

"Rachel."

She winked at him with one blazing emerald eye as she strolled serenely through the mass of ogling men. Never in the history of *Les Gargouillen*, as far as Nathan knew, had a woman attended Council.

"The woman"—she cut a hard look at Elder Price when she reached the front—"is willing to bear him as many sons, and daughters, as he wants."

Her voice softened as she stopped chest to chest with Nathan and met his dumbstruck stare. "As long as they raise them together."

A few of the men gasped out loud. Others frowned, or shrugged and scratched their heads.

"This is outrageous." Price's cheeks reddened as he blustered. "It's unheard of!"

"It's not unheard of," she answered, but her gaze never left Nathan. "There is precedent. My father was—"

Her breath hitched. The words caught in her throat, and Nathan sent her a gentle mental brush. A caress of reassurance. Of strength.

"My father was one of you. He was one of the Old Ones, the original Gargoyles of Rouen."

Heads turned all around the room. Men whispered to each other.

"It's true," Teryn said. "I've spoken to the Wizenot of Damien Paré's—that's Rachel's biological father—congregation personally. He's substantiated the story. Damien had broken from the congregation. The Wizenot at the time didn't know where he'd gone. But he did know he'd had a child before he left. A little girl."

The room hushed.

He'd also had a son, Nathan thought. Rachel had figured out quickly that meant her father might very well have already reincarnated. With so few Gargoyle children being born, it wasn't a certainty. There simply weren't enough bodies for all the souls waiting. But Nathan knew she would want to find out. She would want to look for him.

"He married my mother and stayed with her even after I was born," Rachel continued. "Even after my brother was born."

"She has a brother," one man mumbled. "The son of an Old One."

The man next to him nodded.

Her lips trembled. Nathan reached for her, but she held him back with a look. "Best we can piece together from old newspaper articles, he lived with his family in peace until one day he saw a neighbor child fall through the ice of a pond. He saved the boy, but unfortunately some of his neighbors saw the Awakening. They killed him because they were afraid of what he was."

The buzz of whispers around the room rose, subsided.

"What I am," she finished, lifting her chin. "I am of the blood of one of the Old Ones," she said, "and I want to amend the petition." Her gaze blazed around the room. "I petition the Council to restore Nathan Cross and his mate, Rachel Paré, to the congregation."

"A woman?" someone asked.

"This is blasphemy," Price said. "It's indecent!"

Connor looked up from his wheelchair, and Nathan couldn't tell if the expression on his swollen face was a smirk or a smile. Maybe a little of both. "I call the petition to vote," he said.

"I second the call."

Nathan turned his head and got a nod from Ethan Keller, Rhys's father, and Patrick's grandfather. Ethan had been away the day of the fire and, to Nathan's knowledge, had never met Rachel, but he was sure the man had been told what she'd done for his grandson.

Teryn held up both hands to quiet the room. "The petition's been called and seconded."

Nathan looked back at Rachel. "You don't have to do this."

This time he was pretty sure the look on Connor's face was a grin. "Shut up, Nathan."

"All in favor?" Teryn called.

Connor and Ethan's hands struck upward, but no one else moved. By tradition, Teryn couldn't vote except to break a tie.

Seconds passed, but Rachel kept her head high, giving away none of the anxiety she felt churning in her mind, until one by one, every man in the room, even Elder Price, held one hand in the air.

Standing before the massive window in the darkened living room of his condominium, Nathan couldn't help but think what an amazing night it had been. What an amazing woman Rachel Vandermere—now Rachel Paré—had turned out to be.

Not so long ago he'd stood in this very spot and his eyes had been drawn to the still, black waters of Lake Michigan. He'd longed for the peace of a place like that. The everlasting darkness. Now when he looked out, his eyes weren't drawn to the darkness, but to the light. The life. The crossword-puzzle patterns in the windows of nearby office buildings. The red-and-white lines of headlights and taillights streaming up and down Lake Shore Drive. The blinking neon beckoning passersby into stores and bars and hotels.

He saw a future for himself, and it was all because of one look across a crowded art gallery.

A look of female appreciation. Of curiosity.

A look not unlike the one on her face now as she climbed out of the bed behind him, watching him watch her reflection in the window, her cheeks still flushed and her hair tousled from lovemaking.

"Hey, you." She padded up behind him in her bare feet, belting his old robe around her waist, and put her arms around him, her palms flat on his chest and her cheek against his back. "What're you doing over here?"

He clasped her hands in his and leaned back into her. "Just thinking."

"Good thoughts, or bad?"

"Mostly good."

"Mostly?"

Smiling, he trailed his fingertips up and down her forearms. "You set me up today. You and Teryn."

She propped her chin on his shoulder. "Busted."

"You could have told me he planned to petition the Council. Or that you did."

"It's good to be surprised once in a while." She hugged him more tightly. "He and I had a long talk. He told me what happened between you and your people, how he excommunicated you."

Nathan hated the involuntary stiffening at the mention of his banishment, and forced himself to relax. "He had his reasons for what he did."

"He said he made a mistake. A big one." She smiled, and he felt the curve of her lips against his newly healed shoulder blade, and in his heart. "I like him. He reminds me of you."

"He should. He's my son."

She lifted her head and looked questioningly at his reflection in the window.

"My *saytreán*, actually. The son of my soul, fathered in another life."

"Marabella's child," she breathed, and he nodded.

"It happens once in a while. One of us has a son, then dies and is reincarnated while that son still lives. Our souls recognize each other. The son is called his *saytreán*, son of his soul; the father is the child's *paytreán*, father of his soul."

"You didn't think to tell me this any sooner?" she asked incredulously.

"It's good to be surprised once in a while."

She laughed softly, flexing her arms around his waist.

He smiled, and his gaze was drawn to another light in

their reflection—the sparkle of the marquis diamond set in white gold—his ring—on her finger.

His smile grew. "I can't wait to see his face when you ask him to call you 'Mom.'"

She'd given him an incredible gift today, committing her life, her love to him. Restoring him to his people.

He just wondered if she really understood what it would cost her.

What it would cost both of them.

He was willing to pay the price—any price—to have her.

One day they would die. Only he would be reborn. He would live another life, and another, missing her. Loving her.

But what the hell. One life with her, one *day* with her, would be worth the torture of living the next thousand lifetimes without her. Besides, she was *Les Gargouillen*. The daughter of one of the Old Ones. She could make the Calling. Who knew what other powers she had.

Maybe she would reincarnate.

If she did, he would find her. No matter how long it took, he would find her soul.

He would pay his price gladly enough, but he had to know she was willing to pay hers, as well.

He turned in her arms, kissed her, savoring the sweet heat of her a moment, then drew back while he still could. "Teryn believes there are dark times ahead. Worse than what we've already been through."

"He told me. But I can't walk away from you or our people now. He said he could help me find Levi."

"He was adopted while you were in foster care?"

She nodded. "I tried to find him later, once I was out on my own, but the courthouse in Jackson County had burned down a few years before. The records were destroyed. I've posted on every one of those adoption reunion websites on the Internet, but gotten no response."

"There must be someone who remembers."

"It took years, but I finally found a nurse who gave me

the name of a doctor who kept some old patient files. I really believed I was going to see my brother again, but by the time the investigator I hired tracked down the adoptive family, Levi had run away. They had no idea where he was. He was just fifteen when he left." She pulled her robe tight across her chest as if she'd caught a sudden chill. "God, no wonder he ran away. What must my brother's life be like, being so different, and yet not understanding how or why or even *what* he is?"

"We'll find him."

"I know you'll do your best. And I'll do my best to help you through whatever is going to happen. All of you. You're my family now."

He took a deep breath, wishing it could be so easy. "Not everyone in the congregation is going to accept you. Hell, half of them still don't accept me. You'll have to deal with . . . our ways."

"I'm prepared."

"Are you? Will you be prepared the first time one of the brothers comes in with blood on his hands and you wonder who he's killed? Will you be prepared when one comes in with a baby, and you wonder where its mother is?"

"Are you trying to scare me away again?"

"I'm telling you that if you need to leave here, go live someplace else, just the two of us, that *I'm* prepared."

He didn't want to leave his people now that he had them back, but he would. As long as he had her, he didn't need anyone else.

She thought for a moment, then shook her head. "My father tried that. It didn't work. We need the congregation, Nathan. We're stronger with them."

"Stronger, but not necessarily better."

"I can't say I agree with all of our people's ways. I'm not sure how I'll deal with every situation, but I hope I'll be a positive influence, make them see they have choices."

"They've never had a choice in what they are."

"But they have a choice in how they live. You, more than anyone, know that. Von has made his choice. He's signed himself up for an alcohol abuse program and is already talking about petitioning the Council to bring Jenny into the congregation, as well." She tightened her hold on him. "Times change. *Les Gargouillen* can change."

"It won't happen overnight."

"No, but they will change."

"I hope you're right."

"Our people's past may be carved in stone, Nathan." She laid her palm along the side of his face, her expression so honest, so full of belief that she made him believe. "But their future isn't."

Continue reading for a special preview of
Virginia Kantra's novel

CLOSE-UP

Coming in July 2005 from Berkley Sensation!

The woman scrambling over the stockade wall had a really nice ass. So it was a damn good thing she wasn't his sister.

At least, Jack Miller hoped she wasn't his sister. Because that would make things really complicated, and he had more than enough complications in his life already.

Concealed in the shadow of trees outside the militia's compound, he watched as the woman's head followed the rest of her over a ten-foot wall of rough-cut pine. The sunlight fired her short blond curls.

Nope. Definitely not his sister. His sister Sally wore her hair in a long, dark braid. Or she had the last time he saw her—what was it now, seven years ago? Eight?

Ignoring the familiar twinge of guilt, Jack narrowed his gaze on the blonde. Okay, so the hair was wrong. But the getup was right, the long skirt and sandals, sort of Haight-Ashbury goes Amish. She must be one of them. The Holy Rollers. The Disciples of Freedom or whatever the hell they called themselves.

But if Blondie there was a member of God's little army,

why was she tearing up her clothes and her hands going over the wall?

So far, none of the compound's sentries had noticed her break for freedom. Lax of them, Jack thought. But then, what did they have to worry about out here? Bears? Timber snakes? They were in the middle of the Nantahala National Forest, eight and a half miles of rough backcountry from the nearest access point and a long day's hike from the closest town. The deep gorges and steep hills all around probably made even paranoid militia men feel safe from intrusion.

At least, that's what Jack was counting on.

But the blonde wasn't taking advantage of the guards' inattention to make a run for it. Scared? Jack wondered. He was too far away to see her face or her knuckles, but she sure seemed reluctant to let go of that wall. His muscles tensed. Come on, sweetheart, he urged silently. It's not that far. Three feet. Four, tops.

Her sandal dropped. And then Blondie did, too, crumpling as her feet hit the hard-packed ground. There were no bushes to break her fall. The Disciples had cleared the area around the compound of brush, which explained why Jack had set up his stakeout thirty yards away, outside the perimeter of trees.

He watched as the woman lurched to her feet. Was she hurt, or just jarred? Jarred, he decided, as she stooped for her sandal. At least she had the sense not to stop to put it on.

She hopped toward the tree line, her shoe clutched in her hand, angling for the thick laurels on Jack's right. Good. So she wouldn't lead her pursuers straight to him. Assuming she attracted pursuit. As long as Jack didn't do anything stupid to call attention to himself, like offer her shelter or help. . . .

But he wouldn't.

He couldn't.

He had to think of Sally.

His blood pumped. Adrenaline flooded his body. He had no ties to the mystery blonde, no stake in her escape.

But he caught himself rooting for her as she stumbled for cover, ungainly as a mother partridge distracting a fox from her nest. He sure hoped she had some goal, some thought, some plan beyond making it to the bushes.

She didn't carry a bundle. No sleeping bag or supplies. What was she going to do tonight when the sun went down and the temperature dropped thirty degrees? Spring was beautiful in these North Carolina mountains, but fickle. And cold. Kind of like his ex-wife, actually.

Yep, the blonde definitely needed a plan to survive.

A shout sounded from inside the compound.

Jack stiffened. Shit.

The blonde's head jerked up like a startled deer's. At this distance, Jack could see she was young. Cute, too. Under her loose pink top, her breasts were nice and round. No wonder somebody didn't want to let her go.

After that one frozen second, the woman dropped her chin and ran like hell over the rocky ground. Her skirt snagged behind her as she plunged into the bushes, a flag to watching eyes, and then it, too, disappeared.

Jack released his breath. Time for him to do the same, before Locke sent his thugs out after the pretty fugitive.

He withdrew silently through the trees, grateful for his drab jacket and camouflage pants. Poor Blondie. Her pink shirt and full, flowered skirt would show up against the browns and greens of the forest like tracer bullets in the night sky. He heard her crashing through the woods on his right and scowled. She'd be better off lying low until her pursuers had passed. Plenty of hiding places in this wilderness.

Like that oak over there . . .

Jack's gaze narrowed. The forest giant had toppled many seasons ago. Its leaves were gone, its branches broken, its roots raised in a broad wedge of crumbled clay and rock. The gaping hole left behind was an obvious hiding spot; the depression under the trunk, sheltered by a tangle of brush and leaves, made a much better one.

Jack was no Daniel Boone. He'd gone camping with his old man exactly once, and the trip, like most of their attempts at father-son bonding, had been a disaster. But he'd picked up some basic survival skills, at Uncle Sam's insistence and taxpayer expense.

Squatting, he poked under the log with a stick. The hollow appeared dry and snake-free. He'd need to squeeze his shoulders through the narrow opening, but beyond that the ground fell away. He wasn't crazy about being stuck in a hole in the ground, but this one had plenty of room to move and breathe.

Jack tossed the stick away. Shrugging out of his pack, he shoved it out of sight, under the trunk, and crawled in after it.

Lexie ran, blind with pain and panic.

Her ankle jarred with every step. Her breath grunted and whistled. Branches lashed her arms, tree roots tripped her feet.

She snatched at a sapling, keeping herself upright through sheer luck and force of will. Her heart hammered. She had to get away. She couldn't let herself be captured, wouldn't let herself be used again. . . .

The ground heaved, and a man rose up practically under her feet.

Oh, God. She was caught.

He was as massive as the mountain, dusted in dirt and leaves, and dressed like a nightmare out of *Soldier of Fortune* magazine.

Whirling, she bolted.

He grabbed her from behind, yanked her against his large, hard body, and covered her mouth with his hand.

She bit him.

"Shit." His breath hissed against the side of her face as she kicked and clawed his arm. "Hold still, will you? They'll hear us."

His voice penetrated her panic. He didn't sound angry. Exasperated, maybe, but Lexie exasperated lots of people. Typical male reaction, really.

And that *us . . . They'll hear us. . . .* Wasn't he one of them, then?

She stopped struggling.

"You okay?" he growled close to her ear.

She was not okay. She was scared out of her wits. Her side ached, her ankle throbbed, and she had Locke the Lunatic and his band of baddies hot on her trail.

But she nodded. At least, she tried. It was hard to signal agreement with that big hand clamping her jaw.

The hand relaxed slightly. "You won't scream?" His breath was hot against her cheek.

Why would she scream? Nobody would hear. No one who would help, anyway.

She nodded again. And then, fearing he'd misunderstand her response, she shook her head.

"Right."

Those fingers eased their grip. Slowly, as if her captor was as suspicious, as reluctant, as she, he released her.

Lexie twisted in his arms and took a step back. Pain shot to her knee. She staggered.

Oh, dear Lord.

Lexie had seen enough militia-style getups in the past few days to recognize trouble. And this man, with his slouch hat pulled over burning eyes and his stubbled jaw, would look dangerous with or without the uniform. Dangerous, disreputable, and—despite his intimidating attitude and the three days' growth of beard—very, very hot.

Lexie licked her dry lips. She didn't *do* intimidating men, she reminded herself. Growing up with an overprotective, ultracontrolling father had put her off tall, dark, and dangerous for life. And if her upbringing hadn't already convinced her to steer clear of macho males, the past couple of days surely would have.

She never should have trusted Ralph.

Just because this guy wasn't one of the crazies inside the compound didn't mean she could trust him, either. As much as she'd railed and rebelled against her father's paranoid view of the world, she had to admit now there were some seriously bad people out there. Man Mountain could be anyone. Anything. A hunter. A hillbilly. An escaped convict.

She shivered. "Who are you? What are you doing here?"

He looked at her as if she was the crazy one. "At the moment, I'm saving your ass. Get in."

Lexie blinked. The drugs they'd forced on her were out of her system, but she still felt woozy. Get in what? Get in where?

The woods crackled behind her.

The big man swore. Grabbing her elbow, he dragged her toward a fallen log and shoved her to the ground. Lexie caught herself with her hands. A hole gaped in the earth, dark and spidery and uninviting.

Her stomach quailed. In *there?*

But she had no choice. Anyway, the man behind her wasn't offering her one. He nudged her into the crack, crawling and sliding in after her. Lexie fought a burst of panic. How could they fit? There was no room, no air. . . .

And then he levered his body somehow, bracing himself on his hands and his toes, and stretched out on top of her.

That was better. And worse. His thighs trapped hers. His chest flattened hers. His arms were heavy with muscle. She could feel the tension in them as he splayed above her.

He weighed a ton.

"They're coming." His voice was a vibration at the back of her neck. "Don't talk."

Talk? Lexie wasn't sure she could breathe.

She turned her cheek against the cool, decaying leaves and inhaled carefully through her mouth. Her ankle throbbed in time with her pulse.

The man on top of her moved his lips to her ear, his jaw rough against the side of her face. "Dogs?"

Lexie's heart lurched to her throat. Oh, God. If her pursuers were hunting with dogs, their hiding place was worse than useless. They'd be caught. Trapped.

She swallowed her panic. She hadn't seen any dogs within the compound. Of course, drugged, tied, and confined, there was a lot she hadn't seen. And some of the things she had . . . she shivered.

Don't think about that now, she ordered herself. There's nothing you can do about that now.

"No dogs," she said.

He grunted, apparently satisfied. The sound, low and intimate in her ear, made something inside her clench and then soften. She lay still, her senses straining. No shouts. No gunfire. Only the pounding of her heart and the slow, steady breathing of the stranger above her and—

There. He must have heard it, too, because he stiffened. A stealthy disturbance of the forest floor, too loud to be a bird and too deliberate to be a squirrel, moving away to their right. Footsteps? Someone was after them. After her.

Lexie squeezed her eyes shut and held her breath. She was acutely aware of the man pinning her to the soft, damp ground. His size. His strength. His . . .

Oh, my goodness. Her eyes popped open. He was aroused. That wasn't his belt buckle pressed hard against her bottom. It was too long, too hot, too thick, to be mistaken for anything but, well, what it was.

Lexie exhaled. Now what?

Under normal circumstances, she would have made a joke and moved away.

But things had slid from normal to nightmare three days ago.

And nothing in her past experience, none of her father's dire warnings or her mother's frank instructions, offered a clue of what to do when you were being hunted through the woods by armed religious zealots and a significant portion of your rescuer's anatomy was poking your backside.

Lexie's hands fisted against the cool, soft earth.

Well, fine. If he could endure it, if he could ignore it, then so could she.

Lexie bit her lip. Anyway, she could try.

Don't miss the next sizzling adventure
as Gargoyle Connor Rihyad
takes center stage in Vickie Taylor's

Flesh and Stone

Coming in April 2006 from Berkley Sensation!

The only thing stronger than Gargoyle Connor Rihyad's loyalty to his people is his outrage at the abominations to his race that have turned on their own kind. Two months after the fire and attempted kidnapping at St. Michael's in which Connor almost lost his life, *Les Gargouillen* of Chicago have tracked down their enemy, and Connor has been sent to infiltrate them. What he learns is even more chilling than what he already knew about the evil clan. Not only are they stealing Gargoyle children, they're kidnapping human women into sexual slavery, forcing them to bear sons to grow their dark army.

For the last six years, Mara Kincaide has run a shelter for women in crisis. A few weeks ago, a client she'd become particularly close with disappeared. Mara wants to know what happened to her, so she traces her friend's movements, and as a result, falls victim to the same fate. But when Mara is "given" to Connor Rihyad, she senses something different about him. With the potential for betrayal and explosive violence sizzling around them, she must decide if he is the man of her dreams . . . or the monster of her nightmares.